P[illegible]
THE INV[illegible]

"Jeff Wheeler weaves a deep and unique world filled with magic, danger, and hope. Readers will fall in love with the characters and root for their triumphs. (And I may have a crush on Robinson now.)"

—*Wall Street Journal* bestselling author Charlie N. Holmberg

"What a ride! Jeff Wheeler really brings out the big guns—literally, there are cannons—with this amazing introduction into the world of *The Invisible College*. From the prologue, I was absolutely hooked! With a world of inventive magic, a doomsday war on the horizon, and a romance you can't help but want to cheer for, this story showcases some of Jeff Wheeler's best work. Old and new fans of his masterful storytelling are going to gobble this right up and come back begging for more."

—Allison Anderson, author of the Cartographer's War series

"Jeff has written an engaging story full of ancient magic, secret handshakes, devious antagonists, and a charming hero just discovering his power."

—Luanne G. Smith, author of *The Vine Witch*

THE INVISIBLE COLLEGE

ALSO BY JEFF WHEELER

Your First Million Words

Tales from Kingfountain, Muirwood, and Beyond:

The Worlds of Jeff Wheeler

The Invisible College

The Invisible College

The Dresden Codex

Doomsday Match

Jaguar Prophecies

Final Strike

The Dawning of Muirwood Series

The Druid

The Hunted

The Betrayed

The First Argentines Series

Knight's Ransom

Warrior's Ransom

Lady's Ransom

Fate's Ransom

The Grave Kingdom Series

The Killing Fog

The Buried World

The Immortal Words

The Harbinger Series

Storm Glass

Mirror Gate

Iron Garland

Prism Cloud

Broken Veil

The Kingfountain Series

The Queen's Poisoner

The Thief's Daughter

The King's Traitor

The Hollow Crown

The Silent Shield

The Forsaken Throne

The Poisoner of Kingfountain Series

The Poisoner's Enemy (prequel)

The Widow's Fate (prequel)

The Maid's War (prequel)

The Duke's Treason (prequel)

The Poisoner's Revenge (prequel)

The Legends of Muirwood Trilogy

The Wretched of Muirwood

The Blight of Muirwood

The Scourge of Muirwood

The Covenant of Muirwood Trilogy

The Banished of Muirwood

The Ciphers of Muirwood

The Void of Muirwood

Whispers from Mirrowen Trilogy

Fireblood

Dryad-Born

Poisonwell

Landmoor Series

Landmoor

Silverkin

THE INVISIBLE COLLEGE

JEFF WHEELER

47NORTH

This is a work of fiction. Names, characters, organizations, places, events, and incidents are either products of the author's imagination or are used fictitiously. Otherwise, any resemblance to actual persons, living or dead, is purely coincidental.

Published by 47North, Seattle

www.apub.com

ISBN-13: 9781662521867 (paperback)
ISBN-13: 9781662521874 (digital)
ISBN-13: 9781662525964 (hardcover)

Cover design by David Curtis

Printed in the United States of America

First edition

AUTHOR'S NOTE

I've always ended each of my books with a note talking about where the inspiration for a story may have come from or other tidbits that I think may interest my readers. For *The Invisible College*, I thought readers would be better served if I opened with my reasoning for certain details you'll find in this book, especially since one of the characters is deaf.

I'm inspired by history, settings, and events that are very different from our own.

Writing from the point of view of a deaf character was especially challenging for me since I had to use my imagination and research to try to bridge the gap of understanding. Societies throughout history have regularly mistreated individuals who are considered different from what may be considered "normal." The world of *The Invisible College* is no different and exposes some of the injustices that can and often still do persist despite more modern research and methods.

For example, in this book deaf children are considered pariahs and unwelcome in Society. Those in power make false and injurious assumptions about their abilities and potential. Unrealistic expectations are also contrived, such as lipreading and vocalizing being preferable to other forms of communication, like sign language. In reality, lipreading and speaking might prove inaccessible for some individuals born without hearing.

Such themes are in this book, but I wanted to point out to my readers that while I write about many topics and do a lot of research in my world-building, it doesn't reflect my personal beliefs or attitudes. I wanted to state this because authors have to make hard choices about what goes into a book and what gets left out, and some of these choices may be viewed as perpetuating debunked ideas. It's never my intent to injure or offend my readers. The teaching methods in the book were typical of the time it is based on—New England in the 1870s. Back then, many deaf children were sent to asylums to endure lives of misery because it was supposed, incorrectly, that they were incapable of learning.

I hope you enjoy the story and how it shows that individuals of all abilities have the capacity to do amazing things.

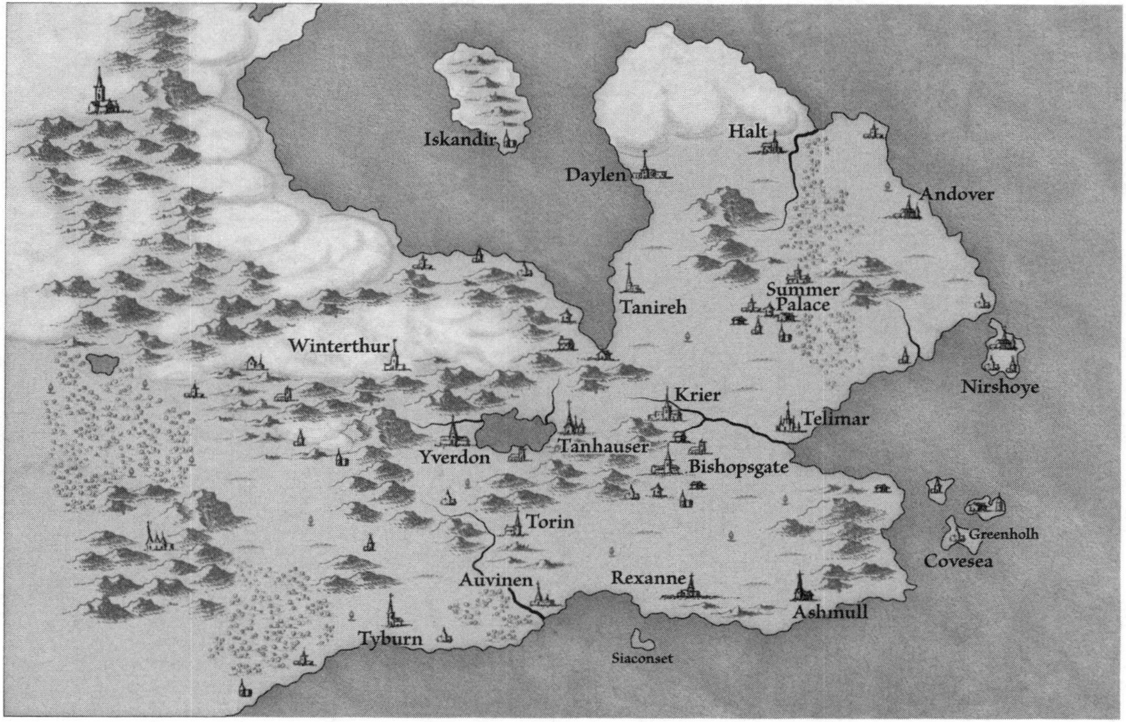
Iskandir
Halt
Daylen
Andover
Tanireh
Summer Palace
Winterthur
Nirshoye
Krier
Telimar
Tanhauser
Yverdon
Bishopsgate
Torin
Greenholh
Covesea
Auvinen
Rexanne
Ashmull
Tyburn
Siaconset

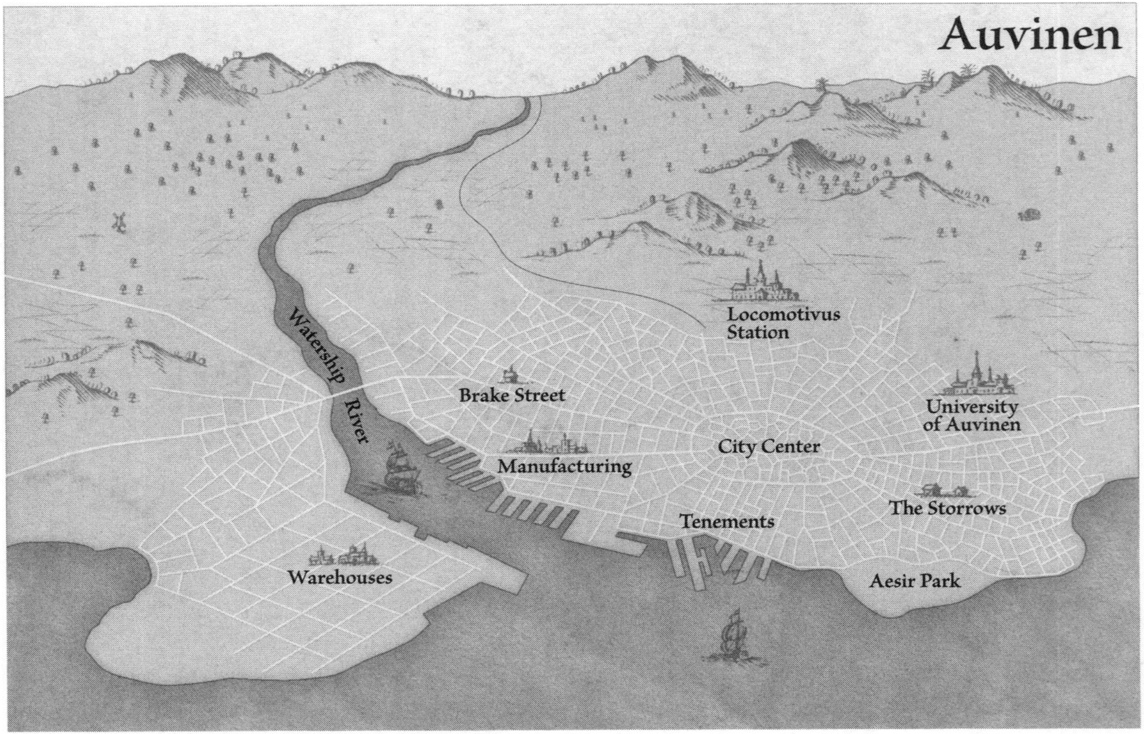
Auvinen
Locomotivus Station
Watership River
Brake Street
University of Auvinen
City Center
Manufacturing
The Storrows
Tenements
Warehouses
Aesir Park

Truth is the offspring of silence and unbroken meditation. That is the last and the first of it.

This is a truth we hold evident: There is another species on this world other than our own. They first came here from a moon orbiting a planet orbiting a dying star. Theirs was a world of unrelenting cold. When they came to our soiled world, they built cities out of ice and stone, made gardens carved from massive glaciers. They are beings of impeccable justice, which they consider the highest of all virtues. But do not be fooled by their cold beauty, the splendor of their magic, or their awe-inspiring songs.

The Aesir are no longer our friends.

There is no history describing our earliest contact with them, but songs and legends imply there was once harmony. Harmony that eventually led to them sharing bits of their magic with us. Something must have shifted, however. Perhaps they watched our ranks grow and gain enlightenment and knowledge, some of which they themselves had provided. Regardless of the cause, we know one thing: they now seek to destroy us.

Our life spans are pitifully short compared to theirs, and they seek cold where we seek warmth. When they go to sleep, a state of semi-awareness they call Skrýmir, to purge their bodies and minds of excess heat, it can last for centuries. And when they awaken, they see our encroachments on nature and their dwelling places, our development of new technology, and our experiments with magic alchemy, and they begin to hunt us again. Like rats.

That is another truth: they consider it within the bounds of justice to exterminate us.

—Isaac Berrow,
Master of the Royal Secret,
the Invisible College

Joseph Crossthwait

PROLOGUE

The Ice Trenches

The sled dogs gobbled up the chunks of meat thrown to them, and several began fighting each other for the scraps. Joseph Crossthwait whispered a musical Aesir command, and the metal skis of the sled began to warm, melting the ice crusts that had formed along the journey from the glacier's front.

Joseph felt comfortably warm despite the frigid temperatures as he hiked over the icy crest toward the encampment below. He'd veered off the main supply route earlier to ensure he would arrive unseen. The metal buckles and button studs on his uniform produced heat through the magical effect of incalescence. As he walked, he gazed across the interconnected maze of trenches cut into the embankment. These trenches had been built in every mountain pass, every hollow valley, every border where the permanent ice field stretched edge to edge in the empire. There were always guards stationed in them, even in summer, but as the season edged toward winter, the reserves were called in. No one knew when the Aesir would next awaken, but to be unprepared was to die.

Evidence suggested it would be happening *soon*.

When he reached the command post, he lowered the silver-edged cowl of his kappelin, which deactivated the spell of invisibility—and frightened the two soldiers standing guard, both wearing thick beaver-pelt helmets.

"Aesir's blood!" one of them gasped in shock. "Where'd you come from?"

If he had been an Aesir, he could have slain both of them without a word with the harrosheth blade fixed to the bracer on his left arm.

"Where's Colonel Wickins?" Joseph asked, ignoring the guard's impertinent question.

The soldier chafed his gloved hands together. Like many of the soldiers stationed out here, they were bearded, something that helped against frostbite.

"I'll take you, sir," said the other sentry, who escorted Joseph to one of the command yurts ringing the area.

Joseph entered the tent, while the sentry remained outside.

Colonel Wickins, a man in his midfifties with a balding front, stood next to a table on which an incalescent heater radiated shimmers of heat beneath a copper teapot. The yurt was comfortably warm, and the colonel's possessions were strewn about the space haphazardly.

The colonel's adjutant stood near him, a man half his master's age.

"Ah, good of General Colsterworth to send you," Wickins said gruffly, reaching out to shake hands. He made a hand sign of rank from the Invisible College, revealing himself to be a Knight of the Eagle, a fifteenth-degree sorcerer. Joseph responded with a higher-level sign, which established in seconds the supremacy of his authority despite the colonel's rank in the military.

"Tell me what happened," Joseph said.

"It might be better if I *showed* you," Wickins answered. His expression was equal parts awe and confusion. How would it not be? He'd seen a myth in the flesh. "We still have the body."

"You caught an Aesir? Alive?" Joseph asked incredulously. Eagerly. In all his training, in all his missions, he'd never confronted such a situation. No one had until now.

"No, sir. He's dead. Murdered sixty before a lad took him down with a lucky shot."

"The Aesir don't consider it murder," Joseph answered with a narrowed look. "Take me there."

"I don't pretend to know the Mind of the Sovereignty on such matters," Wickins said, grabbing a beaver-pelt helmet and donning it. "All I know is we each have an allotted time on this planet and now sixty men are dead and frozen. That's why I sent word to Bishopsgate. Come along." He gave the teapot a wistful look before deactivating the heater and leaving it behind.

Their boots crunched in the packed snow, and they started down one of the trench walls. The glacier was an interlocking maze. Joseph heard the colonel mutter the command to activate his buckles and buttons. He probably spent more time in the yurt than he did inspecting the men and positions.

"Your uniform," Wickins said, glancing at Joseph with puzzled and wary eyes. "It's not ours."

"I just returned from spying on the Andoverian lines," Joseph said. "But none of that is your concern. Tell me what happened while we walk."

"I've only got fragments. Some men found soldiers frozen to death, their skin blue as ice. That's how we knew it was an Aesir. An entire line was like that by the time the alarm was raised."

"Were the officers playing music?" Joseph asked. Even a flimsy magical shield conjured by a single sorcerer with a tune was better than nothing. It was a gross neglect of duty to be caught so unaware at the front.

"It was night. They were cold and huddling in the yurts."

Joseph sighed with contempt. "Go on."

"We raised the alarm. Sung the shields. Started firing our rifles to raise a fog of saltpetr. Boxed him in, you see."

It was about as wise as locking yourself in a room with a wolf. In his mind, Joseph could imagine the night, the trenches illuminated by chains of magic stanchions using quicksilver gas. The soldiers bewildered, shooting at anything that moved.

"What happened then?" Joseph asked.

"See for yourself," answered the colonel as they reached the death chasm. There were no guards stationed at the entrance of the kill zone. The colonel, the adjutant, and Joseph entered it and found the frozen corpses littering the way. Joseph stopped and knelt by one of them, seeing the telltale marks of blue on the vacant face. It wasn't frostbite. It was too soon for that. The Aesir only fought during the wintertime or near the network of glaciers inside the mountain ranges. They could come and go at will, quiet as the morning haze.

Joseph straightened and nodded to the colonel to lead the way. Each network of ice trenches had a command hub with a respite shelter for the men to warm up in. That's where they'd dragged the Aesir's body. The incalescent heater had been shut off, so the space was frigid. Their breath could be seen.

Awe washed over him, though he did his best not to let it show. Unlike a stone effigy or a centuries-old painting, this was real and startling and vivid. The Aesir was seven feet tall, wearing the thin bands of armor of his race. The hair was silver. The skin like snow crystals. The eyes were open, pale as diamonds. The skin beneath the eyelids showed violet smears—not paint, it was part of their anatomy. A jewel wrapped in white gold was embedded in his forehead. Looking from face to neck to chest, he found it. A bullet rupture. No blood, of course, but that was to be expected. The wound had already cauterized. The body was dressed in a kappelin, the famous cloak of the Aesir. Like the one that Joseph wore, the cowl had a silver duckbill fringe decorated with magic runes that would shield the wearer's thoughts. The kappelin was untouched by the damage, so it would be worth thousands on the open market. A bidding war in the Invisible College would be held soon.

"The man who shot him," Joseph said, examining the Aesir's body with great interest, seeing the flesh of the enemy for the first time. It had been a century since the last Awakening. "Who was it?"

"Lieutenant Snell," said the colonel. "Lucky shot, as I said. He was the only one who survived."

"Bring him here," Joseph ordered the adjutant.

"Yes, my lord," replied the man, a young sorcerer himself no doubt. Only someone from the Invisible College would have been allowed to serve such a high-ranking officer.

Once the adjutant departed, Joseph turned to Wickins.

"What do you make of it?" asked the troubled colonel in a worried tone. "You think . . . you think it's the Awakening?"

"We have to assume so," Joseph answered in a near whisper, afraid that saying it too loudly would make the nightmare real. This wasn't the first indication the Awakening was upon them, but it had been the most deadly event so far. "There has not been one in well over a hundred years. I must reprimand you for your dereliction of duty, Colonel. You'll be demoted. We cannot afford such lapses in security. Where is the lieutenant colonel?"

Wickins grimaced, but the demotion could not have been unexpected. He had failed at his most important obligation, one they'd all trained for their entire lives. Vigilance was necessary, even if it was a nearly impossible task to stay vigilant against a threat last active during the time of one's great-grandparents. "Dead, sir. He came rushing into the fight."

"And where were *you*?"

The man stiffened at the rebuke. "I had to send orders. We needed reinforcements. What if there were more of them?"

"Your ignorance is appalling," Joseph said. "The last time the Aesir attacked, we were using flintlock pistols, muskets, and silver-rune bayonets. The Industry of Magic was still in its infancy. Why do you think we have so many soldiers living in trenches during the heart of winter, year after year, decade after decade, century after century! When they awaken, it's worse than a slaughterhouse!"

The colonel's eyes began to water with fear. "I'm sorry, sir. It won't happen—"

"How wealthy have you grown because of your rank, your position in the college? Hmmm? You think your life is worth cuppers if the Awakening is upon us? You're fat and lazy and contemptible. You would have abandoned your men and fled for your life if not for a lucky shot from a greenling who doesn't even know why we're here adapting to the cold, to be ready for the real danger when it comes. A time like *now*!"

Joseph Crossthwait was furious. He needed to get back to Bishopsgate. If he could sprout wings, he'd *fly* there. But there was something that needed to happen first. He could not go back to General Colsterworth without being able to answer one question about the attack. He'd seen enough evidence of the damage *one* Aesir could do. On rare occasions, a single Aesir would rise before the rest to test the boundaries. But the tales agreed on one thing—usually the sighting of an Aesir in the flesh meant more were on the way.

What would mankind do when thousands of them emerged from their glacial fortresses and began to wreak havoc on humanity? Again. The humans, the deaf and the whole, would be massacred like sheep. Some, a few, would be chosen by the immortal race to be servants and slaves. The gifted of all ages—the poets, the musicians, the craftsmen, the scientists. Slaves. All of them. The innocent people farther south had no idea what was about to come. He'd hoped, as had his commander, that they would still have more time to prepare.

While Wickins cowered in shame and fear, they waited for the adjutant to return. When he came back, he was with the lone survivor. A young man in his early twenties.

"Lieutenant Snell," Joseph said.

The young man had light brown hair and blue-green eyes. He looked so young and was clearly shaken by the ordeal he'd been through that night. As Joseph watched, he rubbed his arm with a gloved hand, trying to coax more warmth from the incalescent buckles.

"Yes, sir. Who are you, sir?" asked the young man in a troubled voice.

"I'm General Colsterworth's adjutant," Joseph said. "You were very brave during the attack."

"I did my duty, sir." He looked at the body of the Aesir with bewilderment. "What is that . . . thing? Is it really a man?"

"No," Joseph replied curtly. "No, they're not like us. They speak. They sing. But they have no feelings for our kind. The Aesir are our enemies. And you killed one."

"I shot him," Snell said, "but he didn't bleed. Why didn't he bleed?"

"Blood is too hot for them," Joseph answered. "Were you injured, Lieutenant?"

He rubbed his breast muscle nervously. There was a sizeable gash in his jacket, Joseph noticed, and the fabric was stained with blood.

"He . . . he cut me," Snell said. "Medic gave me stitches and bandaged it up. Still hurts."

That's all Joseph needed to know. He drew his pistol and shot Lieutenant Snell. The crack of gunfire was loud in the hut. As the young man crumpled to the ground, Joseph turned, drew a second pistol from his belt, and shot the Aesir in the temple.

"What in the Sovereignty's name—!" Wickins shouted in sudden terror, gazing at Joseph with abhorrence. The delicious tang of saltpetr flavored the air as smoke curled from the weapon and seeped into the hut.

Joseph ignored him, watching the dead lieutenant's lips part and a single puff of icy breath emerge from them.

"Now he's dead," Joseph said, holstering the weapon. He turned to the two shaken men. "Snell died last night. That wasn't him. It was a Semblance."

The Mind of the Sovereignty gave living things self-motion beyond our understanding. If the Sovereignty is without doubt able to implant the other principles of motion into bodies that we may understand as "little," then It may also do so in bodies that are "large." If mere thought causes muscles to dilate and contract, if forces of attraction subdue and repel, then the wonders of magic are perhaps without limit. If the Unseen Powers, which when exhibited by a colony of ants, can power a factory, what will happen, I wonder, when we finally learn the secrets of harnessing the intelligences of mortal beings such as ourselves.

The Aesir have mastered this secret. They can inhabit a mortal body and imposter us at their whim and will. We call these beings Semblances, and creating them is perhaps the most dangerous of all the Aesir's powers.

All we know about the working of this magic is this: someone on the very verge of death is susceptible to being overwrought by this arcane magic. We have enemies among us.

—Isaac Berrow,
Master of the Royal Secret,
the Invisible College

Robinson Dickemore Hawksley

CHAPTER ONE

A New Life

The iron-studded hull of the *Hotspur*-class warship loomed over the edge of the smaller merchant vessel that Robinson and his parents had just disembarked from. He gazed at it in awe. He'd never seen one up close before, but the fleet rarely did more than sail past the isle of Covesea, the home they'd left behind to make changes. Hopefully for the better.

He helped his mother climb onto the street tram, which was already crammed with passengers. It was pulled by a literal iron horse, a complex mechanical invention animated by intelligences that pulled the trams without tiring. The river quay teemed with ships carrying various cargoes, the waters befouled by seagull dregs and the smell of decomposing fish, but those were familiar smells and comforting in a way.

A big meaty hand clamped onto his shoulder. Robinson turned his neck and saw his father's agitated eyes. "I put two coins in the head. Why don't you go to the hotel with your mother? I'll follow with the cart and luggage."

Robinson had had another coughing fit as they'd walked down the gangway, and he was still wheezing. The dreaded disease that had killed both of his brothers was still lingering in Robinson's lungs, but he was determined not to be a burden on his parents. He was twenty-six and should be able to manage such a simple task as transporting luggage, which had already been loaded onto the cart and was waiting. Gripping his violin case in his free hand, he shook his head.

"You go ahead. I've got it, Father. I haven't been to Auvinen since you took me when I was a boy. I want to see the city with fresh eyes in that two-wheeled gig, not in a cramped tram. I'll see you at the hotel."

"Are you sure?" Father asked. He was nearly twice the breadth of his only living son, but that was because of Robinson's illness and his propensity to ignore mealtime while working on his experiments.

"I'll be there soon."

The sorcerer driving the tram whistled the tune that would power up the iron horse pulling it. Father gripped the rail and climbed aboard, wedging his hips into the small space left on the bench. Robinson waved to his mother, then watched in awe as the contraption began to move. The whole city was crisscrossed with iron rails embedded in the cobblestone streets, and these magical contrivances hauled people all over the city. It fascinated him. Indeed, the whole of Auvinen did. It was the thriving hub of the Industry of Magic, and he knew he'd be able to see some of the inventions he'd only heard about in Covesea.

Ambling through the crowd, Robinson reached the gig and plow horse hauling the luggage. The driver scratched his bristly bearded neck and gave the newcomer a sour look. "Hop on, sir. Let's get moving."

Something felt off. Wrong. Robinson held up his hand and walked to the back of the gig where the trunks had been stowed. It was missing a bag. His alchemy trunk was gone.

"One of the trunks is missing," Robinson said.

The driver turned and looked confused. "I watched the porters load it myself. It's probably at the bottom. Let's get going."

Robinson could *sense* it was missing. A nagging feeling, a sense of wrongness. Of loss.

"It's not there," he insisted, but how could he explain the truth to a fellow that wasn't part of the Invisible College? One who didn't have any rank on the rites of sorcery.

"Sir, we need to get going. I don't have all day."

"Then go ahead and take the freight to the hotel without me. My parents took a street tram. I'll meet you there."

"Or you'll get lost," grumbled the driver, giving Robinson a look like he was being ridiculous. "Hip, hip," he commanded, and the horse tossed its mane and started. As soon as it moved along, a little mechanical device on wheels scooted over from its position at the edge of the street. It began to scoop up the manure the horse had dropped during the wait. Robinson stared at the little machine in fascination, wondering where it took the manure, then reminded himself of his missing trunk.

"Calex epso," he sang under his breath, summoning an intelligence within the trunk to activate, one that would guide him to it. Immediately, he felt a pop of connection. It wasn't far away.

Robinson strode forward purposefully, feeling another itch of a cough in the back of his throat, but he subdued it as he passed the people along the edges of the road. There were dockworkers aplenty, loading up other ships with merchandise. The rank odor of the water was momentarily blotted out when he smelled a delicious creamy soup and baked bread from a shop just across the street. The same kind of shop he'd visit at home in Greenholh for a mess of pottage, which would invariably lead to a particular floppy-eared stray dog following him and whining for a bit of meat. That stray had been run over by a carriage on the day of his brother's funeral. It still hurt to think about cradling the bloodied animal in his arms and then burying him no more than an hour after he'd witnessed his brother's burial. But he stuffed the memories away and wound his way toward some buildings with soot-choked windows, which meant there were no magical braziers inside and the inhabitants were forced to burn coal.

His stiff leather shoes thumped on the paving stones, and then he saw two men hoisting the trunk and heading down an alley, a third man leading the way. He called out to them, but his yell caused a coughing fit, which made him put his hand against the wall of the alley and pause to catch his breath. After it subsided, he set off after them and, after turning a corner, caught up to them.

"Excuse me!" he said, huffing. "That's my trunk. I . . . I need it back."

He wasn't strong enough to carry it back on his own, so he'd probably have to hire the men to do it for him. Robinson had a little money saved from tutoring and teaching, though he was loath to part with the funds he would need to establish himself in the new city.

The one walking in front of the two carrying it turned and looked at him. He was a big fellow. A sturdy dockworker wearing the cap and shirt of his trade. His muscles bulged beneath the shirt. Robinson was a scarecrow in comparison.

"Run along, little man," the fellow said in a dangerous tone.

Oh, so they were *robbing* it on purpose! Robinson rubbed his nose, feeling a fool. When the men at the dock in Greenholh had carried the trunk on board, they'd commented on its unusually heavy weight. The various instruments in Robinson's alchemy trunk were naturally heavy—stone grinding bowls, quicksilver measuring devices, lead ingots, jars of chymicals, various sizes and shapes of magnifying glasses and burning tools. All packed carefully, wedged together with sawdust to prevent them from breaking. Surely one dockworker had told another that the trunk belonged to a sorcerer of the Invisible College and would fetch a hefty price in Auvinen.

"Please set the trunk down; it's very precious to me," Robinson said as he lifted his violin case and unlocked it. He could use magic with solely his voice but feared another coughing fit if he were to try.

"Imagine so. You're pale from axioma. Can hear it rattling in your breath," said the leader in a taunting way. "You won't be needing this stuff for long."

"All the same, I'd rather not part with it," Robinson said. He set the case down on the street and pulled out his violin and bow.

"Get on," the leader said to the two men straining to hold the trunk. "I'll deal with him."

Robinson lifted the violin to his chin and played an offset chord, summoning a magical shield to block the trunk from leaving the alley. With another chord, the trunk began to move *toward* him, while the two men wrestled powerlessly to stop it.

Robinson gazed at the biggest fellow and began to play his instrument fast, vigorously, and with skill. The magic worked quickly—a flare shooting up into the sky and exploding like a firework. The alert would summon other sorcerers—hopefully those in law enforcement—to rush to his aid. Robinson quickly shifted the tune to invoke a protective spell to safeguard himself from their fists.

"Can't stop it!" growled one of the men, shoving his whole body against the now floating trunk as it pressed inexorably toward its owner.

Robinson arched an eyebrow at the leader, who was advancing on him with open menace. Surely the man wasn't *that* stupid? Three thugs against a sorcerer? Even in his weakened condition, Robinson was more than a match for them. If they had any sense, they'd run, although they wouldn't get very far since he'd blocked the alley.

The burly man reached behind his back, under his shirt, and withdrew a dagger. The blade glittered with the sheen of magic.

"A harrosheth blade," Robinson said, impressed, still playing music, shifting from one tune to another. "A blade so cold it can pierce anything." He was summoning intelligences to aid him, and they came to him in droves. In Covesea, it took much more coaxing, but Auvinen was clearly bursting with them. It was a startling response to such a simple magical request.

"I know what you are," the burly man said grimly. "And I know what this can do."

Robinson changed the tune again, going into a minor chord, and the dagger was yanked out of the man's hand. The man watched, dumbfounded, as it embedded itself into the stone wall. A harrosheth blade could cut through metal, stone, or wood. It was an Aesir weapon, very costly. This one was undoubtedly stolen.

The burly man's eyes bulged as he continued to watch it. The blade was worth three trunks like Robinson's. Maybe four. With wild eyes, he rushed to the dagger and grabbed the hilt, which was exactly what Robinson had expected him to do. He'd noticed the ring on the man's littlest finger. The thief wrenched and pulled, trying to free his weapon, but no amount of physical strength was going to do the trick. Not when Robinson had the Unseen Powers at his command. The man might as well try lifting the entire building off its foundation.

Robinson shifted to another chord, and the ring on the man's finger and the hilt of the dagger fused together with an alchemical bond. Shrill whistles from Marshalcy officers came from both ends of the alley, and a force of six men appeared around both corners, wearing their dark blue uniforms with the brass buttons in rows and odd-shaped little helmets, which reminded Robinson of his previous childhood visit.

The other two would-be thieves had already tried to flee, but they were clawing against an invisible force that was blocking their escape. The burly man, realizing his danger, was now trying to pry his hand *off* the dagger hilt and failing miserably.

Robinson let a final strain of music linger in the air and then tucked the violin and bow back into the case and released all the magical constraints except the one holding the trunk aloft. For that, he asked the intelligences to set it down gently, which they did.

A young officer approached Robinson. He had a neatly trimmed handlebar mustache and keen eyes, and they quickly shook hands. As expected, the clasp he used identified him as another ranking member of the Invisible College.

"I'm Detective Lieutenant John Prescott Bigelow of the Marshalcy," the officer said before releasing the clasp. "Thanks for the timely summons."

"I'm Robinson Dickemore Hawksley. Thank you for the timely response. These three tried to steal my alchemy trunk."

"Do you go by Rob?"

"Robinson will do."

"Well enough. I can tell by your outfit and speech that you're new to Auvinen. I apologize for the sordid welcome. Are you visiting?"

Robinson watched as the officers apprehended the dockworkers, one of whom earned a thump from a club for his resistance. The sight made him reflexively grimace. He didn't like to see any creature suffer. Even if earned.

"A change of scenery was needed. Just arrived with my parents. My father has given lectures at the university before, and he secured an interview for me with one of the deans."

"Who?"

"Lennox Warchester George. Do you know him?"

"I know *of* him. He's part of the Storrows. One of the better quorums of the Invisible College in Auvinen. You could do much worse."

"How many quorums are here?" Back home, there'd only been one quorum; here, they were probably scattered throughout the city.

"Dozens," the detective lieutenant said. "Preensby, Gaulter, Wellrip. That's mine . . . Wellrip. If you need a situation, you could always start there. I'd speak for you. For now, I need you to come to the station to make a statement about these fellows and what they did."

"My parents are expecting me at their hotel. Can we do it there instead? I could use some help with the trunk as well."

"Brother to brother," said the officer with an accommodating grin. "I'll bring you myself. We can talk on the way. Your word is all we need."

"Thank you," Robinson said, shaking the man's hand again, this time without the secret clasp. "I'm much obliged to you."

One of the officers approached with the harrosheth blade, showing it to the detective lieutenant. The burly man's ring was still affixed to it. It would take some time in an alchemy to break the bond between metals. “He could have done some damage with this,” the officer said grimly.

The detective lieutenant snorted and, with a twinkle in his eye, said, “He picked the wrong man to rob.”

Robinson shrugged self-deprecatingly at the quip. Rob was a nickname only his most intimate friends called him. He hoped he would make such friends here in such a vast, formidable city.

A city teeming with magic.

The practice of magic is the study of invisible things.

The most delicately ground glass scope, which can amplify vision twenty-fold and show the head of a pin to be full of cracks and seams, still cannot reveal its underlying nature or the various elements of its construction. Yet even if we could see between the gaps, so to speak, vision alone would not reveal what is there, what sorcerers in ancient times described as Unseen Powers. Even the tiniest of gnats has an intelligence—although quite a small one. A bird with its wings, feathers, blood, and organs may be despoiled by a cat. But its inner spark, its life source, cannot be extinguished by a claw. A cat has intelligence as well. And so does a horse. The Unseen Powers can connect such intelligence to a form of matter, be it iron, a tree leaf, or the twitch of a mouse's whisker. And so, by harnessing the Unseen Powers, we can make an iron horse that can move and respond to simple commands, such as pulling a street tram along its tracks. But a sorcerer must always be there to give the command to stop, or the horse will go on and on until it collides with a brick wall and keeps trying to go, or its iron sinews melt with the heat and friction of its cause. The more intelligence, the greater the power to be harnessed.

—Isaac Berrow,
Master of the Royal Secret,
the Invisible College

CHAPTER TWO

In Need of a Situation

The hotel Robinson's family was staying at, Harrington's, was located in a shabby part of the city by the locomotivus station. Father said he always stayed there because it was less expensive than the fancier hotels and an easy walk to the railyard. Detective Lieutenant Bigelow had brought Robinson there, and he helped him lift his heavy trunk off the luggage rack of the Marshalcy carriage. Two hotel workers quickly rushed up to handle the load for them.

"Thank you again," Robinson said, shaking the officer's hand.

"The secret entrance to Wellrip is a fighting club," the officer said. "Tell the bookie you want to bet on the Berrow fight, and he'll get you to the entrance quick as that. Hope to see you again, Professor Hawksley."

"A pleasure," Robinson said. He hefted the violin case under his arm and followed the hotel workers inside. Immediately within the lobby, he saw his parents talking worriedly to a stately woman with a wide-hoop dress and her hair done up in curls. She was in her forties, judging by the laugh lines at her eyes, but she noticed Robinson's entrance and beamed.

"I think the lost has been found," she said, gesturing.

Robinson's father hurried forward and hugged his son violently. "Where have you been, my boy? I was so worried, I summoned help."

"There was a mistake with the luggage," Robinson said. "It took some time to sort it out."

Mother came and kissed his cheek, then patted his shirt.

"Who is your friend?" Robinson asked, extending his hand. The woman took it in a sorcerers' clasp, startling him, but he responded in kind.

"Sarah Fuller Fiske," she said. "What an honor. Two Professor Hawksleys in my acquaintance now! I understand from your father that you taught his method of elocution at the university in Greenholh?"

"A small university, to be sure," Robinson said modestly.

"My son is a gifted teacher and tutor. I arranged for an interview with Dean George before we came, and he said he would *make* a position for the Hawksley method to be taught here." Robinson's father beamed proudly. "I made a demonstration at Mrs. Fiske's school last year."

"The Physiological Alphabet is an important method," Mrs. Fiske agreed. "There are many young men and women in Auvinen who struggle with the diction required for sorcery. Your father says you are also quite musical? I judge by your violin case that he's correct."

"I do love music," Robinson said. He didn't want to boast about what had happened in the alley, but the woman seemed very affable and pleasant. He wanted to know more about her. "Tell me about your school, Mrs. Fiske. Is it a music school for singing or instruments?" Achieving a precise combination of voice and tone was crucial to anyone who wanted to learn magic and tap into the Unseen Powers.

"No, none of our students can sing, Professor, or play instruments. They are deaf. I was just commenting how impressed I am with how well your mother can read lips and is so attuned to conversations. It's really quite remarkable."

His own mother was deaf, one of many victims of the redoubtable fever caused by the Aesir, having lost her hearing as a teenager. She was gifted at reading lips, however, and could speak with perfect diction. He knew Society in Auvinen would probably be unwelcoming to her, as they were to all with such conditions, but if all went well, his parents would enjoy a comfortable retirement here.

"Indeed? I thought the deaf were sent to live in asylums in Auvinen."

"Many are. But thanks to the generosity and influence of one of our barristers, our school was chartered by the government. We've welcomed children and people of all ages to our school. We teach them to communicate, Professor. That is our goal. Some use voice and some their hands."

"Astounding," Robinson said. "I am so pleased to hear that."

"My son has a soft heart for the oppressed. I'm sure he could be persuaded to give an occasional lecture or two to your staff. Nothing that would interrupt his teaching at the university, of course. Maybe some private students?"

"Father," Robinson sighed. He was keenly interested in his own experiments, ones he funded with the money from his teaching, and didn't want to overcommit to tutoring or lectures. Still, he'd always been generous with his time and would willingly make an exception for those truly in need.

"You're right, of course. Dean George is your ticket to a new life here," Father said. "But perhaps there are one or two promising students you could help? Just a few?"

Mrs. Fiske studied Robinson closely. She didn't seem the kind of person to take advantage of someone. "Actually, there *is* a family I'd recommend. Our sponsor . . . founder . . . our *friend* Mr. Foster the barrister has a daughter, McKenna, who was stricken by redoubtable fever as a small child. She inspired Mr. Foster to seek remedies for her situation. The family hired a governess, who teaches at my school, to educate their three daughters. McKenna was the eldest, and they treated her no differently than the younger two who could hear."

That was very interesting. "How has she fared?"

"She can speak well, just by reading lips, and is highly educated. The family recently returned from a year-long trip to Tanhauser. McKenna learned the language and became fluent in three months. People cannot believe she's deaf. But . . . there are still telltale signs. Now that she's eighteen, her parents have stalled on the coming-of-age celebrations, worried she may still be shunned by Society."

After all that effort, it would be heartbreaking for a young woman to be treated so callously. Robinson felt a little surge of indignation.

"I see the look in his eyes." Father sighed.

"But if he can help the poor girl," Mother said, "I think he should."

"With your permission, Professor Hawksley," Mrs. Fiske nudged, "may I introduce you to the family after you're settled into a situation?"

"What kind of law does Mr. Foster practice?" Father asked.

"What does it matter?" Mother said.

He patted her arm. "The name is familiar to me."

"He is an esteemed patent attorney, specializing in magical patents," Mrs. Fiske announced proudly.

Robinson was even more interested. Any sorcerer who invented a new way of harnessing the Unseen Powers could become quite rich if the idea were properly safeguarded. He himself was brimming with ideas. It wasn't the money that appealed to him, though. It was the thrill of discovery.

"I knew I'd heard of him," Father said with a self-satisfied grin. "I'm sure Robinson would do very well. His own mother shares the girl's condition, and he has tutored other young people before. He can teach anyone. I know he can."

"I would be honored to get an introduction," Robinson said. "My parents need a situation as well. A place to live and a quorum my father can join. I won't rest easy until they are secure."

"How expensive is rent in the city proper, Sarah?" Father asked. "We could stay here at the hotel for several weeks if needed, but it is more expensive than I remembered."

"The city has grown considerably since you were last here," she said sadly. "Many are leasing cottages in the country to enjoy their golden years somewhere more relaxing. With the locomotivus lines connecting Auvinen to Bishopsgate and far-flung locations in the empire, traveling has become less of a hardship. I can make inquiries for you."

"Oh, thank you, Sarah. If you would!"

Mrs. Fiske clasped his parents' hands, not in a perfunctory way, but with an easy, friendly manner. Then she clasped Robinson's hand. "I hope your interview at the university goes well, Professor. I like you already. If I had additional space in my own home, I'd offer it to you, but two young officers are renting out my basement apartment. I should have liked to have you as a boarder. Please come and visit the school when you can. You would *love* the children."

His heart was already softened toward the notion. "I shall. Thank you."

⁂

It was the autumnal plum trees with the vibrant red and orange leaves that caught Robinson's notice upon entering the majestic campus of the University of Auvinen two days later. He could tell by the growing chill in the air that the leaves would drop soon. In addition to the colorful foliage, he'd witnessed some exciting signs of the magic flooding the city. A factory chimney that belched purple smoke and a mechanical frog outside an eating establishment that used its flicking tongue to rid the air of flies. He wondered what other bewildering inventions he would find while living there.

There were three smaller magical universities in town, each prestigious in its own right and chartered by private donations instead of government funds. They specialized in different aspects of the Industry of Magic, whether it be medicine, music, law, engineering, politics, or speech—the last a specialty of the university Robinson was heading toward. The air was full of birdsong and the rival orchestras practicing throughout the massive city, along with the hammering iron noises of complex machines working in the factory district. The Watership River bisected the town and was itself another highway of transportation deeper inland.

Robinson carried his violin case tucked under his arm as he walked hurriedly across the students' yard. There were students everywhere, and his dark attire from Covesea made him stand out as an anomaly. The young men wore frock coats, vests, striped pants, and knee-high boots with fancy buckles—and the ladies likewise wore splendid, colorful gowns in silks and taffetas over corsets, their hair done up in elegant coils. Gloves were the rage for both sexes.

It was all for the good that Robinson cared nothing for his appearance. He was here for a job—to teach, not to impress others with his appearance.

He found the office of the dean of speech and rhetoric, Lennox Warchester George, and arrived promptly for their appointed meeting. Dean George was a solid man, about forty-five, and gave Robinson a crushing handshake encoded with a tap of the Invisible College, which Robinson returned.

"Well met, Professor, well met!" boomed the boisterous dean. "Take a seat, take a seat." He waved at a nearby chair opposite him. "Where have you and your family been staying?"

"A little hotel near the wharf," Robinson said, taking the offered chair and sitting down.

"Which one? Maybe I know it?"

"Harrington's."

"Excellent, though on the rough side of the river, no doubt. How old are you, Hawksley?"

"Twenty-six."

"You look run-down. It's that terrible sickness, isn't it? Your father said you were on the mend, but you look twigs and skin."

"Thankfully my illness hasn't impaired my speaking or playing," he said, trying to steer away from the topic of his gauntness. "I still get headaches, on occasion, but nothing I cannot endure. It will not impact my lectures, I assure you."

"Oh, don't bother with that. I've heard accounts of both you and your father, of course. I was thrilled when he said you'd be coming here to stay. You can imitate any sound you hear, is that true?"

"I can," Robinson said, adjusting his pants. "My grandfather taught rhetoric at the University of Greenholh. I trained under him—and my father too, of course." They both knew that was why he was here. His father was known across the region for the revolutionary elocution technique he'd developed—one Robinson was qualified to teach.

"Excellent!" He paused, then added, "Say, in Tanhauser, they have a more guttural speech than ours. More abrasive on the ear."

"Indeed."

"Their word for 'penmanship' is '*schoonschrijfkunst*.' Beastly word for an elegant topic. How would you write that word in your father's teaching method?"

He was testing Robinson. It was a difficult word. But just like with musical chords and notes, so could he hear the sounds distinctly.

"Schoonschrijfkunst?" Robinson repeated effortlessly.

That earned a startled nod. "Yes. Do you speak Tanhauser?"

"No. But I'm familiar with the pronunciation of most languages. When I was eight, my father had me pronounce a word in Iskandir I'd never heard of before. Do you know the language, sir?"

"I've heard it, but it's unfathomable to me."

"Well, with his Physiological Alphabet, the symbols do not reference letters but the positioning of the mouth. May I?" He gestured to the slate board fixed to the wall behind the dean, which had some calendar items and tasks written on it in chalk.

The dean leaned back and nodded in eager affirmation.

Robinson rose and scuttled around the desk to reach the slate board and picked up the nub of chalk. "'*Schoonschrijfkunst*' is composed of several sounds." He jabbed the chalk on the slate and drew the various symbols, repeating each one in order. "It is how one shapes the lips, orients the tongue, the palate, and the nasal cavity. 'Sch-oon-schr-ijf-kun-st.' Six symbols compared to . . . let me see . . . a dozen letters? I do not know how to spell the word, sir, but these symbols teach you how to pronounce it correctly, assuming, of course, that you *are* pronouncing it correctly. If I heard a native speaker, I could alter the symbols accordingly."

"Incredible," said the dean. "This is what impresses me most about your father's system. It is so compact. It is not about the etymology of the word, the linguistic origins. It is . . . well . . . you know . . . the . . ."

"Physiology of the mouth," Robinson said.

"Naturally." The dean leaned forward to look at the strange symbols written in chalk.

Robinson returned to his seat, feeling satisfied he'd made a good impression, and indeed, the dean said, "We would like to start you off with four lectures a week. I believe the demand will grow as word spreads. You take private students?"

"On occasion. I had several before coming here and tutored university students as well. I was very active in the Invisible College, however, trying to discover new uses for magic."

"There are many quorums of the Invisible College here in Auvinen. Like in the days of Isaac Berrow centuries ago, many of the quorums align with the universities they are near."

"I understand you completely. Do you have a recommendation?"

"Since you are in need of a situation—a place to live and a quorum to belong to—I might suggest starting with the Storrows. Its quorum has many wealthy patrons. It is the one I attend."

Robinson felt a flush of gratitude. He'd only been in town for a couple of short days, and he'd already been invited to two quorums. This would be the smarter one to join, however, as it would give him a chance to mingle with potential investors. In Greenholh, only a few people held financial power, and appeasing them could be arduous. "That would please me greatly," he said with a genial smile.

"What rank have you achieved, if you don't mind me asking?"

"The ninth degree," Robinson said deferentially.

"Impressive. Truly, I think the Hawksley method will be a great asset to our esteemed university. Mrs. Eunice Fletcher Jacobs will arrange for your stipend. We will pay in advance for . . . three lectures? Does that sound reasonable?"

Robinson had been hoping for a longer commitment up front. He was dangerously low on funds, considering the current prices for alchemical materials here in town, which he'd quickly realized upon arriving. Still, he didn't want to seem greedy by asking for more. He could live on very little and expected to find a modest dwelling.

So he waved his hand as if the fee meant nothing to him.

"Settled, then. If you go to the Storrows, I'm sure you will find another young man who has a spare room or knows of openings in a lodging. There are many vacancies this time of year. The deployments are heading out to the front day by day as winter draws near. Classes begin in two weeks, if that suits you."

"Of course. I'm ready to start immediately," Robinson said. "I will talk to Mrs. Jacobs about my classroom?"

"Since you are part-time, you will be sharing a room with other professors. You might wish to remain part-time, for private tutoring can be quite lucrative, if you catch my meaning."

Not to mention it saved the university a great deal as well. There was comfort in consistency. But Robinson had no false modesty. He was an excellent teacher, and although his true passion lay in invention, he loved helping others improve—seeing them struggle and then rise above it. He would also talk to Sarah Fuller Fiske about getting introduced to the Foster family.

He noticed the dean giving him a very intense look. Like he had a concern he wasn't sharing. A feeling of disquiet congealed in Robinson's stomach.

"Is there anything . . . else?" he asked the older man.

The dean pursed his lips. He was debating within himself, wasn't he?

"Can I ask . . . ?" He didn't finish the question. He let the silence dangle instead.

Robin leaned forward. "By all means."

"You don't have any predilection for joining the military, do you?"

That question surprised him. "I've never given it a thought before. Why do you ask?"

"I can't say. Not now. It's very confidential. But as with all sorcerers in the Invisible College, we may be expected to fulfill certain duties if called upon."

"Naturally."

"Good. Well then. I'm grateful you've come to Auvinen. I think you've come just in time."

CHAPTER THREE

INDUSTRY

Ignoring the tug of the violin case on his arm, Robinson gazed at the city that would be his new home as he followed the dean's directions toward the Storrows. Nothing about the old city was flat, except near the river, where he'd disembarked two days before. There were plenty of horse-led carriages in this part of town, in addition to the street trams pulled by iron horses and countless people walking along the boulevards.

There were more magical devices here, near the university, than what he'd seen by the river. There were flickering quicksilver lamps that came on and off at sunset and sunrise, brought to life and extinguished by a sorcerer's hum. Shops with little, tiny musical chests powered by the intelligences of grasshoppers, for those unable to afford to live near the conservatories and concert halls. Even the variety of dress had its roots in magic. He'd heard that the mercers of Auvinen used machinery enchanted with the intelligences of spiders so that each pattern was distinct and different.

After turning a corner, he saw the major intersection of streets leading to the state legislature building, roads forking away from that central plaza. The building had a modern design with columns and a triangular roofline. The aroma of glazed sugar and peanuts caught his nose, and he saw a little wheeled booth with a fire burning under a copper kettle with contents sizzling. The smell was intoxicating, and he bought a bag of spiced peanuts from the woman and enjoyed them as he walked past the government building.

As he ventured farther away from the hub of Auvinen into the thick of the industrial zone, the delightful songs humming through the air were replaced by the percussive hammers of machinery, a drumbeat that rattled Robinson's teeth. The clothing became drabber, the people more hard-faced and less sociable. This was the factory quarter, where the different mills operated.

It was in the center of the industrial district that he encountered the Storrows, the chapter of the Invisible College recommended to him by Dean George. There was no mistaking it, for the building was set at a major intersection and had a triangular design, a solid wedge made of stone with no lower windows, only upper ones. An enormous bell tower and cupola topped the front facade. It was larger than most banks and definitely decorated like one. The crowds in the street walked past it, most in a hurry for business. There were no obvious doors leading inside, nor would there be. The grand pillars at the apex showed a decorative bronze sheet with two handles carved with symbols of the order. It looked like it should be an opening, but there existed no seams or hinges. On either side, there were three forked bracers of quicksilver lamps.

Grateful he'd found the building so easily, he bypassed it for a quick visit to the heart of the old downtown. A medieval castle overlooked the Watership River and the inlet of the bay, but there was something older than the castle there. He'd beheld it on a previous visit and wished to see it again.

At the mouth of the harbor, above the highest spot of its looming promontory, was a suspended wedge of stone. It was not held aloft by ropes or chains. In fact, a rope fence had been set up beneath it to keep the curious at a distance. The block had been sheared off a mountain somewhere, all jagged and broken-edged. It was three stories tall, longer than it was wide, with a bodkin-pointed upper half, wholly unshaped but vaguely resembling a teardrop. Nothing physical could be detected above it for it to hang from—but hang it did.

Robinson approached the phenomenon, feeling the same sense of awe and wonder he had when he'd first seen it as a child. On one of its faces glowed an Aesir rune.

He shook another clump of warm peanuts into his mouth as he gazed up at its majesty. Robinson's father had explained to him, on their first visit, that some principles of magic simply were not yet understood by humans. The promontory had once belonged to the Aesir, back during the last ice age, when the whole planet had been sheathed in ice. That ice had been receding for generations, and it now subsisted only in the mountains, forming a borderland between the Aesir and the mortal world. It had been at least a century since the last Awakening, and some were hopeful, probably unrealistically so, that another might never happen. Robinson thought that was an overly optimistic sentiment. In all likelihood, the war would come again, and soon. Wars always started in the borderlands, though. At least there would be a warning before the Aesir attacked.

This floating stone was just one more remnant of their magic that had been left behind.

There was no obvious meaning attached to it. Had it once been a lighthouse of sorts? A warning beacon against invaders? Centuries before, sorcerers from earlier times had chipped into the bottom of the great rock, breaking off loose chunks and fragments of it, which was why the lower half had gouges and cracks. Eventually they'd stopped, for fear of breaking whatever magical grip was holding the stone in place. No one had studied it for years.

But Robinson felt drawn to it.

It played a chord of invisible magic, a thrum just below the register the natural ear could hear. He'd always possessed exceptional hearing, the ability to differentiate the minutest sounds, but he could not remember hearing this particular sound out here as a boy. And yet . . . it felt oddly *familiar* to him. It reminded him of something he couldn't quite remember. Like a dream that had been lost. Or was the difference in the sound an indication that the Awakening would soon be upon them? Perhaps, indeed, that was what the dean had alluded to at the end of their meeting.

He set down his violin case, folded the paper top of the half-eaten bag of peanuts and stuffed it into his jacket pocket. From his vest, he withdrew the device he'd taken to carrying around with him, a family heirloom his father had bestowed on him on the occasion of his brother's funeral. It was a curious device that had no obvious purpose. It was magical, undoubtedly, but no one in the family knew where it had come from or what it could do. Father had been given the device from his father, who had gotten it from his, and so on.

Since it couldn't actually do anything, every attempt to explain it or find a value for it had turned fruitless. The most expensive Aesir artifacts, like a harrosheth blade or a kappelin cloak, were typically auctioned to the highest bidder. This device, which didn't even have a proper name, was an enigma. Worthless, yet potentially worthy.

And it was now *his* enigma.

Robinson opened it, gazing at the strange patterns and dials within. It fit in the palm of his hand, an instrument that could easily be mistaken for a pocket watch with its hinged rounded cover. But there were no hands to point or any other possible way to tell time. Rather, the device contained a multicolored stone set in the middle with dials all around it. Since he'd last opened it, the center stone had rotated slightly, but the number at the top—the Aesir runes signifying the numbers nine, nine, eight—never changed. Robinson twisted some of the dials around the inner stone. They ticked quietly but revealed no further manifestation. Neither did pushing the twin buttons at the top near the hinge.

Indeed, he hadn't expected otherwise, for no amount of fiddling had ever made the numbers change or anything else of substance happen. Still, it didn't stop him, or his brother before him, from trying.

He closed the cover with a snapping sound, stuffed it back into his vest pocket, and walked a circuit around the boulder, gazing up at the jagged underside. He'd heard in his studies that farther north, in the web of mountains and glaciers, there were statues carved out of the mountainsides so tall that no mortal could possibly have lived long enough to carve them. The brave and overly adventurous oftentimes took dogsled teams to visit those wayward scenes. The idea of that appealed to Robinson, but he knew he was still too unhealthy to chase such fancies. Nor did he have the money. Only the very wealthy could afford to waste their resources on mere curiosity. Robinson himself had an equal mixture of dread and fascination about the Aesir. They intrigued him. So little was known about them. But considering the violent history of past wars, he was uneasy about any change in the status quo.

Sighing, he tucked the violin case under his other arm and headed back to the Storrows, his legs weary from all the walking. Once he reached the building, he gazed at the other buildings around it. Sure enough, he found the symbol he was looking for directly across the street from the doorless edifice—carved into the stone of the opposing building was the octagonal cross made of two intertwined strands with a braided circle around the middle intersection. A pub sign hung from the display board beneath it.

That had to be the entrance.

Robinson strolled into the establishment, which smelled strongly of port and hummed with the low rumble of many voices. The bartender looked like an amiable fellow and greeted him warmly. "You're not from these parts, sir."

"Covesea. What gave me away?" Robinson replied.

"We get a few now and then. Are you thirsty?"

"For knowledge." He set down the case and touched his hands together, connecting his thumbs at the right angles to demonstrate he was a ranking sorcerer. An outside observer would have just seen his lifted hands, not the symbol he made with his thumbs.

It was typical to find an entrance to the Invisible College in a neighborhood with any number of vices—some were positioned near bawdy houses. Some were associated with gambling dens or fighting clubs, as the detective lieutenant had mentioned when he'd arrived. A true sorcerer was expected to have the strongest will, the most impeccable morals, the most sober commitment. One did not develop those traits without enduring fierce opposition. It was common for a newcomer to be tempted away from their commitment. It was a final test, as it were, and one that could bar them from the quorum doors forever.

Robinson had already passed those tests, however.

The bartender nodded and then invited over a tall, brooding man who escorted Robinson to the back room of the establishment. Underneath the table was a trapdoor, which he pulled open before nodding for Robinson to descend.

The stairs creaked as he went down, and then the trapdoor slammed shut atop him, the sudden darkness making him flinch.

"Hoxta-namorem," he sang succinctly, meticulously, precisely. It was the first spell every sorcerer learned to cast. It meant, literally, "light . . . where once was darkness." They were powerful words. Hummed words that summoned the intelligences of phosphorescent creatures to light the way forward in dark places. No true sorcerer ever needed to endure total darkness. There was no smoke, no burning stench of tallow. Just a ring of wispy illumination.

Robinson followed the underground path down and then forward. He imagined he was crossing the street above. At the end of the tunnel waited a bronze door in a stone frame, a miniature of the one above, including the heavy handles. This door, however, had a seam.

Robinson set down his violin case and gripped the handles of the door with both hands. He had not been taught the password for entering this particular quorum. That meant he needed to pass a test, to prove his competence and membership in the Invisible College. He would not be accepted into the Storrows immediately, but with the dean's invitation, it was all but a formality.

He felt a pulse of warmth against his palms, and a voice spoke through the bars. It was not an animating intelligence but someone on the other side who watched the door.

Having undergone such exercises before, he knew he would be asked questions related to each of the three pillars of the order—mind, spirit, and heart. The first question he was asked was a random advanced-arithmetic question. He answered it easily, grateful his grandfather had filled the gaps of his earlier education.

The second question was a philosophical one about the creation of the universe. He answered it as well. There was no strict ecumenical ideal required of a sorcerer, only the acknowledgment of a higher, controlling power orchestrating the universe.

"I believe in the Mind of the Sovereignty," Robinson answered honestly.

The third question was one of fellowship.

"Are you a true sorcerer?" the man asked.

Robinson felt a surge of pride. He'd been part of the Invisible College since he was fourteen, the minimum age required to join. Being born into a family of sorcerers helped, to be sure, but it was no guarantee of admission. Character mattered more than heredity. And ability mattered most of all—those with no talent for singing or music wouldn't get very far, no matter how pristine their character.

Many quorums had their own rites of passage. But this oath, the Honored Oath, was the same for them all. "With all my blood, with all my heart, with all my soul, I am true. I swear fealty to no king, emperor, or bishop. All earthly kingdoms must fail. But I will remain true to the Invisible College to the end of my life and to the end of all time."

The lock was turned and the door opened partway. A young man's hand extended, and Robinson saw the fellow on the other side, probably three years younger than himself. "Brother to brother," the man greeted, and they gripped hands in the sorcerers' clasp.

"Brother to brother," Robinson answered. The door opened enough to reveal the young man's dress uniform. He was regular army, the rank of lieutenant on his shoulders. Double-breasted buttons went down the front of the rich blue jacket, which bore an octagonal cross at the collar. He had a thin beard and mustache.

"John Kelly Wickins, at your service," he said, squeezing Robinson's hand in a friendly way.

"Robinson Dickemore Hawksley. A pleasure. I've recently moved to Auvinen. I'm staying at a hotel with my parents at the moment, but I'll need a place to live."

"Dean George told us as much, and he also said you're younger than you look, old chap. Welcome. I have a distant cousin who is a Dickemore, I think. I like you already! I'm stationed here at the barracks in Auvinen, but I have my own private lodgings nearby. A basement apartment. My roommate died at the front recently. He was going to come back and take over while I train at signaling school here in the city. You can have his room if you like. It's a nice place. The previous tenant was a teacher."

His words jogged loose a memory. "Who owns it?"

"An incredible woman—Sarah Fuller Fiske. She's one of the leaders here at the Storrows."

"I know her! She mentioned the apartment was already let. I'm sorry to hear about your roommate. Isn't it too early in the season for war games?" During the seasons of spring, summer, and autumn, the soldiers trained and studied. It was during the winter months that they conducted field exercises in the trenches at the glacier walls.

"It didn't happen in a war game," Lieutenant Wickins said cryptically.

"Do you know what did happen?" His tone had set Robinson on edge. Like Dean George's. Some rumors were floating around that weren't common knowledge. Yet.

Wickins shook his head. "No details. Come in, let me show you the college. Mostly university and industry here. A few officers in training, like me and Lieutenant Snell. That was my roommate. He was a brother to me. He'd been assigned an outpost where my father is a colonel. The news was . . . sparse on the details."

"I'm sorry," Robinson said. "I lost both of my brothers to axioma. I've had it myself, and that's why we moved here. I'm still a little weak."

The lieutenant clapped Robinson's shoulder. "My sympathies as well. Poor chap. Well, let's introduce you. There are some uncommonly handsome women in the college too, I'll have you know. Smart as pistols. Come on."

He pushed the door fully open, and the sight of the red velvet carpet stretching before them struck Robinson with another familiar pang. There was something about the color that just made him feel welcome. He ducked and grabbed the violin case before following Lieutenant Wickins down the corridor.

When Wickins opened another door at the far end, the sight revealed took Robinson's breath away.

The Storrows was a mansion compared to the building used by his former quorum in Greenholh. Rows of dazzling chandeliers, lit by quicksilver bulbs, provided a soft but vibrant glow. There were at least forty tables, separated by aisles, where sorcerers were gathered, reading, talking, or demonstrating bits of magic. By Robinson's estimation, the room could easily hold a hundred and sixty sorcerers at once, and it was probably at half capacity at the moment. Along the walls were rows and rows of books, and there were floating mechanical hands that were delivering books or returning them to their proper locations.

Three young ladies approached them in the center aisle.

"Is this the new professor?" one of them asked with a pleasant smile.

"Indeed it is, may I introduce you to Robinson Dickemore Hawksley. This is Irabella Grant Swanson, Mildred Peter Smythe, and—" He snapped his fingers, trying to remember.

"Lavinia Horrocks," said the final girl, introducing herself. She reached out and took Robinson's hand, giving him a sorcerers' handshake.

Robinson repeated his name and then proceeded to greet the rest.

"Are you looking for a situation?" Irabella asked. "My father has a spare room! He also teaches at the university." She ducked slightly as a floating hand clutching a book sailed dangerously close to their heads. It caught him off-guard but in a delightful way. Surely the hand had been spelled to return books to their rightful places. He'd never seen such an invention before.

"I've decided I'll be staying with Lieutenant Wickins," Robinson said.

"Oh, that's a lovely home," Mildred added. "But what about Lieutenant Snell? I thought he was your roommate?"

"He . . . uh . . . he won't be coming back," Wickins said. "He died several days ago."

"Poor thing," Irabella said with real concern, touching his arm. "An accident?"

"I'm not sure. They don't send the bodies back, you know. Just the ashes. Ashes to ashes, dust to dust, and all that."

"I liked Lieutenant Snell," Mildred said sadly.

Lavinia looked troubled. Not just about the unexpected news, Robinson guessed, because her expression was worried as well as sorrowful. "Do you think it was the Aesir? My cousin was killed in action at the front as well. Very recently. We were told to keep it quiet. Not to cause alarm."

"Why would the military say that?" Irabella asked. "Do you *know* something, Wickins? Your father's a colonel."

He pursed his lips. "Not anymore. He was . . . demoted. He wouldn't say why."

"That's not common, is it?" Robinson asked. Until now, he'd never had any friends or acquaintances in the military, but he'd never heard of such a thing.

Lavinia's eyes widened with fear. "You don't think the Awakening is upon us?"

Wickins shrugged. "I don't know. If there were multiple casualties, it will be difficult to keep it secret for long. I certainly hope not."

"It's been over a hundred years," Irabella said, her brow wrinkling. "Thousands were killed in the last Awakening."

"Tens of thousands," Mildred declared. "I read a book on it once. But surely we have better magic now than then. It won't be as easy for the Aesir to slaughter us as they did before."

Robinson felt his stomach clench with dread. They were talking so casually about the death of a generation. With Robinson's health problems, he doubted he'd be conscripted, but many others would be. Certainly, his new friend would be expected to join the fight.

"I hope it's nothing," Irabella said. "An accident maybe. Poor Lieutenant Snell. Such sad tidings, but you are welcome here, Professor Hawksley. Truly."

He was grateful for the warm welcome, but a sense of foreboding hung over him. When the Aesir chose to come, wishes would not make them stay away.

To comprehend the Invisible College, it is best to first understand what it is not. It is not a university. There are no professors, headmasters, provosts, or deans. There is no curriculum, no distinction based on societal rank outside the college, and, intriguingly, no doors to enter the college from the outside. Discovering how to get "inside" is the first of its many tests.

Magic is not solely the dominion of the wealthy. The educated. The august. It is the privilege of the persistent. The curious. The autodidact. There are no artificial boundaries imposed by age, experience, or sex to attaining the highest degrees of distinction within its order.

The study of the magic of the Aesir was, to the best of my knowledge, founded at the University of Nirshoye in Andover. It was a secret even then, operating within those hallowed walls without the knowledge of its learned professors.

Who was the first Master of the Royal Secret? No one knows.

—Isaac Berrow,
Master of the Royal Secret,
the Invisible College

MaKenna Aurora Foster

CHAPTER FOUR

A Step toward Society

McKenna clasped the newly purchased book in her hands and walked along the busy boulevard to the carriage waiting at the end. It was easily distinguishable as belonging to her family, what with its royal-blue glossy paint and bronze trim and hubs. The team of two horses—Braden and Jenny—were also recognizable and so very unlike the multitude of iron horses that crisscrossed the neighborhoods and businesses of the thriving city and tugged on their heavy trams without complaint while leaving no dung to be swept up by the enchanted little street sweepers. A parcel rushed overhead, borne on magical wings that carried it whipping past the crowds, the sight coaxing a smile from her lips. The various manifestations of magic in the city never ceased to delight her. It made her hunger to be part of it somehow, someday. Maybe a deaf girl shouldn't dream of such things, but McKenna dared.

The women walking the streets had their hair in fashionable coifs and designs, marking them as adults in Society. McKenna, although eighteen, still wore hers loose. She had not been officially presented to Society yet. Because of her condition, because of the Aesir curse of the redoubtable fever, which had struck her as a small child, her acceptance into Society was far from a foregone conclusion.

Sighing to herself, she put on a burst of speed to reach the carriage, whereupon she greeted the driver. "Good morning, Mr. Thompson Hughes."

He tipped his hat to her. "Good morning, Miss Foster." She was close enough now to read his lips. He had a heavy coat over his suit coat, and gloves sheathed his hands. It was cool, but the brisk autumn air didn't bother her.

McKenna tugged on the handle and climbed up into the carriage where Father sat expectantly. His graying beard was long and full, a respectable length for an esteemed barrister. His pince-nez glasses rested on the crook at the top of his nose. He was reading some legal papers, but he set them back in his leather case and shut it.

"And what book did we purchase today?" he asked, a twinkle in his eye, after she sat down across from him.

"*The Incurious Mind of Chester Malcolm Weathersby*," McKenna pronounced, holding up the leather-bound book and admiring the gold foil embossing the title and the edges of the pages. Book manufacturing was also part of the Industry of Magic, the printers powered by the intelligences of ink beetles, while machines fueled by ox intelligences hoisted the heavy pallets of paper. It took a great number of sorcerers to keep the presses running. Father had explained the basics of magic to her, but he did not share the secrets of the Invisible College. Not like he'd done with her younger sister Clara, the nearest to her in age.

It was a fact universally acknowledged that the deaf could not learn magic.

"And why did you choose that one?"

"I'll admit the title piqued my interest at first. I read the beginning chapter while standing by the shelves. I think the authoress shows great promise."

"So the title is whimsical?"

"I believe so. From what I can tell. But this exercise was not merely about buying a book. You were here when I got off the street tram. Did I follow all your stipulations properly?" She felt like teasing him a little because of all the demands he'd made prior to this exercise in proving her competence to maneuver in Auvinen alone.

"You did indeed. You displayed cautious judgment before crossing the street by looking multiple times each way. You maneuvered through the foot traffic with grace and dignity. I saw you stop and ask someone for directions to Dredge & Magleby's, and you followed their directions right to the door."

"Even though I already *knew* where it was," McKenna declared. "I've been there enough times, Father."

"Yes, but always with an escort. You demonstrated, to my satisfaction, that you can wend your way in the city even after getting off at the wrong stop. Ah, here's your mother."

McKenna shifted her attention to her mother, dressed elegantly, complete with an eye-catching hat. Mother seated herself next to Father, but immediately reached across and squeezed McKenna's hand.

"What is your verdict?" Father asked Mother. "Did anyone comment on McKenna's speech after she left?"

Mother was always honest. "One of them did. Not the one who served you, McKenna, but another attendant came forward and asked about the interaction afterward. She said you spoke a little oddly and wondered why."

Father pursed his lips and then banged his cane against the roof, signaling to Mr. Thompson Hughes it was time to leave. McKenna's heart sank as the carriage jerked forward and joined the street traffic.

"If I can't fool a few shopgirls," she said, her throat tightening, "how am I supposed to convince someone like Lady Harpendon or Lady Challister?" It wouldn't matter to them that she could read any book given her, that she knew advanced arithmetic, that she had mastered the Tanhauser tongue in less than three months. Not even Lady Harpendon could speak it! Society would be fixed against her for the mere fact that she was deaf. It made her furious and frustrated at the same time. Indeed, it made her incandescent with rage.

McKenna loved words. She loved them passionately. "Incandescent" described her feelings perfectly. She set the new book down on the seat next to her and folded her arms, trying not to sulk.

Mother touched her arm, but McKenna waited to look at her. Throughout her childhood she hadn't realized that people touching her to get her attention was different from what they did for each other. Her parents, her sisters, her childhood governess—Mary Trewitt—had all contrived to treat McKenna as an ordinary child, one with no disadvantage at all. She'd learned to read lips and pay close attention to people's faces. To be aware of her surroundings in an inner world void of audible cues. Even though she couldn't always follow every single word someone was saying, her quick mind had learned to fill in the gaps intuitively. Now it was rare when she couldn't follow a conversation completely.

If she'd been stricken with the fever earlier, she likely would never have achieved such fluency in speaking and lipreading. But she'd been just the right age to adapt to the situation remarkably. Her abilities astounded everyone, in fact, and yet they still might not be enough to grant her what she wanted.

Sighing, she looked back at her parents' concerned expressions. Time was running out and they all knew it. Once McKenna turned nineteen, she would miss her chance at formally being acknowledged in Society. Her opportunities would shrink. It might not be horrible—because of her parents' wealth and reputation she could likely find someone to marry who might overlook her deafness. Someone who might not secretly fear that those who'd fallen ill from the Aesir's curse might pass the infliction on to another generation. A nice young barrister perhaps, one willing to take a blow on the social ladder to earn Mr. Foster's favor. She'd resigned herself to that notion, but she wanted more than to be an *appendage* to someone else's career. That word made her smirk.

"What?" Mother asked, noticing the expression.

"You've done so much for me already," McKenna said. "We went to Tanhauser, one of the most illustrious cities in the Lake Country. We visited every school we learned of that trained in speech." She remembered, with fondness, the ladies who favored bustle skirts to hooped ones and elaborate furs to hats. The men wore smart suits with dangling magical ribbons and had thick side whiskers but no beards. She'd even gone to an opera performance. The singers had sung in the language of the Lake Country, so although her parents hadn't been able to understand the words, they'd reported that the music had conveyed feelings both strong and passionate.

It had been a performance of the opera everyone was raving about, the famous Aesir story about the Erlking's daughter, who had been cursed into falling asleep while her husband forgot her and married another. It was a famously *tragic* story, one that ended with the destruction of the world. She'd read the tale to understand the plot, but watching the performance had grown tedious. One could only admire the costumes and props for so long. Singing words was different from speaking them, so her ability to read lips, especially at such a distance, had failed her. Even the little ocular glasses, enchanted with bird vision, didn't help her to see well enough, and she could only look at one face at a time, thus suffering in boredom throughout the performance.

Mother had been moved to tears. Father had thought the tickets too expensive.

"There is the new professor who recently came to Auvinen," Father reminded her, jostling her from her thoughts. "He has already given a talk at the school for the deaf. Sarah Fuller Fiske believes strongly he can help you."

"I respect Mrs. Fiske. And I'm grateful Mary wrote to us about him," McKenna said, trying to ease the tension from her shoulders. But she was skeptical of his ability to help her.

In all honesty, she was just stubborn enough that she wanted to prove them all wrong. To find a way to improve her speech without anyone else's help. But that attitude would do nothing to help her.

"His father taught a series of lectures years ago," Father said. "I recall hearing about the Hawksley method but didn't know much about it back then. Mary is convinced it'll transform the teaching at the school and also that it's the very thing to help you."

"What if this method takes years to learn?" McKenna asked with a sigh, thinking again of the ticking clock.

"Dearest, you learn things very quickly," Mother reminded her. "If this gentleman might have the ability to help you, we must at least try. You'll be shunned unless you can demonstrate your speech is equal to that of the daughters of the leading sets."

She knew what that meant—she'd be unable to form her own life, would remain an appendage to her family.

"If he can improve my speech, do you think it will be enough for me to try learning sorcery?" McKenna resisted the notion that her deafness would stop her from being what she wanted to be or subject her to limitations not of her own making.

Her father's eyebrows scrunched together. "I wouldn't get your hopes up, McKenna. No deaf person has ever learned to cast a spell. Without hearing, it's considered impossible for a person to sing the proper tones. It's been tried for centuries, since the days of Isaac Berrow. At first it was thought that perhaps playing music on an instrument would be the key—but there is more to music than learning to play the proper notes, and it has never yet worked, even with properly tuned instruments. Being self-aware of the sounds being made is apparently a necessity. For that reason, or some other, deafness and operating magic are incompatible."

McKenna generally liked that word—"incompatible"—but not in the present context. While she was enormously grateful that her parents had not consigned her to an asylum, as did many parents of deaf children, regardless of class, she didn't like to feel she was limited in anything. Still, she recognized what a rarity it was that her father, a wealthy patent barrister specializing in the Industry of Magic, had chosen to fight so proactively for her education.

"I guess I shouldn't set my hopes on anything, then," McKenna said, toying with a lock of her long hair. "I'll have to be content marrying a diligent barrister someday. That is all."

"While I admire your future husband's trade," her father quipped and adjusted his spectacles, "that is not as loathsome a fate as you imply. Love is not a tedious burden but a joy." He reached over and squeezed Mother's hand.

Mother smiled at the compliment.

"I know you will excel with the Hawksley method," Father said. "It is not easy to understand. It involves learning different symbols for how to shape your mouth and say certain words properly."

"You mean enunciation, elucidation, and articulation?" McKenna asked, using some powerful words that rhymed.

Mother smiled indulgently at her brashness.

"It will take more than well-chosen diction to overcome prolonged prejudices," Father added. "When I first invested in the opening of the school for the deaf, years ago, the experts refused me because they all agreed that the deaf could not be taught to speak. You know, I had considered taking you to Hawksley's father's university years ago, but Professor Winston Clarke from Auvinen had already been to that school. It was his advice to hire Mary. For all of us to treat you as though you could hear."

"And I'm grateful, Papa," McKenna gushed. "I know I cannot truly be part of the hearing world, but I'm not sad. I'm grateful we have traveled. I'm grateful to live here. I'm grateful for books. I'm grateful for tastes. I'm grateful for the feelings of different fabric." She ran her hands down her legs. "And I'm grateful to Mary for telling us about Professor Hawksley. I'm eager to meet him, although I think what I really need is *her* again. To let me know when I'm speaking too loudly or softly. Maybe we could bring her back?"

Mother patted McKenna's hands. "It's not just volume, dearest. You haven't heard in twelve years, and you don't even remember what it was like." She bit her lip, the memories clearly painful. "You've come so far. But you are not ready for Society. I'll ask Mary to escort you to your first appointment. If Professor Hawksley cannot help you cross these final steps, if only your sisters are accepted in Society, please don't resent them, McKenna. This is still difficult for all of us. I've seen the tension between the three of you increase so much over this last year."

McKenna shook her head. "I don't resent my sisters except for when they tease me. And they never tease me about being deaf. They are just silly creatures. I can't help being taciturn."

"That word doesn't describe you at all," Father observed. "You're lively, McKenna. Spirited. And not one bit silly."

Perhaps not, but the "silly" truth was this—her true goal was not to join Society but to learn magic and become a high-ranking member of the Invisible College. Because "impossible" was one word McKenna Foster did not wish to have in her vocabulary.

CHAPTER FIVE

Professor of Defective Utterance

A few days later, McKenna and Miss Trewitt disembarked from a street tram near the university. Anticipation made her stomach flutter. She was excited to be trying something new, even if it didn't work. Being in a different part of the city was also interesting. There were students everywhere, distinguished by their youthful appearances, suits and walking dresses, and the silk armbands attached to their sleeves denoting their academic status. It was an unfamiliar district for her, which was why Miss Trewitt had been summoned from her teaching job at the school for the deaf to escort McKenna to her first lesson. She'd balked initially, wanting to demonstrate her independence, since it was far from unusual for young women her age to attend such appointments on their own, but her parents' protectiveness had won out, and she was glad of it.

"How old is this professor?" McKenna asked, glancing at Miss Trewitt's face for a response.

"I'm not sure," Miss Trewitt said. "He's been very sick most of his life. Very frail. But quite passionate about what he knows. He's brilliant. You'll respect him, I know it."

"We shall see," McKenna said. But while she trusted both Miss Trewitt's and Mrs. Fiske's opinions, she would reserve her judgment about her new tutor until she'd learned his character for herself.

Since the street trams only operated in the major thoroughfares, they had to walk several blocks afoot until they reached their destination: a stately building with a mansard roofline and dormer windows—very chic. McKenna was surprised. She'd pictured more of a hovel than a stylish upper-class home.

"He does well for himself," McKenna said.

"He's only a boarder here," Miss Trewitt said with a laugh. "This is Sarah Fuller Fiske's house. He and another young man share the basement room, and there's a little schoolroom down there, set up by a former tenant, as well as space for his alchemy."

"His what?" McKenna asked. She hadn't caught the last word well enough.

"Alchemy," Miss Trewitt said, facing her and enunciating more slowly.

"Oh, he has an alchemy?"

"Oh yes. He has several different experiments going on. He's not just a practical sorcerer. He's an imaginative one."

"Which quorum is he part of?"

"The Storrows, naturally."

That was another word McKenna adored. *Quorum*. It was an archaic Aesir expression that meant, literally, "of whom we wish you to be one." Such an eloquent expression, she'd always thought.

She longed for the chance to join a quorum someday. All sorcerers were adept at grinding powders, mixing interesting-smelling reagents, and animating objects. She would love to learn how all of that worked. If she were trained, she could help oversee a loud printing press factory and not be bothered by the noise!

There were steps leading up to the main door, which was on the left side of the property, and another set underneath those that went down to the basement apartment. Miss Trewitt descended with her and knocked on the door.

Feelings of anticipation and reluctance warred within McKenna. What if she didn't like Professor Hawksley? What if he had halitosis or overly watery eyes or limp hands? She wasn't disposed to detesting people in general, so the fanciful thought *did* make her embarrassed about herself. At the same time, she was also concerned this man who was supposedly brilliant might not be impressed with her.

Why did that even matter?

They stood there, waiting, no one answering.

"Are we on time?" McKenna wondered, and quickly withdrew a little round pocket watch from her vest. No, they were early, not late. The appointment was imminent. Where was he?

Miss Trewitt knocked again, harder this time.

"Maybe he can't *hear* you?" McKenna said with a hint of disdain in her heart. Her father had taught her punctuality. It was an obligation of Society. A demonstration of integrity. If the professor had forgotten about the appointment, then—

She saw the door slowly open, revealing a gaunt man with a mass of dark hair, a single curl spilling onto his forehead. His shirt collar was unbuttoned. Unbuttoned! No cravat. A wrinkled shirt no less.

Miss Trewitt looked predictably appalled and embarrassed. She patted her bosom. "Professor Hawksley, it is Mary Trewitt. We had . . . we had an appointment with you this morning at this time? I am here with Miss Foster. Your new student."

The man looked positively confused, his eyes going from one face to the other.

"It is . . . morning?" he said, gazing at Miss Trewitt. "Already?"

McKenna saw the chain and the bulge of a pocket watch in his vest pocket. He should probably use it more often. Her opinion of him sank.

"Yes, Professor Hawksley. It is . . . time. We took the street tram, you see." Miss Trewitt was clearly mortified. This was not the introduction she'd anticipated after singing the teacher's praises to McKenna and her parents.

He had overslept. That was the only explanation for his state of undress, his bloodshot eyes, and his wince at the sunlight splashing across his face.

"Excuse me," he said suddenly. He shut the door in their faces.

McKenna's eyes opened wide, aghast. All she could do was look at her teacher in bewilderment.

"He is retching . . . rather violently," Miss Trewitt mouthed to her. McKenna could tell when someone was mouthing versus speaking—it put a different look on their faces, and the words were harder to discern.

"Oh dear," McKenna said. So it wasn't merely a matter of oversleeping. Was he . . . was he *intoxicated*? A sorcerer of the Invisible College?

After a pause, the door opened again, and the haggard professor reappeared. He looked even more run-down this time.

"Was it one of your headaches, Professor?" Miss Trewitt asked with a stiff hesitancy.

He winced at the sunlight again. "It came on last night," he breathed. "As soon as I heard the news. These headaches are quite debilitating."

"What news?" McKenna asked, even though it had hardly been a proper introduction. Society would have frowned on her for speaking to such an unkempt man who hadn't been prepared to receive them. But judging from Miss Trewitt's remarks, this wasn't intoxication. She knew some people suffered from cephalalgia, which rendered them quite incapacitated.

The professor's eyes met hers again. A look of anguish was on his face. A brooding darkness. "The Awakening has begun," he said. "The Aesir war is starting again."

To McKenna's and Miss Trewitt's dismay, Professor Hawksley urged them to come in. They were brought to the little schoolroom, which had been set up with a few haphazard chairs. Other than that, it was nothing like the schools she'd visited in the Lake Country of Yverdon,

Mrs. Fiske's school, or any other. The walls were covered in teaching materials, drawings of human faces without the skin, some with teeth, tonsils, and tongues. Professor Hawksley wore his trousers and suspenders, a billowy white shirt with a high collar, and shoes that were practically falling apart.

They sat down on a bench while he pulled up a chair across from them and leaned close. His dark hair tumbled over his brow, but it was cropped at the nape of his neck, just above the collar. He really was ghastly thin.

Mary, as was her custom, put a hand on McKenna's shoulder each time she asked a question, then they both awaited the professor's answer.

"This is dreadful news, Professor," Miss Trewitt said, a worried look on her face. "There has been nothing in the press about it. At least not in today's paper. Nor is it winter yet."

"No, it will not be for another several weeks. But it is colder up north. Winter comes earlier there. My roommate is a lieutenant. He was just notified of it and may get called to the front. Every available soldier is being sent to the ice trenches. Several breaches have already occurred, so war is imminent. The time for training and balls is at an end."

"It has been at least a century since the last Aesir war, has it not?" McKenna asked in astonishment. She'd heard the stories, of course. They'd all been raised on them. And she'd seen Aesir relics in museums, as well as the floating rock in her own city. But it was quite a different thing to know that it was happening again. That her generation would be the one that knew war.

Professor Hawksley gazed at her inquisitively. "Miss Trewitt, you have done yourself credit. Your speech is exemplary, Miss Foster."

So was his. Despite his unconventional attire and greeting, she'd noticed at once that he was the most articulate person she'd ever met. Not only did he have an astonishingly reliable vocabulary, but his expressive face and pronunciation made his lips easier to read and understand.

"I have devoured books since I was a child," she told him. "I love language, literature, and learning in general."

"Miss Trewitt told me you learned the native tongue of the Lake Country in only a few months. A second language is difficult under ordinary circumstances. I am bewildered you could make out sounds you had never heard spoken before."

"Is it really so strange, Professor? When I watch people speak, I notice their expressions, gestures, and other clues that help me understand the meaning behind the words. Then I do my best to imitate what I've seen. And books are an inexhaustible way to expand one's vocabulary." She knew she was showing off. A little.

"Miss Foster has been an exceptional learner," Miss Trewitt said proudly. "I think she's always been brilliant."

He looked impressed as well. "Extraordinary. You have a natural gift for communication for one in your situation. But imitating what you see is not enough. You must learn to *feel* your words."

"I don't understand, Professor."

"Speech is vibration." He popped out of the chair and suddenly knelt before her, breaking every code of Society as if they meant absolutely nothing at all to him. Then he put his hands on her face! Not just her face—he touched her earlobes and then the corner of her jaw, pressing his fingers gently but firmly into her skin and sinews. Then he put one hand on his own throat and the other on hers. "Your larynx produces the vibrations. Your eardrums are meant to receive them. Your ears were permanently damaged by redoubtable fever, of course. They will not function. Impossible. But can you still feel the vibration when you speak?"

"Yes," she said, feeling flushed by his hand resting on her throat in such an intimate way. Not intimate like lovers—the skies forbid!—but intimate like they had been friends or acquaintances for a long while instead of having just met on the doorstep.

"And you can feel the vibrations through your nose as well, can you not?" he asked, moving his hand from his throat to his nose and his other hand to hers.

"I suppose so?" She hadn't ever thought about it.

He lowered his hands, still crouching in front of her, hands now on his knees. "What you cannot hear, but the rest of us can, is that your speech has a little honk to it."

"A honk?" she said, uncertain she'd understood him.

"Like a goose. It is a sound you have not heard before, but all animals make their own kind. It is what is known as a defective utterance."

"I beg your pardon!" McKenna said with a surge of offense.

"Oh, I apologize! In my training in elocution, that means any form of speech that isn't correct. I didn't mean to ridicule you, Miss Foster. Many hearing children exhibit the same issues. One of my students from Covesea cannot say his *s*'s. Would you say that letter for me, please?"

She was becoming more and more fascinated. He didn't treat her like an invalid or inferior. He knew she was educated, well read, and he was already starting to teach her, not waiting to see if she was willing to learn. This wasn't an interview at all—it was a lesson.

"Ess," she pronounced.

"Where are your teeth when you finish the sound? The tips of your front teeth are touching." He gently lifted her chin. "Now try saying the letter with your tongue in between those front teeth."

"Eth," she said, then giggled. She couldn't help it.

"I corrected a young man's defective utterance by showing him where to put his tongue while he spoke. Not by sound. But by the position of his lips, his tongue, his jaw. This amazing apparatus, your mouth, is capable of so many splendid words and sounds. You should not be feeling the vibrations of speech in your nose so much"—he patted his own upper chest, and she was more than relieved and grateful when he refrained from doing the same to hers—"as from here. I believe we can eliminate that little honk in no time. With practice, and I know you will practice because of all you've achieved thus far, it will vanish completely, for you will recognize how correct speech feels on your face, in your throat, in your chest."

McKenna felt the squeeze on her knee.

"Professor Hawksley, how often would you need to meet with Miss Foster at the beginning?"

"Every day for two weeks and then once a week after that." He stared at McKenna as he answered to make it easier for her to read his lips. "Once I teach you the forms, the symbols, you will do much of your practice at home. I will offer correction and practices."

Miss Trewitt had another question. "Is it true your father taught an urchin how to speak correctly, and she tricked a parlor full of ladies and gentlemen into thinking she was one of them?"

He smiled at the memory. "Who told you that story?"

"Mrs. Fiske did."

"It is true. And that young woman went on to join the Invisible College and no longer sells flowers at locomotivus stations."

What a change of fortunes for her. "Do you think, with training, I can be part of Society?" McKenna asked him.

"Undoubtedly," he said without a moment's hesitation. "You would make an excellent dancing partner as well."

"Truly?" Miss Trewitt said excitedly. "But she cannot hear the music."

"All the Society dances are practiced steps performed at a regular tempo." He clapped his hands to the beat. "One, two, three, one, two, three. The waltz, for instance, invented in Tanhauser a century ago, is a repetition of the beat while twirling in a circle. Your inner ear is damaged, Miss Foster. You may have noticed that you rarely get dizzy. That is why I suggested you would make an excellent dancing partner."

Something unlocked in McKenna's mind as she watched his lips. She had never considered dancing before. It had always been an impossibility. But Professor Hawksley had insisted she could not only learn it but excel at it.

"You really think so, Professor?" she asked, growing more animated as she thought about it.

"I have no doubt whatsoever. As I said, you would excel. It will take several days to teach you all of the symbols of my father's method, the one I recently shared with Miss Trewitt's school. If that is agreeable, we can begin today."

"Yes," McKenna said eagerly. There was another question burning inside her. The very same question she'd just posed to her parents several days previously. "Do you think, Professor, that I can learn spells? If I can say any word, can I not join the Invisible College someday?"

The brightness in his eyes wavered and dimmed. "Miss Foster. I cannot say it is impossible because I do not know for certain. But if you were to ask anyone at the Invisible College right now, they would declare it to be just that. Impossible."

"But why?" She felt a stab of disappointment. Her cheeks began to flush. Was she going to cry? No, not in front of him! She bottled up her feelings, refusing to give way to them.

He looked at her with a sympathy that suggested he knew she was hurt. "Let me try to explain what we know. If we visit my alchemy, I can do a better job of it."

CHAPTER SIX

The Alchemy

McKenna's father had an alchemy, but it was a very small one. In his career, he no longer required the regular use of one. Professor Hawksley's room was eye-popping with its array of quizzical instruments, mortars and pestles, and varying sizes of magnifying glasses, tuning forks, jars, tubs, bottles, and heating coils. The smell of it—like burnt toast with a hint of overcooked eggs—was strange but not unpleasant. She gazed around the small room equipped with benches, a worktable, and two chairs. Everything was cluttered with hand drawings, calculations, and nubs of pencils and charcoal. Miss Trewitt touched McKenna's arm, signaling that Professor Hawksley was trying to get her attention.

"I beg your pardon," she apologized. "Do go on."

"Sorry for the mess. My father was going to help me organize things, but he and my mother found a situation in a little community outside the city, and I helped them move. I've been so busy since, I haven't made time to rearrange things. I have three different experiments going at once."

"Oh? What are they?" McKenna asked, intrigued.

"I can explain those later. Every sorcerer starting out needs an alchemy in order to practice and experiment with sound, light, and chymicals. It was a trade, long ago, used to create substances like saltpetr to be used in the war. There is a specifical chymical sequence that must be followed with great precision in order to harness the Unseen Powers. Saltpetr has three ingredients—bat droppings, charcoal, and sulfur. It's the combination of those three, after being ground to minute particles for hours in a very specific ratio." The professor took the mortar and pestle and went through the motions as he explained. "Extreme care must be taken, of course, because when they are combined, the Unseen Powers are ready to be unleashed. Certain sounds can cause an immediate explosion. Many sorcerers, in the early days, died learning the craft. Or burned their houses down."

"That's terrible," McKenna said in surprise. Father had never explained the dangers to her before.

"How do you know when you've reached the proper combination? We know it *now* after centuries of practice, but back then, a sorcerer would grind until they *felt* it was done. That feeling was transmitted to them by invisible intelligences. You are familiar with intelligences?"

"Yes," McKenna said, nodding. "Father has explained that every bit of life has a spark of intelligence to it. Even cockroaches. But can you explain the difference between the Unseen Powers and intelligences? They aren't the same, are they?"

Professor Hawksley chuckled. "Even cockroaches. You are right, they are different. An intelligence is an undividable essence of sentience. A stone is not sentient; therefore it does not have one. A shrubbery does. A very small one. It can die and decompose, but the intelligence will live on. Those intelligences can be beseeched upon to help us. They are . . . agents of the Unseen Powers, if you will, which are phenomena that exist in the universe. Laws. Powers. Organizing principles set in motion by the Mind of the Sovereignty. If I drop something, it falls, even though I cannot see what pulls it down. There are many aspects to such laws that we are still only primitively aware of."

"Oh," McKenna said. "That makes more sense. But how does a sorcerer learn what is known or unknown? I haven't read a single book about it. Are none published?"

"Well, you've already learned things from your father. I was a little more patient with my grandfather's teaching methods than my father's, so he was the one who taught me the beginnings of it. But yes, there are books. They are kept within the quorums of the Invisible College. Therefore, anyone who wishes to join the Invisible College must first have a mentor."

"And how is someone unconnected to the college to find one? I've heard it said there are no doors on the quorums."

"As with anything else, you must ask questions. Seek advice. Study and learn from those who are willing to teach. Many schoolmasters are part of the Invisible College, and when they see promise in a student, they are often willing to provide extra coaching, additional insights."

"But you haven't explained why *I* can't be part of it," McKenna pleaded. She was engaged in the conversation, impressed by his mind and hands-on approach to teaching. Literally hands on.

He nodded sympathetically. "Language. What is it used for?"

"To communicate?"

"In its simplest form, it allows a thought in my mind"—he tapped the side of his head with his index finger—"to transfer to yours." He touched her temple next. "To hasten that transfer, we have invented words, language, names, parts of speech, grammar. We agree that what I am wearing is a shirt. These are hands." He waggled his at her. "But words are sounds. And sounds transmit by vibrations." He walked over to the worktable and picked up a tuning fork. He whacked it on the edge of the table. "You can't hear it."

She shook her head. "No."

Miss Trewitt tilted her head, looking perplexed.

"Come closer," the professor said, gesturing with his other hand for McKenna to approach. When she did, he whacked the edge of the table again and then held the tuning fork near the lip of a cup of water. She watched with fascination as he dipped it toward the liquid. The water bubbled and frothed as he touched the tuning fork to it, making her start with surprise.

He dried it off on his shirt and thumped it again, then pressed it against her hand. She felt the quivering of the tuning fork still. She knew about vibrations from touching things at home, like the strings of a violin. But she'd never given it this much thought before. "Music is more than just a metaphor for teaching magic. It's the conduit for resonance. Two tuning forks, held near each other, will resonate the vibrations of music. If you put your hand on one, the other still carries the sound. You can speak, Miss Foster, but I'm guessing you were never trained to sing."

"Indeed not," she said.

"They likely believed it was impossible. Perhaps they were correct, perhaps not. I don't have the training to teach you to sing, and it may be too late to start, but let's see where things go with what I know. We may yet discover another way to make the resonance happen—one that does not require song."

She noticed the professor's eyes looking over her shoulder and realized someone must have entered the alchemy. Turning her head, she saw a man in military uniform in the doorway. It was not a dress uniform, the kind she had seen officers wearing on military parades or at guard posts. No, she rather thought this was the sort of uniform an officer donned before heading to the trenches. According to her father, whom she'd asked how soldiers stayed warm in the trenches, the buckles and buttons were enchanted to provide warmth. The soldier had a pistol holstered at his side, a bayonet blade strapped to his front pocket. He was a young man, much closer to her age than the professor was. A brooding young man about to go to war, from the look of it.

The professor gestured to the young man. "This is my roommate, Lieutenant John Kelly Wickins."

"Pleasure to meet—" he said, but bowed so quickly she wasn't sure what else he mumbled. After he straightened, he gave the ladies a curt smile.

Miss Trewitt positioned herself slightly ahead of McKenna so that her face could be seen by her charge. "Is it true you are heading to the front, Lieutenant?"

"So my friend has told you the news, has he? Not yet. I'll be spending more time at the barracks first. None of us believed another Aesir war would happen in our lifetimes."

"Indeed so," Miss Trewitt said. "What do you do in the army?"

"I was studying ancient languages so that I might read older texts and learn about the Aesir. Now I have been reassigned to Signals Intelligences. We use the . . . uh . . . the Geager Code . . . to transmit messages along the front."

"What code?" McKenna asked. "I didn't catch that word."

"Oh, the Geager Code. Tonal sounds transmitted along wires."

"I see. Go on."

"The mountains are vast and so are the glaciers. The problem is that we don't know where the attack is coming from. The Aesir are not predictable. Until recently, no one living had ever encountered one before."

"Oh, I do wish they would stop attacking us!" Miss Trewitt said, looking fearful. "My grandfather used to tell tales he'd heard from his father about the last war. Dreadful. And they always come in the winter."

"I know something on that score," Lieutenant Wickins said. "I'm a bit of a history and ancient literature student. In addition to my other pursuits, I study the language of the Aesir."

"You do?" McKenna asked, impressed.

"Yes. Uh. It was a hobby at first, admittedly—a challenge I set for myself—but now that hobby is in precious demand at headquarters at present, which is why I won't be shipped to the front right away. If we encounter one of *them*, I may be called upon to translate."

"I would imagine so," McKenna agreed. She was finding it more and more difficult to concentrate on the conversation now with the additional speaker. One who was not as precise in his words as her new teacher.

"The Aesir believe we have abrogated . . . um . . . 'violated' is perhaps the better word, my apologies, an ancient treaty. A treaty no country can remember agreeing to or even knows the terms of."

"Wasn't this treaty written down?" Miss Trewitt asked in confusion.

"It likely was. But it could have been centuries ago. Longer even. There is nothing left of it now. Yet they hold us to it. They believe we mortals have violated the terms. Lucky us. Unwitting as we are, they continue to attack us."

"Is there any pattern to their invasions?" McKenna asked. "The last time was a century ago, but it hasn't always been thus, has it?"

"Ah . . . the timing is inexplicable. The Aesir are not mortal by our understanding, and thus their timeline is completely different from ours. They attack us when they awaken. Our kind needs six to eight hours of sleep each night. Our bodies require it. Well, except for Dickemore here, who gets by on three. Poor chap. The Aesir bodies have different needs. They are dormant for a time and then awaken. Sometimes it is longer, sometimes shorter. There is no pattern. When they do awaken, they instantly seek to destroy us. Until the next time they fall into dormancy. It is a strange affair, this hatred between our peoples." He looked awkwardly at them a moment before shifting his gaze to the professor. "I need to head to the barracks across town. We'll get some tea when I get back?"

"Yes. I'd like that," the professor said. He looked several years older, but the two seemed to have a natural camaraderie.

"Your headache still troubling you, poor chap?"

The professor nodded and rubbed the side of his head. "It started after the news. Like a bell is ringing in my mind and I can't shut it off. Thankfully these delightful young ladies came over to distract me from it."

"We should probably leave," Miss Trewitt said. "What time would you have Miss Foster return for her next lesson?"

"I finish my last lecture at four," the professor said. "Is that agreeable? Each day except for Closure?"

"It is agreeable," McKenna said. "I will take a street tram here. That is no trouble."

"You travel alone?" the professor asked with surprise, which shifted to a look of approval.

"I can come with you," Miss Trewitt offered. "Just until you are more certain."

"I would have no trouble finding this house again. I can manage it on my own, Mary."

He flashed her a genial smile and nodded in approval. She was grateful he and the lieutenant were part of the Invisible College, for that made the propriety of doing private lessons in the house less problematic. So did its ownership by Mrs. Fiske. It would have been considered untoward to take private lessons from someone without such impeccable reputational credentials.

"A pleasure meeting you both," McKenna said. She longed to be part of the tradition of handshaking, but that was only done sorcerer to sorcerer—another aspect of the order that her father had refused to teach her. It had to be earned by ascension through the ranks. And maybe, just maybe, Professor Hawksley was the one who could make that happen for her. With the onset of war, she felt more determined than ever.

CHAPTER SEVEN

Uproar

The last two weeks with Professor Hawksley had opened a new world to McKenna, consisting of a secretive language of symbols, the science of vibration, and teaching methods she'd never encountered before. None of the lessons had been boring—far from it. The professor was easy to understand, determined to challenge McKenna's limits, and quick to praise when she'd accomplished something or even when she'd given it her best effort and failed.

Her parents had both commented, independently of each other, that they'd noticed a substantial improvement in her speech and, because of it, had requested she invite the professor to dinner on Closure. Her subtle honk had been totally obliterated. She'd sung Professor Hawksley's praises so many times that her sister Clara had teased that she was infatuated with her teacher. Which was utterly absurd.

She did admire him, however, and looked forward to the daily lessons. As she walked briskly down the boulevard to get to her next appointment with him, having already disembarked from the tram, she noticed the unusually large number of soldiers in uniform preparing to leave for the ice trenches. Indeed, there were signs everywhere that the empire was mobilizing for war. Enlistment recruitment posters were plastered on the sides of buildings, and street hawkers gave out proselytizing handouts to every young man who passed by. Some citizens had even started wearing flag pins on their clothes to signal their support for the military. Papa had said during breakfast that it was almost impossible to get a ticket to Bishopsgate because most of the locomotivus lines were being used by the army to transport equipment and send in troops. Winter had not yet set in, but their world was changing. Her parents had even talked about sending her and her sisters to winter at Mowbray House, Aunt Margaret's estate on Siaconset Island. That little island off the coast had very mild weather and would thus be safer.

Climbing down the steps to the professor's residence, she knocked firmly on the door and smiled when the professor opened it. He was suitably clothed this time, unlike their first meeting, but she'd learned he had a total disregard for modern fashion.

"Welcome, Miss Foster," he greeted, inviting her in.

"Mama would like you to come to our home for dinner on Closure," McKenna said. "Should I say you will come?"

"I would be honored, of course. I admire the tradition of Closure in Auvinen," Robinson said. It wasn't common in Covesea or other regions of the empire. The one day off each week that every worker looked forward to. A day for machines and mortals to rest.

"Lieutenant Wickins is invited too, of course."

"He is working late hours at the railyard this week. I do not know if he works Closure or not, but I will ask."

"We would love to have you both," McKenna said, eager to get started on her lesson for the day. He brought her to his teaching chamber, but a young woman awaited them there, something that had never happened before. She looked to be twenty or so and wore a modest fashion, like someone from a lower class.

"Miss Foster, let me introduce you to Miss Ella Florence Hurst. Miss Hurst, this is McKenna Aurora Foster."

"Pleased to meet you," McKenna greeted, feeling confused. She'd never shared lessons with someone else before. Papa had paid for *private* lessons.

"I look forward to working with you," Miss Hurst said with a kindly smile.

McKenna glanced at the professor in confusion.

"Miss Foster, I've asked Miss Hurst to continue your private lessons. She works at the school your father set up and is an excellent teacher, who has already mastered the principles of the method. Under her guidance, you will flourish."

This did more than confuse McKenna. Indeed, she was struggling to keep her composure. She didn't *want* a new teacher. The rush of violent disappointment was startling in its intensity.

"Why?" she demanded, probably a little too hotly.

"I am afraid I have a tendency to overcommit myself," he said with a sheepish grin. "I have enjoyed our lessons, Miss McKenna, I m-mean Miss Foster, but it would be better if you continued on with Miss Hurst. I will oversee your progress, rest assured, and indeed, I believe you will be better suited with her."

"Is my father aware of this change? He did not mention it during breakfast." McKenna worried she was starting to sound rude, and judging by the look on Miss Hurst's alarmed face, she was feeling the awkwardness of the moment keenly.

"I did not mean to offend you, Miss Foster," the professor said placatingly. "It is entirely my fault. I took on more work than I can realistically perform to satisfaction. You have made such amazing progress so far. Your grasp of the method, your work ethic, they are above reproach. I implore you. Just give Miss Hurst a chance. She will earn your regard. I promise you."

Peevish. That's how McKenna felt. She was being peevish. And it was unseemly for a young woman of her station to act like that. If Papa were there, he would shoot her a scolding look from beneath his spectacles.

"I apologize," McKenna said. "This just . . . came as a surprise. That is all."

"Why don't we go to the lesson room? I will linger a moment and make sure things are going well. I'm excited to listen to your progress on the lyrics of the Poundstone canticle. It trips up many students and would-be sorcerers."

That was another thing that galled McKenna. Although Professor Hawksley had made it clear he didn't think it likely she could ever become a sorcerer, he'd said he would be willing to work on her goal with her. Was he abandoning that promise? Had he forgotten he'd even made it?

"The seething sea ceaseth and thus the seething sea sufficeth us," McKenna said with a toss of her hair before marching primly into the classroom.

*

"How was your lesson with Professor Hawksley today?" Mama asked with a bright smile as McKenna entered the parlor. She was sitting on the bench at the Broadwood grand, its onyx keys beneath her fingertips. Clara and Trudie were playing a card game in front of the fireplace, and one of them paused to look up at her before returning to the game.

In the mornings, the curtain had to be shut because of the sun's direct rays shining brightly through the glass. The curtains were open now, though, revealing a glass greenhouse and garden in the yard.

McKenna leaned against the entry door, still wrestling with her feelings of disappointment. She'd even let a few tears fall on the way home, which was mortifying.

Mama seemed to notice her dour expression. How else to describe it? Truly, McKenna felt dour. She felt dark, determined, and decided.

"I think I will quit the lessons," she said stiffly. "The professor has taught me all he *can*, apparently."

"In two weeks? You've made so much progress already, but—"

"He doesn't want me as his student anymore," McKenna blurted out. "I'm to be educated by a young woman only a few years older than I am. A beginner at the method, no less. It's appalling. I should just quit. I'm determined to."

Mother rushed to McKenna and brought her to the little sofa by the bay window overlooking a leafless cherry orchard and gardens. She looked sympathetic and more than a little concerned.

"Tell me what happened, dearest," she said coaxingly.

"I arrived for my lesson a little late, but it wasn't my fault. The first thing he said to me was he was overworked and had to let a student go. And he chose me. He arranged for another teacher from Papa's school, but she's barely older than I am."

"Who? What is her name?"

"Miss Hurst," McKenna said with a sigh of disgust. "She's perfectly . . . adequate."

"And she knows the method? She taught you today?"

"Yes, but I want to study with Professor Hawksley."

Mother glanced toward the fireplace. "That isn't helping, Clara."

McKenna turned and looked at her sister, who had a devious smile. "What did you say?"

"Nothing," Clara said with a simper, looking down at her cards. Clara was the second oldest and was always vying for attention with her acerbic wit. It didn't help that she would be coming of age herself and looked at her big sister as an impediment to her own success in Society. They'd been really close when they were younger, but Clara and Trudie had joined an unspoken truce.

McKenna glared at her before turning back to Mama. "What did she say?" she asked tightly.

"Darling, so he didn't cancel the lessons? He just has another teacher helping?"

"Yes, but she doesn't know the method as well as he does. His father invented it. It's not fair. He just assumed that I would be fine switching like this. With what Papa pays him, you would think he would be more deferential to our family."

Mama squeezed her hands. "McKenna, darling, I am certain Professor Hawksley had a good reason for what he did. With the war starting, perhaps he has more sorcerers to teach now? More people to help train to defend us?"

"It's not that," McKenna said. Now Mother's patient coaxing was making her feel like she was being peevish again, which would not do. Not at all. "I get the sense he's always working in his alchemy on some invention or other. He stays up way too late at night working. The man hardly sleeps. That's why he is so thin, so bedraggled all the time. He hardly *eats*."

Mother bit her lower lip.

"What?" McKenna said, feeling exasperated.

"You speak of a silent concern your father and I have had these last few weeks."

"I don't understand."

Mama gripped her hands more tightly. "Did you invite him to dinner at Closure?"

"Yes, but only because I invited him first thing. Before he told me he didn't want me as a student. I wouldn't have otherwise. It's too mortifying."

Mama looked down in relief. Then she met McKenna's gaze again. "Dearest, Mrs. Fiske expressed her worry that he does not have enough food to eat. Living in Auvinen is so expensive. Even with his salary at the university and his income from private students, he does not eat more than once a day. She's often invited him to dinner because she worries he will not ask for food. That is why I wanted you to invite him to dinner, McKenna. He's a proud man. He will not ask for help."

That was something she had not even considered. She felt a splash of hot shame on her cheeks. The professor was unbearably thin, but she'd assumed it was a legacy of his illness.

Mother released her hands. "If he loses you as a student, McKenna, it might go badly for him. Papa does pay generously. But if he is like other young sorcerers in this city, he must purchase his own experiments, equipment, and materials himself. You mentioned he has an alchemy."

"Yes, and it's amazing," McKenna said.

"He probably spent everything he has on it. I just think . . . just consider . . . that he could use our help as much as you need his."

Her cheeks were too hot. She felt like crying again, but not for the same reason she'd been stricken on the way home. She'd been foolish. No, worse. She'd been blind to the suffering of someone she valued. She, whose family had so much to eat that they gave to the poor and invited people to dinner to share their abundance. She was proud of Papa and Mama. They were good people. Exemplary. And she was just a peevish child.

"I will . . . persevere," McKenna said, her throat catching. She patted her mother's hands. "I hope his invention is a triumph and that he becomes as wealthy as the emperor. It is kind of you and Papa to invite him and Lieutenant Wickins to dinner."

Mama gave her an approving look. "His work with you, darling, has been nothing short of astounding. If you can enter Society as a peer, it will change your future forever. Some young man may see your beautiful character, your shining example, all you have been through and triumphed over, and he will not care that you are deaf. He will love you for who *you* are, McKenna Aurora Foster."

McKenna felt giddy inside at the thought. She was just over eighteen. In a few months, she would need to enter Society or be rejected from it permanently. She believed in herself because her parents believed in her—and Professor Hawksley believed in her too.

"I will marry for love or not at all," McKenna announced with as much of a dignified air as she could muster. "Like Aunt Margaret. Even if I can't join the Invisible College, I could still invest in inventions." Like her teacher's. Having some power, even if it was only financial, was better than none, although she was not ready to give up her dream. It wasn't in her to give up.

She decided she would be kinder to the professor at dinner. She would watch for signs of hunger. She would pay closer attention from now on.

"Clara," Mother said, shaking her head.

"What did she say?" McKenna demanded.

"She's being incorrigible," Mama said with an arch look.

"What did she say this time?" McKenna said.

"She was teasing about you being alone with Professor Hawksley if his roommate heads off to the war. Saying you'd need a chaperone then."

"Don't make light of the war," McKenna scolded her sister.

"Why not?" Clara said. "With our inventions, we'll obliterate the Aesir. They'll scurry back beneath the ice. Just you wait."

McKenna shook her head. It was easy to believe such things when the ice trenches were so far away. But what about the soldiers who had to survive in the cold? Lieutenant Wickins would likely keep his station at the barracks in Auvinen due to his training. But if things got bad on the front, he could be called there.

The thought opened a pit in her stomach.

They say there was a time, deep in the past, when we were not at war with the Aesir. A time when they taught us some of their ways—language, music, magic. In that order most likely. Our cities are just a pale comparison to theirs. It is said that hearing one of their arias could make someone tire of food or drink or even sleep. Many mortals attempted to live in their frigid kingdom—and died. Our races are not compatible.

But we still learned what we could from them. You can learn from anyone. Even your enemy. Perhaps especially your enemy. Their magic is a combination of sound and feeling. That is what draws on the Unseen Powers. Discordant sounds can unravel magic. Harsh noises can frighten away those powers. That is why the sorcerers use saltpetr in cannons to make loud explosions. The sound disrupts hearing their magic. And we learned, quite by accident, what saltpetr and elfshot do to their bodies.

—Isaac Berrow,
Master of the Royal Secret,
the Invisible College

Joseph Crossthwait

CHAPTER EIGHT

The Stillness

Joseph's breath formed a thin trail of mist in the frigid air. Although the buckles and buttons of his uniform kept him warm, he could still feel the hairs inside his nose responding to the subfreezing temperatures in the mountain pass. He walked down the colonnade of cannons, each one staffed with soldiers and one sorcerer who would ignite the blasts. In the last war, it had been discovered that one of the Aesir's greatest weaknesses was the smoke of burning saltpetr. For some reason beyond understanding, the gritty smoke that belched from firearms hindered their magic. It could slow their deer-quick speed and empower the balls of alloyed shot to penetrate their armor. Maybe the loudness of the blasts and concussive aftershocks of the cannons also interfered with the spells they cast. It had been too long since the last Aesir war. This new generation lacked the field experience and resolve required to face such foes. They relied on their artillery, believing that when the inevitable came, the scale of firepower would determine the outcome.

Joseph stopped beside one of the cannons to examine the fire symbol etched into the metal. The soldiers had fearful looks in their eyes, highlighted by eyebrows white with frost beneath the beaver-pelt helmets they wore to protect their heads from the cold. The guns were all pointed toward the mountain pass ahead, burrowed in a devastatingly beautiful range of mountains that dominated the skyline in all directions. In some parts of the front, the glaciers still intruded into the lower valleys, forming giant walls of vertical ice. And the Aesir, through their magic, could pass through the crystalline structure of the ice without any impediment. To them, it was like walking through fog.

"Which parts of the line were struck yesterday?" asked the sorcerer assigned to the gunnery. He'd noticed Joseph's pause and decided to risk a question for the benefit of his men.

"The Eau Claire Pass," Joseph said. "Just a skirmish. About a dozen dead, impaled with seeking arrows."

Seeking arrows were imbued with intelligence and could arc around obstacles to hit their prey. Each arrow was a death shot, and the kill released the intelligence that had been bound in service, thus preventing the human sorcerers from gaining any information from them.

Joseph tugged his gloves on more tightly. One of his fellows had inspected the dead to be sure none had miraculously "revived"—bringing another Semblance into their midst. There were more of them in the population, though. There had to be. He knew from experience that the Aesir used Semblances to infiltrate the mortal world and glean what they could of their societies and defenses. They could be just as deadly in mortal form as in their own.

"Have you ever fought an Aesir, sir?" asked the sorcerer timidly.

Joseph glanced at him and the interested eyes of his men. The next group of gunners were also keenly paying attention.

"I have," Joseph answered simply. He didn't elaborate. They were encounters he wouldn't have survived without his training, and especially not without his kappelin.

Centuries ago, a band of knights had been formed who dedicated themselves to the lore and ways of the Aesir in order to defend their war-torn kingdoms from them. Joseph Crossthwait was one of the few remaining members of that order, a deadly order directed by the Invisible College.

"And if we get attacked today, what should we do?" asked one of the soldiers, his voice quavering.

"Follow your training," Joseph replied with a snap in his voice. "Aiming is useless. By the time you see one, it's already too late. They move too fast. Keep up a heavy fire to fill the sky with smoke. That will give the sharpshooters a chance to pick them off. We outnumber them a thousand to one. The arithmetic is in our favor."

That awful arithmetic also meant the Aesir had learned to become more brutally efficient at killing over the centuries-long or perhaps even millennia-long war. They could only mount their attacks during the winter, when conditions for their race were tolerable outside the glacier mountains. During spring, summer, and autumn, they retreated back to their crystalline palaces hidden beyond miles of solid ice. No amount of elfshot or cannon could reach their hidden lairs. Might as well try to blow up a mountain range.

Not wanting to answer any more questions, Joseph began to walk away, the ice cleats on his boots offering steady footing. He continued down the line of cannons, gazing at the mountain pass repeatedly. He felt a tingle go down his spine, a prickle of apprehension.

The first blast of cannon fire told him his instincts had been correct. Whirling around, he saw the graying smoke belching from the cannon's throat. Then all the cannons were igniting, creating a cacophony of noise, shattering the stillness. His heart began to race and he withdrew his ice axe. It was an Aesir weapon, one he had been gifted by his commander.

The best way to defeat them was to mimic their ways of fighting and defense.

The Aesir came from the skies, appearing just over the crest of the mountains that loomed above the glaciers. They rode nightmares made of bog flesh and cormorant wings. This was as close to the glaciers as the military dared go, having learned from previous mistakes that the concussions of artillery could unshackle avalanches. Attempts had, of course, been made to attack the Aesir while they slept, but the ice in which they lived was impenetrable.

An otherworldly sound permeated the blasting cannons, and Joseph's pulse began to race. This was an advance guard, the ranks of the Disir, who swept down on mummified beasts that had been reanimated by their powerful magic. Beasts from another era that looked more like monsters than birds. The Disir were female, all of them, and it was said their battle songs could drive men mad, causing them to clamp hands over their ears and shriek uncontrollably. Joseph was already wearing the hood of his kappelin, which protected him from the mental onslaught of such magic. To this day, they had been unable to deduce what magic empowered them, which meant they could not be replicated in factories. The complexity was just too advanced.

The thunder of artillery rocked the entire front lines as the Disir swooped down and began throwing spears. As each one landed in the ranks, a pop of light sent up a blinding flash, followed by the purple-and-orange crackle of magical energy, which shocked and killed soldiers in an area. The cannons were largely ineffective because of their inability to fire at a high enough arc.

A breach in the front was happening before Joseph's eyes. Real terror wriggled in his chest. It would be a slaughter. All the books and strategies and learning of the past one hundred years was being proven useless before his eyes.

He marched down the row, screaming at the soldiers to keep firing. The thicker the saltpetr fog, the more it would slow everything down. He caught a glimpse of one of the maiden warriors, her skin the strangest shade of blue, an otherworldly beauty bedecked in armor on arms, shoulders, breasts, and knees as she rode the monstrosity in a felling swoop, unleashing another spear that exploded into the command tent.

She flew low enough that a cannon shattered the monster she was riding. With preternatural swiftness, she leaped from the beast, spinning in the air before landing amidst the soldiers. Arming herself with twin axes that had been holstered at her sides, she began scything through the shrinking ranks of human soldiers before they could grab their pistols and start firing at her.

Joseph sung a spell-song, and his boots launched him into the air straight at her. In the leap, he activated his bracers and knee guards, which would absorb the painful impact of his landing and prevent his bones from shattering. The Disir had killed dozens by the time he reached her and swung his ice axe at her back. His cloak shielded his thoughts and prevented her from sensing the attack before it was made, but still she moved impossibly quickly.

He met nothing but air and had to defend himself from her counterstrokes with the haft of the axe until he could time another strike. They were face-to-face now, and he was beguiled by her hair, the color of diamonds, glittering in the light. She spoke to him, but her words were lost in the deafening concussions of battle. Was she casting another spell or trying to communicate? He couldn't tell.

He watched as her mouth continued to form words he couldn't hear. Would he understand them even if he could? Her face was trying to implore him—at least, that was the sense he had as he defended against her attacks with reflexes enhanced by the magic he wore.

And then a sharpshooter pierced her with a shot. He saw the implosion of her armor, watched in horror as her eyes rolled back in her head so only the whites were showing. The blue-tinted skin began to gray as she crumpled onto her back.

Sadness struck him viscerally, like a dirge ending in tragic tones. Another Aesir had died. And he couldn't help but mourn, even though she was his enemy. He'd only fought Semblances before.

It was a truth known to few that Semblances walked the earth—even fewer were aware that Semblances were active even when the rest of the Aesir were asleep. There were far fewer of them, true, but they did exist. The one he'd executed in the ice trenches had not been the first he had killed. However, more and more had begun to creep into the world. A first wave, so to speak. Still. He'd never felt like this after killing a Semblance.

From the knowledge passed down to him, he knew Aesir magic impacted emotions, and at this moment, he realized how powerful that magic could be. He stared at her corpse, shocked, grieving, disillusioned, even though he was grateful she had fallen.

This was war unlike anything he'd studied in books. The ferocity of the fighting had taken him aback. And he had been trained! These common men were fodder. His mind could hardly grasp the number of casualties they'd suffer. A generation of youth would be lost. At least. What if they reached one of the cities?

How could creatures of such beauty be so relentless in their desire to exterminate his people? Yet he felt complicit. He didn't understand why, other than that they were creatures of such uncommon beauty. Seeing a dead Aesir had not prepared him for seeing them living.

"Sir! Sir!" shrieked a terrified sorcerer, gloved finger pointed skyward.

Joseph Crossthwait followed with his gaze and couldn't believe what he saw. The sky was no longer aswarm with Disir. Huge billowing clouds were forming, thunderheads of massive and unnatural dimensions. The sky had been clear previously.

Then the vaulted skies parted, and from the rift emerged what could only be described as a ship made of stone. The shape was unlike anything he'd seen in the fleets of the mortal world. No record of such ships existed in any of the oldest stories of the Aesir. The one overhead had no masts or sails, but giant wedges of curved stone, at least three, jutted upward from the top of the vessel. The prow sliced through clouds now swelling around the mountaintops. It was thin, with spars and staves protruding from the bottom like fin keels, except not in water—was that to stabilize it in the air? Did it operate under the same magical principles as the famous floating boulder in Auvinen?

In all the histories of all the sorcerers from all the quorums of the Invisible College, Joseph had never heard of such a thing. It was too high to hit with cannon. It was huge, at least the size of five or six of the emperor's largest vessels.

And then he saw another one. And another. They came, piercing the clouds, heading over the stretched-out army—silent except for a vibration that thrummed through the very ice around them.

"Sir! What are they? The Aesir . . . the Aesir have ships!"

Then the whistling sounds started—a series of piercing shrieks that penetrated their eardrums—and explosions began raining from above.

Joseph gazed down at the prostrate body of the Disir warrior. Her skin was gray now, not blue, her eyes still wide open but sightless. A quiver of intuition struck him.

She had been trying to boast to him about what was coming. The war wouldn't be contained in the trenches along the front as it had been in times past. The fight would not be relegated to the periphery between the human world and that of ice, towns lost in winter only to be regained in spring. No. These flying ships changed everything. The Aesir could leapfrog over the defenses in some places and attack the larger cities directly. And pin down the soldiers in the trenches as well.

The war would be different this time.

To understand the order of sorcery, one must first acknowledge that wisdom we have now is based on what was lost long ago. Every quorum of the Invisible College contains copies of journals and notebooks of sorcerers past, handed down to be studied and researched by the young.

Every sorcerer who lives must write down an accumulation of their wisdom and knowledge. Upon their death, that work is handed over, and copies are made and disseminated. Hence, once the founder of a spell is dead, others may copy it and reproduce it and engineer it. To shield their work from the unworthy, who would only use it for profit, most authors cloak their work in symbolism, parable, and sometimes ciphers.

There are infinite variations of how the Unseen Powers may be attached to inanimate matter. There are specialties, of course, which can take a lifetime to master. No one sorcerer can harness all the Unseen Powers.

This collection of knowledge must be the most valuable thing the Invisible College possesses. It is how new sorcerers will be trained. How new inventions will be made. But we must never lose sight that this knowledge is of ancient origin. It was first passed to mortals from the Aesir. How they must rue that occasion now. We would be so much easier for them to destroy had they not given us the means to fight them.

—Isaac Berrow,
Master of the Royal Secret,
the Invisible College

Robinson Dickemore Hawksley

CHAPTER NINE

The Treasure of Friendship

"We don't want to be late to the Fosters' dinner," Wickins said with a tone of impatience. "Shut the book!"

Since all shops were closed on Closure, many sorcerers used the free day to explore the collections of the Invisible College and further their knowledge of magic. Robinson had been so engrossed in his reading he had lost track of time—again—but his friend was right. He'd learned that Mr. Foster was a meticulous man and extraordinarily punctual, and he expected the same of others. Robinson had found him exceptionally interesting, and they'd discussed several topics, including the Physiological Alphabet, patent law, and favorite composers. After several Closure evenings spent at the Fosters', he'd come to look forward to their standing dinner date.

With a sigh, Robinson shut the book, written by Isaac Berrow two hundred years ago, and summoned a wandering hand with a thought. The nearest metallic gauntlet swept up to him, and Robinson held up the book. The gauntlet seized the book in the gentlest of grips and floated away with it, returning it to one of the shelves gracing the massive walls. Although he'd seen it happen any number of times now, it never ceased to entertain him.

"Come on!" Wickins urged.

Robinson didn't need the urging. He took his small leather notebook, wrapped the ribbon around it, and stuffed it into his pocket. He was excited to go to the Fosters' again. Dinner with the family was the highlight of his week.

"What time is it?" Robinson asked.

"You should really get a pocket watch," Wickins chuckled. He snapped open his watch and announced the time. He wore his lieutenant uniform proudly, and McKenna's sisters always praised him for his rank. None of the Fosters' daughters were part of Society yet, but they were eagerly practicing the social graces, along with some harmless flirting, with both their visitors. After they came of age, such behavior would be considered highly inappropriate.

They walked briskly together through the esteemed hall. The Invisible College was open night and day to vested sorcerers, and Robinson often found himself there in the middle of the night, trying to hunt down a source or glean knowledge from one of the old texts. The newer texts were less prudent, but he still found a lot to be learned from the older works. He read voraciously.

When they reached the street, which was excessively crowded on Closure, Robinson realized they didn't have enough time to walk and still get there in time. He only had a few coins left in his pocket, which meant no breakfast or lunch the next day if they took the street tram. He was inclined to invest every cupper he earned from teaching at the university and doing repairs on magical trinkets in the purchase of additional equipment and raw materials he needed for his alchemy. Sometimes he also completely forgot to eat because he was so engrossed in his work. Thankfully, he knew his appetite would be sated at the Fosters'.

Wickins reached the street corner first. Luckily, a tram was heading their way, the iron horse plodding across the cobblestones, dragging the heavier carriage along on the rails. It stopped at the corner and many got off, which was a relief. They wouldn't be hanging off the sides during the ride uptown. They both deposited their coins in a slot in the iron horse's head and then gripped a railing and stepped aboard. With fewer passengers, they didn't have to sit crammed next to one another. The nearest civilians were talking fearfully about the sky ships that had been unleashed by the Aesir and the slow progress they were making as they approached the northernmost cities.

"I'll never miss these dinners if I can help it," Wickins said. "The rations at the barracks aren't nearly as delectable as Mrs. Foster's banquets."

"Hear anything from your father at the front?" Robinson asked.

"Not since the last ambush. The Aesir slaughtered about fifty soldiers in the trenches before reinforcements came. Something else may have happened since. You know how long it takes to get messages."

"I heard that Elizabeth Cowing has an invention where communication signals travel by light. Would that not make things faster?"

"Don't get me started on Elizabeth Cowing's *inventions*," Wickins said in a disparaging tone. He shook his head slightly.

"Isn't she the *wunderkind* at Bishopsgate at the moment?" Robinson asked drily.

"Oh, do not get me wrong, Dickemore. She may be all they claim her to be, a prodigy tantamount to Isaac Berrow himself. I work in Signals. Do you know how much money it will cost to create the infrastructure she claims is needed? Make no mistake, she stands to make a great fortune if she's right."

Robinson blinked at his friend's unusual use of his name, but let it pass. "You say 'if' with some trepidation, sir."

The tram turned left at another major crossroads, and unfortunately, more passengers boarded it. Robinson and Wickins quickly gave up their seats to some older women, thus putting an end to their private conversation.

Elizabeth Cowing was indeed very popular at the moment. She had been born out of wedlock, hence she lacked the double surname, but she had risen above the scandal of her birth due to her excellence in magic. Since light traveled faster than sound, her idea was an interesting one, if she could get the animations to work correctly.

A very large company had hired her directly from her quorum in Bishopsgate, and it was said she dressed very smartly and kept her own private carriage. She was not even thirty years old, but Robinson didn't resent her for her success at such a young age. If she had seen something no one else had, it was due to her innate intelligence and to the fact that she, like all the rest of them, stood on the shoulders of the giants who had come before. That's what Isaac Berrow had famously said in one of his keepsake letters, for he too had been a prodigious sorcerer at a young age.

There were problems working with light, however. Isaac Berrow had discovered this centuries before. Light could be bent, but it still needed to travel in a straight line, which made relaying it difficult and costly. Robinson's own idea was more revolutionary. Rather than encapsulating messages in light, he was trying to encapsulate them in *thought*. His instincts told him that a mind-to-mind connection could hasten communications on the front. The idea had been captivating his attention lately, although he always had multiple ideas to wrestle with at once.

The tram reached the Fosters' neighborhood, and the two young men hopped off before it stopped, then began to walk quickly toward the Foster home on Brake Street. It was a picturesque neighborhood with stately elm trees and the occasional hemlock. The leaves were all gone and swept clear, and the bite in the air and the diminished crowd in the city streets were constant reminders that the Aesir war was underway farther north. This winter, particularly, would be a somber time. No festivals celebrating another reprieve.

They reached the door exactly on the hour, and Robinson sighed with relief as the butler answered the door. Soon they were greeted by McKenna's exuberant sisters and by Mrs. Foster herself.

But when his gaze fell on McKenna, the rush of anxiety of being late melted away, and he felt that timid, lovely glow of delight inside his chest. She was looking at him, smiling in welcome, and he wondered if his sudden faintness was from her smile or his empty belly.

Robinson greeted the sisters and mother cordially, but he then excused himself and approached McKenna. She had such an expressive countenance that it charmed him every time he saw her.

"I look forward to our dinner gatherings," she said. "I was watching the grandfather clock. You were perilously close to being tardy, Professor. Unforgiveable." She said it with a slight teasing smile and light touch on his arm.

"Alas, I do not own a pocket watch, so I am subject to the vagaries of time," he apologized. "But I am never deliberately late, Miss Foster."

"Is yours broken, then? You have one in your vest pocket. I know I have seen you look at it."

Her diction was better and better. More precise. More harmonious to the ear. She was mastering the method faster and better than any of his other students had. Even though he had handed over her tutoring—and its income—to Ella Florence Hurst, he'd made it a point to drop in during their weekly lessons to check in on her progress.

He'd never intended not to see her regularly. Indeed, he'd only put a halt to the personal lessons because his admiration for her was beginning to distract him from his work. He'd thought to temper those feelings by having another teacher guide her personal development. And yet, his feelings had not abated. And visiting her and her family for dinner at Closure had only increased his regard for her. He loved her smile, her friendly manner. He craved her conversation.

"Ah, but this is *not* a pocket watch." He corrected her playfully. He withdrew the device his father had bestowed on him from his vest and handed it to her.

"It certainly resembles one," she said, studying it. "The cover and body are round. The lid hinge gives it that appearance. The tapered ends are distinctive. May I?" She looked up at him with anticipation.

"By all means, Miss Foster."

She carefully opened the rounded lid and revealed the striated polished stone and dials. Her eyebrows narrowed with curiosity as she studied it. Then her brow wrinkled.

"What is it?"

"I don't know," he said, waiting until she was looking at him to answer. Given her remarkable fluency in speaking and lipreading, it was easy sometimes to forget she was deaf. But she was always alert for cues when someone was speaking to her. She had to be.

"It measures something. I'm sure you'll figure out what it is. It's a puzzle, that's all."

The butler cleared his throat. "Dinner is served."

McKenna quickly offered the device back to him. It was still warm from her hands—and he clasped it more tightly than need be.

⁕

The meal—amazing. The company—impressive. But it was the time of friendship spent afterward that Robinson relished the most. They had the habit of gathering in the parlor. It was a spacious room with a Broadwood grand, a cozy fireplace, thick velveted curtains, and a variety of stuffed chairs. The barrister had his special chair, which no one else sat on, and he would sit and preside like a judge at court as the family and guests interacted. Sometimes one of the daughters or the lady of the house would play the grand. Wickins would regale them with stories from history, and often they would ask Robinson to play the violin. He could mimic any tune any of the women played or even blend two or three different songs together without any rehearsing at all.

It was Wickins who had embarrassingly mentioned his talent at that first gathering, and now every week they expected him to play some ditty or other. Sometimes one of the sisters would hum a few notes and ask him to invent a song just for her. But as much as he enjoyed the attention, he knew it shut McKenna out because she couldn't hear any of it. And he didn't like the thought of her being shut out. It must happen frequently, though. And would have even more if she hadn't had such a strong ability at lipreading.

"Professor Hawksley, if you would?" said the stern Mr. Foster with a subtle wave of his hand.

"Do you want him to play, Papa?" asked Clara, the middle sister, eagerly.

"Oh, do make him play!" echoed Trudie, the youngest.

"I have some questions for the esteemed professor first. You may bother him with your requests later on."

"He's not bothered by them, Papa, surely," said Clara with a mischievous grin. "Are you, *Professor*?"

The barrister gave his daughters a wry smile. "Ignore them if you can, Professor Hawksley. Although it does not prove successful every time."

The girls tittered again, and Robinson gave them both a helpless shrug and then sat on the ottoman near his host's oversized chair. His gray whiskers and pince-nez spectacles gave him such an intense look when his gaze was set upon something. He had immense powers of concentration.

Robinson noticed from his peripheral vision that McKenna had changed seats. She was across the room still, but now she could see both their faces. Which meant she was eavesdropping on the conversation.

"I have some familiarity with Lennox Warchester George, the dean of your university," Mr. Foster said. "He informed me that you are working on an invention in your spare time. My daughter was quite impressed with your alchemy as well."

"I am indeed working on something, sir," Robinson said meekly. He was too modest to speak more.

"It is my understanding also that this invention is related to the transmutation of thought. Is that true?"

"It is, sir." He felt his neck growing hot. He wanted to talk more about it, but he was waiting for an invitation to elaborate. Most people started a conversation because of what *they* wanted to communicate.

The barrister pulled off his spectacles and rubbed the lenses on a handkerchief. Then he put them back on.

"I would appreciate hearing more about your research if you are willing to speak of it? I sense some reticence to discussing it on your part, Professor."

"I would be happy to express myself more candidly, sir. I was awaiting an invitation to do so."

That seemed to please the barrister, who gestured with his hand for Robinson to speak freely.

"I don't need to explain to you, sir, the science of how the transmutation of thought works. It is indeed the core principle of harnessing the Unseen Powers. I've been studying and researching some arcane Aesir magic, their thought shields specifically. If one wears a *tarnkappe*, or a 'kappelin' as we call them, it can render us practically invisible to our enemies. I think we could harness this form of magic inversely. Rather than shielding a thought, we can amplify it. Right now, when we wish to communicate a message, we must instigate it, transmit it, then pass along that communication from person to person. What if we could bridge that gap? What if the speaker and the listener, or audience, no matter how distant, could comprehend the message simultaneously—as quickly as your body understood your wish to clean your glasses?"

There was no change in the barrister's facial expression. But there was a twinkle in his eye. Maybe just the slightest wrinkle of interest in his brow.

"Go on," he said coaxingly.

CHAPTER TEN

The Investor

Robinson discovered a ready and sympathetic mind in the esteemed barrister. They spoke for nearly an hour about the experiments that Robinson had been conducting. Mr. Foster asked probing questions, demonstrating his deep knowledge of the Unseen Powers, and Robinson found himself again in the role of teacher, and this to a man twenty years his senior.

"I am impressed with your depth of knowledge," Foster said at last. "I knew you were an expert on linguistics, but the variety of your experience and interests is admirable."

"Thank you, sir," Robinson answered. "When I was a young man, my brother and I made a partially working mechanical head, which we empowered with the gift of speech."

"Indeed?" the barrister said with a laugh. "How did you actuate it?"

"With the intelligence of a parrot. It could only repeat what we taught it to say, but it was a convincing apparatus."

"Where did you get the parts?"

"My father had commissioned an artificer to make a human head for his demonstrations of the method. It was a prop, really. My brother and I added the soft tissue and enchanted it. We tried to sell the invention, but it was a bit too unnerving to look at. No one wanted a mechanical head in their home repeating odd sayings."

Foster chuckled again, shaking his head. "Professor, I see some promise in your future. You've a canny mind and a propensity to make intuitive leaps. This idea you've shared tonight . . . I would like to be an investor in it."

Robinson blinked with surprise and felt a flush of pleasure. "Well, thank you, sir. I appreciate your offer, but Dean George has already been supporting me. I do not feel it would be appropriate to take on another investor without consulting him first."

"Your integrity does you credit. It is no surprise to me that Dean George has expressed interest in your work as well. I will speak to him and discuss his feelings on the matter. I have significant resources I could bring to bear, and patent law happens to be my expertise. My connections in Bishopsgate would be advantageous to your venture, and I could provide a stipend that would allow you to focus on this project."

"That does indeed sound favorable," Robinson acknowledged. "If you wouldn't mind speaking to him and coming to an agreement?"

"I will do so on the morrow and send word to you. Not only would the army benefit from your work, but I think the university system would as well. Do you keep journals of your research?"

"I do, of course."

"And are they ciphered?"

"Naturally."

"Well done. You can expect to hear from me tomorrow, then."

"I will look forward to it, sir."

Robinson took the final words as a dismissal and rose from the ottoman. He stretched his back and neck as he glanced across the room. Wickins was playing a card game with Mrs. Foster and the girls and seemed to be enjoying himself. He noticed McKenna approaching and met her midroom.

"I didn't catch all of what you talked about. But I'm pleased Papa wants to invest in your research," she said. "If I were as wealthy as my Aunt Margaret, I would do the same."

"Thank you for saying that. And I'm more than pleased. Your father is a noteworthy man in Auvinen and throughout the empire. His backing will be helpful. Yours would be no less."

"I think Papa is right. You do have a propensity for intuitive leaps." She smiled as she said it.

"Your vocabulary is impressive, Miss Foster."

"I like words. I always have. When Miss Trewitt taught me to read, it opened up a new world for me. Why settle for boring words when there are others far more magnificent to use?"

"Language is a wonderful thing. I noticed you were not playing cards with the others. Why not?"

"Card games are diverting sometimes, but I would rather be lost in a book or have interesting conversations. Can you show me your . . . What do you call it? That thing that is not a pocket watch but looks like one?"

Fishing it from his pocket, he offered it to her again, and she opened it and began studying the markings.

"This is so interesting," she said, gazing at it with wonder. "Was it made by the Aesir, do you think?"

"I do think so. You see that little piece of glass at the top? There are Aesir runes there. Numbers."

"Really? What is the number?"

"Nine hundred ninety-eight."

Her eyebrows lifted in surprise. "How curious."

"Oh, it is very curious indeed. But it is worth next to nothing."

"Why not?"

"Well, as I explained to you earlier, one of the principles of the Unseen Powers is that an intelligence indentured must be released after a term of service. An iron horse, for example, will pull a tram for so many miles, so many hours, so many years. They agree to the service because there is an eventual release from it. They would not be willing to serve indefinitely. Why would a device such as this reach its limit before one thousand? Seems an appropriate time period for the Aesir race, does it not? A thousand what, though?"

"A thousand years?" she suggested.

"That is a logical guess, naturally, considering the Aesir's dramatic longevity. But this device has been in my family's possession for years, and I have never seen this number change. Not once. Neither did my father or his."

"Oh, so it is not bound by time, then?"

"Precisely. What is it bound by? No one knows. As far as I know, no one else has one. It is an oddity, really."

McKenna twisted one of the inner dials, and it clicked softly. "Are these rings like the tumblers of a safe?"

"There are four inner rings, each with different markings and tick mark sizes. I do feel it is like a combination lock of some sort, but mathematically, there are a staggering number of possible combinations. It would require an Aesir's life span to attempt them all. Still, this is something I've put some thought to. I expect the polished stone in the middle gets released once the right combination is put in. And only when that happens will the buttons on the top work and activate whatever spell is configured here. My guess is that there are only two more spells left before it no longer works. Hence the number."

"How fascinating," she said, gazing at the strange device. "It's . . . mathematical."

"That's what I believe. Or . . . sadly . . . it is just a broken curiosity devoid of any magic whatsoever. A relic of some past age that stopped working ten thousand years ago but cannot fade."

"Surely the metal would have fatigued after that much time?" she said, which was an excellent observation. Even an iron hinge would fail after enough swinging on a gate.

"I've tried to open it, to see what's inside, but there is no mechanism to pop it open. The hinge on the cover has never wearied. I believe it is immune to entropy, like the other relics we've found from the Aesir. Did you know they found a sword in a burial mound that was three thousand years old? The skeletons were nearly dust, but the sword still held its edge and its sheen, still brimming with magic. They think it was an Aesir gift to honor someone and it was buried with him. It sold at auction for an astonishing sum."

"I had not heard of that. How interesting." She examined the device again before clicking the lid shut and handing it back to Robinson. "I really hope you discover its purpose someday, Professor."

How he wished she would call him by his given name. He detested the formality of Society.

He tucked it back into his vest pocket. "It is a puzzle, to be sure." He glanced at the grandfather clock and sighed. "I don't want to overstay our welcome. We should probably be going."

She caught him by the arm as he was about to motion to Lieutenant Wickins, her touch sending a tingle down to his fingertips.

"Don't leave. Not yet."

She wanted him to stay? She'd never said so before. It made his insides buzz with energy.

"I just wanted to ask you something," she said, eyes imploring him.

"Very well," he said, gesturing back to the couch where she'd come from. He followed her there and sat on one side. She took up a position on the other so they sat facing each other. She looked so hopeful, so intense, that he felt a spark of hope in his breast that she might, someday, come to care about him as he did her.

"What I wanted to ask, Professor Hawksley, is if you've changed your mind about whether *I* might be able to learn about the Unseen Powers? Do you still feel it is likely hopeless?"

That little spark of hope within him withered. She looked at him as a teacher. A respected one. But it was not in her nature to develop fondness for someone who was so different from her.

"I have not given up all hope, Miss Foster," he said, speaking from his heart. "There are nearly insurmountable obstacles, to be sure, but you have the determination required to overcome them. I have no doubt on that score."

"But will you start teaching me? Maybe after my lessons with Miss Hurst? Just for a quarter hour? More? I don't know what would be required."

He bit his lower lip and involuntarily began rubbing the heel of his palm against his legs. "I will . . . have to think about it, Miss Foster."

Being alone with her would be difficult for him. Could he hide his growing feelings from her? Feelings that distracted him from his work? From his invention?

"Are you afraid I'll be disappointed? I'm expecting to fail. I'm not afraid of failing."

"It's not that," he said, feeling itches all over his body. He felt his cheeks were in danger of blushing.

"What is it? I know you are busy, but it would mean so much to me. I can't tell you how much. It is almost past time to enter Society. But I don't want to be just a marriageable prospect. I want to go as far as I possibly can. I want to be part of the Invisible College. Not just an observer from afar."

His insides clenched with unease. Was marriage something she felt was beneath her potential? He was secretly hoping he could start courting her. It was why he had voluntarily relegated her to another tutor.

"We will . . . try," he stammered. "But it could take some time—"

She looked so relieved, so pleased, that he couldn't stop himself from smiling.

"Thank you, Professor Hawksley! I cannot thank you enough. I will pay you for your time."

He held up a hand and shook his head no. "I couldn't accept it."

"But you *must*. I have my own money, you know. Papa trusts me to buy the things that I require."

"It . . . it would not be right," he stammered. "This is more like an . . . experiment. It just requires time and curiosity and a lot of patience. I cannot, in good conscience, charge you for something that has no guarantee of success. I will give you my time, Miss Foster, because you ask it of me. And because you will be doing all the work."

Her eagerness had faded, just a little. Maybe she didn't want to feel indebted to him? He wasn't sure he could read her expression.

"Is there anything I should do to prepare for our first lesson?" she asked after a prolonged pause.

Such an easy question. Such a baffling one. For a young person learning magic, they usually first attended voice lessons sponsored by members of the Invisible College. Such a beginning was impossible for her because she could not hear her own tones in order to modify them. Maybe he could invent something visible, a dancing flame perhaps, that would respond to her breath and help her see when she hit the notes properly? Was such a thing possible?

"Have I baffled you with my question, Professor?" she asked. Again, meeting her eyes, he wasn't sure how to interpret her mood. Had his silence offended her? In honesty, her question had launched him into the paroxysm of an existential quandary.

"She does that, Professor, quite often," said Clara, who had approached unheard behind them. "Poor thing. She always wants to know too much."

"You weren't part of this conversation, Clara." McKenna gave her younger sister a little scowl.

"I had to rescue the poor professor, though. Mama wants him to play a song for her before he goes. You and Papa claimed him too long tonight."

Robinson sensed he was causing a little disagreement between the sisters. He still didn't have a good answer for McKenna's question, though. Was there another way, outside of music, that would work? Simply saying the words was not enough. It required more . . . precision and intention. She loved literature. Could there be an opportunity there?

"Please, Professor, you must play Shopenhauer's piece from the opera," Clara begged. "The aria of the Erlking's daughter. You must."

"Please, Professor Hawksley! Oh, please!" tittered Trudie. "I love that one!"

It was one of Robinson's favorite pieces too. How he wished he could afford to travel, to visit the grand opera houses in Tanhauser and hear some of the famous performances in person.

"Let me think on your question some more," he said to McKenna, just mouthing the words. She nodded and watched with what must have been a little disappointment as he went to the Broadwood grand and began to play the majestic song using that instrument instead of the violin he preferred. He wanted to be able to play more notes than the combination he could do with so few strings. Even so, the music began to vibrate inside him as he played the lovers' song by the Erlking's daughter. It was a piece that had always brought him to tears. Music was powerful that way. Something about it was so visceral.

The opera was a tragedy. The Erlking's daughter had fallen in love with a mortal man, but he had rejected her. The aria was her lament.

And there was something about playing that night in the Fosters' home that made the hair on the back of his neck stand on end. He felt a kind of magic he rarely felt.

Mrs. Foster was dabbing her eyes with a kerchief when he was done. "That was so well done, Professor. So well done," she said, sniffling.

Robinson's arms were trembling from having played it so vigorously. Trudie was fanning herself with her hand dramatically. Clara was smirking, looking at her sister over Robinson's shoulder.

He glanced back at McKenna and found her lost in a book.

It broke his heart that she could never experience such a song—or music in general. It was precious to him, but it never could be for her. And if music were the only path to magic, she would never experience that either.

CHAPTER ELEVEN

Poverty

The temperature had dropped precipitously since the dinner at the Fosters' home two days earlier, and still lacking a long coat for winter because he'd been too busy to try to find one, Robinson compensated by walking more briskly. Still, he caught the tempting scent of spiced peanuts from the seething pot a woman was tending at the corner.

"You want some peanuts, Dickemore?" Wickins asked, keeping stride with him.

"I'd rather not," Robinson answered. His roommate always offered to buy him food, but he was steadfast in his refusal. He'd chosen his situation. He'd bought the equipment to furnish his alchemy deliberately, knowing he would skimp on meals as a result.

"I was going to get some myself. I'll share mine with you." They approached the woman, and Wickins bought a fresh bag. The scent was maddening.

It was dusk already, the days waning faster and faster. In the distance, the bells tolled and the music continued to play over the city of Auvinen. There were donation machines at every intersection, with parrotlike voices updating passersby about conditions on the front, casualty lists of soldiers to be honored, the current location of the enemy's slow-moving sky ships—thankfully still far to the north—and requesting funds for more winter gear. The waist-high metal-riveted boxes had slots for coins to be inserted and would croak a thank-you for each donation. He felt a little guilty every time he passed one on his way from street to street.

Being perpetually short on funds, Robinson was already looking forward to the next family dinner at the Fosters' house. They always prepared a veritable mountain of food, and Mrs. Foster invariably insisted they both accept little packages of the leftovers before heading home. He hadn't eaten since lunch the previous day, and his stomach gnawed with hunger.

Wickins took a handful of the sizzling peanuts and popped some in his mouth before offering the bag to Robinson, who shook his head.

"C'mon. I know you're hungry. I haven't seen you eat anything today."

"I haven't eaten anything because there is nothing in the cupboard. And there is nothing in cupboard because I forgot to make time to purchase groceries yesterday."

"I'm willing to share some of mine."

Robinson shook his head more vehemently. "That's kind of you, but it's my own fault. I accept the consequences of my absentmindedness. Now, this breeze is frigid. Let's keep walking." He started off again at a quickened pace, and Wickins had to double his steps to catch up.

"At least you can afford more groceries now that Foster invested in your invention," Wickins said. "I remember that little jig you danced when the contract came through. It's a generous stipend."

Robinson looked at Wickins's baffled eyes. "The stipend pays for the experiments. For the materials I need to buy. Quicksilver and cobalt and thoss iron aren't cheap. None of the chymicals are."

"I don't think the barrister would begrudge you using *some* of the stipend to eat, Dickemore. There's a tram. Let's take it back. It's faster."

"Obviously I'm not going to let myself starve. But I'm happy to save the money and walk the rest of the way back."

"You are too fastidious by half, my friend. I'm going to the Storrows to enjoy *my* peanuts."

He went the other way, hailed the street tram, and boarded it. Robinson gritted his teeth in irritation, partly because he knew his friend was right.

A passerby knocked into Robinson's shoulder, nearly throwing him off balance. He gave the fellow's back an icy glare and was about to step off the curb onto the street to cross when he noticed something in the grime. A coin.

Robinson felt a ripple of excitement and stooped down to pick it up. It had been stepped on with dirty shoes and even run over by a tram wheel. But it was a twenty piece. The ridge of copper around a silver core gave that away. He rubbed the face of the coin with his thumb, revealing the imperial crest. A twenty piece. That was enough to buy two bags of peanuts. Or a supper of stew and bread and something to drink. His mouth began to water as he fantasized about what he could do with such a discovery.

He stared at the grimy piece in his hand, feeling the crowd walk around him. Someone had dropped the coin. Maybe someone who needed it even more than he did. Robinson looked around, trying to see if anyone was searching. How long had it been in the street? A few days? Longer? It could belong to anyone.

A little throb of anxiety flickered in his chest.

He was a ninth-degree sorcerer of the Invisible College. In order to keep advancing, he had to demonstrate—not just to others but to himself—that he lived the principles of the order with exactness. He could find the true owner of the coin. Or he could keep it for himself. It was in just that sort of moment that character was tested and defined. No one else was watching him. No one else knew about his internal dilemma. But he was unflinchingly honest. He *chose* to be.

He stared at the coin and sent out a thought. *Help me find the owner of this coin. I seek to return it.* He considered the situation. He needed an intelligence that had a prodigious gift of scent. Also one that would have compassion for the feelings of someone who had lost something of value. Losing a coin was a common anguish. What animal . . . ?

A dog. A retriever. Not all pets or animals behaved the same way or had all the same instincts. When Robinson was young, he and his brother had befriended street animals. Even though it made Robinson's eyes itch, he loved petting and scratching the poor mongrels, and they'd always followed him through the streets. He'd been fond of that one floppy-eared fellow in particular and thought of him still.

He closed his eyes and hummed the incantation. "*Anoxo-memora.*"

Words did not always need to be spoken loudly to be effective. His thought contained the bounds and conditions, as well as the tune. The spell would last until daybreak only. If the owner of the coin could not be found before then, the intelligence would be released. Then Robinson could, without guilt, keep it. He was under no obligation to incur an expense to restore the coin to its owner. That would not be just. But if they were in the city, and he could reach them on foot, then he would do so.

A throb in his chest came surprisingly quickly. The coin began to vibrate in his hand, and he closed his fingers over it. It pulled him down the street in a different direction.

⁂

It was long after dark when Robinson reached his destination. The coin had taken him to a ruined and dilapidated part of Auvinen. Here, there was no music. Indeed, there was none where the Storrows was located, but that was only because the noises of industry would have drowned it out—if the threat came close to them, music would be played there, and loudly. Here? There were only trivial sounds—voices, closing doors, rattling windows—and no music at all. There was no lyceum here, no concert hall. No gift of magical protection. This dark part of the city was where the most impoverished lived, and he saw how privileged he was in comparison to these poor souls.

The coin took him to a ramshackle tenement with multiple levels and some broken windows. There were no quicksilver lamps lighting these streets. Only a few had candles inside. He opened the main door and went down the hall, the floorboards creaking ominously. It smelled of sickness. There was no warmth.

The coin tugged at his hand, bringing him to the stairs.

"Hoxta-namorem," he said crisply, distinctly, and the feathery wisp of light appeared ahead of him, preceding him as he climbed the steps. It took him to the highest floor and to the third door before the end of the row. He heard noises coming from inside. With his wind-bitten knuckles, he knocked on the door timidly. Quiet.

He heard some creaking and then a whisper at the door. "Who's there?" It was a woman's voice.

"A friend."

The door unlocked and parted a crack. The woman gazed at the floating light, which illuminated her filthy face. She was missing several prominent teeth.

"Who . . . who . . . ur you?"

The coin stopped vibrating in his hand. The intelligence sighed as it left the coin, but Robinson felt the presence linger a moment. It did not rush away.

"My name is Robinson. I found this in the street." He opened his palm and held out the coin so that the glimmer of light shone on it. "It's yours."

The woman opened the door wider, her face registering confusion and then wonderment. "You f-found it?"

"In the street. Near Oxenby Road and Tanil, I think. It is yours." He offered it to her again, smiling as the look of wonderment began to get wet with tears.

"You're a sorcerer," she whispered reverently.

He nodded as she took the coin.

"Bless you, sir. Bless you! It's been missing since yesterday. I searched the whole place. Under every nook. Oh, bless you, sir! Bless you!"

He felt his throat thicken, and he backed away. There was something otherworldly happening. The intelligence he'd summoned had lingered to savor the happiness he'd given this woman.

"Children! Children, look!" she said, gesturing to the chamber behind her. "The coin! The one we've been searching for!"

The feeling intensified as three grubby little faces appeared next to her, each one looking more delighted than the mother.

"Did that nice man find it, Mama?" one of them said in a puckish little voice. A girl. She was adorable.

"He did. He's a sorcerer. A *true* sorcerer," said the mother. "Bless you, sir. Oh, bless you!"

He sensed the intelligence swirling around them all, like a puppy wishing it could jump and lick them all with pleasure. Very much like that dog he and his brother had frolicked with in Covesea. An insight struck him. Without knowing how, he was certain that it *was* the intelligence that had been attached to that dog. Had his connection to the dead animal induced it to follow him? Had his care of its remains made a connection somehow? Perhaps those shared feelings had drawn them together like a magnet.

He'd known that the Unseen Powers could find the woman. What he hadn't realized was that intelligences could be particular. The intelligence had willingly chosen to help him restore the lost coin because it wanted to help *him*, and now it wanted to help the family.

The intelligence's delight burned inside him, chasing away his own hunger. How many other sorcerers had missed such an opportunity to employ their magic for good because they'd been too busy to notice the need? And now the suffering had flipped. It had been *inverted.*

His mind felt the edges of an idea: Emotions could be amplified. Thoughts encapsulated in emotions could be transmitted by intelligences. There were stories, of course, of lost pets who were so loyal to their masters they traveled great distances to return to them. That was the vehicle, not strands of wire for current or glass relays for light.

"It was my pleasure to help," Robinson said. "Good night. Bless you."

"Thank you, kind sir. Thank you a thousand times!" the woman said, weeping with gratitude.

Robinson felt as if he were walking on clouds. He didn't have money for a street tram, so he walked the rest of the way back. The positive feelings lingered. He wasn't cold anymore, even though the onset of darkness had dropped the temperature.

He unlocked the door and went inside and smelled something. Freshly baked bread. He couldn't have mistaken that smell for all the world. Following the scent to the kitchen, he saw a plump loaf wrapped in a cloth with a jar of jam. A note was written on a folded card near the bread.

Professor Hawksley:

I had the urge to bake bread today and made an extra loaf to share with someone else. I kept thinking about you and how much you have done for our children at the school. We are so grateful you came and instructed us in the method. It has made such a difference in so many lives. I believe you were sent to us for a reason.

With warm affection,
Sarah Fuller Fiske

Robinson bowed his head, wiping a tear from his burning eyes, and he felt the throb of the magic again. The little intelligence had followed him home. It filled him with warmth to think of it as that little floppy-eared dog.

History is plagued with those who have attempted to manipulate nature for wealth beyond the bounds of every mortal avarice. I foresee a day when magic will be used in all forms of industry. Not to benefit the lives of all but to prevent it from blessing the lives of all.

The Invisible College must be open to everyone, regardless of status, regardless of rank, regardless of stature. Those who are willing to accept its demands must be privileged to walk the hallowed halls, be they peasant or king.

—Isaac Berrow,
Master of the Royal Secret,
the Invisible College

MaKenna Aurora Foster

CHAPTER TWELVE

The First Falling of Snow

"I am leaving for my lessons, Mama," McKenna said after poking her head into the parlor. Mother was at the Broadway grand, teasing the keys with her fingers. McKenna had tried playing the instrument herself once, but Clara had demanded she stop making such hideous noises.

That selfsame sister glanced up from her primer on arithmetic and gave one of her conspiratorial looks to Trudie, who was seated next to her on the sofa.

"Do give our highest regards to the professor, won't you?" Clara then said, her eyes looking rather devious.

"Miss Hurst is my teacher," McKenna reminded her. "She's not a professor yet."

"Oh, but doesn't Mr. Hawksley always end up in your lessons anyway?"

Trudie grinned.

"What are you getting at?" McKenna demanded. There was some scheme between the sisters against her. McKenna was the eldest child and felt more and more at odds with both of her sisters lately.

"McKenna, you don't want to miss the tram," Mother said with a wave of her hand. "Do remember to tell the professor that my sister is coming to stay with us this winter. She'll be here in time for dinner at Closure."

Clara blinked innocently, but her smile was insincere.

No matter. McKenna bundled up for the cold and hurried to the door. Brake Street was a private neighborhood in the upper part of Auvinen, but there were tram tracks at the nearest intersection, which made getting downtown convenient. When she reached the corner, she gaped in dismay, seeing the tram had already stopped and moved on. If anything, it was usually late, not early.

Panic seized her, and she started to run after it, but her shoes were unsuitable for such exertions, and she knew she was likely to fall or twist an ankle if she persisted.

Why had she let Clara distract her from leaving? Clara would turn eighteen in the next year and would be the first daughter of the Foster family to enter Society. She'd always been a tease, but her words were lately spiced with innuendo and sarcasm that continued to go over McKenna's head. And Trudie had begun acting as her accomplice. It was so aggravating.

McKenna wondered if she should turn around and ask to summon a carriage, but that would take too long. Papa used the family carriage every day for his trips to his barrister's office. He rarely took the street tram.

Instead of running, she pumped her legs hard and hoped the tram would stop and that she might be able to catch up to it. But alas, that was not to be. She kept pulling out her small pocket watch and saw the hour of her appointment looming closer.

She had never been late to a lesson before. Never. It was mortifying and distressing. Worse, this was supposed to be the first lesson in which Professor Hawksley would attempt to teach her to harness the Unseen Powers.

After forty-five minutes of walking, she reached the main crossroads of town. It took several tries before she found a street tram heading toward Mrs. Fiske's. She took it, breathing hard and feeling sweaty under all her layers of garments. At least she had a moment to rest and catch her breath.

She arrived for her lesson quite late and offered a contrite apology to Miss Hurst. There was no sign of Professor Hawksley, which caused an acute stab of disappointment. He'd likely forgotten his earlier promise. Or, worse, he'd gone to continue his research when she hadn't shown up for her scheduled appointment. They walked into the little classroom, and there were several phrases written on the slate. On the wall were several handwritten sets of symbols from the method written in the professor's penmanship.

"Now, Miss Foster, let's make up for lost time. We will dispense with the mouth exercises this time. The professor has some challenging exercises for you today. Shall we start?"

"So he is gone?" she asked, feeling awful again for being so late.

"Yes. I don't know when he will return. Let's start with these phrases." She used a rod to point to the first one.

McKenna sighed. "Brisk brave brigadiers brandished broad bright blades, blunderbusses, and bludgeons—balancing them badly."

"Excellent. The next one?"

"Near an ear, a nearer ear, a n-nearly eerie ear."

"You stumbled on that one. Try it again."

McKenna tried again but fouled up twice. Without being told, she took a deep breath, tried to calm her agitated nerves, and mastered it on the third attempt.

It went on for a while, each one requiring positive pronunciation. The professor had gotten these from his grandfather, he'd said, who taught at a university in Covesea. Some of the sayings were rather silly and fun, and her mood began to brighten despite her disappointment.

"Well done, Miss Foster," Miss Hurst said, moving along to a different board. "Now we have these sayings. Just do your best. They are challenging."

McKenna screwed up her face when she saw the first one. It did not even look like her language at all.

"Alles . . . komt . . . op . . . zin . . . no, that's not right. Zijn? Zijun? Tigg . . . no, it's tijd!" Then she grinned and said it easily. "*Alles komt op zijn tijd.* That is Tanhauser, isn't it?"

Miss Hurst nodded and grinned. "He knows you've mastered that language. He wondered how long it would take you to realize it. I don't know what it means, but you said it correctly."

"It's a proverb. It's similar to one of ours. 'Patience is a remedy for every sorrow.' It's beautiful."

"What about this one?" Miss Hurst asked, pointing to the next drawing of symbols.

McKenna studied it first before attempting to speak it. *"Alles heeft zijn reden."*

"And what does that mean?"

"'Every why has a wherefore.' A reason."

Miss Hurst's head jerked suddenly, and she looked at the open door of the classroom. McKenna turned and saw Professor Hawksley striding into the room.

"There's no sign of—" He stopped abruptly when he saw her. His face had been quite agitated, alarmed. Then a look of relief overtook his features. "Miss McKenna!"

"I apologize, Professor, but the street tram came early today, and I missed it. I hurried, but I was very late."

"No, no, I'm just grateful you are all right." His brow was dappled with beads of sweat. "I went out looking for you."

He'd worried about her? That meant he hadn't forgotten his promise. "I am sorry."

"No need. Carry on with the lesson. I do not mean to intrude. Go on."

McKenna felt pleasure and relief. And he stayed there for the rest of the lesson. That meant he was truly going to try to teach her magic. Her heart became quite giddy in anticipation.

⁂

Miss Hurst had to leave early for another appointment, so the lesson was thankfully brief. McKenna was so eager to get started that she felt she could not wait another moment.

Professor Hawksley sat on the bench across from her and put his hands on his knees. His suit was so shabby it was almost ridiculous, but she knew he cared not a fig for fashion and that he was also quite poor. Thankfully, Father had agreed to invest in his research and invention. But he wasn't spending any money on new clothes, that much was obvious.

"Let us begin with your questions," he said to her. "I am sure you have many."

"Why are there no entrance doors at the quorums of the Invisible College?"

"Because finding the entrance is one of the first tests a sorcerer must pass."

"Are they below the streets?"

"Are they?" he asked with a canny smile.

"You won't tell me?"

"Should I tell you?"

"Are you going to answer all my questions with more questions, Professor?"

He grinned and shrugged. "What else?"

"I want you to *teach* me," she said. "Something. Anything. Clara earned her fourth degree when she was fourteen. But she has not done much since then. Why are there so many degrees? So many levels?"

"At the fourth degree, you know the basic principles in the operations of magic. You know the *why* behind it. What do you already know, Miss Foster?"

"I have learned this and that from eavesdropping, as you might say, on others' conversations. When Clara was being taught by Papa, I wanted to learn too. As I understand things, matter and spirit are quite separate, but the spirit can act upon matter. This spirit substance is called intelligence."

"Indeed so. Where does this intelligence exist?"

"It's all around us, for the most part. But there are degrees of intelligences. The intelligence that drives a gnat is different from that which moves a bird."

"Intelligences can progress," he told her. "It takes time. A long time. The Aesir can coax an intelligence from one life-form into another. Why?"

"Because they live so long. A mortal only exists for seventy years or so, but the Aesir can live permanently. Their bodies do not atrophy."

"But they do, you see. Under certain conditions. They live in a realm of extreme cold, but the other seasons are too warm for them. That's why we'll have our respite."

"I have seen paintings of them in museums. They seem regal."

"I suspect very few painters have seen one. They wouldn't sit for a portrait, you know. Lieutenant Wickins's father has seen one. A dead one, anyway. I read the description in a letter he wrote."

"I should like to read that! But I would not like to meet one. If I did see one, it would not be a good occasion."

"We don't live far enough north. In olden days, during winter, they would come to our lands. They had palaces here, even. But we've managed to keep them isolated in the mountain ranges and farther north. Now, back to the lesson. These intelligences are sentient. They can hear our thoughts. The iron horse that pulled the tram you missed is empowered by the intelligence of a beast—a beast that can only respond to simple commands, however. And that is why we think or use words to summon magic. The first spell that all sorcerers learn is Hoxta-Namorem."

"Hoxta-Namorem," McKenna repeated. "Did I say it correctly?"

"You did indeed. However, it must be sung. At least at first. But many trained sorcerers can also learn to invoke the magic through an instrument. That is the barrier we are facing. But you should know the word first. We can try singing."

"That must be the one Mama has used at night! When she would comfort us because of the dark, she would leave a ball of glowing strands in our bedroom to help us fall asleep."

"And the spell probably only lasted until you fell asleep. And she likely sang it to you. A lullaby, really. Once you were asleep, the purpose was served and the intelligence was dismissed. No light came when you said it just now because there was no melody." He raised his hands and splayed his fingertips, holding them apart from each other. "Words," he said, wagging one hand. "Music." He wagged the other and then brought his fingers together. "Ideas. Needs. The universe is driven by thoughts and desires melded together."

His words fascinated her, and she found herself leaning forward intently.

"The words represent thoughts. They mean, literally—"

"'Light where once was darkness,'" she interrupted.

He smiled approvingly. "Exactly. But then comes the other part. Something I've begun to understand more recently. Your mother summoned light because you and your sisters were *afraid* of the dark. The intelligence came in response to her desire to quench your fears." He pulled his hands apart and then tapped his fingertips together. "Thought and need. Together. The door to the Invisible College is in darkness, which forces us to summon light. It is designed that way to test the sorcerer's will. To create a little fear, a little apprehension. Does that make sense?"

"Entirely," she said with enthusiasm. "Can we go to the basement, then? Can we practice down there?"

He grinned and chuckled. "I am afraid it would prove difficult teaching you down there, Miss Foster, where you cannot see my face and know what I'm saying."

"Obviously, that. But that's not what I—"

"It would also be rather inappropriate for me to bring you down into a basement all alone. Most sorcerers are trained by someone of their own sex in order to prevent . . . Shall I put this delicately? Tempting circumstances. Am I being clear?"

She blinked with surprise, and then her cheeks began to heat. "Oh. I understand."

"For now, I want you to practice at home. The words. The need. I will try to find a way to navigate the music part."

"I shall. We have a cellar below our home on Brake Street. It smells . . . strange. I would be quite alone. Trudie is afraid of going down there."

"A good place to start, then. I suggest we go outside. For a walk."

"Where?"

"A park in the old downtown with an Aesir relic."

"The floating stone? Papa has shown it to me."

"That's the one." He rose and offered her his arm. "Shall we?"

That was the first of her private sorcery lessons with Professor Hawksley. She knew she would never forget how she felt, walking down the street that first night, clinging to his arm.

He was opening a new world to her imagination. A new language of words. A web of ideas. She could almost imagine what it felt like to hear the world.

But still the magic was silent to her.

It was the first night it snowed that year.

CHAPTER THIRTEEN

Aunt Margaret

McKenna sat cross-legged in the dark cellar, again, and repeated the word Professor Hawksley had taught her. Again. Nothing she did coaxed the spindles of light to appear. Not her need. Not her frustration. Not her anger. But still she tried.

It was snowing outside. In her imagination, she could see the fluffy flakes descending on the yard. She'd asked her sisters if snow made a sound when it fell, but they'd told her it was completely silent. Just like the accursed cellar.

"Why?" she finally blurted, bursting with frustration. Clenching her teeth, she rose and went toward the sliver of light peeking in from the upper door. She had done everything she could, but something was missing. The music half, no doubt. She'd hoped her need would be enough to summon the magic. Her desire. And yet, the simplest spell that the youngest *child* could manage, she could not. Because she was deaf. Why did the magic even care?

She climbed the steps, feeling the wood vibrate as she stomped up. She knew she was acting peevishly again, but she couldn't help it. Why was her inability to hear sound blocking her from communing with intelligences?

When she reached the top of the steps, she gripped the bronze door handle and twisted it. It didn't turn. She tried again. It was stuck in place. Had someone locked it?

She knocked forcefully at the door. "Open the door!" she cried out.

Nothing. Of course, if someone had heard her and answered, she wouldn't know. She waited, feeling her indignation growing. Clara had to be behind this. Or perhaps Trudie acting under Clara's orders. Her nose wrinkled with fury, and she started to pound on the door. "Open. The. Door!"

Mother and Father had taken the railway to Bishopsgate and were due back the day before Closure. Aunt Margaret Aurora Blatchford was at the house, however, and she'd be staying for the duration of the winter. Why wasn't she coming? McKenna pounded on it more furiously.

"This is so rude!" she yelled. "Open it!"

Frustration began to metamorphose into worry. Had Aunt Margaret taken the girls outside to see the snow? Was McKenna alone in the house? Had they forgotten about her? She opened her hand and slapped the door more swiftly, a twist of fear blooming in her stomach. The darkness was oppressive, reminding her of childhood fears. And with that thought came a sudden surge of irrational terror. Something was in the dark. It was drawn to her fear, and it approached with silent steps. Its invisible claws would reach out . . .

She began hammering on the door, her throat tightening, her mouth too dry to cry out. "Help me!"

But no one did. No one would. She'd be here alone, until—

Then a will-o'-the-wisp of light appeared. McKenna stared at it in shock, watching the blue flickering light hovering in front of her. It chased away the dark. There was nothing coming up the stairs. Or if there had been, the magic had driven it off.

She stared at it in relief, in fascination, in wonder. She hadn't even used the word! And still it had come. It had come in response to her fear. To the spasmodic terror that had gripped her heart. It had come—

The door swung open, and Aunt Margaret was standing there with a key in hand, a stern look on her face. She was Mother's elder sister and had crow's-feet, and her hair was set in a heavy voluminous bun. The high-necked blouse and affixed brooch were her typical fashion, a dark green with a diamond-web pattern.

McKenna wiped tears from her cheeks, relieved at her deliverance and the magic she'd summoned.

"I-I did it," she sniffled. "I made the light."

"No, McKenna. *I* did." Her aunt frowned and snapped her fingers sharply, and the will-o'-the-wisp vanished.

McKenna watched the light wink out and felt a horrible feeling of shame and failure. She was acting like she was eight, not eighteen. It embarrassed her that she'd become so distraught.

Aunt Margaret held up the key. "When will it get through your thick pride that you cannot summon magic? The Aesir created that sickness *deliberately* so fewer of us could use the magic." She shook her head, looking frightening in her certainty. McKenna's courage wilted under her austere gaze. "Now, come with me while I scold your sisters."

"Please, don't," McKenna begged, but Aunt Margaret was a force of nature. She scowled and turned, expecting to be followed. And so McKenna did her part.

When they reached the parlor, Clara was sitting primly on a sofa, her hands clasped in her lap, her gaze down and subdued. Trudie was bawling.

"Whose idea was it," Aunt Margaret demanded with an imperious gaze, "to lock your sister in the cellar?"

Trudie lifted her hand timidly. "M-My idea. I'm so sorry, McKenna. I'm so sorry."

"You haven't the brains to plot it yourself," Aunt Margaret stated, her gaze boring into Clara's downcast head. "Would you please explain yourself, Miss Clara?"

"It was only a little joke," Clara said, glancing up at McKenna and then looking away.

"Did her shrieks feel like a little joke?" Aunt Margaret asked.

Clara shook her head no.

"You will be eighteen next," Aunt Margaret said. "You are about to enter Society. Such insults and trickery are not becoming of a young lady. Especially to a sister who has enough challenges to deal with."

"I apologize," Clara said, her cheeks flaming. "It will not happen again."

"I should hope not, young lady. One might expect such jests from a common family. But this household is not common. Now, wipe your nose, Trudie; you're making a mess of yourself."

"Y-Yes, A-Auntie," Trudie said, rising from the sofa and hurrying from the room with a hand at her nose to collect the drips.

McKenna hadn't wanted to see her sisters rebuked so forcefully. Now that the terror was over, she thought she had overreacted and was embarrassed.

"May I go now, Auntie?" Clara asked with a humbled look.

"You may."

Clara rose meekly from the sofa, hands still clasped together, and left the parlor with a subdued air. As she passed by McKenna, just out of sight of Auntie's stern gaze, she looked back at her sister and mouthed *"I'm sorry"* to her.

McKenna wanted to go comfort her sisters and reassure them that she was fine, but as she started to walk, Aunt Margaret caught her sleeve.

"Yes?"

"Please sit down, McKenna. I would speak to you as well."

That was a foreboding pronouncement. McKenna went to the sofa where Clara had just been sitting. After seating herself, she looked at Aunt Margaret inquisitively.

"My sister tells me you are taking private lessons from Professor . . . ?"

"Hawksley."

"Professor Hawksley. I understand he is trying to educate you in the knowledge of the Invisible College. Is that so?"

"Yes, Auntie."

"To what purpose?"

"Pardon me?"

"To what purpose is he instructing you? So that you might be more conversant in the ways of Society? I should think your good father has suitably instructed you on that score?"

"No, well . . . yes. Papa has—"

"McKenna. Such endearments are no longer suitable at your age. 'Father' is the appropriate term to use now."

McKenna felt her cheeks flush. "Y-Yes, Auntie."

"And your father is best suited to educate you in the matters of sorcery to improve your ability to hold educated conversation on the subject."

"I am not taking lessons to improve my conversation," McKenna objected.

"Oh? Please enlighten me."

"Professor Hawksley believes it may be possible for me to learn sorcery. He's made no promises, of course. That would be rash."

"I look forward to meeting Professor Robinson Dickemore Hawksley and seeing for myself the intimacy he shares with this esteemed family. I've heard your sister call him . . . Rob."

McKenna swallowed. "He has come for dinner for several months now, Auntie. We are past the formality of surnames, surely."

"Formality is protection," Aunt Margaret said. "He would not be a sorcerer without impeccable standards of conduct. But he is your teacher, and you are his student, and so there must be extra safeguards in place to protect your reputation. Your dignity. Your mother tells me you take the street tram to your lessons unaccompanied?"

"I am not a child." She felt a stab of guilt saying it since she'd just behaved like one.

"You are not. You are vivacious and intelligent and surpassingly eloquent in spite of your affliction. I have heard the results of Professor Hawksley's influence on your speech for myself. And it gives me hope, deep hope, that with proper training you may . . . just may . . . be able to enter Society. To earn respect. To rise in status when so many with your affliction fall. Imagine the possibilities. To be respected for your mind, your capabilities. I am grateful to your teacher for the help he is providing you to reach your full potential. But he is also a man, and I have heard enough impertinent remarks from your sisters about him that I feel things have become too casual."

"Have you spoken to Papa—"

Aunt Margaret's eyes flashed with hostility. McKenna cut herself short. She wrestled with her feelings, not liking being the subject of Aunt Margaret's high standards. Especially when they made her feel lacking.

"Have you spoken to Father about your concerns?"

"I have not. Yet. I was waiting to see for myself at Closure. But I have spoken to your mother. She holds the professor in high regard. And the young lieutenant Wickins as well. I withhold judgment, of course, until I have made my own observations."

"As you should, indeed," McKenna said, but she had the feeling her aunt had already made up her mind about her teacher.

"You may go," Auntie said with a nod of dismissal.

McKenna rose from the sofa and approached her aunt. She was grateful that Aunt Margaret had saved her from her hysterics. But she felt a throb of stubbornness too. That she could also make up her *own* mind on things.

"I do believe that I can learn the magic," McKenna said, keeping her chin up, holding herself with all the poise she could muster. "Just because I haven't done it yet, does not mean it cannot be done. There may be thousands of wrong ways of doing something. But through persistence, by not giving up, we can discover another way. The deaf children at the school are learning to communicate well because of their implementation of the Hawksley method and hand signs."

"I admire your tenacity, McKenna," Aunt Margaret said, touching her niece's chin with her thumb and forefinger. "Maybe you will prove me wrong in this. But I doubt it."

CHAPTER FOURTEEN

The Last Lesson

The snow was relentless. McKenna had gazed out the window at least a dozen times throughout the afternoon, hoping the onslaught would ebb. Yet it did not. There was little to no wind, so the large flakes came straight down, covering the trees, the grass, the walkways. Everything visible was blanketed in white.

McKenna fastened the buttons on her cloak, gazing out the front window. Mother was gone with Clara, clothes shopping for winter and some preliminary exploration for her not-too-distant debut, assuming McKenna succeeded in her own entrance to Society. They'd taken Father's carriage. That meant the only option for attending her lessons that evening was taking the street tram. She had no intention of being late to catch it this time and was willing to wait out in the snow to make sure she did. The iron horses worked in all weather conditions and without pay or complaint.

After tugging on her gloves, she walked to the parlor and found Trudie tinkering at the Broadwood grand.

"Tell Aunt Margaret I've gone, Trudie," McKenna said.

Trudie looked up, confused. "But it's snowing so hard!"

"It's not that bad," McKenna said, although it felt like an untruth. "Just tell her I've left."

"All right. I hope Clara gets home soon. I'm bored."

McKenna shrugged and walked to the front door. In addition to the cloak, she had her lace-up boots on and extra layers beneath her dress for warmth. The conversation with Aunt Margaret earlier in the week had only stoked her determination to prove her elder wrong. Whether or not it was hopeless, McKenna was determined to keep trying. Passion and determination could yield amazing outcomes. A little recalcitrance was often necessary, was it not? Oh, how she loved that word.

McKenna had beaten the odds once. She could do it again.

She'd already made it down the first step in the deep snow when she felt a hand grab her cloak and stop her. Startled at the interruption, she turned and saw Aunt Margaret, her eyes flashing with anger.

"You are not possibly going to your lesson in this weather," her aunt stated with an authoritative air.

"Of course I am," McKenna answered, realizing just then that her aunt had probably overheard her conversation with Trudie and had immediately set off after her, knowing her niece wouldn't be able to hear her calls.

Which is another reason she'd wanted Trudie to deliver the message when it was already too late for the older woman to intervene.

"McKenna Aurora Foster, it's a blizzard!"

McKenna adopted a dumbfounded expression. "Is it? I hadn't noticed the weather at all. I don't want to miss the tram. I must go."

She turned to leave, but her aunt yanked her around again. "I do not think it is safe for you to be wandering out at this late hour during a storm. Come back inside."

The obdurate part of McKenna's heart revolted at the command. She stamped her foot in the snow, crushing it down. "It's only a little snow, Auntie. I'll be fine."

Already her aunt was bedecked with snowflakes just by standing there for so long. She was beginning to shiver, but McKenna felt perfectly warm. "If the street trams are called off, I'll walk directly back. Mother knows I was planning to go."

"But she didn't know about the storm."

"It's fine, Auntie. You'll see. I don't want to miss my lesson."

With a firm and determined heart, she began to walk briskly to the front gate, opened it, and was relieved when Aunt Margaret offered no more interruption.

The snow became progressively deeper as she went up the street. Some children were throwing snowballs at each other, but they were respectful to her as she passed and didn't pelt her with any. The splotches of white against her dark cloak were pretty, but her hands were feeling cold, so she folded her arms and bent her head against the snowfall until she reached the intersection. Judging by the crisscross markings along the iron rails, the trams were indeed still running. The gray slush of snow was wedged near the tracks.

Soon, thankfully, her street tram arrived and she hurried onto it. She nearly fell down on a patch of ice, but managed to keep her footing and inserted the coin into the iron horse. There were very few riders and plenty of room on the seats.

During the lumbering journey, she saw fewer iron horses and pedestrians than usual. Gripping the guardrail, she let her imagination wander. Auvinen had been transformed by the unusual winter spell. It struck her that while she was bundled up because it was too cold, an Aesir would be bundled up because it was too *warm*. Maybe during the night, when the temperatures dropped further, an Aesir would feel safe exposing his or her face to the night air and breathing in the smells of such a remarkable city.

When the iron horse reached her stop, the snow was even thicker, and she had to tromp through it to reach the professor's apartment. The laced boots had been the right choice, but the hem of her dress was wet with snow by the time she'd climbed down the steps and knocked on the door, breathless from the effort.

Miss Hurst opened it with astonishment in her eyes. "Miss Foster! Come in at once!"

McKenna unbuttoned her cloak and left it to hang near the door. "It is a little wintry today," she said, feeling grateful for the warmth. She took off her gloves and then noticed Mr. Hawksley approaching from the hallway.

"You came?" he asked in surprise.

"It's only a little snow," she said with a toss of her hair.

Her teacher and the professor exchanged a look of disbelief. "We didn't think you were coming, Miss Foster," Miss Hurst said. "I was about to head home myself. But you're here, so we'll do our lesson. If the snows gets much deeper, the trams won't be able to keep up and I don't want to be stranded."

"Oh," McKenna said, realizing the wisdom of her teacher's words. "Let's get started, then."

The lesson was different in that Professor Hawksley stayed the entire time. He praised her for her diction, her mastery of the phrases, and her persistence when she struggled to get something right. She basked in his approval and really thought it quite silly that he'd handed her off to Miss Hurst the way he had, especially since he always appeared during their lessons regardless.

"I should get going," Miss Hurst said with a nervous look. "I can walk with you to the tram, Miss Foster?"

"I haven't had my private lesson yet," McKenna reminded her. "I am sure if the weather gets worse, Father will come in the carriage to get me when they return."

"Your parents are out?" the professor asked with concern.

"Mother and Clara took the carriage. Clara is getting a new wardrobe for her Society balls. The number of hairstyles she has tried . . . It's all rather overwhelming."

He nodded. "That's right. It is the fashion here for girls to sport rather elaborate configurations."

"Is that not so in Covesea, where you are from?" she asked him, genuinely curious.

"It is very different," he replied. "The girls who wear their hair up in Covesea do so because they work in factories for the Industry of Magic. Many a young woman has been nearly scalped by the machinery. The idiom 'letting your hair down' comes from the factories, you know. In Covesea, you'd be considered a great beauty, Miss McKenna, just the way you are, not for any stylish way you wore your hair."

It was high praise indeed, and it took her by surprise. Had he just told her she was beautiful? She felt a little sting on her cheeks. He looked a little embarrassed for having made the compliment, but he didn't retract it.

"I cannot stay longer," Miss Hurst apologized. "I need to go back to the school before I go home tonight. But I worry about—"

"I'll see that she reaches home safely," he said with a reassuring nod. "You go on."

"I am grateful for the courtesy, thank you," McKenna said, giving them both smiles. "I'll pay for your tram fare."

"No need, Miss McKenna. No need."

Miss Hurst excused herself again, and then she was gone, heading out into the snow.

"Is Lieutenant Wickins here?" McKenna asked, suddenly wondering if the two of them were actually alone.

"He is," Robinson said, which gave her a little twinge of feeling she wasn't sure how to interpret. "The signals cannot be read in snowstorms, so his captain sent him home early. Shall we begin?"

She started the lesson by telling him about her misadventure in the cellar and how she'd believed she'd conjured a will-o'-the-wisp out of terror, only to find out her Aunt Margaret had done it. She told him forthrightly about her aunt's opinion on the matter of her lessons and of her own determination to continue them.

"I told her what you said about persistence and will," McKenna concluded. "You are right. Some people like to think for others. To put their beliefs on them. Maybe she's afraid I'll be too disappointed if I fail. But I don't care how long it takes. I'll keep knocking on your door for lessons as long as you keep opening it. I enjoy them. Truly. You are a very good teacher. And . . . and a friend."

A look came over his face. He seemed pleased by her compliment—she'd expected that—but there was something else in his eyes. What was it? Had she offended him?

"You're an excellent student, Miss Foster. I've not known anyone who has worked so hard as you. I know it's discouraging that you haven't seen results yet, but I believe it is because there may be some underlying principle we have yet to discover. I am working on an instrument to help you see your voice in a flame."

"Truly?" she asked, so startled by the news she involuntarily reached out and touched his wrist. They were both surprised, and she hastily withdrew her hand. But his thoughtfulness made a flame of its own ignite in her heart.

"It is taking longer than I thought," he confessed, cheeks slightly flushed, "and I have a duty to keep working on the invention for your father. But I want you to keep practicing with your emotions. If a fearful situation didn't trigger the Unseen Powers, perhaps we try another emotion instead? Whom do you love and admire the most?"

"Do I have to pick between my parents? That's unfair."

He smiled at her jest. "You can love them equally, but they are different. Your mother is an accomplished musician, a patron of poetry and the opera. Your father is a distinguished barrister. He has a cunning mind, high status, and is a relentless advocate for the underprivileged."

"As I said, I love them both. And admire them. I admire you too, Professor." She touched his arm in a familiar way and saw his fingers suddenly flex. Strange.

"And you love your sisters?"

"I do, but of late they have been vexing me. Deliberately. I think Clara has been jealous because my parents are so intent on launching me in Society that she feels she is more of an afterthought. We're both nervous about meeting expectations. I understand why the formalities exist, but it all seems so unnecessary at times."

"Much of what we do every day happens because of habits created long ago by people we no longer remember," he said with a slump of his shoulders. "Our choices in food. Our conversation. What is appropriate to talk about versus what it not. If we could peel back the curtain of history to see what times were like before, we'd think it all very strange."

"I couldn't agree more," she said enthusiastically. "I've often wondered what it would have been like to live in Isaac Berrow's day! When the Invisible College was being established. I should think that must have been a wonderful time to live in! What discoveries they made."

"It was not all tranquility, I am sure, Miss McKenna. When he was a young professor at the university, the Aesir unleashed a new plague on them. The university was hit hard, and he had to return to his estate to ride out the flood of infections. So many died."

"Was that when the redoubtable fever first struck?" she asked him.

He shook his head. "That came later. A new plague gets added every generation or so, and it's no coincidence that they always wreak havoc on our ability to speak and hear, or that they coincide with the waves of war. The Aesir would prefer for us not to use magic. Alas, we are distracting ourselves from the topic at hand."

"Sorry. I enjoy talking to you."

"I do as well. My assignment for you this week is to imagine loss."

McKenna wrinkled her brow. "Loss? You do not mean to lose something?"

"More particularly to lose *someone.* Someone you love and care about. What if you could never see that person again? Let those emotions build inside you. This is, again, where music is so poignant."

She *adored* that word. Poignant.

"The greatest arias in the opera strike those feelings. But even if you cannot hear the tune, you can still imagine the feeling. Do that and then summon the magic to comfort you. Let's see what happens."

"Father has warned me that our thoughts can bring the very terrors we fear. That we should eschew such feelings."

"He's not wrong. We are exploring the unchartered mountain passes, Miss Foster. For one week, I want you to be fixated on this idea. Then we will try another. We're explorers, you and I. Now, I am growing more and more concerned about the accumulation of snow. Let's get you home, shall we?"

She didn't want the lesson to end, but she knew he was right. She retrieved her gloves and cloak. When Robinson returned, he was wearing a military jacket over his usual threadbare suit. He'd borrowed it from Lieutenant Wickins.

The accumulation of snow just from the last hour or so—to be honest she'd lost track of time—was substantial. They tromped through the thick barrier, which was now nearly up to her knees. To her dismay and astonishment, when they reached the upper street, there were few pedestrians and no sign of any street trams.

Robinson caught a man and hurriedly asked him a question, but with the flurry hazing her vision, it was hard to read lips. He turned back to her. Under the glare of a quicksilver lamp, she could see his mouth moving.

"The trams have been canceled because of the weather. The last one just left here five minutes ago. If we hurry, we can catch it!"

She nodded and the two stepped into the street, following the fading tracks the tram had made in the snow. They'd gone a few paces when they both hit an ice patch and Robinson windmilled his arms with a look of terror.

"Are you all right?" she asked, half giggling at the look on his face.

"There's a sheet of ice under the snow," he said. "Come on! Let's go together! We'll anchor each other." He held his hand out to her.

She grinned and seized his offered hand. He had no gloves. Of course he didn't. He didn't even own a winter coat.

Together they raced up the street, a dash that would either allow them to reach the tram or see them both sprawled in the snow. McKenna felt giddy with excitement. When he detected an icy patch, he pulled her around it with a surefootedness that surprised her. They nearly slid into a drift, but somehow, almost magically, they kept upright and were both laughing as the tram came into view, grinding its way ahead after stopping to disgorge a single passenger.

She saw Robinson waving his other hand, calling out to the sorcerer compelling it. Low-level sorcerers were the ones employed for such tasks, activating and halting the magic through a whistled command. Either the man didn't hear or he wasn't stopping, and the tram lurched away.

"Come on!" Robinson said with a grin, tugging on McKenna's arm.

With a final burst of speed, they reached it. He grabbed the rail first, even though the tram didn't stop, planting his soaked shoe on the ledge. Then he pulled her up beside him with an iron grip. They collapsed on a bench, breathless, the sorcerer bundled up at the front looking back at them and shaking his head.

McKenna gasped for air and couldn't stop laughing. She had the strangest urge to snuggle up against her companion, to sigh and laugh and remember the magic of the evening. But she shoved that thought away and just smiled at him.

Too soon they reached the corner of Brake Street. "I'll go on from here," she told him. "The tram will head back to the city center. You should just take it."

He shook his head. "I said I'd see you home, Miss McKenna. I'm a man of my word."

He was that, for certain. She trusted him. She felt safe with him. He climbed off the tram and reached in his pocket for a coin, but she hurriedly put two in before he could put one in.

"I insist," she said, giving him a firm look that brooked no disapproval. They were the last passengers. "And driver. Please wait for him to come back. It won't be long. I don't live far."

"You don't have to," Robinson said, shaking his head.

McKenna burst out laughing again, not because his words were particularly funny, but because she was unable to help herself. Taking his hand in hers, she put her other hand on his arm and let him guide her through the thick snow. The curb was impossible to discern, so they just walked up the middle of the street. It felt strangely right being with him that way. What a peculiar feeling.

When they reached the porch of the Brake Street house, the front lamp glowing white against the drift, it cast their shadows on the snow behind them.

"Thank you for escorting me," she said. "That was very gallant of you. Reckless too. But fun."

"It was my pleasure," he said. "I'll see you at dinner on Closure?"

"Yes. Good night!"

The door opened on its own. Aunt Margaret stood there, looking at the two of them with consternation in her eyes. No, it was severity. She did not approve. McKenna realized she was still holding her tutor's hand.

"You must be Aunt Margaret," Robinson said, then bowed. "The roads were icy. I wanted to be sure Miss McKenna made it home."

"Duty required, no less," Aunt Margaret said with a half snarl on her lips. "The family thanks you for your pains, Professor."

"I should be hurrying," he said, releasing her hand and giving a little wave. "I don't want to keep the driver waiting."

"Yes, I expect it will be wise not to delay, so neither McKenna nor I will detain you!"

Auntie grabbed McKenna by the fringe of her cloak and dragged her into the house, practically slamming the door on her teacher's grinning face. Even her aunt's rude treatment hadn't wiped the smile from his mouth. McKenna was grateful for that.

Papa approached them with a worried look.

"I'm fine, Father," McKenna said with exasperation, tugging at her gloves and thinking about buying a set for her teacher. "He brought me back himself to be sure I made it home safely."

Father's look became even more stern. He came right up to her. "McKenna."

Her stomach flopped. "What is it? What's wrong?"

"An Aesir sky ship appeared at dusk over the northern part of the city. It came with the storm."

The Aesir have a ruler known through the ages as the Erlking. Names are powerful, but we no longer remember the origin of his title or even his name. He rules in the frigid north and his domain comes to the crest of the world. To the Erlking, mortals are but a brief spark of light existing between two eternities of cold and darkness.

Based on the legends, some wrong was committed against the Erlking's consort. We know not what it was but believe it was the impetus for the vengeance they have unleashed upon our kind for thousands of years. This vengeance has taken many forms—blade, poison, pestilence, hailstones the size of fruit, even the cunning artifice of their music. That is their most dangerous magic. When an enemy rages against you with sword, axe, or javelin, swooping down atop bog creatures terrifying and beautiful, their rage reveals their intent. But when they sing softly, lullingly, we become pacified and complacent. Hence there must always be a shield of music hovering over our cities to disrupt this most dangerous of ploys they can use. In the silence, their melodies kill.

—Isaac Berrow,
Master of the Royal Secret,
the Invisible College

Joseph Crossthwait

CHAPTER FIFTEEN

The Stormbreaker

The locomotivus slid to a halt at the station, letting off plumes of billowing ice fog as the magnetized rails connected with the tracks. The magic of the locomotivus was one of the most impressive feats created by the Industry of Magic. It was not a faultless magic, however, and often the machines could be stranded on the tracks for hours while the sorcerers battled to get the various parts harmonizing again.

Joseph had experienced such a delay, so when they reached the station at Bishopsgate, he hurried out the doors and activated the vesper wings, a temporary set of magical wings that sprouted from his cloak and vaulted him up into the air, away from the crowds of soldiers, women, and children who were on board. With his cloak, he was nearly invisible to any onlookers and soared over their heads and then over the station buildings. On the other side were the trams and conveyances ready to transport the coming rush of passengers.

He dimmed the magic and alighted smoothly on the street, then lowered the cowl of his cloak, making himself fully visible. He approached an anxious-looking driver sitting atop a single-person coach.

"Gresham College," Joseph ordered the young man as he climbed up into his seat.

"Aye, sir," mumbled the young man before he whipped the crop against the horse's flanks. The streets were devoid of snow, for the enchantments inlaid in them warmed them and made the snow melt. Flurries were still coming down hard against Bishopsgate. It looked very different from the last time Joseph had been there. He was grateful for the street-warming spells, however, which were rare in most cities because of their expense.

"Come from the front, sir?" asked the driver.

Joseph remained silent, not wanting to add to the gossip undoubtedly swirling through the city.

Bishopsgate was the intersection of the war effort, with direct links to the imperial city. He gazed out the window as the masses began exiting the station. So many women and children, bundled against the cold, fleeing to a place they knew would be heavily defended.

The carriage jolted down the road, avoiding the congestion of other vehicles in transit. Those who could afford to flee the epicenter would go to relations in distant parts of the empire. But many were coming here to Bishopsgate, which had the most formidable magical defenses. In the coming weeks, every hotel, boardinghouse, and cellar would be full of people escaping the coming devastation unleashed by their immortal enemies.

They were approaching Gresham College, a distinctive building that had been added onto over the centuries since its founding. It had started as a private university before being donated to the Invisible College. It was a formidable building, but there was, in fact, a square cloister in the center of it, hidden from public view by the walls. The southern side was longer than the northern one, and the east and west sides contained dormitories that the old students had once lived in and that now housed the many visiting sorcerers who arrived at all hours in Bishopsgate.

As they got close, the driver took one more shot at attempting to get information from him.

"Is it true the Aesir have a flying ship now?" the young man asked. "Did you see it?"

"I was there when it was first sighted," Joseph replied, tendering his coin to the driver as he disembarked. "It's not a ship as we know them."

"What is it, then?" the young man asked. "What should we call it?"

Joseph looked in his eyes. A name had already been approved by the committee. How to describe something that cleaved the skies and brought winter with it?

"It's called a stormbreaker," Joseph said as he dismounted.

The driver whistled in awe and then tapped his horse with the crop and went on. Joseph walked through the slush on the street and approached the looming gatehouse. The building was showing its age, but it was a familiar place to him. His stomach rumbled with hunger after the long trip from the front, but he knew the general was expecting him and wouldn't appreciate any further delay.

When he entered the gate, he didn't pass through it. He went to the blank brick wall, smudged with soot, and uttered a magical command.

"Extressis." The wall shimmered and revealed a porter door.

A soldier opened it from the other side and extended his hand. Joseph took it in the secret way, and the soldier nodded and let him through. Even though he was recognizable to the soldier, he had still needed to demonstrate he was part of the quorum. An Aesir's glamour could deceive the senses, after all.

"General Colsterworth was expecting you hours ago," the officer in charge said after Joseph passed the sentinel.

"The machine malfunctioned in the storm," Joseph answered. His kappelin repelled snow and water, so it was perfectly dry. He activated the heating buckles and hurried to follow the officer upstairs to the general's office—the old headmaster's private residence.

There were two guards stationed in front of it, both wearing kappelins and armed with harrosheth blades on their arm bracers. They nodded to Joseph as he passed them and entered through the door, which the officer held open for him. He'd once stood guard in that very spot. He much preferred the action of war to bodyguard duty.

"Crossthwait, there you are," General Colsterworth said gruffly. "It's a nuisance having to wait so long for you."

The general had a distinctive bushy mustache that angled sharply upward beneath his nostrils with waxed tips. His hair was buzzed short, mostly gray, and he had deep, penetrating eyes. His uniform was crisp and ironed with twelve brass buttons, one of which had an obscure folded ribbon marking his command of the secret society of which Joseph was a member.

"Something malfunctioned and we were trapped on the tracks for a few hours, sir," Joseph replied. Everyone knew the pitfalls of the magnetized locomotivuses. When the magic stopped working, they stuck to the tracks like a mountain. No amount of horses would have been able to dislodge or move the apparatus. It took at least a team of six sorcerers to staff each locomotivus.

"What a nuisance. I'm glad you are back. You won't be staying long."

"Sir?"

"That blasted stormbreaker settled over Auvinen."

A jolt of shock and surprise went through Joseph's chest. "That far?"

"Yes. And it immediately unleashed thunder and burning hail."

Joseph shook his head. "Sir?"

"You heard me, Crossthwait. The ice is burning with magical fire. Setting fire to any unprotected building. And the thunder is terrifying the citizens. Like the sky itself is speaking. Very strange."

"How much damage has the city sustained?" Joseph asked worriedly.

"The shields over most of the factories held, although some had lapses in vigilance and caught fire. During a blizzard no less! We've ordered a general evacuation of the citizenry other than able-bodied men and sorcerers, with the exception of mothers who must lead their children to places of safety. The evacuation will take days. I need you there, Crossthwait. Immediately."

"Yes, sir. I will leave at once."

"Not yet. I'm not sending you to shore up the city's defenses. Colonel Mack Harrup has that duty. I believe there is a Semblance operating in Auvinen. Your mission is to hunt it down and kill it."

Joseph blinked in surprise. "You think it has been there all this time?"

"Why not? In a city that size it could blend in with the population without drawing notice. It could be male or female. Of any age, but I would propose you start looking at newcomers to Auvinen, say within the last few years, or a native with strong connections to the Invisible College."

"But what about the evacuation? Was that deliberate?"

"It wasn't just to save lives, Crossthwait. I believe this Semblance is operating within Society. But I may be wrong. Do not let me prejudice your investigation. I have a list of several suspects provided by local sources. One man, in particular, should be surveilled. A young elocutionist from Covesea arrived in Auvinen several months ago. Robinson Dickemore Hawksley is the name, I gather. He came because he was sick with axioma. Same that took his brother's life."

Joseph squinted. "Axioma is fatal in most cases."

"Now you see what I'm getting at, lad. He could be one of them and not even know it. He's become something of a favorite down there for his work with the deaf. Tread carefully. But if he's the one who betrayed us to the Aesir, put a bullet through his skull."

"Who are the other suspects?" Joseph asked, feeling the weight of the task. A city the size of Auvinen . . .

It could be anyone.

But it did stand to reason that the stormbreaker hadn't randomly appeared over the industrial center of the region, a city that would provide enormous resources for the war effort. Uniforms, ammunition, saltpetr, and a host of magical contrivances—the empire would need to stave off the enemy. No, it did not have the appearance of a coincidence.

"I have reports in that satchel. You can read them on the way. There is also a briefing on a new development in Andover you should be aware of."

"Andover? That's where I'm from."

"I know that, lad. I know. A quorum in the Invisible College in Tanhauser is advocating surrendering to the Aesir. A composer has even written a canticle espousing the idea. It's gaining followers."

"How does that impact Andover?"

"The emperor has asked to listen to the canticle. Someone *told* him about it."

Joseph frowned. Over the centuries, there had always emerged factions that thought, naively, that survival ultimately depended on submitting to the Aesir.

One community, deep in the mountains, had attempted it. They'd all been slaughtered. Every man, woman, and child.

The Aesir experienced no mercy. They were incapable of it. A memory flashed in his mind. Of the female warrior, the Disir, he'd faced at the front. He could still see the beauty of her face, the haunting memory she'd left.

It was natural for mortals to desire to worship such beings of transcendent beauty and power, but they were a completely different species. There were legends of mortals who were abducted and taken to their frigid lands never to return. They were kept as drudges used only to serve the whims of their immortal overlords.

The Awakening had come. And the terrors were only just beginning.

The sentient intelligences of the universe are drawn to and respond to emotion. They are highly susceptible to the influence of music. In the dark ages of the past, children were taught to hum or sing protective songs as they crossed the woods, especially during winter. Their fear, mingled with song, would attract will-o'-the-wisps to guide them back to the safety of their homes. These intelligences, if we harness them in clever devices, could be used in the future to defend mortal cities.

—Isaac Berrow,
Master of the Royal Secret,
the Invisible College

Robinson Dickemore Hawksley

CHAPTER SIXTEEN

The Midnight Guardian

Hunger nagged Robinson as he sat on one of the benches in the middle of the Storrows. The room was full, each seat taken, the low murmuring of voices of a hundred hushed conversations playing out. When he'd gone to the Fosters' for Closure the previous day, the servants had said the dinner was canceled because the barrister was busy making arrangements to safeguard his family. The Fosters had a second home in Bishopsgate, and Aunt Margaret was taking McKenna and Trudie there. Clara, who was a sorcerer herself, was not allowed to leave Auvinen because she was deemed old enough to help, and her commitment to the Invisible College required it. She and her parents would join in the city's defenses.

It had grieved Robinson to miss the family dinner. It had grieved him even more that he'd been unable to bid McKenna goodbye before her departure.

A hush fell over the room. Robinson looked around to determine the cause of the sudden silence, and noticed the familiar face of Sarah Fuller Fiske, his landlady and the headmaster at the special school of the deaf in Auvinen. She was standing on an upper balcony, overlooking the hall.

"If you please," she said in her kindly way. "I know there are many questions, but there is little time to address them. You should each have been given your assignment on which part of the city you have been called upon to defend. The bombardments are happening suddenly, with no notice or warning, and they strike randomly through Auvinen. When they come, we need every available sorcerer to hasten to that location to amplify the shields. However, those of you who are assigned to the manufacturing district must remain at your posts at all times until relieved by another sorcerer."

Hands shot up in the air, wagging for attention, but Robinson just folded his arms and tried to ignore the empty ache in his belly. His roommate was at the military base and hadn't been home in days. There was no food in the house, and Robinson was once again very short of funds. He'd invested both time and money into the voice contraption he was working on for McKenna. The pinch was especially keen now that the private lessons he'd been giving had been canceled due to the Aesir's stormbreaker appearing over the city.

"Please. There is more. If you would remain patient a while longer." Some, but not all, of the hands and murmured questions stilled. "Thank you. We've been told reinforcements from Bishopsgate are on the way. The heavy snows have made travel difficult, and more, it is hampered by those who are fleeing the city. It will take time for help to come. Our brothers and sisters in the Invisible College are aware of our plight and the injuries we've suffered. We assume our city was chosen for attack because of its importance in manufacturing. But the people are depending on us to use our gifts and training to defend them. It is imperative that you come to the Storrows at the beginning and ending of your duty. The noise of the bombardments is truly frightening. Nerves are fraught. But we must stand together and defend our society. Now, I only have time for a few questions. Please be sensitive that we just don't have many answers."

Robinson did not envy the situation she was in. But she was one of the highest-ranking sorcerers at the Storrows, and so it fell on her to provide leadership during the crisis.

"Yes. Mr. Dagget Brown?" She pointed to someone in the crowd. She had an amazing ability to remember people's names.

"I haven't slept in two days. We're all exhausted. How are we supposed to maintain the defenses like this?" He sounded fearful and annoyed.

"Get as much rest as you can during the lulls in between the bombardments. For many decades, our soldiers at the front have borne the brunt of war preparations and cold winters while we've been safe at home. Now is our turn to show equal courage. Next question? Yes, Miss Forsythe?"

"How are the children at the school, Mrs. Fiske? Have they been evacuated?"

Mrs. Fiske smiled at the question. "That is very thoughtful of you to ask, Miss Forsythe. We have been evacuating the deaf children at the other schools first. You can imagine how terrified they are. They cannot hear the bombardments coming, but they can feel the tremors, smell the smoke from the fires, and see what's happening outside the windows. We are trying to evacuate them, but there are many deaf people in Auvinen, as you can imagine in a city of our size. Next question?"

Robinson felt a throb of warmth in his heart at the news. If he could make a breakthrough with McKenna, it would help open the way for so many others. Their defenses could be multiplied exponentially then. What a discovery that would be!

"Yes, the gentleman with the blue cravat, over there," Mrs. Fiske stated, pointing to the young man.

"How long will the university be closed?"

"I spoke with Dean George early this morning. The deans of all the universities have agreed to the temporary suspension of classes. Each professor is needed in the defense, and each student who can cast spells has been called upon to assist. We hope this will be a temporary measure. Next question?"

Robinson's stomach rumbled again. He raised his hand and was surprised that she called on him so promptly, for there were many other raised hands.

"Yes, Professor Hawksley?"

He raised his voice so it could be heard. "What is being done to defend the slums, Miss Fiske? Is another quorum assigned to defend them? I have not observed any of our sorcerers being sent there."

Mrs. Fiske did not answer right away. Some faces turned toward him because he'd asked a question no one else had yet posed.

"At present, we are doing nothing, Professor. No quorum has been assigned to defend that part of the city."

Some audible gasps of concern followed her answer. The murmuring grew louder. Robinson respected her for being truthful. She hadn't evaded the query. He had gone into that quarter himself, at night, to verify his hypothesis that it was undefended and to check on the widow and her children he'd befriended after restoring their coin. The building next to theirs had already burned to the ground.

"There is no more time for questions, I'm afraid," Mrs. Fiske announced. "Remember, return to the Storrows before and after each duty. When you hear the raid sirens, please gather in that area unless you are in the manufacturing district. Thank you, all."

Some of those gathered began to shout questions, but Mrs. Fiske turned and spoke to one of the high-ranking sorcerers up on the balcony with her and then disappeared through the doors.

The men and women of the Storrows spoke anxiously to each other as they prepared their cloaks and coats to return to the blizzard outside. Robinson didn't have a coat. Wickins had taken it back when he returned for duty. So there was no urgency to leave the warmth of the room.

While the commotion was ongoing, a man with a beard and balding pate approached him. "Mrs. Fiske would like to speak with you, Professor."

That was surprising, but he rose and followed the man through the crowd to a private study on the second floor. Mrs. Fiske was tugging on traveling gloves when he arrived.

"Why did you ask that question, Mr. Hawksley, when you already knew the answer?" She gave him a questioning look. She wasn't upset. She looked harried, the lines in her brow showing the weight of the responsibility on her shoulders. Not only was she headmistress of her own school, but her rank in the Invisible College—a twelfth degree—meant the organization demanded more of her than of others.

"I haven't seen you in days, Mrs. Fiske. I wanted to corroborate my assumption before taking action."

"'Taking action'?" She tipped her head. "What do you mean by that?"

Robinson sighed. "I'm going to help them."

"You have an assignment to defend the university," she said severely.

"They're not attacking the university. And I will keep to my assignment. But at night, I am going to bring my violin and play music on the rooftops."

"You are *needed*, Mr. Hawksley. The invention you are working on would be very helpful. If we could speed up communications between cities—"

"I'm no closer to figuring it out than I was before, and the noise of the bombardments is too distracting. It feels wrong to try and sleep when so many are suffering."

"But when will you sleep?"

"I get by on very little, Mrs. Fiske. You know that to be true."

And she did. Indeed, in her capacity as a leader in the quorum, she'd spoken to him often about his late hours and bouts of intense concentration that led to headaches.

"You cannot change the slums by yourself," she said. "The intelligences recoil from such a place. There is too much suffering. Too much poverty there."

"Actually, they do not," Robinson said. "They *want* to help. I cannot defend the entire area by myself. One sorcerer with a violin? But does that mean I should do nothing at all?"

She looked at him seriously, her brow softening from concern to respect. "Maybe some of the others will follow your example."

"I've met this lad, you see," Robinson said. "A widow's boy. He asks me about the Invisible College. I've started teaching him arithmetic. If he sees what we are really about . . . what we really stand for: integrity, self-discipline, compassion . . . If he works hard, he can join the college. One little boy. Maybe others will as well. Maybe that is how it all started in the first place?"

She pursed her lips and nodded at him. "I won't forbid you to help in the slums."

"I knew you wouldn't."

"Do what you must, Mr. Hawksley. Do what you must." She gave him a fierce look, one that eased his hunger pangs for a moment, and then she hurried away with the man who had been waiting for her at the door.

"The carriage awaits."

After his shift was finished at the university, he still hadn't found anything to eat but went to the widow's apartment with his violin case tucked under his arm. He shivered with cold, but the fast pace of his walking helped stir some warmth. He sensed the dog's intelligence tagging along behind him. Indeed, the intelligence followed meekly every time he headed this way. And even though an invisible companion wasn't much of one, it felt better than making the journey alone. He couldn't afford a trip on the tram and still felt indebted to McKenna for having paid his return fare the other night.

Memories of holding her hand made him smile as he made his way down the snow-packed street. Her laughter and the gaiety in her eyes had made her look even more beautiful to him. But her intense focus and determination were equally appealing. When he spoke, she truly listened, listened with her eyes, her whole body slightly leaning forward.

It was rare for someone to be such a good listener, and he knew she was one out of sheer practicality—it was the only way she could understand! But it wasn't just that. She hungered to know what he knew. And she willingly shared what she knew as well. She'd read hundreds of books and knew facts on subjects he'd rarely bothered to cover on topics unrelated to magic. It was a mutual confiding, a connection between two sensible people despite the gap in their ages. He sorrowed that she was gone but was grateful she was on her way or at Bishopsgate already. Men like Mr. Foster had resources. He had two homes in two exclusive neighborhoods in two prominent cities of the empire.

When he reached the widow's apartment, the family was huddled around the little brazier that Robinson had repaired for them. It burbled heat, night and day, good for heating soup or warming a slice of bread or cold hands. The mother and children slept huddled around it at night.

"Mr. Robinson?" the boy asked. His name was Jake. "Are you hungry?"

"I came to play my violin," Robinson answered.

The other children looked at him eagerly. He gazed at the widow, Trest Hallow Farmer. They'd developed a friendship of sorts. She was so grateful for his visits. Grateful for the brazier he'd enchanted. Grateful for the coin he'd brought. And that gratitude had spawned a friendship between Robinson and the family. He cared about them and wanted to check in with them.

"Would you play for us, sir? Would you?" Trest asked.

"I'm going to play on the rooftop so all can hear it," he said. "Jake, can you move that chair over by the skylight, please?"

"Yes sir!" He obeyed with alacrity.

Robinson climbed up onto the chair, stretched his arm to unlatch the skylight, and then pushed it open. He handed the violin case to Jake. "Hold this a moment, good fellow."

Then he gripped the icy frame and pulled himself up onto the steeply slanted roof. He fixed a foot on either side of the roof and then dropped into a crouch. The temperature was frigid up there, but thankfully there was not even a breeze. Jake climbed up onto the chair and handed him the case.

"Undo the buckles and hand me the violin if you please."

"Is the ship bombing anywhere? Do you see it?"

"It's been quiet for hours," Robinson said. "Most of the hail hit the docks earlier today."

"Did any catch fire?"

"Not a single one. We stopped them."

"My goodness, I should have liked to see that!" Jake said. He opened the case and then stretched to hand Robinson the violin.

"The bow as well. I can't play it very well without that," he said. "Unless I just plucked the strings." Which he proceeded to do, solely to make them laugh, before reaching down and taking the offered bow. The snow started to fall again. It had been coming down off and on all day.

Robinson closed his eyes and thought of McKenna. Without planning to, he began to play the aria of the Erlking's daughter. He felt the snow grazing his hair and hands as he closed his eyes and lost himself in the music. It was a hauntingly beautiful melody. It made him think of the last time he'd played it, at the Fosters' warm and sweet-smelling home. Of laughter and games and McKenna, sitting on the cushion reading a book, unable to hear the notes he played.

He poured himself into the piece, hearing it echo back from the stone walls of the tenements. What would it be like to live in a world of silence? To be unable to experience music the way it was intended?

He thought of her as he played on the rooftop. Of her inquisitive eyes, her vivacious conversation, of her hands when they were close enough to his to almost touch.

And those were the thoughts that kept him warm.

CHAPTER SEVENTEEN

Unseen Powers

A dull throb of pain radiated in Robinson's skull. He was averaging three hours of sleep at night, and his body was exhausted by the constant threat overshadowing the city. Thankfully his belly wasn't as cramped with hunger as usual. The grateful citizens of Auvinen were providing food to the weary sorcerers defending them. And the locomotivuses were arriving hourly, bringing the first phalanxes from the army to assist in the city's defense. And more were on the way.

Robinson rubbed his bleary eyes as he walked from the university to his apartment. The walks were treacherous with long stretches of ice, trampled by so many feet, but at least he had a basket of leftover food and would have supper tonight before going to the tenements to play his violin.

An hour or so later, when he reached his street, Robinson jogged down the city steps and fished the house key from his pants pocket. As he was about to insert it into the lock, he noticed that one of his wards had been disturbed. The regular hum of magic had changed—one of the notes was off-key. An ordinary sorcerer probably wouldn't have noticed such a subtle change. To him, it sounded like an oblique chord on a Broadway grand, the notes sending invisible strings of magic in crosshatch patterns around him. Someone had entered the apartment earlier, and it wasn't Wickins, because the ward was already attuned to him.

Frowning, Robinson inserted the key and unlocked the door. He entered cautiously, summoning a web of magic to shield himself from harm. The value of the equipment and materials in the alchemy would be tempting to someone driven to desperation by the circumstances of the Aesir conflict. And just about everyone in the city knew the sorcerers were working around the clock.

Robinson set down his basket and went directly to the alchemy. When he went inside, he immediately noticed his things out of order. Someone had been there, rifling through his papers. Most sorcerers, Robinson included, wrote their notes in a cipher just as Isaac Berrow had role-modeled in a previous century.

The lid of the quicksilver vial was askew.

Robinson lifted it and noticed that none of the liquid metal had been taken. A frown furrowed his forehead. One of the most valuable ingredients in the alchemy, it produced a poisonous gas, which would be harmful to anyone not careful in transporting it, but also very helpful in the manufacturing of lamps—the agitated gas was what made them glow. He settled the lid back on properly to prevent more of the fumes from escaping and summoned a portion of the Unseen Powers to begin purging the air in the room.

He found several other articles out of place, but nothing had been stolen. A quick search of the rest of the apartment revealed its condition was much the same—someone had been there but had only made passing changes. It was the alchemy that had been the most disturbed.

A burglar's motives he could understand. Want, stress, and the threat of sudden violence could induce someone to lower their morals and temporarily coax them to illegal action. This was different. Another sorcerer had likely been the intruder. And this act of violation was expressly against the order of the Invisible College. A trustworthy character was the bedrock principle required for those who wished to harness the Unseen Powers. Someone untrustworthy had done this, but there was no way of knowing who.

He ate his meal in silence, ruminating on the evidence his unwanted visitor had left behind. The door had been unlocked and locked again. Perhaps it had been done by one of Lieutenant Wickins's comrades? That was plausible. The fellow might have agreed to retrieve something from Wickins's room as a favor and gotten sidetracked.

Robinson never intruded on his roommate's quarters without permission, so he couldn't know if anything had been retrieved. That seemed the most likely scenario, however. It would explain the ward, the lock, and possibly the curious rifling through the alchemy. So he put the incident from his mind and sprawled out on his bed to rest for a few hours before going to the tenements.

He awoke to the sound of the chime he'd magically set, before falling asleep, to wake him at the correct time. Lethargic and with a throbbing head, he ate a little more from the basket, determined to save some for breakfast. Then he tucked his violin under his arm, locked the door behind him, and reset the ward.

It wasn't until he was in the quiet of the tenement district that he had the sensation he was being followed. Not by a friendly intelligence. The previous feelings of wariness and unease returned, but he glanced back at the dark street and saw no one at all. He stopped, stifling the sound of his own shoes crunching on the brittle snow, and listened.

There were no lights burning from the windows of the tenements. There hadn't been any since the stormbreaker had come. And, as ever, there was no music invoking its soothing and protecting power. The silence was eerie, but there was something beneath it. He discerned the subtle thrum of magic coming from behind him.

Fear constricted his throat.

Once more, he summoned a shield of protection for himself. He was being followed by something invisible. Was it an Aesir? That thought caused a spasm of dread inside his chest. Ordinary sorcerers such as himself were not capable of defeating an Aesir. He wasn't a soldier. He had no pistol, no saltpetr, nothing to use to slow an Aesir's magic. His magic was primarily defensive.

Robinson began to walk again, this time increasing his pace. That preternatural feeling of dread lingered. No, it *followed* him. He dispatched a spell to try to discern the nature of his pursuer, but no response echoed back. If he had a harrosheth blade, at least he'd stand a chance, albeit a small one, for that kind of blade vibrated at a frequency that could penetrate an Aesir's armor.

His mind raced for ideas of what to do if he were suddenly attacked. The shield spell would be helpful, but he'd need a way to summon help. He sensed the dog's intelligence suddenly padding along beside him and could feel its distrust and worry. If it could have growled in warning, it would have.

He was nearly to the widow's building when he realized he was bringing danger to her. It would not be wise to proceed. In fact, it would be safer if he went directly to the Storrows. The magical defenses imbued in that building would be a better help to him than anything in his humble apartment. So he changed directions and took a side street so he could circle back and make his way to the safety of his quorum. The foreboding feeling persisted, however. He was still being followed.

Robinson increased his pace again, trying to put some distance between himself and his pursuer. But the nagging feeling didn't recede. His invisible companion didn't retreat either. It matched his stride soundlessly. He ducked into another alley and then cast a defensive web at the entrance, one that would entangle a man. He hurried to the other end of the alley, ducked around it, then peered back the way he'd come.

A strum of magic sounded, followed by a small flash of light. It gave him just a glimpse, in the darkness, of a figure wearing a cloak with a silver mark on the cowl. He recognized it instantly. A kappelin cloak.

An *Aesir* cloak. One that could make the wearer invisible. The complex spell Robinson had cast at the entrance had revealed the figure for just an instant before the cloak's magic had smothered it.

Robinson ran. It was impossible for a mortal to outrun an Aesir, but he at least had to try. He was halfway down the next street when the starlight was obscured by something overhead plunging the street into shadow. Robinson felt the ice, and suddenly he was unstable, his arms windmilling. The violin case flew from his hand and crashed into an icy embankment nearby, and he heard the sickening crunch of wood. He went down on his back, feeling his muscles wrench violently, and as he gazed up, he saw the underside of the stormbreaker. And he could *hear* it. The notes were far too soft for most mortal ears, but Robinson had always had exceptional hearing. It was *singing*. And the Aesir melody struck his heart and made him gape in shock at the glory and splendor of it.

Little red particles began to slough from the Aesir craft, drifting down like snow, except they were glittering red. They hissed as they struck the ice.

Robinson hurriedly recast his broken shield, which had come apart when he'd fallen and lost concentration. The web of magic surrounded him, and the dots of crimson lights bounced harmlessly off it. They made little popping noises as they fell. It was as if motes of bloodred dust were swirling over the tenements. His stomach wrenched with dread. This was not the sound of the ice-fire hail that had devastated the city earlier, but surely they meant ill.

He needed to do something.

The motes were raining down on the tenements. Robinson groaned with the strain in his back and hurried to his violin case. He opened it and saw the instrument inside was broken. His instrument couldn't help him counter whatever the Aesir were raining down on the city.

Kneeling in the snow, Robinson looked up and began to sing. It was one of the shield canticles he'd learned in his formal education at his grandfather's quorum. It was meant to be sung with eight parts, and he only had one. His voice. He sang into the night, willing the Unseen Powers to shield the population of the tenements. Knowing the protection would only extend to the distance his voice could travel. His voice faltered when he realized he was too far away from the widow's building. His voice wouldn't reach her or her children.

But he started again, lifting his voice in a song of defiance. Before tonight, he'd never heard the music of the Aesir. It was otherworldly. It was beautiful. It penetrated to the bone. Yet still he tried to counter it, singing louder, his voice beginning to crack.

The blast of a pistol rang out in the night. The bullet ricocheted off his shield. That made him falter too. What were the odds of his shield deflecting such a direct hit? They must be incredibly low.

Had his invisible companion aided him somehow?

He thought he heard a cacophony of whispering voices inside him, commanding him to run, to flee before he was slain.

Another idea came into his mind and exited his lips before he could stop it. He cried out in song, uttering a magical command to aid in his defense. It was a complex shield spell, one to be used against another magic wielder. Had the thought come from him, or the dog?

A shriek of magic blasted the alley, directed toward his unseen attacker. A shocked groan rose in its wake.

Run!

Robinson left his broken violin and fled the tenements while the crimson rain continued to fall across them like hoarfrost. When he'd cast that spell before, in practice, it had never been so powerful. So jarring. So potent.

He had no idea what had just happened, but he knew it had saved his life.

CHAPTER EIGHTEEN

Unheard Sounds

The barracks in Auvinen were near the locomotivus station on the north side of the river. After crossing the bridge, Robinson witnessed the evidence of devastation caused by the bombardments in the rubble-strewn roads and scorched timbers. He was still rattled by his experience of recent days and felt uneasy being in public. He'd twisted his mind into knots trying to unravel the sequence of events.

A magically shielded person had come after him. The dog's intelligence had saved him. Had his compassion toward the beast tied them together inextricably? He did not have enough clues to put all the pieces together. But that didn't stop him from trying.

Glancing both ways to ensure he'd miss two street trams crossing in front of him, Robinson slipped behind one, following it for a moment, then finished crossing the crowded street to the entrance of the barracks.

Two soldiers in uniform were at the gate. "Hold there, friend, this area is off limits to civilians."

"I'm meeting someone," Robinson explained.

"Who?"

"Lieutenant Wickins, Signals division."

"Are you Dickemore?" asked the other sentry.

Robinson nodded.

"He left a pass for you." The soldier reached into the jacket pocket of his uniform and withdrew a folded slip of paper. "In the commissary. The big building yonder. You can't miss it."

Robinson took the paper gratefully, nodded to the soldiers, and entered the compound. Wickins had been living in the barracks since the stormbreaker had arrived, and Robinson hadn't seen him in several weeks. He was grateful his roommate had responded to his cryptic message. If his discovery was correct, he would have an early warning if the invisible fellow came hunting him again. In order to test it, however, he needed someone he could trust.

Once he reached the commissary, he had to show the pass to the guards at the entrance. There were a surprising number of civilians there, and it took him a moment to discern Wickins from the rest, sitting at one of the rows of benches with a half-eaten plate of food.

Robinson passed through the maze of people and sat down on the bench across from his friend.

"Good to see you," Wickins said with a grim smile. "I saved you some of my dinner. You look unwell. Go on . . . eat it. I took my fair share, nothing more. I'm not hungry. Everything is butter and sauce in here."

Robinson looked at the half-eaten plate, his hunger suddenly surging, accompanied by the realization that he hadn't eaten much, if anything, over the last few days. He took a mouthful of chicken thigh smothered in gravy, and his stomach murmured with pleasure. He ate ravenously, demolishing the plate in a few minutes before washing down the meal with a few large gulps of water.

"You've been starving yourself again," Wickins pointed out. He stared in disbelief. "Literally."

Robinson wiped his mouth on the back of his hand. "Not deliberately. There are just more important things to do than eating sometimes. But that's not why I came to see you."

"It's about the break-in. I tell you, I don't know who—"

"I couldn't care less about that right now."

"Then what do you want?"

"Do you remember the night the Aesir ship attacked the tenements with the red sparks?"

"What of it? It didn't damage anything."

"Not that we know of, anyway. I was out there that night."

Wickins's eyebrows shot up. "Whatever for?"

"I'd been helping defend that quarter with my violin." He'd gone back the next day with a trinket that would play music. It needed to be wound up, but at least it would provide the family with some protection should the ships came back. The widow and her children had been so grateful.

His friend looked even more dumbfounded. "The obsessed violinist? That was *you*?"

"I'm not sure what you mean."

"I've heard stories of a rogue sorcerer playing his violin on the rooftops of the slums."

"I did it on my own time."

"I should have guessed it was you. Well, that mystery is solved. So what's this all about, old chap?"

"I need access to an Aesir cloak. A *tarnkappe* as they're called in Tanhauser. I need to borrow one to test a new invention."

Wickins seemed flummoxed. "They don't sell those here, nor could I afford one in a time of war!"

"I know that. I've asked at the university, and the only one they had was requisitioned by the military because of the Awakening. But I *need* one."

"And are you going to tell me why?"

Robinson lowered his voice. He had to be very careful about what he revealed. "I think I can break through their enchantment."

Wickins leaned closer. "Say again?"

"I think I know a way to break through their enchantment." And if he was right, it wouldn't help only himself but could possibly help the entire military on the front lines.

"Why would anyone want to lend you an Aesir cloak if you're going to attempt to break it? Do you know how valuable they are?"

"I don't mean *break* it. A kappelin can render the wearer invisible to mortal eyes. It even veils their thoughts, overriding a preternatural ability we have to sense the unseen. The night the stormbreaker came to the slums, I heard the ship's magic as it flew overhead. As clear as can be." He decided he should trust Wickins about the attacker. Someone else needed to know.

"Do you need to see a doctor? Their music can derange someone!"

"So they say, but I'm not deranged. It opened my ears. And now my eyes. What if we could hear them coming without being susceptible to their power? What if we could harness the Unseen Powers in such a way that we can hear an Aesir approach and be forewarned?"

Wickins was interested now. The intrigue shone in his eyes. "That would be an incredibly valuable invention, Dickemore. We have to defend miles and miles of borders because we don't know where they will strike. Their invisibility to our senses is their greatest strength."

"That night, someone in an Aesir cloak was following me."

Wickins's brow wrinkled. "Where? Into the slums?"

"Yes. And I felt them because it was too quiet. I felt them because the Unseen Powers knew they were following me and warned me. I thought it was an Aesir, but the individual shot at me with a pistol, so . . . I rather think they were mortal."

"Good grief, Dickemore! Why didn't you tell me?"

"Because I fear it is a faction within the military. Common gents do not have pistols with elfshot or try to kill rogue sorcerers who play violins on rooftops. I've been obsessing over this thought for days. I even moved out. To another location."

"What? Where?"

"I can't tell you. Not yet. But if I'm right, if it is possible to discern intention behind an Aesir's veil of invisibility, it would be a tremendous invention. I've been working the last few days on some ideas that have borne interesting fruit so far."

"You've tested this, then? How?"

Robinson nodded. "A park near the shore has a floating boulder that was originally set there by the Aesir . . . who knows how long ago? Do you know of it?"

"Yes. I've seen it."

Robinson reached into his coat pocket and removed a glass tube, the kind used in quicksilver lamps. A small one. "Take this to that park and see for yourself. It will start glowing when you get near the stone."

Wickins held his hand out for the tube and then took a moment to inspect it. "It's an ordinary tube. Doesn't it actuate when the sun sets?"

Robinson shook his head. "Not this one. It will only activate when it *hears* an Aesir's song. It will only start glowing when you go near that floating boulder, and it will stop when you walk away. Try it for yourself. I need you to help me get a cloak so I can conduct further tests."

"How does it work?" Wickins asked curiously.

"It operates under the same principle as any quicksilver lamp. This one is just a little more intelligent. It doesn't get excited when darkness falls. It gets excited when it hears something we rarely hear. A perfect Mixolydian chord. That stone radiates a harmony that is at a pitch almost inaudible to us. But I can hear it . . . well . . . it's more like I can sense it. I attuned the intelligence to that chord, and it responds every time it hears it. Your father is a colonel. See if you can borrow an Aesir cloak. If I'm right, this tube will start to glow immediately when it is nearby."

Wickins turned the tube over in his hands, gazing at it with keen interest. "What intelligence did you harness?"

"Mr. Foster has encouraged me to keep that confidential until the patent is secured in Bishopsgate. I asked if he could get me access to a cloak, but the military has exclusive rights to them during the war."

Wickins tapped the glass bulb against his palm. "Let me test it out myself first. How do I reach you with an answer if you've moved?"

"Sarah Fuller Fiske knows where I'm staying. She helped arrange for my alchemy to be moved during my shift at the university."

"So we're not roommates anymore?"

"The new place is in a dingier neighborhood than our current situation. It would be better—"

"I'll hear none of that," Wickins said, shaking his head. "I'll ask her to move my things as well. This invention, Dickemore, this is serious. I will head there as soon as possible to test it out. I want to be part of it if you'll let me. You know the music, but I know the language of the Aesir. I think I can be of assistance."

A loud chime cut through the noise of the commissary. An alarm. Heads swiveled and the room fell silent.

"All officers, report to your duty stations. All officers, report to duty stations immediately!"

Robinson felt a deep thrum inside his bones, for the bulb in Wickins's hand had started to glow.

"It's the stormbreaker," Robinson whispered. He could hear it, but not with his natural senses. It was the same feeling he'd had that night in the alley. "It's passing overhead right now."

Wickins stared at the tube, seeing its glow increasing.

It was more the vibration Robinson felt than anything else. A chord of magic so deep that his ears could not hear it, but he felt it throb in the wood of the bench seat, the tiny quiver radiating from the tabletop. It made him excited and afraid at the same time.

"Shields!" someone in the room screamed. The sorcerers rose in unison and began to sing the canticle of protection. It was not all officers, for rank was of no significance to the Invisible College. Robinson and Wickins hurried to their feet and added their voices to the impromptu choir. As webs of magic began to assemble overhead, the light from the bulb grew brighter and brighter, radiating in Wickins's hand like a torch.

Long have we studied this rift between our kind and the Aesir. Did we become too obstinate for their sensibilities? Or was it that, as the historian Lord Babington Thomas surmised, "With the dead there is no rivalry, with the dead there is no change." Was it our predisposition to change the world before they woke up that finally broke their long-suffering with us?

They have created every vexation we face in our lives—war, pestilence, famine. And yet these selfsame vexations might perhaps bring us to another level of wisdom, one we may never have achieved without being forced to face our true natures when pressed to our extremities. That is the penultimate end of the Invisible College. Not inventing trinkets of magic.

—Isaac Berrow,
Master of the Royal Secret,
the Invisible College

McKenna Aurora Foster

CHAPTER NINETEEN

The House at Bishopsgate

McKenna missed her home on Brake Street. She missed her lessons with Professor Hawksley—truly, she missed those most of all—but she also missed the dinners at Closure and their lively conversations. She missed the smell of syrupy cooked peanuts and her mother's lavender perfume. She missed the library as well. Oh, the books! And now she missed Clara. Surprise of surprises.

Clara was living an adventure, helping to defend Auvinen from the Aesir attack. In her letters, she described all the soldiers she'd met and the fear caused by the bombardments. After several months of them, though, things were becoming quite normal again. People no longer hunkered down in their homes. Businesses and the factories were thriving.

McKenna was grateful no harm had come to those she loved the most, although she felt sadly removed from it all.

The Foster house in Bishopsgate was on a curved street where all the homes were bunched up together in a row, no separation between them. It was within walking distance to the Great Rotunda, the seat of government in the region. During McKenna's walks on the wintry streets, there was an endless procession of soldiers and wagons full of matériel for the war effort. That was a new word she'd learned since the war came. "Matériel." It meant something other than manpower that was needed in war, like elfshot, saltpetr, and cannons.

And in this war, which was creating mass casualties in every attack, giant vats of saltpetr were needed. Racks and racks of elfshot. Cannon wheels. Rifles with silver-tipped bayonets that could pierce an Aesir's armor.

McKenna felt a tap on her shoulder. She'd been sitting at the front window, chin on her hands, watching the people and equipages passing along the street. Turning her head, she saw it was Trudie who'd tapped her.

"Another letter from Clara just arrived," her sister said, offering it to McKenna with a worried look.

"Is anything wrong?" McKenna asked, taking the paper from her sister's hand.

"Read for yourself. It's dreadful."

McKenna turned around on the couch and began to peruse the letter. Clara had a keen wit and a deliciously wicked sense of humor, but all that was absent as she described a new illness spreading through Auvinen.

It had begun in the tenements. After a ship had passed over them and dropped a mysterious substance, they'd immediately begun developing symptoms, the most prevalent of which was a sore throat and coughing, followed by swelling of the throat and fever. Gray pustules then formed in the mouth and, coupled with the swelling, made breathing difficult. This illness didn't affect the ear but the *voice*. Those suffering had barking coughs that rendered speaking magic impossible.

McKenna read with growing horror. It was a new abomination sent by the Aesir to destroy mortals.

"This is awful," she said, looking at her sister.

"Why do they hate us so much?" Trudie asked, blinking with fear.

"Father said it isn't hate so much as indifference," McKenna said. "But maybe it has grown into hate. You know how there are so many here in Bishopsgate? I see them scurrying about all the time. Picking at garbage. Maybe the Aesir see us as rats. They don't see any use for us anymore."

"But we're not rats, McKenna. We're people. Don't we have a right to exist?"

"I don't understand it either, Trudie." McKenna looked down and continued reading the letter. It was a well-written letter, but the tone bothered McKenna deeply.

Clara had said people in the tenements were being barred from working in the city. Many wealthy families had already become sick because of their serving staff, however, and the disease was starting to spread quickly. Clara lamented that when summer came, it would impact her coming-of-age ball when she entered Society at last. McKenna thought it rather shallow of her sister to worry about others' death and misery interrupting a social event. Clara could be so self-centered sometimes. People were dying. That was infinitely more important and terrible than delaying a ball.

Then she remembered that Father had told her Professor Hawksley had spent some nights in the tenements with his violin, helping to protect the people living in squalor. Surely Mother or Father would have mentioned if he'd gotten sick? The thought of him slowly choking to death filled her with dread. How awful that would be. And not just because it would impact her own lessons and dreams for the future. She cared about him as a *person*, not just as a teacher. He was a friend of the family.

"Do you think Papa will return soon?" Trudie asked. She wrung her hands. "I miss him."

"So do I," McKenna confessed. Aunt Margaret had excised McKenna's use of the endearment "papa," but since Trudie was younger, she could get away with it without a scolding. McKenna liked her aunt well enough, but she was so prim. So full of self-importance. Her imposing manners had driven away potential suitors long ago. She was, technically, a spinster, although she wouldn't have used that term for herself. She had wealth and an ample estate on the island of Siaconset. McKenna and her sisters loved visiting there, although the tides could be treacherous. It was full of wildflowers, the smell of the surf, and seagulls that danced in the air with the wind. It was never fully winter at Mowbray House.

"I'm worried now that I've read Clara's letter," Trudie said. "I should *hate* to get sick and choke to death."

"We are much better off than the people living in the tenements, Trudie. We can afford doctors and medicines."

"I overheard Aunt Margaret talking to Papa. The war has been hard on us. Their investment in the school takes up so much money, and they've two houses to maintain. Aunt Margaret said Papa can't afford to keep up both forever, partly because the school hasn't yet grown enough for him to see yields on the investment. But I don't want to go back to Brake Street. Not when everyone is getting sick."

"You think we're going back to Brake Street?"

"We have to go back someday."

McKenna pursed her lips and patted her sister's shoulder. "I think Father would tell us if we were going to return. We are safer here. I don't think we'd go back unless it was absolutely necessary."

"I hope you're right."

Trudie left and McKenna read the letter once more. No news about her teacher. Sometimes Clara liked to tease about him in her correspondence. But this letter had focused on the outbreak and, of course, the potential impact on Clara's future.

McKenna folded the letter up again and set it on the sofa, turning to look outside. The snow was more gray slush than fresh powder now. Winter was soon coming to an end. The Aesir might be powerful beings with powerful magic, but they could not prevent spring from coming. Once it did, they would be forced to retreat to the glaciers again. They had a fixed limit of time in which to cause their mischief.

She missed Auvinen so much. The family time. The cherry orchard. She and her sisters used to overeat the fruit so much as little children they'd stain their fingers and their dresses. They were too old for such antics now, but spring was full of good memories. Memories she'd miss if they stayed in the rich neighborhood in Bishopsgate.

⁂

That night, McKenna sat in the dormer room she shared with Trudie and brushed out her hair. She had a thick mane of hair that hung all the way down to her waist. She gazed at herself in the mirror as she brushed, turning her head a little to the side and trying to picture her hair done up in one of Clara's new styles. Once her sister turned eighteen, she would be expected to adhere to the styles approved by Society. There would be corsets and handkerchiefs, little parasols for walking around town. McKenna set the brush on the table and gazed at her reflection. Mother said she was pretty. She'd told Mother that the professor had called her a beauty. It still made a little giddy feeling in her bosom when she remembered that night, walking hand in hand with him in the snow. He was just being gallant, though. He was probably more than twice her age, and she was still very young, even if Society would consider her ineligible for a role once she turned nineteen in a few months.

Picking up the brush again, she began some more vigorous strokes, succumbing to a fanciful thought of seeing herself as she'd imagined she'd look in the future.

She'd observed Mother, as a child, doing her hair up. She lacked the dexterity to complete such a task, but she did the best she could to contain her locks with the pins she found on the vanity table. Her hair was so long that she couldn't contain it all, however, and the effect made her laugh. She tilted her head a little and tried on a smile. The nightdress was incongruous with the fancy hairstyle, so she unbuttoned the top buttons and tucked the ends of the collar in to expose her throat and some skin. In her imagination she wore a necklace made with three ornaments, like one of Mother's favorites, with a larger center piece and two smaller ones on either side. Slowly, she turned her head from one side then to the other. Instead of smiling, she tried on a mysterious look instead, an expression of someone older, more sophisticated.

She hadn't heard the door creak open. And so she didn't notice Aunt Margaret until she appeared in the mirror.

McKenna felt a stab of embarrassment for her whimsy, but the look on her aunt's face wasn't scolding or taunting. Her aunt stared at her reflection, her mouth slightly open.

McKenna wrung her hands. "It was just a little fancy, that's all," she said apologetically.

Aunt Margaret stepped forward and put her hand on McKenna's shoulder, her eyes serious. "Every daughter does it, McKenna. I can help you next time if you like."

"Oh . . . would you?" McKenna said, surprised, feeling a surge of pleasure. "Could you do it like . . . yours?" She'd secretly admired her aunt's lavish hairstyles.

Aunt Margaret nodded, but there was a sad look in her eyes. Or was it worry?

"I just received a letter from your father," she said.

Trudie had already fallen asleep on the bed, but she sat up quickly, rubbing her eyes. "Papa? Is he all right?"

"Yes, the family is well. All are in good health."

"But something is wrong," McKenna observed.

Aunt Margaret nodded slowly. "The infection has spread to the school. Your father's school. Mrs. Fiske has fallen ill. So has your tutor, Miss Hurst. They've been tending the sick children all by themselves. Some have died. It's . . . it's very sad. The disease is spreading so fast."

"Oh dear," McKenna said, her heart constricting in pain. The unfortunate children. Away from their homes, their families. She felt horrible for them. Poor Miss Hurst! "What's to be done?"

"The first case in Bishopsgate was discovered this evening. In your father's previous letter, he gave instructions that when the first confirmed case of the illness hit here, he would like me to dismiss the servants and close up the house."

"We're going? Where?" Trudie said, beginning to sob. She rushed off the bed and hugged Aunt Margaret.

Their aunt stroked her hair. "We're not going back to Auvinen. Not until it's safe."

"If the house is being shut down," McKenna said, "then where will we live?"

"Mowbray House."

Trudie looked worriedly at McKenna.

"For how long?" McKenna asked, her heart constricting. She didn't want to be even farther away from home.

"Until it is safe."

Aunt Margaret suddenly turned her head toward the dormer window. Trudie did the same.

"Do you . . . do you hear something?" McKenna asked them both.

Then she felt the vibration. The impact. All three of them rushed to the window and watched the bombardment begin over Bishopsgate. Blue oval shields were forming over the sky, summoned by sorcerers to protect the city.

Bishopsgate was under attack.

CHAPTER TWENTY

Siaconset Island

McKenna's heart raced as she was jostled through the crowd. She pulled Trudie along through the chaos of the locomotivus station while her aunt in turn pulled her along. Aunt Margaret had given the orders to shut down the Bishopsgate house, and the servants, those who wanted to, would follow to the island of Siaconset. But they had left at once.

There was no decorum at the station. It was mass panic.

Women and children were crowding into the crammed box cars, which had been designed to transport war matériel but now needed to include passengers. The smell of saltpetr fumes filled the air. It was a sharp smell that permeated everything.

For a moment, McKenna lost her grip on her sister, and she spun her head around in a panic, finding the space filled with other distraught people.

"Trudie! Trudie!" McKenna called out, yanking on her aunt's hand to stop her from going farther. Then her sister was back again, her face pale with terror.

Aunt Margaret nodded curtly and pulled them toward the passenger compartment at the head of the train. Plumes of white smoke billowed from the front as the magical energy chilled the tracks and the metal parts. When they reached the compartment, a soldier barred the way.

"We're full, ma'am. You'll have to wait for the next one," the officer said. McKenna could tell he was a lieutenant by the rank stripes on his shoulders, which matched the ones Wickins wore.

"I have tickets," Aunt Margaret said. "Three tickets!" She shoved them at the officer's face.

"So does everyone else, ma'am. I'm sorry."

"We're getting on board," Aunt Margaret said, her nostrils flaring. "Stand aside!"

"Ma'am, there will be another locomotivus coming just behind this one. You'll be the first to board, I promise."

The young officer would not be denied, and the two clashed until the locomotivus started to screech. McKenna sensed the vibrations in her body—she felt them in her chest. Disappointment flooded her.

The door of the passenger car opened, and a uniformed rail worker called out. McKenna, reading his lips, saw he was declaring there was room for two more.

The lieutenant whirled back and then looked at Aunt Margaret. "I can bring your two girls. They can go on ahead if you hurry!"

Aunt Margaret shook her head. "It's all three or none of us. Please, sir! I'll stand the whole way. I don't need a seat!"

". . . And get them on board!" shouted the worker. McKenna had missed part of the dialogue with her attention being fixed on her aunt.

They all started following the locomotivus, which was slowly moving from the station. The lieutenant lifted Trudie up to the worker. Then McKenna. Aunt Margaret had to run, but she took the outstretched hand of the railway worker and was soon on board. The passenger car was crammed indeed, with faces of women and children of varying ages spread throughout. One small row of seats by the windows was left, and the worker escorted them there. Everyone else squeezed closer together, and the three were able to press in until they all were seated, with Aunt

Margaret in the middle. She was flushed but triumphant, her broad-brimmed hat cocked on her head, and she squeezed both of her nieces' hands as the machine picked up speed.

McKenna turned her neck and gazed out at the city as the locomotivus slid on the tracks before the magic kicked in and it began to levitate off the rails. Soon the magnetic forces were propelling it faster and faster, and Bishopsgate became a blur before disappearing into the distance.

Trudie leaned her head against Aunt Margaret's shoulder and promptly fell asleep. McKenna wished she'd been able to bring some of her books along, but they'd fled in too much haste. So, to pass the time, she thought about the Hawksley method and began to practice some of the diction phrases under her breath. She hoped Miss Hurst and Mrs. Fiske and as many children at the school as possible would be all right. It worried her that they were suffering from a new menace unleashed by the Aesir. It felt unjust for so many to suffer.

She grew bored of practicing after a while and, unable to sleep, examined the other passengers. One set, a mother and two sons, were wearing the fashions of Jevena, which were much less colorful. Watching their lips in confusion as they spoke, McKenna realized the language they were speaking was Tanhauser and that she actually knew what they were talking about. The mother was telling her sons, in a low voice, that the Aesir war would only end if the mortals unconditionally surrendered. Mortals had stolen their magic, and the Aesir would not be satisfied until it was abandoned and forgotten. Until there were no more sorcerers or floating locomotivuses.

McKenna was baffled by the sentiments. Disarming oneself against a relentless enemy didn't feel like a wise course of action or a viable option. According to the accounts she'd read in books, previous attempts at submission had proved fatal.

The southbound locomotivus took them to Rexanne, which they reached by the end of the next day. The passengers all disembarked, and McKenna made a point of trying to help the mother and sons communicate with a porter to get their luggage transported to a nearby hotel. Her proficiency in their language was greatly appreciated, and Aunt Margaret complimented her on being so helpful. They retired to a hotel themselves because the ferry to the island had already left and wouldn't return until the next morning.

Aunt Margaret had accounts at all the draper shops in Rexanne and secured a change of clothes and some necessities for them before they took a meal at the hotel to assuage their hunger. McKenna liked that word too. "Assuage" had such a soothing pronunciation. It meant *to alleviate or pacify something*. And that is exactly what needed to happen to their hunger pangs.

Her mind had wandered back to the Physiological Alphabet of the Hawksley method, and she found herself focusing with such concentration on the placement of her lips and jaw for the *g* sound that she missed Aunt Margaret's question and Trudie had to tap her arm.

"Yes, Aunt?"

"You look like you are muttering something under your breath. What are you doing?"

"Oh, it is just the Hawksley method. I was thinking of the proper pronunciation for certain words. The *g* sound, for example, can be hard or soft, and the proper way to do it softly is—"

She felt Trudie tap her shoulder. "It looked like you were practicing *kissing* someone. I'll bet I know who."

"That's absurd, Trudie." She turned her gaze back to her aunt.

Aunt Margaret had lifted her eyebrows imperiously. "Whom do you mean?" she asked.

"Clara and Trudie like to tease me," McKenna said.

"He said you were beautiful," Trudie said.

"Who did?" Aunt Margaret looked even more concerned.

"They like to tease me about my teacher. They are being silly, Aunt. That is all."

"He talks to you more than he talks to us," Trudie said. "He *likes* you."

McKenna felt her cheeks starting to flush and squeezed her hands into fists beneath the table. "Trudie, this isn't the time for such nonsense. We just escaped with our lives!"

Her sister gave a sullen pout. "I miss Clara. She's more fun."

"But McKenna is right," their aunt said in an admonishing tone. "You are being childish. Enough of such nonsense."

"Yes, Auntie."

After that, McKenna felt the teasing would cease and she could get some relief for a while. But Aunt Margaret noticed everything, and she had already made it very clear she disapproved of the informality between Robinson and McKenna. No doubt she'd noticed the way McKenna had been blushing.

*

The ferry to Siaconset was rowed by a young man and took passengers and their cargo safely across the waters to the island. Most of the residents lived in Newdale on the coast, but there were farms and homesteads all across the tiny island.

Mowbray House, Aunt Margaret's saltbox home, was on the main street in a prestigious neighborhood. The outer walls and roof were of shake shingles, with a platform on the top, framed around a central chimney. At the back of the house was an extended structure with a clock, a cupola, and a bell tower. A white picket fence surrounded the shrubs and the two-sided staircase leading up to the front door. As with all the other homes in the area, it was built with the main living quarters starting on the second floor because of the occasional typhoon that caused storm surges.

A carriage was stationed in the alley next to the house, and similar saltbox houses flanked each side, but none were as large or grand as Aunt Margaret's. She was the eldest child of the family, so she'd inherited the estate, whereas Mother had gotten a sizable dowry instead.

It was a beautiful home, with white-trimmed windows on the lower and upper floors and bright pink flowers that seemed to bloom year-round in the mild climate, and it was large enough to house twenty or more, including servants' quarters. The air smelled of the sea as, just behind the established trees of the elegant homes, there stretched a long beach.

The wind was a constant presence on the island, and McKenna brushed her hair from her face continually. They walked up the steps and were greeted by the housekeeper, Mrs. Foraker, a no-nonsense woman after Aunt Margaret's heart.

"Heard yesterday about the attack on Bishopsgate," Mrs. Foraker said with relief in her eyes. "I thought you might be returning in a hurry. And look at your two nieces. They've grown so much! You are both jewels. I'll have Mr. Swope make up two rooms for them at once."

"Thank you, Mrs. Foraker. A bit of tea would be helpful."

"I'll bring it to the parlor at once, my lady. It's good to see you, Miss McKenna, Miss Trudie."

"Can I have the corner room upstairs, please?" Trudie begged. "The one with the rocking chair?"

Aunt Margaret nodded and Trudie bounded off.

McKenna didn't care which room she had. There were enough that they usually got their own rooms. She was about to wander toward the kitchen, but Aunt Margaret caught her arm and motioned for her to stay. Mrs. Foraker left to get the tea.

"Please sit down," Aunt Margaret said, gesturing to the stuffed chair in the entryway.

McKenna wrinkled her brow but complied. She was desperate to write a letter to her parents, to let them know she was safe and to ask for news about the children at the school.

"Yes?" she asked inquisitively.

Aunt Margaret's brows were nettled with concern. "Do you wish to marry, McKenna Aurora Foster?"

The use of her full name was quite unusual. More formal than the situation required. "I imagine someday, yes."

Aunt Margaret frowned. "That would please your father, certainly. And add to the reputation of the family."

"Surely I shouldn't only do it to increase our reputation," McKenna said.

"There are many reasons young ladies choose to marry and many reasons they choose not to. I would caution that sympathy is not a good reason to choose a mate."

"I don't understand you, Aunt. Sympathy?"

Her aunt pressed her lips firmly together. "When we spend time with people in more relaxed circumstances, forms of sympathy begin to develop. They are natural, of course. Appropriate even. But sympathy can turn to pity." She shook her head emphatically. "And that is entirely the wrong reason to marry someone."

McKenna felt even more confused. She also felt flustered. What was Aunt Margaret getting at? She didn't know what to say, but her aunt seemed determined to lecture her, so she remained quiet and gazed carefully at the woman's posture, her serious eyes, as well as what she was conveying with her lips, so as not to miss a single nuance.

"Professor Hawksley. He's going to ask you to marry him. Out of love? Out of pity?" The way she cocked her head slightly, McKenna could tell that these were questions instead of statements. There were so many subtle clues in communication.

"Has Mother . . . told you something?" McKenna asked in a faltering voice.

Aunt Margaret shook her head again. "I have eyes, McKenna. You are an attractive young woman from a distinguished family. You are also deaf. And there is no guarantee that your children will not be born with the affliction. So I ask you. Do you want to marry Professor Hawksley?"

McKenna felt her cheeks flaming at that. This was not what she'd expected upon her arrival at Siaconset. "I'm . . . it's still . . . it's only been a few months since I came of age, Auntie. I'm . . . I'm still not in Society."

Aunt Margaret shook her head again. "You are a young woman. He cares for you in his own way, I suppose. He is older than you. Sickly. Probably not the sort of man who feels valuable. He is a professor of speech, and you need his help. How can he not pity your situation, McKenna? Perhaps he thinks he is trying to save *you*"—this was said with a rolling of the eyes—"but it is *himself* he is really trying to save. From poverty, from disgrace, from failure. Men of his sort are driven by ambition and, unfortunately, more times than not, never succeed. Your father has invested in that success, but it is still an unlikely venture. This is what will happen. He will sink lower and lower into poverty and ill health until, at last, he enters an early grave. I've seen this over and over and grow wearied of the tale. I would spare you this tragedy, McKenna. You must have an answer when he asks you."

The words Aunt Margaret had used summoned horrible images in McKenna's mind. Father believed in Professor Hawksley. McKenna did too. He was not like other people. But she didn't have romantic feelings for him. Did she? He was so much older. But he was kind, thoughtful, and a brilliant teacher. She respected him deeply.

McKenna felt her cheeks burning even more. "N-No, Auntie. No, I don't want to marry him."

There was a self-satisfied look on Aunt Margaret's face. "Good. Then I suggest you consider ways you can express your feelings properly and prudently. For he *will* ask you. Your sisters aren't the only ones who see his clumsy attempts at affection. I saw it myself that night you came back in the blizzard. Trudie's comment last night at dinner made me resolve to intervene. Pity isn't a reason to marry someone. Pity for you. Or pity for him."

"Pity" was such a guilt-provoking word. And she knew her aunt had used it deliberately, for those were exactly the feelings that McKenna started to have.

If we could instill the phenomena of magic into mechanical principles, it could be harnessed in devices and constructs. Intelligence woven into matter. I have a suspicion that all phenomena may depend on certain unknown forces by which the particles, by causes not yet known, either are impelled toward one another and cohere or are repelled from one another and recede. Attraction and repulsion. This is the core of how the universe and magic both work.

—Isaac Berrow,
Master of the Royal Secret,
the Invisible College

Robinson Dickemore Hawksley

CHAPTER TWENTY-ONE

Secret Attraction

Robinson gazed at the words written on the page. *Attraction and repulsion. This is the core of how the universe and magic both work.* The young professor was not the first who had pondered this particular passage. It was a particularly famous one, written during a sequestering caused by another Aesir plague. The university had been shut down, and Isaac Berrow had returned to his private estate. Something had happened to him during that time. Something had happened to the fastidious professor, to alter his way of thinking, resulting in a prolific series of inventions and discoveries that eventually became the Invisible College. Berrow might not have been the discoverer—or *re*discoverer—of the methods of sorcery. So many of the Aesir lessons had been lost over the centuries. But Berrow's impact on the history of magic could not be understated. Scores of sorcerers had since pored over copies of his private journals in the hopes of discovering what the "something" might have been. Such a copy lay on the reading-room table in front of him at the Storrows.

Robinson glanced at the clock and saw that it was nearly time for supper at the Fosters'. It hadn't been the same since McKenna had left. When he'd heard Bishopsgate had been attacked, he'd been desperate for news of her safety and was relieved to learn that both she and Trudie had gone with their aunt to Siaconset. So she was no longer in immediate danger. But not seeing her had put a dull ache in his heart, one that tormented him day and night. At least the invitation to dinner at the Fosters' hadn't been rescinded. Robinson would not turn down a free meal, not when his personal circumstances were so acute. The University of Auvinen had been closed due to the raging illness now called the inspiratory stridor, so the rest of his lectures had been canceled. His private students were all gone. He had money and time to work on his invention, but he could not, for integrity's sake, use those funds to feed himself or pay rent.

His situation was grim. He felt like a scarecrow some days, those characters of sticks and straw used to frighten away birds.

"There you are, Dickemore," Wickins said, coming up from behind him. "I thought I'd find you here."

Robinson was about to greet his friend with a grin, but he saw his troubled look and the quicksilver lamp in his hands. Wickins presented it to Robinson, who took it with a wrinkled brow.

"I'm glad I didn't send a request to my father for testing with that Aesir cloak. It doesn't work. Not at all."

That was preposterous. "What do you mean it didn't work? You saw it work that night at the commissary."

"Indeed. But I finally took it to the floating boulder, the one in the park, and nothing happened at all. It must be broken."

"Nothing at all?" Robinson said, his emotions churning with incredulity.

"Shall we go for supper, then? I'm famished."

"Hang the dinner, it can wait. We need to stop by the park first. I can't believe this. It worked perfectly. I tested it for hours."

"I'm sorry, poor chap. It is what it is. But if you don't believe me, let's stop there first."

Robinson returned the copy of the Berrow journal to the levitating floating hand and went with Wickins through the underground exit and into the pub. The clamorous noises there were soon forgotten as they exited onto the slushy streets. Robinson tucked his hands deep into his pockets and was grateful he had the Storrows to get warm each day. At his new quarters, there was just a little automaton brazier that only worked half the time.

"Can we take a street tram? I don't fancy the walk."

"I can't afford one."

Wickins sighed. "I'm happy to spring for the expense."

"It wouldn't be right if I accepted it."

"You accepted help from Foster's daughter, remember."

"That was different. I couldn't let her wander home in a blizzard unaccompanied. Honor demanded it."

"Have you told the girl you dote on her yet?"

Robinson gave him a scowl. "Of course not."

"Cheer up, then. You haven't a cupper to your name, your clothes are threadbare, and you're as gaunt as a corpse. What could go wrong?"

"Thank you for the vote of confidence."

"I only jest. She's a handsome girl, to be sure, though I like her sister better. But with her condition, she'll not likely find many suitors."

"She is an incredible young woman and I'll not have you disparage her."

"I'm not disparaging her, Dickemore. Most girls in her situation end up in an asylum. If her father weren't the man he is, with his means, her life would be very different."

"And if I hadn't caught the same disease that killed my brother, I'd still be in Covesea. Ashes to ashes, dust to dust. Justice claimeth its own."

"True. And we'd never have met either. You're a strange fellow, but I like you. Now, listen here, we're going to the park to experiment with your invention. Is that not grounds to use Mr. Foster's funds for transportation?"

Robinson thought a moment and realized the argument did make sense. He was so used to being tight-fisted that he hadn't thought the matter through.

"Don't be obstinate just because I suggested it," his friend said with shining eyes.

Robinson chuckled. "No, your argument makes perfect sense. When I purchase supplies, I take the tram because it saves so much time."

"Precisely! There's a good fellow. Let's catch that one!"

Soon the two were riding swiftly on a tram, tugged along the tracks by the iron horse. The smell of burnt sugar peanuts wafted by, but there was no sign of a cart. They reached their destination near the park and hastened the rest of the way. The rubble-strewn area had already been cleaned up. Despite the continual Aesir bombardments, the citizens of Auvinen were quick to repair any destruction visited on the city.

As they approached the floating boulder in the park, Robinson held out the glass tube with the quicksilver vapor trapped inside. His heart beat faster as he approached the boulder, but just as before, it activated the lamp, which started to glow.

"I told you it worked," Robinson said with a victorious smile.

"I'll be flummoxed," Wickins said. "It didn't work for me. Let me handle it."

Robinson gave it to him, and the light remained on. "It's the frequency of the sound that activates the magic. It shouldn't matter which of us holds it."

"Yes, I know. Here, let's try this again. Back up a few steps, and I'll approach it alone."

Robinson shrugged and complied, and the two friends retreated until the light dimmed and then extinguished. Wickins gripped the tube and then walked forward alone. The tube did not react at all.

"See here, that's what I meant," Wickins said when he reached the boulder. He wagged it at Robinson. "Not a thing."

Robinson started toward him, and the tube immediately sparked to life, surprising them both with the sudden luminescence.

He halted, then retreated back a few steps. The light winked out.

What was going on? Robinson had attuned the apertures in the lamp to react to the subliminal chords of Aesir magic thrumming from the stone. It should work according to the proximity of the tube to the boulder, not because of who held it.

"How strange," Wickins said after approaching him and holding out the tube.

Robinson took it and examined it again. "What degree sorcerer are you again?"

Wickins replied, "Sixth."

There was not much difference between the ninth and the sixth. Could that be the reason? Or was there something about Wickins that repelled the magic?

The light tube operated because of an agreement between the intelligence and the object. Once the bargain was struck, the law of justice demanded compliance. Unless another law superseded it. It should work the same way regardless of who wielded it. It *should.*

Robinson stepped forward again, and the tube began to glow. He retreated and it stopped.

"Sorry, Dickemore. It seems it only works for you. You can't be everywhere at once."

The disparity was unbelievable. He continued to walk closer, observing the light increasing in intensity. What was he missing? What principle had he neglected to consider? Feelings of frustration began to roil inside him. They were followed promptly by their cousin, despair. He would never figure it out. He was nothing but an insignificant elocutionist from a backwater province of the—

Robinson cut off the thought immediately. Such insidious thoughts repelled progress. Over the centuries, sorcerers had to learn how to fortify the walls of their thinking against such intruding thoughts. For the effect to work, a mind needed something to focus on, so Robinson focused his on McKenna's smile, the gleam in her eyes, the sound of her laugh. Immediately his emotions began to alter, shifting from despair to delight. He wondered what her aunt's house looked like. Was it very grand? Her presence there would make it all the grander. She was like the tube clenched in his hand, brightening everything because of her presence. If only she would let him woo her, when the time was right. He'd decided already that communicating his intentions to her mother, Mrs. Foster, would be for the best. Who better to open his heart to than a loving, devoted mother who would want nothing but the best for her daughter? If Mrs. Foster believed there was no chance for him to win her daughter's heart, he would remain an admirer from afar.

He wished he were holding her hand and not the cool bulb.

And that's when the spark of insight struck him.

It's the device.

Robinson halted, standing right at the brink of the floating boulder. His heart began to pound with excitement. He recognized that whisper of thought. Had the dog's intelligence spoken to him unbesought before? He couldn't remember it doing so. But he could sense its presence, the energy it exuded as if wagging a tail expectantly, hoping he would understand.

"Come here," he bid Wickins.

The lieutenant sauntered up with an inquisitive look. Robinson gave him the glass tube, then he dipped his hand into his pocket and took out the Aesir device he always carried—the one that resembled a watch. He tucked it into Wickins's pocket and then walked briskly away.

Wickins stood there, tube glowing in his hand. The light was undiminished.

"I'm flummoxed again," Wickins said. "It's working for me now."

"Walk away from it and then go back," Robinson instructed. Wickins obeyed, and the light dimmed and then guttered out. As soon as he approached it again, the light blinked awake and shone. They tried it several different times and different ways. Whoever had the device in their possession could make the lamp work.

Something about the device was aiding the magic. Robinson didn't understand what, specifically, but he felt certain he could in time discover the principle that aided in the transfiguration of quicksilver gas into light in the presence of a perfect Mixolydian chord that mortal ears could not actually register. He was giddy at the thought of it.

Wickins could not persuade Robinson to take the tram to the Fosters' house on Brake Street since the experiment was over, and so the two of them chuffed quickly until they reached the sloping street leading up to the house. The sun was already down by then, but the streetlamps illuminated the way. Mrs. Foster greeted them at the door and welcomed both of them inside, where the delicious smells of clam chowder and rolls lingered in the air.

Robinson's appetite was voracious. He hadn't eaten a proper meal in two days, not since his last shift defending the university. He was so enjoying a buttery roll that he had to ask Mrs. Foster to repeat her question.

"I said, isn't it such a shame about Mrs. Fiske?"

Robinson blinked in surprise. He hadn't seen Mrs. Fiske in several days but had attributed it to her heavy responsibilities at the Invisible College and the school.

"Is something wrong?" he asked after he'd swallowed the bite and could properly speak.

Mr. Foster looked stern and serious. "The inspiratory stridor is at the school. There have been four deaths there already. Mrs. Fiske has been struck down with it."

Robinson was shocked by the news.

"Grim tidings," Wickins whispered under his breath. He gave Clara a sympathetic look.

Robinson had been so wrapped up in his work, he'd heard no such tidings. "W-When?" he stammered.

"One of the servants came in with a cough. Infected so many. Mrs. Fiske insisted everyone remain inside so as not to infect others. She sent word to the city council for assistance, but none of the doctors are willing to go minister there."

That shocked Robinson even more. "None?"

Mr. Foster shook his head. "The hospitals throughout the city are already overwhelmed. There is nothing they can do."

"Surely there is something," Robinson insisted. He was horrified at the thought of all the suffering children, frightened and fainting and slowly dying of asphyxiation.

"No medicine yet can cure it," Mrs. Foster said. "The young perish faster because of it." Her throat caught with emotion. "I hear Mrs. Fiske is on her deathbed."

"What about Miss Hurst?" Robinson exclaimed.

"She is ill also. The fever and ague is terrible. But what can be done?"

"Ashes to ashes," murmured Wickins. "Dust to dust."

In their world, death was routine. An inescapable part of the mortal condition that impacted philosophers, emperors, or orphans. Its primeval regularity was a burden every soul had to reckon with. The universal wheel of justice ground relentlessly.

"Justice claimeth its own," Clara added as she tenderly patted Wickins's hand. They usually sat near one another. Hearkening back to Wickins's earlier comment, he did spy some marks of affection that could be interpreted as mutual.

Robinson pushed away from the table. His brothers had died from an illness brought by the Aesir, and now a new disease spread by their kind was claiming other people he esteemed. The indignation he felt was combustible. *He* wasn't prepared to write it off as inevitable.

"Where are you going, Professor Hawksley?" Mrs. Foster asked, looking at him in alarm.

He stared at her in confusion. There was only one thing to do.

"I'm going to comfort those sick children," he said thickly. And as they stared at him in stunned silence, he strode from the dining hall, rushed out the door, and slammed it shut behind him.

CHAPTER TWENTY-TWO

Suffering

The school for the deaf had no lights on inside. The quicksilver lamps from the street cast skeletal shadows on the walls from the winter-dead trees. As Robinson walked up the front path, he saw a smear of paint across the door, a warning sigil in red. *Danger.* The doglike intelligence had followed him here as well. He could sense an alteration in its playful mood. The somberness of the occasion, of his mood, was affecting it. The unseen suffering within those walls.

Brushing aside his fears, he strode to the front door, gripped the handle, and turned it. As soon as he opened the door, the stench struck him in a powerful wave. The odor of human filth was strong, but equally so the reek of death.

"Hoxta-namorem," Robinson said, invoking the gossamer strands of light. As he walked down the main hall, he listened for sounds other than those his shoes made on the wooden floor. Coughing could be heard upstairs. He stopped by the classrooms first and found them all empty. Then he went to Mrs. Fiske's office and found it despoiled. The

desk had been ransacked, papers strewn everywhere. The safe had been pried open, its contents stolen. He clenched his teeth with disgust at whoever had taken advantage of the situation.

Before he went upstairs, he walked to the kitchen and found a dozen children inside, huddled together in the dark. He blinked with surprise at their dirty faces, their baffled and fearful expressions.

"Professor Hawksley?"

A girl no older than twelve rose from comforting the others and came to him, her eyes widening with hope. Her name was Averi. She'd been one of the first to master the Hawksley method, which she added to the finger signs she'd already mastered.

With the strand of light illuminating the room, he saw their sorry state, but the children looked hale.

"Yes," he said, moving farther into the kitchen. It smelled of tomato soup, the kind packaged in cans. "Where is Mrs. Fiske?"

"She's upstairs with the sick children," Averi said. "She told us to stay down here, away from them. I haven't seen her in two days. Is she . . . is she dead?"

"I don't know," Robinson answered honestly. One of the littlest rushed up and gave him a hug. Then they were all crowding around him, some making signs with their hands, showering him with questions. He only understood some of them, however. He was an elocutionist and had only recently started picking up sign language by observation.

"Did you bring any food, Professuh?" asked another child, a little boy.

"When did they last eat?" he asked Averi.

"We had the last can of soup this morning. Cold. We can't start the heaters either. No magic. Some food was delivered yesterday, paid for by Mr. Foster, and left by the front door. It was stolen before I could bring it in. The original message was found discarded near the gutter rail."

That was vexing news. Who would dare? Robinson hugged and caressed the children and then went to the oven and activated it with the proper spell. It began to glow, and the children gathered around it, warming their hands and smiling hopefully.

"I came as soon as I found out," he told Averi, taking her aside. "I'm going upstairs to check on the sick ones. Once I go there, I cannot come back to you. But I'll send for help. For food and blankets."

"We have blankets," Averi said, pointing to the various piles. "And the oven will keep us warm."

"I'll make sure to put a stop to the stealing," Robinson said. He felt terrible they'd been sitting in this darkened place, hampered from communicating. He asked the light to linger in the kitchen and stay until morning. He did the same for the oven and felt a throb of willingness from the intelligences empowering them.

"Is there anything else that I can help you with? Anything that will help make the confinement easier for you?"

"The cold box. It hasn't worked in a while. If you can fix that?"

Cold boxes were enchanted by the intelligences of creatures preferring very cold climates. They were complex, but he knew how they worked. "I will. You've been very brave, Averi. I'm so proud of you. Stay here. I'll have food brought to you."

"Thank you, Professor Hawksley. Thank you!"

He smiled at her and then left, summoning another will-o'-the-wisp to guide him. Before going, he sent a thought to the dog's intelligence to warn him if intruders came. Then he went to Mrs. Fiske's office again and used her writing materials to craft a note stating the need for food for the uninfected children in the kitchen on the first floor. Taking the note with him, he made his way to the front door, where he set a ward that would shriek if more intruders came. That would alert him of their coming, and he'd be able to instigate the kind of magic that would make them less courageous to return.

He tacked the note to the door and then summoned an emergency flare, one that another sorcerer would recognize as a cry for help. The magical response was quite strong, much like it had been after his things were stolen upon his arrival in Auvinen. A dozen intelligences had responded rather than a single one. The violet, flickering flare would continue to rain sparks down over the house until a sorcerer responded to it. Someone would come, read the note on the door, and hopefully provide food for the children.

That done, he went upstairs. The smell of death was strong. The sound of coughing suggested there were survivors, but it took every bit of courage in his heart to enter the living quarters above. He found Mrs. Fiske languishing on a bed, struck down by fever. Miss Hurst was there too, coughing, unable to move. There were two dead children lying still, sharing a bed. Another girl, maybe three years old, sat up in bed, coughing and wheezing, and had bloody flecks on her nightdress. Three more children, two girls and a boy, were lying in beds near her, gasping for breath. The pitiable scene wrenched his heart. There was blood, vomit, and filth everywhere. Attempts to contain the illness could be observed in rags and a bucket, but it was obvious the situation had moved beyond control.

The light he'd brought with him made Mrs. Fiske shield her eyes. She didn't seem to recognize him, just pushed her hand at him, as if warning him to stay away.

He came to her bed and knelt by it.

Her eyes bulged as she recognized him at last. She shook her head. He gripped her hand, so weak and limp it was powerless.

"I'm going to help you," he said firmly. "I've summoned a flare so someone will bring food for the children downstairs. Averi has been taking care of them in the dark." With his other hand, he pressed his palm against the headmistress's forehead. It was burning with fever. She tried to speak but couldn't. Her throat was swollen, as were her cheeks. The illness had devastated her ability to use magic.

It was obvious she wished him to go away, to save himself, but there was nothing she could do to stop him. He went to the two dead children and washed their bodies with a zinc solution—the water and zinc were already on the tabletop. Their bloody clothes he gathered into a pile to be burned. Then he began to clean the room, bit by bit, removing the source of the oppressive odors. He worked hard, scrubbing, wringing, washing, trying to banish the stench of death. He comforted the sick children until help arrived in the form of a couple of officers from the Marshalcy, who shouted from the front door when they arrived. Rushing from the sickroom, Robinson called to the officers downstairs, telling them the contagion had not reached the kitchen, and the children there needed food. By then, he knew those who were upstairs were too sick to eat, their throats nearly too inflamed to drink.

He went back to his care, bathing Mrs. Fiske's face with a cool, wet towel before doing the same for Miss Hurst. He needed to burn their clothes as well and asked for their permission to assist in undressing them so he could do it. They understood the importance of removing infectious sheets and clothing, and he helped undress them to their underclothes and then heaped the blood-flecked articles into the same pile, which he then carried downstairs to the back alley and burned on the street with a summoning of magic. Stars glittered overhead, and he gazed up at them, feeling a deep and growing hatred of the Aesir, festering within him. Such misery they'd unleashed. Such wretchedness. He watched the clothing burn for a while, feeling the cool breeze on his cheeks and hands. Then he went back inside and continued to help.

It was the longest night of Robinson's life.

Another child died before midnight, strangled by the lack of air. It was a blessed relief when it came because it ended the girl's suffering. Robinson wept as he went from person to person, trying to offer relief as best he could. When silence came from Miss Hurst's bed, he thought she had expired too, but she'd only fallen asleep, the unsteady rise and fall of her bosom the only sign of life. When he bathed Mrs. Fiske's face with a damp rag again, she tried to speak, failed, and then took his hand and kissed it, her eyes shining with gratitude and despair. Then another series of racking coughs started from the boy, and Robinson hastened to him, rubbing his back, trying to soothe the fit. The boy died an hour later. Another body stripped, washed with zinc, and laid to rest by the others.

The battle raged on after morning came. More food had been delivered. The final few in the sickroom were in the throes of the illness. Robinson was exhausted, but he'd cleaned every stain, stripped off every soiled piece of clothing and sheet and burned them. Miss Hurst's cheeks were so pale she looked like a corpse, but still she breathed on, though each was a struggle. Mrs. Fiske was delirious by now, and nothing soothed her.

One of the sick girls, hardly older than a toddler, began the death throes next. She sobbed and coughed, and Robinson lifted her up and held her, walking gently, patting her back. The girl coughed bloody spume in Robinson's face, but he could not put her away from him. He could not let her last mortal moments be comfortless. He felt a trickle down his cheek and wondered whether it was blood or his own tears.

In a fit of final agony, the little girl died in his arms. And soon her body joined the others. He wiped his face on a rag, saw the stains of disease, and added it to the burn pile. A wagon came to collect the bodies of the dead, going down the street. Robinson hailed it and carried each child to the awful pallet in the back. Then he went back to perform his lonely vigil over the three remaining in the sickroom.

He knew he would likely get sick. His constitution was already weakened from his earlier illness, and now he'd been exposed to the worst of it. His clothes would have to be burned as well. Only he didn't have another set to wear, other than a second shirt. At his lodging he had no food. Not even a can of old tomato soup.

But he wouldn't have—he couldn't have—made any other decision but to help. Even though nothing he'd done had spared any of their lives, he just could not bear the thought of anyone dying comfortless. He stared at the floor, trying to master the raging storm of emotions inside him. Poverty and death stared back at him. Growing up in Covesea, he'd had enough to eat. His father had trained him in a profession that would have supplied a steady income if Robinson had not been so blasted curious about everything. Or was his curiosity just a means of trying to escape the monotony and boredom of doing the same thing day after day?

He felt a little tickle in the back of his throat. He had breathed the same air as the sick for hours. He'd mopped up their bodily fluids with his bare hands and soiled rags. His own mortality became vividly real to him in that moment. He'd watched his own brothers buried in their youths. Who was he, Robinson Dickemore Hawksley, to escape death?

But he had escaped it. More than once. Each time, he'd managed to wriggle out of its grasp. Perhaps it was his time; perhaps not. No one was guaranteed another day of life.

As he sat there, watching the three sleep while the midmorning sun shone through the window, he saw a robin land on the windowsill. The red-breasted fellow cocked his head curiously at him, as if asking why he was lazing about and not flying. But a robin? In winter?

Then he realized it was the first token of spring. The birds knew the changes of the weather better than anyone. The coming of spring meant the Aesir attacks would stop. There would be a season of tranquility and peace.

Sitting there, his heart and mind churning, he made several decisions about what he would do if he survived.

First, he would go to the dean of speech and rhetoric, Lennox Warchester George, and ask for an advance on next semester's lectures. He could not ask for charity, that would be too humiliating, but he felt confident that something could be arranged for at least a partial payment in advance.

Next, he needed clothes. He would write to his parents at the little cottage they'd rented on the outskirts of town and see if there was something he could be loaned for a while, even if it didn't fit. Robinson's father was a stouter man than his surviving son. So be it. Clothing. Shelter. Food. He needed all three.

Lastly, he decided he would write a letter. It was the most dangerous thing in the world. But facing death up close made one fearless. He would write a letter to Mrs. Foster announcing his intention to court

Miss McKenna. He would ask her permission to travel to Siaconset and declare his intentions once the military allowed sorcerers to travel outside Auvinen again. He didn't care one bit if she was never able to enter Society. He loved her, and she should know it. Even if it meant banishment from the family dinners at Closure. Even if it meant earning Mr. Foster's ire and losing his sponsorship. Dissemblance was abhorrent to him in any fashion. He would be honest no matter the personal cost.

He had to let McKenna know how he felt.

Instinctively, he knew that if his body was going to fight off infection, he needed something to live for.

He would write the letter, and if he died, at least they'd discover it and she would know the truth.

Dear Mrs. Foster:

I must humbly beg your pardon for the great liberty I take in soliciting your advice at this time, but I am in deep trouble and need to unburden myself, lest this sickness worsens.

My interest in your family is strong indeed, and it grows stronger still. I have discovered that my attentions toward a dear student—McKenna—have ripened into a far deeper feeling than that of mere friendship. My recent illness has taught me that I have learned to love her very sincerely. In fact, I have for some time.

It is my intention and desire to let her know now how dear she is to me, and I should wish with all my heart to ascertain from her own lips what her feeling toward me may be, if anything at all. I confess I cannot tell what favor or inclination she may have or how this communication may be received. In her eyes, I may be abhorrent. But this I do know—that if devotion on my part can make her life any happier, I am willing to give her my whole heart.

I would make this request in person, yet this illness is still contagious, and so I deem it imprudent to risk your health with a personal visit. By addressing this letter to you, I mean no disrespect toward your estimable husband. I should, with both of your approval, desire to visit Siaconset in person to relate my intentions and feelings to McKenna directly. I understand she is lodging with your sister at present with no return date on the horizon.

I am willing to be guided entirely by your advice. I promise aforehand to abide by your decision however difficult it may be for me to do so.

Believe me, dear Mrs. Foster, I am in earnest.

Yours very respectfully,

Robinson Dickemore Hawksley

The Invisible College is divided into ranks for several purposes. One is to create ambition. Another to subdivide power. Another still, to prevent infiltration. The requirements to gain access to the lower ranks are not complicated or prescriptive, but there are fewer and fewer positions within the higher echelons. Many of the upper ranks are given the term "knight," even though males and females have equal chance to attain it. That is due to the ancient heritage of the order, dating back to darker ages now shrouded in legend. The twenty-first degree, for example, is known as the Knight of the Royal Axe. In olden times, this was the king's executioner, the person entrusted to wield a weapon not on a battlefield but in the killing yard. If a sorcerer betrayed the oaths of the order, or betrayed a brother or sister of the same, they would meet an ignominious death at the hands of the sorcerer holding this rank. Those in the lower ranks do not even know of this system. But the Master of the Royal Secret knows all. There is only one rank higher than that, and only one person who bears it.

—Isaac Berrow,
Master of the Royal Secret,
the Invisible College

Joseph Crossthwait

CHAPTER TWENTY-THREE

The Brotherhood of Shadows

Joseph raised the pistol with his off hand, squinted one eye, aimed, and pulled the trigger. An explosion of saltpetr, a jet of flame, and a wisp of smoke resulted. But all sounds were inaudible to him. He heard only a tinny sound in his ears, a remnant of Hawksley's defensive spell. The distinct smell of the burning fumes stung his nostrils as he lowered the weapon, a steady stream of sand falling from the crack in the barrel. He tilted his head one way, then the next, and stuffed the weapon into his belt near its twin.

Joseph removed the tabs of molded wax from his ears as the shooting range officer walked over and inspected the ruptured target. He turned with an approving nod and an impressed smile.

"You've quite an aim, sir. Even with your off hand."

"Practice," Joseph said with a shrug. That tinny sound persisted. Day and night, that noise would not leave. It was possible, the camp doctor had stated matter-of-factly, that Joseph's hearing had been permanently ruined by Hawksley's spell. After he'd awakened on the dark street, ears bleeding, watching as thousands of red motes fell from the skies, he'd overcome the bewilderment of his circumstances and managed to make it to his feet, then a tram, and received medical help. The spell had ruptured his eardrums, which had required extensive recuperation. Thankfully, mortal bodies were adept at self-healing. A broken arm could be set and it would mend all on its own. It was a fascinating fact about life-forms in possession of an intelligence. A tree could regrow a lost limb, but a broken chair—no longer living—could not fix itself unless it too was imbued with an intelligence. Still, all healing took time.

And Joseph was impatient for that time to be over.

There were only a small handful of men, such as Joseph, who were trained in the hunting and dispatching of Semblances during peacetime. The need was exponentially greater now, but training could take years, and the new recruits were just getting started. And so, Robinson Dickemore Hawksley had been free to wander and wreak havoc.

"Did I pass?" he asked the range master, lifting an eyebrow.

"I should think so, sir. Nothing wrong with your aim."

"Thank you, Corporal." Joseph adjusted a bracer strap, then marched out of the shooting range hall and made his way up the steps to a higher level. The whole time, he heard the maddening chime in his ears, but it faded from notice as the ambient sounds of Gresham College grew louder. Soldiers in uniform were everywhere, rushing to and fro. Female sorcerers were also in the war rooms, directing Bishopsgate's defenses. He could hear the shrill strings of the violins and instruments playing above, casting a shield of protection over the college and spreading that protection until it overlapped with other orchestras. He nearly collided with a young officer dashing down the corridor with a report in hand.

Joseph continued to maneuver his way through the compound until he reached General Colsterworth's office, which was crowded with underlings. Joseph's Aesir cloak kept him invisible as he sidestepped through the maze of people and took up a place by the window where he could gaze out at the city. Booms in the distance meant the cannons were still firing. He lowered the cowl, rendering himself visible.

"Crossthwait! What are you doing here? Shouldn't you be in a sickbed?"

Joseph turned and saw the general gazing at him with a wry smile, standing by the desk.

"I've been discharged. The doctor felt I had recuperated sufficiently. Sir."

"Good to see you on your feet again. That's the spirit! Are you healed enough to go to the front? We're taking heavy casualties at every breach. Two branches are overrun."

"I would like to finish the other matter first, sir."

"Oh. Ready to return to Auvinen, I see?"

"Yes, sir." Joseph was eager to finish his mission. To get revenge on the Semblance who'd thwarted him.

"Everyone out!" the general shouted. "I need a moment with my adjutant."

The office cleared and moments later the two were alone. Joseph approached the desk and looked at the map. Leaden figurines of Aesir stormbreakers were set on Bishopsgate, Andover, and Iskandir. Soldiers were massed at Krier, represented by little jack-like pieces.

"The weather has shifted," General Colsterworth said, picking up a piece of paper from his desk. "Temperatures are warming day by day. It will be spring soon. A reprieve."

Joseph gazed across the piles of missives and orders. "Any news from the imperial city?"

"Tanireh? Bah! They're too busy holding concerts and throwing balls. The emperor has no interest in the war at all. Foppish, vainglorious wretch that he is. May he live forever!" the general added in an undertone with a gleam in his eye. Ceremonial power helped keep the power-hungry preoccupied. The real war effort was being run out of Bishopsgate. Run by the Invisible College.

"Balls serve their purposes," Joseph said in an offhanded way. "Have your men found where Hawksley has moved to?"

"No. The attack here has drawn all our resources. I don't have a man to spare at the moment. What I do know is that his landlady was stricken down by the inspiratory stridor. She survived, thank the Mind, but she's mute presently and has had to forsake her leadership of the Storrows. Our only lead is Colonel Wickins's son, Hawksley's roommate. He's at the barracks in Auvinen. Pay him a visit when you arrive."

"Yes, sir," Joseph answered.

"Try not to kill him," the general said dispassionately. "His father is, after all, a lieutenant colonel. But I trust your judgment, Crossthwait. If Hawksley is a Semblance, I'm certain he's already done irreparable harm. This newest plague, this stridor, has a high mortality rate. Truly, the suffering it has caused cannot be measured."

"I watched him summon it," Joseph said, feeling the anger throb inside him. "He'd been playing music on the rooftops for days previously. The stormbreaker came to him, drawn like a moth to a flame. The disease started in that very quarter that very night."

"Then he must die," the general said. "See to it, Crossthwait. Do not miss this time."

Joseph felt the tiny sting of the rebuke, nodded, and exited the general's quarters. It was no good giving excuses, but he hadn't missed his shot. Hawksley had thrown up a shield just before the trigger was pulled. And he'd retaliated with a magical attack that had shattered Joseph's eardrums. The tone of the ringing in his ears shifted, as it sometimes did, to a lower pitch. Sometimes he could ignore it, but the omnipresent noise was infuriating.

How had Hawksley realized he was being pursued? The cloak should have prevented any such intention from being perceived. Perhaps it was one of the unknown powers a Semblance possessed? A self-protection instinct? Since the Awakening, several more Semblances had been discovered and killed by the Brotherhood of Shadows. Most of them had infiltrated the ranks through mortally injured men at the front. One had slipped through the mountain passes near Yverdon and made it across the lake before being killed at Tanhauser, having changed bodies four times along the journey.

Only the Master of the Royal Secret was aware of their order, their rank. Only someone who had knowingly killed a Semblance could be included in it.

Joseph's first kill had happened years before. A woman. That had made it harder to stomach. He'd always remember her, but her "life" had only been the first he had taken. Certainly not the last.

⁂

The locomotivus schedules were so impacted by the refugee crisis that Joseph thought it wiser to take a horse to Rexanne from Bishopsgate, followed by a ferry from Rexanne to Auvinen. The ferry passed the small island of Siaconset along the way. The island had no snow at all, its climate being more temperate than the rest of the empire. It was a popular destination for the officer class during the seasonal truces with the Aesir, and many of the large estate owners were military.

Joseph was grateful the Awakening had happened while he was in his prime, though. He had trained for this his whole career. The most dangerous enemy wasn't an easily recognizable Aesir, with their frost-colored skin and silver hair, the smudges of purple or violet under their eyes. No, far more dangerous were the Semblances who didn't even know what they really were. It was one of the most closely kept secrets of the Invisible College—one that ordinary sorcerers knew nothing about because it would sow mistrust and suspicion throughout civilization. Neighbor would distrust neighbor until an entire community was riven with hostility.

That's why the Brotherhood of Shadows existed. It took a certain kind of officer to aim a pistol at what appeared to be a fellow mortal and pull the trigger. It was only upon their death that the Semblance's true nature revealed itself, as it had with Lieutenant Snell at the beginning of the Awakening. A puff of frosty breath came from the mouth of the Semblance when it truly died, severing the connection between body and host.

It was one aspect of magic the Aesir of old had not taught mortals. What they'd learned about Semblances had come through centuries of observation and the careful dissemination of secrets. No Aesir would willingly divulge the truth, and if a Semblance was caught, the hosted intelligence might flee the body for another recent corpse. That was why sudden violence was the best way to handle them.

The ferry arrived at the harbor at Auvinen, and Joseph quickly disembarked and headed into town. With his cloak and other implements, he didn't need to pay the tram fare. He reached the barracks quickly, anxious to get to work and seek out Hawksley.

After inquiring about Lieutenant Wickins, he was directed to Signals. The earaches had subsided considerably, but just being back in Auvinen triggered defensive feelings. The stormbreaker over Auvinen had moved to Bishopsgate, so the city was no longer in a high alert state. Many of the officers had been transferred to defend the regional capital. But not Wickins. He was on duty, and Joseph told his commanding officer to summon him to his office for a private interview. The officer looked nervous, but he stammered an affirmative response and left the office to get Wickins.

Joseph examined the office, looking for any signs of something out of order. He remembered searching through Hawksley's residence, his private alchemy, his school of elocution with its mystical symbols that were so strange and foreign and reeked of Semblance magic. It was not uncommon for a host to begin manifesting increased acumen in skills and awareness they'd lacked before. A miraculous invention, for example, within the Industry of Magic.

"Inside, Lieutenant." The captain lingered at the door, watching as Wickins glanced hesitantly inside. He resembled his father, the officer Joseph had met near the front. Hopefully he'd be more helpful than him. The captain shut the door, leaving the two in the room together.

Lieutenant Wickins had an inquisitive, almost innocent expression. He was in his early twenties, a young officer. A linguistics man, one who had been studying the ancient tongue of the Aesir. A rather useless skill, for an Aesir would prefer killing a mortal over talking to one.

"Sir," Wickins said, standing at attention, hands clasped behind his back.

"Do you know why I am here, Lieutenant?" Joseph asked, coming around the desk. What would be the best way to persuade this young man to help? Words or violence?

"I assume you've come in answer to my request," Wickins answered promptly.

Joseph guarded his expression. He said nothing, which usually was all the lubrication required to get a man to start talking too much.

"You have an Aesir cloak, sir. I sent my father a request for one for an experiment. I wasn't expecting a response so quickly."

This was all new information. Troubling information. But a helpful coincidence, nonetheless. Joseph cocked his head slightly. "Indeed. I have come to validate the need for the request from such a junior officer in the ranks during a time of war. Help me understand why you need such a powerful article of magic."

"I don't need it," Wickins said. "There's a sorcerer here in Auvinen. A professor from Covesea."

"Professor Hawksley?" Joseph asked, feeling the glow of fortune operating in his favor. "I've heard of him."

Fame—I care naught for it. What I care about is truth. I would hunt it down to the ends of the earth and spend a lifetime digging to uncover but one more shell of it from beneath a mountain of sand. I do not know how I may appear to the world. To myself, I seem to be like a boy playing on the seashore, diverting myself now and then in finding a smoother pebble or a prettier mollusk than ordinary, whilst the great ocean of truth lay all undiscovered before me.

—Isaac Berrow,
Master of the Royal Secret,
the Invisible College

MaKenna Aurora Foster

CHAPTER TWENTY-FOUR

Tangles to Be Untied

McKenna sat at the window seat, legs tucked beneath her, devouring her book with feelings of suspense, dread, and entangled complexity. It was a story she hadn't read before, entitled *Miss Brooke*, about an illegitimate orphan raised by her aunt who fell in love with a forty-five-year-old university professor. And the heroine, Miss Brooke, was just nineteen.

McKenna was so engrossed in her reading she didn't notice Trudie had entered the room until she felt her sister's hand jostling her shoulder, which finally broke the spell the novel had on her mind.

"What is it, Trudie?" McKenna asked, vexed at being disturbed. One of the things she loved best about visiting Siaconset was the new assortment of books in her aunt's library. And every reader detested being interrupted.

"A letter from Mama just came. Didn't you see the post arrive? You're at the window!"

"I was reading," McKenna said.

"But there's news from home!"

That was enough motivation to lay the book down on the cushion. She walked with her sister to the sitting room, where she found Aunt Margaret pacing, the letter in her hands. The look on her face implied the news was dreadful. McKenna's stomach began to shrivel with worry.

Trudie must have asked a question. McKenna's attention was fixed on her aunt's face, so she hadn't heard it, but she did understand her aunt's answer well enough.

"Your parents are well. So is Clara. None of them have caught that foul disease, thank the Mind." She lowered the paper and looked at McKenna with sorrow. "Your tutor, Miss Hurst, died of it, though. This was written the day of the funeral, two days ago. I'm so sorry, my dear. This is unexpected."

McKenna's heart jolted with pain. "Miss Hurst? Is . . . dead?"

"Yes. And Mrs. Fiske is still quite unwell. She's lost her voice."

"That's dreadful," McKenna said, feeling tears sting her eyes. "And the children at the school?"

"Many died, unfortunately. But most were spared because they isolated in the kitchen and didn't go near the infected people upstairs. But that fool Mr. Hawksley did. And now he's sick himself."

The surprise was almost too much. "H-He is sick?"

Her aunt's sorrow shifted to something like contempt. "Of course he's sick! Your mother said he went rushing to the school to help them when no one else would. And he caught the inspiratory stridor and may well die of it as well. Stubborn, reckless fool! He's a sorcerer! He's needed in Society. I can understand Mrs. Fiske not abandoning the children, but to put himself in such danger—"

"Was very brave," McKenna burst out, brushing hot tears from her eyes.

"There's no doubting his courage, McKenna. It's his common sense I worry about. Do you know how much your father has invested in his schemes? All would be lost if he died. Or became mute and couldn't help anyone. If he became a *drain* on Society."

McKenna stared at her aunt in disbelief. She knew about the investment, but surely Father's compassion for the deaf children would outweigh mere self-interest. He had helped found the school himself out of his own resources. She was proud of Professor Hawksley for what he'd done. It felt absolutely wrong to belittle his act.

"Do you think I am a drain on Society?" she asked her aunt with a hot spur of indignation burning in her chest.

Aunt Margaret frowned and lowered the letter. "Of course you are not, McKenna."

"If I had been in Auvinen, I should have gone to help them too!" McKenna said, bursting into tears. She stamped her foot, turned away, and covered her eyes. *Miss Hurst, dead. Ashes to ashes. Dust to dust. Justice claimeth its own.* She wished she had been there for the funeral, to toss a handful of ash in the grave. The woman had always been so kind and patient with her. Her heart ached that she hadn't been able to bid her tutor goodbye or to thank her for all she'd done. And now her favorite teacher was sick too? What if she couldn't see him again? What if he died?

She felt hands on her shoulders, trying to get her attention, but she kept her hands over her eyes and shook her head, crying softly. She didn't want to be comforted. She didn't want to be told her feelings were wrong. If she couldn't see their mouths, she wouldn't know what they were saying.

She wrenched herself away from her aunt or her sister and fled back to the window seat, where she could cry in peace. It was a beautiful day outside and that only added to her wretchedness. Her heart felt like it was splitting apart. Death was a common thing in their world, yet it felt anything but when it struck a dear one. She didn't want to find out, through a letter, that Robinson Hawksley was gone. How awful that would be! She brushed her eyes again, sniffling, then wiped her nose on the edge of her sleeve.

No one came. She suspected they'd leave her alone for a while, and her tears began to subside. She gazed out the window at the tranquil street outside. Miss Hurst was dead and there was nothing to be done about it. She hoped Mrs. Fiske would recover. But she needed her teacher too. Maybe she should write him a letter and have it sent by post? From what she'd heard about the inspiratory stridor, though, it only took a few days for it to kill its victims. He might be dead before a letter could get there.

Looking at herself in the reflection on the glass, she saw her swollen eyes, her downcast frown. These mirrored her brooding thoughts. Robinson himself had told her that negative thoughts attracted negative outcomes. Maybe she should write a letter regardless. Even if it was too late. She admired and respected her teacher. Maybe that liking could turn into something more serious. She didn't know. She only knew that her feelings were in tumult—more so than one would expect from hearing that a respected teacher was ill. This felt personal and crushing.

She noticed her aunt's reflection in the glass and suppressed the desire to ignore her.

Aunt Margaret picked up the novel and examined the title on the front. Then she sat across from McKenna on the window seat and rested the book on her lap.

"So this is what you've been reading the last few days?"

McKenna's eyes were itchy, but she didn't rub them. "She's a good author."

"She is indeed. You've always been partial to a good turn of phrase. Why, you've been reading books like this since you were ten years old. Now that you are grown, you're beginning to see life as it really is. Things are not as simple as they were before. The Awakening has come again. You are witnessing war. It has touched you now personally."

"Why do the Aesir hate us so much?" McKenna asked, shaking her head. She already knew there was no answer. Not a satisfactory one anyway.

"I don't know," Auntie said. "Maybe the Master of the Royal Secret does."

McKenna understood the reference. It was the second-highest rank in the Invisible College, held only by one person. The current bearer of that title had held it for several decades at least and lived at the imperial court. Drusselman? Drusselholt? Something like that. Father mentioned him occasionally. He was a bureaucrat, one who required patents to be made for each magical invention so that the patent holders could be paid. He led the Industry of Magic and was the single voice the emperor listened to.

"Would he tell us if he knew?" McKenna asked.

Aunt Margaret leaned back against the window, gazing outside. "Do you like the novel, McKenna?"

"Very much."

"I worry about the influence he has on you. You are still very young and impressionable. And he is overly scrupulous."

"Doesn't that word mean *diligent, trustworthy, and reliable*?"

"Of course, McKenna. But like all words, there are still more meanings. He is upstanding. He is honorable. But I've known scrupulous men before, those who put duty above all else, even their relations. I'm not fond of such black-and-white thinking. I've learned, over many years of experience, to be wary of those who bear this trait. They can be . . . obsessive. Is that a flattering word in your opinion?"

McKenna shook her head.

"Nor do I consider it one." She handed the book over. "But let's talk about your situation now that you're calmer. I know you'll do the right thing, McKenna. I trust you to." Then she slipped her hand into her pocket and produced a letter.

"Is this the one Mother sent?"

Aunt Margaret lifted an eyebrow. "Read it and you will see for yourself."

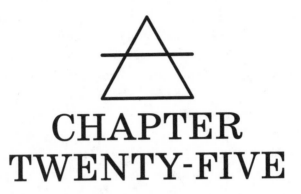

CHAPTER TWENTY-FIVE

A Wicked Tide

Cheeks burning. Eyes stinging. Stomach twisting. McKenna walked along the seashore, the letter dangling from her hand, the stiff breeze blowing her long hair everywhere. She'd read it three times in the study, until anxiety had made her flee Aunt Margaret's beautiful home to allow her some privacy, some chance to reclaim her scattered emotions.

Mother had written her sister to ask for advice in dealing with a potential suitor for McKenna. The person was not named, but it could only be one person: Robinson Dickemore Hawksley. What a tumult those vague words had caused. And even that word—"tumult"—did not do her feelings justice.

Aunt Margaret had insisted that McKenna should firmly reject any overtures or advances from her tutor. It was time to focus on entering Society. Her mind and heart clashed, like the waves pounding the colorless sand at her feet. She looked back and saw her footprints, though many had already been washed away by the surf. Part of her still felt like she was again that ignorant child whose parents had shielded her from the complexities and misfortunes of her world. And now she was supposed to make a decision, one that would impact the rest of her life.

All along, she'd secretly hoped that she would find someone willing to overlook her infirmity. She'd worked hard to improve her defective speech, to win her tutor's approbation. She'd even dared hope that the professor could teach her magic eventually. And then the accursed Aesir ship had broken through a storm and begun attacking her city. So many soldiers had perished in mortal combat along the front lines, their ashes sent back for their families to honor. If these things had not happened, perhaps there would have been time for them to get to know each other better, to be more sure of each other. But now he was sick!

She admired Robinson. She respected him. But those feelings alone did not form her definition of love. She believed the professor was older, much older, than her. But that wasn't truly an impediment. In Society, where so many fell sick and died from the brutal illnesses unleashed by the Aesir, it wasn't uncommon for age disparities to exist between married couples.

She screwed up her face with frustration and unease. She was only eighteen. How could she possibly make such an important decision?

One thing she knew was that Aunt Margaret did not approve of hasty marriages. That much had become very clear to her in previous conversations, as well as the way her aunt had shared the letter. If McKenna joined Society, she would have other options. Her aunt had never married. She'd taken a sort of stubborn pride in remaining unattached to any person and using her wealth to support causes she believed in. Did she have her own reasons for trying to convince McKenna—albeit subtly—to avoid the connection?

"What should I do?" she muttered aloud, gazing down at the letter again. Should she explore these feelings more? Or banish them? Could she banish them? Once more she perused the few lines, and once more she felt that buzzing feeling inside her chest that was uncomfortable, yet somehow thrilling.

Foamy water lapped against her shoes. She stared down at the popping bubbles, imagining the same being inside her chest, popping and swelling and making her feel important and childish and confused and delighted and afraid. Marriage meant intimacy. It meant so many things she'd only read about in books. Her cheeks began to heat again, and she was grateful she was outside. It wasn't proper in Society to speak of such things, of course, of the secret ways between man and woman. Novelists were obscure about it, something that only inflamed her imagination.

Could she envision Robinson kissing her? Her hand, yes. Her cheek, maybe. But kiss her on the mouth? Her nerves rattled at the thought, and she closed her eyes, trying to will away the sudden rush of feelings that flooded her.

That is when the wave struck her.

It hit hard and forcefully and knocked her to her palms and her knees. Her dress was soaked instantly and some of her hair stuck to her face. In startled surprise, she'd dropped the letter. She watched it fly away, the paper seeping up the ocean, the ink already blotting. Crawling away, she tried to adjust her clothing as the wave receded.

How many times had her parents warned her about the possibility of such waves that could appear out of nowhere? Her siblings had the benefit of being able to hear them coming, so McKenna had always been wary of walking the beach alone. Yet she'd been too engrossed in the letter to pay attention to her surroundings. She was upset with herself for being so distracted.

She grabbed the wet letter as it sailed by and saw, to her horror, another wave looming. It struck her in the face, knocking her off balance, and this time she felt the undertow pulling at her. Sand and grit and stinging salty water filled her mouth. She choked and spluttered, flailing her arms and legs. When she surfaced, nowhere near the shore, her reason turned to panic. She tried to scream for help, but found breathing was impossible. She was choking on the seawater. Her dress, soaked now, was pulling her down.

McKenna tried to swim, something she was very inexperienced with, but she knew that her survival depended on it. Kicking her legs and stroking with her arms, she tried to propel herself back toward shore and found, after several minutes, she'd made no progress at all. In fact, she was farther away than before she started. How had that happened? She managed to cough out the seawater but was barely keeping her head above the waves. A pelican soared past her, which was an incongruous thing to be noticing at such a terrifying moment. The ocean was cold too, and her teeth were already chattering.

She tried again to swim back to shore. It got her nowhere. She wasn't just farther away from shore, but also farther down the coast. The trees lining it grew thicker and thicker, meaning she was leaving the area where the homes were built. She cast her eyes for a fishing boat, but the choppy seas had made it inhospitable to sailors.

Why hadn't she paid more attention to the waves? No, self-recrimination would do her no good at all. She had to focus on rescuing herself. She tried kicking again, then alternated with some yells for help, but there was no sign of anyone on the beach. More strokes, then more. Fatigue and desperation battled within her. She'd never been so tired or felt so helpless. But slowly, she began to make progress. The strokes began to bring her closer to shore. Hope ignited within her chest. She could do this. Coming back indoors sopping wet, that would make a story to tell! The letter was lost and ruined, but she would write to Mother. She would ask her if Professor Hawksley had made an announcement of sorts. If he had, McKenna wanted to know. She could only make a proper decision if she had all the facts. And she wouldn't rush her decision either. Good decisions were made after a great deal of thinking about them.

She was panting heavily, writing the letter in her mind, scooping her hands through the waves as she neared land. She wasn't cold now, just trembling from the shock of the situation. She could do it. She could make it to shore. McKenna Aurora Foster was determined. She would live her life.

And she would be the first deaf person who would learn magic.

Another wave was carrying her to shore. She felt it pushing her from behind, bringing her closer to that cherished sandy beach. Faster and faster it went. She looked and saw a monster of a wave building behind her. It was enormous. Would it pass her before cresting? No, it was going to smash her onto the beach.

McKenna had the presence of mind to suck in her breath before she started tumbling head over heels. The sand bit her face. She tumbled, rolling, confused as to which way was up. And then she felt the current again, the undertow dragging her away once more. She tried to claw her way through the sand, to grip onto something that would hold. But everything was seawater and flimsy sand. Nothing solid. Nothing firm.

The need to breathe became desperate, but she was still underwater. There was no way to tell which way was up, not with sand scraping under her eyelids.

She hiccupped and salt water rushed inside her mouth, burned inside her lungs. McKenna fought for life, realizing now that she was too tired to make the swim a second time. She was drowning. She was helpless to prevent it.

Darkness began to blur her mind. She felt herself screaming underwater. Then she was listless, her arms and legs unable to kick or paddle. The ocean had claimed her, a power as inexorable as the Aesir's value for contempt and justice.

Inexorable.

In-ex-or-able.

It meant *impossible to stop or prevent.* But it also meant a person who was unbending, unyielding. Inflexible. Those thoughts danced in her mind. How strange that words were still a fascination to her when she was dying.

McKenna blacked out.

When she revived, she was on the beach once more. The surf had deposited her there a second time. Sand stuck to every crevice of her skin and the folds of her gown. She lifted her head and saw grains of it clinging to her hair, felt them on her lips.

She barely had the strength to lift her head. A gentle lapping wave came up and swallowed her legs. McKenna felt a burst of energy and clambered away from it, digging into the sand, which became thick and solid as she drew away from the water's edge. Her lungs felt strange, like breathing air was wrong.

Sitting up on her knees, she gazed back at the ocean and wondered how she had gotten away from it. A memory that didn't quite feel hers floated by. It was like she was seeing the beach for the first time and was in awe of it. But that was strange—she'd been to the beach many times.

Feelings of gratitude swelled in her breast. She'd survived. She didn't know how. It was a vagary, was it not?

Only . . . what did that word mean? For an instant, her mind blurred and went dark, then the answer supplied itself. It meant *luck*. Chance. A whimsy. Yes, she knew that word. But for an instant, she'd forgotten it.

McKenna struggled to her feet. Her legs wobbled. But that was to be expected. She'd nearly drowned. She needed a bath to wash away all the sand. And a new dress. The wind was still whipping hard, and in her wet clothes, she knew she'd start shivering as she lost body temperature.

Actually, the wind felt nice. Soothing even. She wasn't cold at all. How strange.

A warm bath. A seat by the fire. That would be nice. And then she could finish reading the book she'd left on the window seat.

What book was it? She couldn't remember. Why couldn't she remember?

Mortals are only half-tamed animals who have, for generations, governed others by deceit, cruelty, and violence. Law cannot persuade what it cannot punish, so order must be imposed or disorder shall reign. Chaos always results from entropy. Thus, the Invisible College must provide the structure, order, and higher sensibilities that persuade mortals to rise above their natural inclinations.

—Isaac Berrow,
Master of the Royal Secret,
the Invisible College

Robinson Dickemore Hawksley

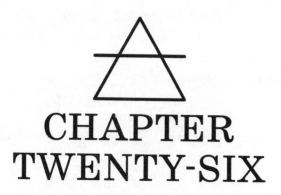

CHAPTER TWENTY-SIX

MISGIVINGS

Robinson was reminded of the time when, as a young boy, he'd worn his father's shoes and coat and thought he'd never grow enough to fill them. His new trousers were baggy, but thankfully the suspender straps could be tightened enough to keep them from falling down his slim waist. The shirt was voluminous too. The jacket, vest, and trousers were brown with dark blue pinstripes. The clothes were modern, fashionable even, and way too big on him.

"You seem less pallid today, Son. And you have not coughed all morning."

The clothes were a gift from his father, who had taken a locomotivus from his Meadowlands home far northwest of Auvinen. He'd given his son his best suit of clothes, and while Robinson would have been pleased with something far less extravagant, he was grateful to have something new to wear since his own suit had to be burned. His father had nursed him back to health. The revival had not been swift, but his swollen lymph nodes had finally returned to their normal state, and the debilitating fever had melted away. Most importantly, he still had his voice.

Robinson sat at the edge of the bed, his father across from him on a small wooden chair. The furnishings in his new lodgings were sparse.

"I feel much better," Robinson said.

"You don't lack for admirers," Father said. James Randulf Hawksley was a proud man, a gentle soul. It had been months since they'd seen each other, the Aesir war having prevented interaction except by post. "Well, at least food keeps showing up day after day. Mrs. Fiske said even the widow woman and her family brought a little stew and wanted to see you and wish you well. The son in particular. He wants some more lessons, I think."

"I'd like to do more for him when I have the time," Robinson confessed. "I am grateful, though. Grateful for all the meals. The well wishes. I don't want to be a burden on anyone."

James gripped his son's knee and shook it. "I'm pleased Dean George granted your request. It's a sign of your integrity he trusts you enough to pay you in advance for next term's lectures. Now that we're entering spring, buildings will be fixed and Society will carry on as we always have. You can take on more students. I'm surprised you don't have more already, Son. You could make a handsome living. I always did."

Robinson rubbed the back of his neck. "It's not so simple."

"What's not simple about it? You gave up a plum student, Mr. Foster's daughter, to that young lady from the deaf school. The Fosters are well-to-do. I'm sorry about Miss Hurst, but you could take Foster's daughter as a student again, and that would solve a great number of your problems."

"Except I can't," Robinson said with a sigh.

James wrinkled his brow. His beard was even grayer than before they'd left Covesea. But there was nothing wrong with his hearing. His eyes became very stern.

"I can't," Robinson emphasized.

"Why not?"

"First of all, her family is not as well off as you believe. The war has hurt Mr. Foster financially, and he is already investing in my invention. I can't take any more of his money."

"If he sees value in your dream, that is for him to decide on. And he will pay for his daughter's lessons regardless of who teaches them. I understand you feel beholden to the man, but this . . . this isn't a suitable reason to decline taking a student you *need*."

Robinson rubbed his face with his hands. "I can't teach the Fosters' daughter because I want to marry her."

His father blinked. "Have you taken leave of your senses?"

"Quite the opposite, Father. I have never felt this strongly about something before."

"Isn't she still considered a child?"

"McKenna is eighteen. She's of age."

"This isn't Covesea. Society matters here. To them, she's a child until her debut. Regardless, you are not fit to marry anyone at present. You're sick, depressed, and financially reckless."

"Reckless?" Robinson felt his heart pang with frustration at his father's rebuke.

"I've seen your alchemy. It's expanded four-fold since you moved here. The materials must have cost the bulk of your income. Your quarters are in a squalid part of the city. You don't have a change of clothes. You ran out of food and have been surviving, barely, on the benevolence of strangers." He leaned forward, his hands jutting out expressively. "If you taught lectures on my method, you could be making a handsome living. You could end up teaching in Bishopsgate! Yes, I would say you are reckless."

"I live within my means, however small. I scrimp and save to afford the reagents I need for my experiments. I don't want to be tied down doing one thing, Father. I have too many ideas, too many thoughts swirling in my head. But none of that matters. I am *drawn* to Miss Foster. She . . . she makes me want to be a better man. I love her."

"You have nothing to offer her. She's a rich man's daughter. You think she would want to live like *this*? Thank the Mind the family doesn't know your desires. You must keep them to yourself for now, until you are in a position—"

"I've already told them."

James was robbed of speech again. And perhaps his expression conveyed a tinge of horror. He stared at his son incredulously.

"When I wrote you that letter asking for help, I also wrote one to Mrs. Foster."

His father looked more and more perplexed, struggling to find words. Despite his exhaustive vocabulary, he settled on a single outburst. *"Why?"*

"Because I felt it is no longer honorable to keep my affection or my intentions secret from the family or from McKenna. I asked for Mrs. Foster's advice and promised I would be bound by whatever she said. But that was before I got sick. I am determined to go to Siaconset and confess my feelings now. And I would like to ask Mrs. Foster to go with me in case help is needed with her disapproving sister."

"When I said you were reckless, I had no idea just how much you are! Son, that is not the way Society works. You don't enlist your future mother-in-law as a coconspirator!"

"I don't care. I *care* about McKenna Aurora Foster. I will care for her, I will support her, I will do *anything* to make her happy. But I don't know if she will have me. And it's the not knowing that tortures me."

"I should think not having six cuppers in your pocket would be more of a torture. I am astounded, lad. You truly wrote her mother?"

Robinson grinned sheepishly. "I truly did. And I'd have more cuppers if I focused on certain experiments instead of trying to do them all at once."

"Have you heard back from her?"

"Yes. She was surprised but not unkind. She counseled me to wait until after McKenna makes her debut in Society. I think her sister, the dragon Margaret, has suspected it all along. She doesn't seem to like me very much."

"Wait until *your* mother finds out."

"Don't you want me to be happy?"

James sat upright in his chair and squirmed. "I do, Son. Truly. But this . . . this is highly unusual conduct for a university professor. Surely you can see that?"

"I think it is fairly typical actually. I have seen evidence of it anyway."

"You mean among sorcerers? I should hope not!"

"No, not within the Invisible College. But there are many professors who aren't sorcerers. Those who pursue relationships with students tend to be clandestine about it. But that is utterly detestable to my sensibilities. I felt . . . attraction to her almost immediately. That's why I gave her over to Miss Hurst."

James sighed and nodded in agreement.

"That is why I must tell her. Even if she rejects me. I could not, in good conscience, teach her without her knowing. And I would do it willingly, without payment, just to be near her. She has so much promise. So much . . . capacity. She speaks Tanhauser fluently, did you know that? Picked it up in just a few months. A natural linguist. And her reading and education . . . higher than most. If anyone with her disability *could* learn magic, it would be her. And I would rejoice."

"It would be a discovery of immense worth, to be sure. However unlikely I deem it to be at present."

"Give me your blessing, Father. I mean to visit Mrs. Foster now that I have recovered. I have an open invitation to dine with the family at Closure."

"My blessing? I think it is imprudent if not *impudent*, Son." He wagged his eyebrows at his own play on words. "The Fosters will probably require you to wait until their daughter has debuted in Society before they agree to let you court her. And they'll require a chaperone at the very least."

"I'm willing to abide by that," Robinson said. "But I must speak with her."

"Do not be too disappointed if she recoils from the idea. She's quite young. You might need to give her some time to get used to"—he waved his hands vaguely—"the *notion*."

Robinson smiled sadly. "That is why I cannot wait any longer. None of us know how much time we have left. I'm not afraid of her rejecting me. I could live with it. What I cannot endure is her not knowing how I feel."

"You have the heart of a wooer," James said with a chuckle. "There was no lass you fancied back in Covesea, eh?"

"Not a one I can remember. But I do fancy Miss McKenna. No, it's more than that. Please don't think little of me, Father."

James shook his head no, and his voice became thick with emotion. "What you did for those dying children. The courage that took is beyond my comprehension. I'm proud of you, Son. I always have been. I hope for your sake she sees the truth I see in you."

"Thank you, Father. I wouldn't have even met the Fosters if you hadn't taught me your method." That praise seemed to please him. It made Robinson even more grateful he had the parents he did. He was their last child. The only one who might survive them.

A knock sounded at the shabby little door. James patted his son's knee, then rose from the chair and went to answer it. It was a messenger boy from the post, a young lad of about twelve years old in his smart little uniform.

James shut the door and examined the letter, his expression showing curiosity. "From a Mrs. Foster on Brake Street? How interesting!"

Robinson hurried to stand only to suffer a miasma of dizziness. It forced him to sit down hard, but thankfully the bed softened the landing. "Give it here," he pleaded, unable to help a silly grin as he took the letter from his father's outstretched hand.

The grin faded immediately after he read the letter from Mrs. Foster.

Dear Professor Hawksley:

I think it would be prudent if you did not share your intentions with our daughter at the present time. I fear McKenna would be startled and distressed if such news were thrust on her while she is at my sister's estate. Now that the season has changed, my sister and our daughters were intending to return from Siaconset in two weeks, but that must be delayed as McKenna had an unfortunate accident on the beach and was struck by a rogue wave and nearly drowned. She has confessed to my sister some misgivings about you that I would prefer sharing in person. They may not be insurmountable, but they persuade me to offer my counsel that delaying would suit your interests (and hers) best. You are welcome, as ever, to join us for dinner at Closure if you feel up to it. Mr. Foster would gladly send the carriage for you if walking is still difficult.

Kindly,

Mrs. Laurel Aurora Foster

CHAPTER TWENTY-SEVEN

Misunderstandings

Gripping his valise tightly with one hand, Robinson knocked on the door with the other. The knock sounded weak in his own ears. He attempted, perhaps in a futile way, to not imagine how he must appear on the Fosters' doorstep, wearing his father's too-large suit, his hair askew and wild, his cheeks sunken and unshaven. He looked more cadaver than man, but none of that mattered to him.

Clara opened the door. It had to be Clara and not Mrs. Foster. The eldest daughter of the family looked at him inquisitively and then opened her eyes wide. Her lips formed a little "oh."

"P-Professor, I scarcely recognized you. And it's not Closure."

"Is your mother at home presently?"

"She was about to leave. But she's here."

"Might I speak with her?"

"Come in. You startled me, that's all." She backed away, opening the door wide, and Robinson gave her a curt nod before entering. He'd missed this home on Brake Street since his illness. But he knew

McKenna wasn't there, and so a feeling of desperate emptiness clung inside him as he gazed at the familiar surroundings. He could have warned Mrs. Foster he was coming. But he suspected his entreaty would be more persuasive in person.

"And how are you, Professor?" Clara asked.

"I'm feeling much better, thank you."

The young woman looked at him with disbelieving eyes, and again he tried not to consider how he must appear to her.

"I'll fetch Mother. The parlor? Would you like to wait there?" Clara looked more stately now, her hair done up in a fashionable look, her dress and corset marking her as a young woman on the cusp of entering Society.

"Yes, please. It's good to see you again, Miss Clara."

She gave him a smile, didn't return the sentiment, and then walked briskly away. Robinson wandered over to the family parlor. He set down his valise on the bench of the Broadwood grand and tapped a few of the keys, playing a minor triad. Mrs. Foster did not immediately come, so he fished the strange device from his pocket and opened the lid, looking at the numbers frozen there, nine hundred ninety-eight. Despite the way it had impacted the quicksilver tubes, everything about it was the same. There were more experiments to be performed, but his rattled mind could not focus on anything but the task at hand. Sleep and work would be impossible until he had gone to see McKenna.

"Professor, what brings you—"

It was Mrs. Foster's voice, but it broke off midstatement as she saw him standing by the musical instrument. When he turned his neck to face her, he saw she was as taken aback as Clara had been.

"Good afternoon, Mrs. Foster. I know I've come unexpectedly."

"I see you brought your valise. Did you come . . . did you come to say goodbye? Are you leaving to recuperate from your illness with your parents? We all think you were exceptionally brave."

"I'm leaving for Siaconset. And I'm here to persuade you to accompany me."

"Professor Hawksley!"

"I am in earnest, Mrs. Foster. I cannot wait another day. The news you sent, which I am grateful for, only adds to my urgency. To think what could have happened."

"Please sit down. Let's discuss this."

Robinson bit his lower lip and then sank down on the nearest sofa, putting his head in his hands.

She sat next to him. "You are distraught. And rightly so. We all are. My sister has assured me that McKenna has fully recovered and is in no danger. She won't be wandering on the beach by herself again. I think she learned her lesson."

"I must tell her how I feel, Mrs. Foster. I cannot understate how important this is."

"But I'm afraid of how she will react if you come in such a state. You are barely recovered from your illness. I cannot see the harm in delaying your confession until she returns. It is only another fortnight."

That seemed an eternity, though. Robinson rubbed his face and looked at her. He saw sympathy in her eyes. She wasn't a heartless woman.

"I will be candid with you, Mrs. Foster. If McKenna were home, I would gladly heed your advice and wait another two weeks no matter how it pained me. But I have a suspicion that my cause is not being well represented by your sister. I fear she has a low opinion of me."

It was probably unwise to be so candid, but Robinson could not misrepresent his feelings or misgivings.

Mrs. Foster put her hand on Robinson's shoulder. It was a sign of intimacy he appreciated.

"My sister wants what's best for McKenna. As we all do. We care a good deal about you, Professor. It is not . . . uncommon . . . for such an age discrepancy among suitors, but usually they are frowned—"

"How old do you think I am, Mrs. Foster?" Robinson interjected.

His words startled her. "I don't exactly know, but I should think you are close to forty?"

"Madame, I am not yet twenty-seven. I have been sick a good deal of my life, and it has surely cost me, but I am not that much older than your daughter."

"Mr. Foster and I . . . well . . . that is better news than we'd expected. It is not uncommon, you see, for older . . . widowed men . . . to desire younger wives."

Robinson threw his hands in the air. "If this is what *you* think of me, what might your sister be saying to her? I must go at once and rectify this misperception. I have tried to be honorable in all regards toward Miss McKenna."

"And you have, Professor. You really have. I apologize for the misconception, but it is not courteous in Society to demand to know someone's age."

"Dean George felt free to ask." Robinson huffed. "I assumed it was common knowledge."

"It wasn't. And Lieutenant Wickins calls you 'old chap' sometimes. You can see how that might be misinterpreted."

Robinson stifled a chuckle, but he was even more determined now. He looked Mrs. Foster in the eyes and then took her hands in his. "Please come with me to Siaconset. I must tell your daughter how I feel, and it would be better if you were there."

"I have engagements here in Auvinen," Mrs. Foster said. "I encourage you to at least wait for her to return. I'm certain my husband would agree."

Robinson released her hands and stood. "I cannot. I can't wait another instant. Has McKenna communicated her feelings to you? I don't ask you to divulge any confidentiality, but I would appreciate knowing what I'm about to face."

Mrs. Foster rose from the sofa. "She did write me a letter. After her accident."

"May I see it?"

Mrs. Foster fell quiet for a few painful moments. "I don't have her permission to share it, so I will not betray her trust."

"Will you tell me nothing of her attitude toward me?" He scrubbed his fingers through his hair.

"I really can say no more."

"I implore you. I am determined to present my case regardless. Honor demands it."

"She is still very young, Professor. And this experience is new for her . . . for all of us."

"And I'm trampling through your ideals of decorum as if it's a flowerbed. In Covesea, there are fewer rules dictating the professions of love."

"But we are in Auvinen, Professor Hawksley. I am not forbidding you to do this. I am advising you on the course of action that will likely produce the best results for you and my daughter. Please stay. Shall we not discuss this with Mr. Foster when he returns from work?"

Robinson sighed. His insides were churning still. He rubbed the edge of his nose. "Then I will miss the evening locomotivus departures and delay even further. I cannot. I must leave at once."

"I will see you to the door, then."

"Will you say nothing about her misgivings? Is it my age that concerns her the most?"

"She has not mentioned that. Not specifically. We haven't really discussed marriage opportunities as yet because it's too soon. That's why we both, my husband and I, proposed that you wait for after her debut before telling her. Our daughter looks at marriage, presently, as a less agreeable outcome. One that she'd be forced into if she is not allowed in Society. Mr. Foster and I are likeminded on this. Your career isn't an impediment. Far from it. We know she's impressed by you."

"But? I beg you. Does she find me . . . repulsive?"

Mrs. Foster sighed and was a little tongue-tied. "I would feel more comfortable if I had her permission to share what she wrote. I haven't told her of your intentions. Neither has my husband. But my sister may have said something . . . indelicately . . . and so McKenna wrote to ask me if you had indeed made any intentions known. She was a little upset that we were concealing something from her."

"Indelicately," Robinson sighed.

"You could leave tomorrow, you see the—?" Mrs. Foster started to suggest.

"I'm leaving at once," he said and hurried out of the room.

"Professor!"

He saw Clara standing in the corridor with a look on her face that revealed she'd been listening in the whole time. It was a sly look, a look that made him feel he was a fool for ignoring the advice he'd been given. That he was going to make a botch of things and she'd delight in his failure.

He reached the door and was again interrupted by a call from Mrs. Foster. "Your valise!"

He was leaving empty-handed. It mortified him. Sheepishly, he met her in the corridor and took it from her.

Clara couldn't suppress a gloating smile and an arched eyebrow.

"Thank you," he stammered, flushing. And off he went to grab a street tram to the station, sensing an invisible, friendly shadow coming along in his wake. He felt encouragement coming from the intelligence, sympathy for his feelings for Miss Foster. He wished in that moment that it were still real, that he could pat the creature on its head and share some food with it as he'd done in Greenholh. At least, he thought wryly, there were no allergies to contend with now.

⁂

The countryside passed by quickly as Robinson stared out the window. The locomotivus was crowded, mostly with soldiers returning home from the front now that the season was changing. Reports of the Aesir sky ships disappearing had spread throughout the continent. Many civilians had been killed due to the bombardments of cities, but Bishopsgate was no longer threatened, and the military was giving soldiers leave in stages. He'd wondered if McKenna might have preferred marrying a soldier, someone like Lieutenant Wickins, but her mother's words had reassured him that his profession, at least, was acceptable. But what were the misgivings she'd mentioned, and could he hope to surmount them?

The locomotivus stopped at every station along the way. He watched the myriad of people getting off and on at each station and wondered about their lives. Each had a destination, each had a family, each had been impacted by the Aesir war. Then the large transportation machine would hum, its magic invoked by the sorcerers on board, and whoosh down the iron tracks, hovering due to the laws of magic and magnetism. Sometimes the journey was delayed when all the components could not be coaxed to action simultaneously, and they'd all be stuck on the tracks until the source of the problem was discovered.

They reached the village of South Horrington after nightfall, and Robinson took his valise from the upper rack and disembarked. The few quicksilver lamps at the station provided a modicum of light. He learned, to his chagrin, that there were no coaches in operation at that hour, and they wouldn't commence again until midmorning the next day. So he made himself comfortable on a bench at the station, used his valise as a pillow, and fell asleep.

The next morning, he found a paper-wrapped pastry and a cup of tea sitting next to him with no one else around. A little scrawled note that had been left with it—*you looked hungry*—revealed it was meant for him. Had his invisible friend coaxed a bystander to help him? Grinning, he wolfed it down and sipped the tepid tea until it was gone. The kindness refreshed him as much as the repast. He wished he could thank whoever had done it, but the crowd was small and no one met his gaze.

He took a coach with several other passengers until he reached the small coastal town of Bleadney. It was a little resort town with a lively waterfront, and it was already occupied with families and soldiers who had come to get away from the bleak winter and the war. Robinson's body ached from the journey, and he was hungry. Would Aunt Margaret allow him to stay for dinner? Would he even be allowed to see McKenna after showing up unannounced?

After asking for directions to the ferry master, he arrived and found the window closed. This caused confusion, so he went around the building until he found someone to ask—a middle-aged gardener tending a little plot of flowers.

"Excuse me, sir!"

The gardener lifted his head. "What's the bob, sir?"

It was a peculiar expression, but Robinson didn't bother to ask about it. Storm clouds lowered on the horizon, and he felt a desperate need to see McKenna now. He wasn't sure why, but the urgency had increased.

"When's the next ferry to Siaconset?" Robinson asked, feeling the throb of another headache beginning to press inside his skull.

The gardener looked at him as if he were absurd. "You missed the last one."

"Pardon?"

"It left at midday already. It's gone."

"I know, but when is the next one?"

"Are you daft? Tomorrow is Closure. There's no ferry on Closure. Morning after that is the next one." He lifted his eyebrows and chuckled to himself. "Penny fool from the big city looking for a ferry. Chaw."

Robinson stared at the island in the distance, his heart sinking into his too-large shoes.

McKenna Aurora Foster

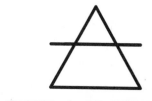

CHAPTER TWENTY-EIGHT

Dream Echoes

It was unlike any dream McKenna had ever had. In it, she could *hear*. She was wandering through a battlefield, but not a modern one. Men in slush-spattered suits of armor gripped swords sheathed in frost. The snowy ground was flecked with blood, and she was crossing it, searching among the corpses for someone. The cry of a hawk sounded overhead, earsplittingly loud. How strange that McKenna understood the cry even though she'd never heard it before. There was such a tumult around her, and the underlying song of war rose and faded like some dark chorus, an anthem of death. Yet McKenna continued to walk through the rubble, an elegant blade in her own hand, curved and glistening silver. The feeling of potential loss was suffocating. She had to find *him*. Someone she loved. Someone she feared she'd lost.

And then McKenna awoke, blinking in surprise, the din of combat hushing to the silence to which she was accustomed. She lay in her bed, the fragrant sea air coming in the open window of her room on the upper floor of Mowbray House. The memories of the vivid dream were there for but a moment, and as she blinked, trying to comprehend them, she felt a mist of amnesia settle on her mind, taking them away.

No! she thought in a panic, trying to clutch the memories. But it was like holding her breath. Eventually, she had to let go, to breathe again, and the dream vanished from her mind. All that remained was the haunting echo of her need to search for someone.

And the memory of what it felt like to hear.

She tossed the coverlets aside, feeling stifled by them. Ever since being sucked in by the undertow at the beach, she'd been uncomfortably warm for some strange reason. She even slept with the top buttons of her nightgown undone and would often wake in the middle of the night feeling oppressed by the room's little magical heater, so she'd started opening the window at night to cool things off. She'd gone so far as to ask Mrs. Foraker to turn off the little creature, a machine shaped like a squatting raccoon.

She swung her legs off the bed and scratched the back of her neck, feeling that the mass of untidy hair needed a good brushing. But she went to the window first to feel the sea breeze on her face. There was a fellow walking down the street, away from the house, wearing an ill-fitting brown suit with darker pinstripes, paired with a bowler hat. Bowler hats were the height of fashion in Auvinen, but this one was too big for the man's head and thus a little comical. She gazed at him, wondering who the strange fellow was walking the street so early in the morning.

She toyed with one of the buttons of her nightgown and then crossed the room to fetch a brush. Trudie burst into the chamber, her hair in cloth ties to add curls. Her eyes were wide with excitement.

"This is early for you, Trudie," McKenna said, tapping the brush against her palm. She started to brush her own hair.

"Professor Hawksley was just here!" Trudie exclaimed.

McKenna stopped midstroke. "Here?"

"Yes! Here! Aunt sent him away."

McKenna tossed the brush back onto the nightstand and hurried back to the window. The trees on the street obscured any sight of the man in the suit.

"Was he wearing a brown suit?" McKenna asked.

"Yes, it was awful!"

McKenna was flummoxed and felt her cheeks start to heat up. Her teacher had come to Siaconset to see her? And he'd come so early in the morning too.

"I heard Aunt shouting at him, which woke me up," Trudie said. "I slipped out to the stairs and listened in. She sent him away."

McKenna felt the flame in her cheeks burn hotter. She'd written a letter to Mother, asking about Professor Hawksley. No response had come yet. Her tutor had come all this way only to be sent away? That was terribly rude.

McKenna felt a throb of indignation and left the room to hasten downstairs, where she saw Aunt Margaret pacing in the entry hall, her eyes flashing with anger, hands gripping several folded pages.

"Did Professor Hawksley just come?" McKenna demanded.

Aunt Margaret turned in surprise upon seeing her niece. "By the Mind, child, go back upstairs and dress yourself! You're indecent!"

McKenna didn't feel ashamed. "Did the professor come?" she repeated.

"Yes. Yes, he did. At such an hour too. Disgraceful."

"What did he want?"

"To see you, obviously. I warned you about him. Please, McKenna, go upstairs. And button up your nightdress before someone sees you."

"Why did you send him away?"

"This is not the proper hour to entertain company."

"But he's not just company, he's our friend," McKenna said, feeling more agitated by the moment. "He was so recently sick. You shouldn't have sent him away."

"What else was I supposed to do? Let him charge into your bedroom and wake you? He was acting desperate. He is desperate. His conduct is beyond unseemly."

"Unseemly? How so? Because he wanted to see me?"

"We are not having this conversation right now. Go upstairs, dress yourself, and then come down. We will discuss it during breakfast."

"What is that in your hands? Is it a letter for me?"

Aunt Margaret's eyes flamed hotter. She did not answer.

"Is it?" McKenna said, marching forward and holding out her hand.

"Yes." The tight lips on Aunt Margaret's face showed she was mortified at having been caught reading her niece's mail.

"Why are you reading it, then? Give it to me."

"I don't think it's for the best," Aunt Margaret said. "A true gentleman wouldn't have written this to a young woman who has not yet entered in Society."

"For the last time, I'm not a child!" McKenna said firmly. "In another few months, I'll be considered too old to enter Society. Let me have it, please."

For a moment, she was afraid her aunt would resist. If Trudie hadn't awakened McKenna when she did, she might never have learned about the letter, or at least not for several days.

Reluctantly, Aunt Margaret handed over the letter and envelope, which had the embossing of a hotel. McKenna seized it, thanked her aunt stiffly, and then retreated back to her room.

Trudie was at the top of the stairs, looking at McKenna in amazement. Her sister started following her into her room, but McKenna shook her head and shut the door. It was a long letter, handwritten, with blotches of ink and crossed-out words. But she recognized the professor's handwriting. She would have known it was his even if it weren't signed.

Sitting on the edge of the bed, she began to read it with equal parts eagerness and foreboding.

Dear Miss McKenna,

I've come to Siaconset in hopes that you will see me and let me tell you all that I long to say.

She felt her pulse quicken and her eyes became very hot. Involuntarily trembles started down her arms.

You may not know, McKenna, you might be utterly unconscious of the fact that I have for some while learned to respect and love you. I have loved you with such a passionate attachment that will be incomprehensible to you, but my feelings are real. They are new to me as well. I've not felt this way for any other person. I wish to make you my wife if you would let me try to win your love. To earn your affection. Not now, not until you are ready. I do not mean to frighten you, but I must confess my feelings. It would be dishonorable to do anything less.

She was blushing. She was blushing fiercely. Had her parents known this for some time and kept it from her? Why would they? Because she was still a child in their eyes also? Had Clara persuaded them to shield the news from McKenna? To give her a chance to enter Society first?

She kept reading, totally engrossed and feeling unsure of herself. When she had last written to her mother, she had expressed confidence in her ability to make a stable life for herself on her own terms. Like Aunt Margaret had.

I communicated my feelings and intentions to your parents. Your father has reproved me for being too impulsive. He sent a letter via sky parcel that reached me at the station, informing me that I go against his wishes and the wishes of your mother by trying to communicate my intentions to you directly. He thinks I'm carried away by unmanly feelings. Your father is a wise man. He may also be right. But these feelings are not unmanly. I am a man. I know I'm in love with you. And I consider myself honor bound to communicate my feelings to you, come what may. If you are too young to receive such tidings, I stand rebuked and prepared to admit my wrongdoing. But I trust you will be comforted to know there is someone who wants to devote his life to your happiness.

Your parents requested I wait to tell you until your return from Siaconset. I confess that to wait in silence would be impossible. Utterly impossible. Not only can I no longer suppress my emotions, but it would feel like the deepest of wrongs for me to continue to meet and dine with your family and for you to be the only one who did not know. You may have come to distrust me already because of what you've been told about me. I cannot bear that.

You do not know, you cannot guess, how much I love you—how much I desire to have the right to shield and to protect you. Had I any confidence in your love, I believe that you would mold my life into any form you could wish it to be.

She paused in her reading, trying to tame the bucking beats of her heart. Had she truly awoken from a dream, or was she dreaming still? There was something nagging at her mind, a suppressed memory she couldn't unlock. She was flattered, surely, but his age . . . He was so much older than her. Swallowing, she read on.

I respect your parents deeply. I can be nothing but grateful for the support and succor they have given me since I came to know your family. However, I believe they were operating under a misconception in regard to my age and thus my intentions.

I am not as old as you fear—I hope! I am twenty-six years old, though admittedly I appear older than that due to the illnesses I've experienced. I know you are surrounded by companions who would ridicule and annoy you if they did know I was here. Trust me, dearest McKenna, that I have not come to Siaconset to wound or pain you. I respect and honor you too much for that.

As I have missed the ferry to the island, I must abide at this hotel for another night. Sleep is a stranger to me these days. The rain lashes against the window.

McKenna frowned. It hadn't rained on the island, had it?

I hope, in earnest, to see you in person, to share my thoughts with words. Words you will discern from my lips. If I am not so lucky as to meet you, I leave this confession with my awkward hand instead. If you would prefer more time to consider your own feelings, I will refrain from further expression of my intentions until you are ready. You need time to know me better. You need time to know your own heart. By this confession, I will no longer suffer the knowledge that you are ignorant of my hopes for us.

Whatever may be the result of this visit, believe me, now and ever,

Yours affectionately,
Robinson Dickemore Hawksley

She bit her lip at the way he'd signed his name. Feelings surged inside her, not unlike the waves on the shore behind the row of houses. Rising from the bed, she walked to the open window, hoping against hope that she might find the man in the ill-fitting suit standing there outside, gazing up at the house.

The street was empty. He was gone.

Robinson Dickemore Hawksley

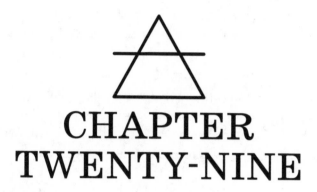

CHAPTER TWENTY-NINE

Changelings

For the third time on the trip back to Auvinen, the locomotivus halted on the tracks, causing another round of disgruntled groans from the passengers. The previous two delays had both taken a long time to resolve. Their arrival at the station would now come well after sunset. Robinson, still in his disheveled clothes, rubbed his cheek, weary from the exhausting journey. After he had left Aunt Margaret's beautiful house that morning, a messenger had found him at the ferry station with an invitation to join McKenna and her younger sister Trudie for a midafternoon lunch and walk along the beach. He'd agonized over what to do. He looked haggard. He could smell himself. He knew any further delays would cause him to miss the ferry back, and therefore be absent from his duties at the university, but that wasn't the true reason he'd held back.

He was terrified she'd reject him. Even if she did it politely and with respect. In his present state, it would have devastated him. It might result in no longer being able to teach her. It could end the lovely dinners at Closure. He wasn't ready for that. Not yet.

So he'd politely declined the invitation and requested an interview with her when she returned to Brake Street. Now that he had delivered his letter, now that he'd made his feelings known, he could wait patiently for a response. The relief he felt at having delivered it was immense. The knots in his shoulders were finally easing, but the knots in his stomach weren't. The headache had begun to ebb. Honestly, he wouldn't have been good company anyway at a beach conversation, especially not if Trudie was in a teasing mood as her elder sister Clara often was.

Robinson rose from his seat, stretched, and then walked down the center aisle toward the front of the locomotivus. There were many murmuring voices.

Passing from section to section, from the crowded seats of the unwealthy to the private rooms afforded only by the rich, he reached the main engine at the front. From the windows, he could see plumes of white smoke gushing from the housing, all part of the magical apparatus that cooled the engine. A young man was guarding the entrance, wearing the uniform of the rail service, but he also had a collar button marking him as a sorcerer.

"What seems to be the trouble this time?" Robinson asked, shaking the young man's hand and giving him a gesture that revealed his own rank within the Invisible College.

"Oh, good evening, sir!" the attendant said, responding to the gesture in kind. "It's above my head. Been difficult coaxing her along the tracks today. Not sure why."

"Can I speak to the sorcerer in charge? Maybe I can help?"

"Even if every passenger on the locomotivus got out and pushed, it wouldn't move an inch. We're stuck to the rails until the magnetism starts working again."

"I see that. Can it hurt, though? I'm a professor at the University of Auvinen."

"Let me talk to Dixon and see if he'd like the help. With the delays so far, he's likely to get an earful from the company when we get there." The young man passed him and opened the door, shouted over the noise from within, then beckoned Robinson to enter.

Three sorcerers were already present, all with looks of mingled frustration and confusion. One scratched his head.

"It should be working, but it's not. I don't know what else to do, sir!"

"This is Mr. Dixon," the attendant said, gesturing to the sorcerer in charge, a man in his forties with side whiskers and a small mustache. "Here's the professor."

"I've ridden the rails ten years now," Dixon said. "Ten years. This is the strangest breakdown we've had. All the individual systems are working, but it's not moving. We're running low on frost ballast too. I'm all open to ideas, Professor."

Robinson approached the riveted panel, which was now open, revealing the intricate structures embedded within. Each system was powered by different intelligences, doing its own part to power the whole. It was an ingenious system, but sometimes the complexity made it difficult to ascertain the problem. Robinson ran his hand over the main screw, trying to get a sense of the thoughts of the embedded entities that summoned the Unseen Powers.

I'd like to get home, please, Robinson thought to them. *I haven't slept well in days.*

Instantly, the screw began to thrum. The engine started to rumble. Then the magnetized fields burst to life and the entire locomotivus began to hover over the rails. A forward lurch signified the propulsion had started. Shouts and cheers could be heard over the engine noise in the passenger cabins.

Mr. Dixon stared at Robinson in disbelief. "How did you . . . ?"

"Lucky guess, I suppose," Robinson said, shrugging, although he was just as startled as the other men. "Looks like she's ready to get moving again."

The other sorcerers gazed at him with perplexed looks, but they were all too grateful to be underway again. It felt good to have helped, but Robinson wasn't sure that he had done anything at all. He'd just made his need known to the equipment, and it had responded with alacrity. That was it.

He brushed off the thanks of the crew and ambled back down to his seat as the locomotivus continued to pick up speed. Folding his arms, Robinson tried to fall asleep, but a renewed throbbing in his skull prevented it. The uncomfortable seat did not help.

They reached the station yard in Auvinen at night, the last locomotivus to arrive, and he grabbed his valise from the upper rack and maneuvered his way through the crowd and back to his new lodgings. As he passed under each of the lights that used quicksilver bulbs, they seemed to grow a little brighter.

Was his imagination playing tricks on him? Or was the device in his pocket interacting with them in some inscrutable way?

Finally he reached the ramshackle district where he'd found his new quarters. There were candles burning inside, so he imagined Father was still there. He'd promised to wait until Robinson returned from his quest to woo Foster's daughter. He was surprised to find Wickins waiting for him as well.

"Look at you, old chap!" Wickins said by way of greeting, gazing at Robinson's new clothes with a look of humor in his eyes.

"What are you doing here?" Robinson asked, shaking his friend's hand after setting his valise down by the door.

"I came looking for you, obviously. I brought an officer with an Aesir cloak, but you weren't here. The barracks are so noisy now with the influx of soldiers, I think I might move in. You shouldn't have all this space to yourself when your father leaves!"

Father rose from the small table and embraced his son. "I can't tell whether she rebuffed you or if you're just weary from the journey."

"I am . . . doing better," Robinson admitted. "I haven't been rebuffed or welcomed yet. I'm in a state of suspense and resigned to my predicament."

"Tell him about the letter," Wickins said to Robinson's father, his eyes twinkling.

"What letter?" Robinson asked.

"One arrived this afternoon from Siaconset," James said. He walked back to the table and retrieved it.

Robinson rushed to take it from his father's hands. He recognized McKenna's handwriting. The flow and curl of her script.

"It came today?" Robinson asked in surprise.

"Read it, Dickemore! Maybe it's your lady love's answer."

His fatigue instantly evaporated. His heart was racing. He wanted privacy, but with both of them gazing keenly at him, he didn't want to disappoint them either. He opened the glued edge of the envelope, pulled out a small sheet of very fine paper, and looked at the clear and unrushed words on the page without a single blot of ink or a crossed-out word.

Dear Professor Hawksley:

Thank you so very much for the honorable and generous way in which you have treated me. Indeed, you have both my respect and my undying esteem. I should be pleased to become better acquainted with you and to see you at Brake Street once again in the very near future.

Even if my present feelings remain unchanged by further intimacy, it will always be a pleasure to regard your visits and friendship as wonderful moments in time.

Thank you, Mr. Hawksley, for giving me time to consider your words carefully before seeing you or responding to them. I also thank you for not pressuring me to provide a response or to approach this subject again until I have had sufficient time to know you and myself. Also, I'm quite honored and grateful for the delicate regard for me that prompted your letter as well as your assurance that this will lessen your suffering on my account.

Believe me, grateful to be your friend,

McKenna Aurora Foster

Her kindness and sincerity made him love her all the more. He perused the letter again, just to be sure he had not missed a word or a misplaced syllable, and again he was impressed with the wisdom of her response. This was not a dictation from Aunt Margaret, who would not have expressed herself so patiently or positively. And the response also lacked the influence of Mrs. Foster, for the letter must have been sent soon after Robinson's departure in order to beat him back to Auvinen.

"Well, old chap? Will she have you?"

Robinson lowered the letter, folded it again, and slid it back into the envelope. "We shall see. Too early to tell. But I am hopeful."

"Mark my words, Mr. Hawksley, your son will be engaged before next winter. If not sooner. Summer weddings are all the rage."

Robinson felt his cheeks heat up a little, but the relief he felt from getting the letter was palpable. He had offered his heart to his pupil, and while not saying yes, she certainly had *not* said no.

"I wouldn't dare hope," Robinson said. "I would wait . . . even longer . . . if it meant she would say yes."

"Well said, old chap. Well said! I'm sorry I wasn't able to persuade Mr. Crossthwait to wait for you. He came down from Bishopsgate to show you that cloak."

"Where is he now?"

"I'm not sure. Men like him, from the military, come and go all the time, depending on their orders. He approached me at the commissary the other day, and we agreed we'd come by today. I didn't know you'd flown from town so quickly until we talked to your father!"

"My trip was unexpected," Robinson confessed.

"He seemed a pleasant fellow, for the military type," James said. "Asked a lot of questions about you. Especially your childhood. I told him you've always had an inquisitive mind. He was sorry to hear about your brothers' passing. And that you nearly died from the same disease."

"Yes, he was especially interested in that part," Wickins said. "But he was a good chap. Pleasant fellow."

James nodded. "Indeed he was. After I told him you'd gone to Siaconset, he excused himself and said he'd return again when the time was right to meet you in person."

"That would be most welcome," Robinson said. "Or I'd be happy to meet him in Bishopsgate."

"He liked your alchemy," James Hawksley said proudly. "Thought you might be on to something interesting. Something useful to the military." He seemed to remember something. "The officer who came, he was quite interested in that little device I gave you, the one that resembles a pocket watch."

"Yes, I told him about our experiments," Wickins said. "How it impacted the response of the bulb to that floating rock. Quite extraordinary actually. I described it to him, but he'd never seen such a thing before. He was very curious.

"Well, I need to get back to the barracks," Wickins said, stifling a yawn. "If you would like, we could continue with the experiments now that you are back? I'm getting some leave soon, now that the war is suspended, so I'll have more time on my hands. Reading ancient Aesir lore is interesting enough, but I should think this is quite fascinating too. I'll need to brush up on my Iskandir."

"I have lectures to start teaching, but yes . . . let's meet again tomorrow. At the park."

"It will be grand! Nice to meet you, Mr. Hawksley. A pleasure."

After Wickins left, James approached his son. "So . . . her answer was ambiguous?"

"See for yourself," Robinson said, handing over the letter.

It was quickly read and his father gave an approving nod. "Exquisite penmanship. I like her already. And she's been deaf since she was a child?"

"Completely. The damage to her inner ear means she cannot even get dizzy. But still she wants to learn magic and join the Invisible College. She's an ambitious young lady."

"Fluent in Tanhauser too, you said. How interesting."

"She fascinates me. It doesn't seem totally hopeless, does it?"

"I would have said a much more mature woman had written this letter, Son. You must bring her to the countryside if you become engaged. Your mother will be so pleased. She worries about you, you know. Worries about you constantly. As do I. But at least you have enough to eat now. Whoever is sending food to you is quite discreet. Not even a knock or a shadow."

Food. There would be enough food. Robinson sighed with relief.

The two embraced, and Robinson's feelings of harmony continued to spread.

He did think it a little odd that Mr. Crossthwait had to leave so quickly, however. He wondered why.

McKenna Aurora Foster

CHAPTER THIRTY

Face-to-Face

McKenna paced near the front window of the house on Brake Street. She and Trudie had returned early from Siaconset, owing largely to her disagreement with Aunt Margaret. Her aunt had remained behind, sending instead her manservant, Mr. Swope, to accompany the girls back to Auvinen by sea. They'd been home for two days now, and it was Closure—the usual day for their dinner with Professor Hawksley. She'd asked her mother to re-extend the invitation so he would be sure to come. Annoyed though she was with her sisters, who were getting more animated with their teasing now that the professor's interest in her was an established thing, she wished to see him. Desperately. Her near-drowning had made her see herself and her feelings more clearly.

Wringing her hands, she walked to the front window and gazed outside. The cherry trees were in full bloom, an exquisite shade of pink that added a dazzling display of color to the boulevards and streets. The snow was long gone, and so were the daily bombardments from the Aesir war. It was a beautiful day, perhaps even a mesmerizing one. Oh yes, definitely mesmerizing. Hypnotic, captivating, thrilling, and—if she were being honest with herself—slightly terrifying.

She was waiting to see the man who loved her. While her own feelings were still tender and new, like all the blossoms on the cherry trees down the lane, she felt a strange sense of certainty that they would bud into fruit and that the fruit would be sweet. The thought made her almost giggle nervously, but she suppressed it. She was eager to see him, face-to-face, to follow the words on his lips and to say her own. To set boundaries, of course. But boundaries that might ultimately bring them closer together.

Finally, she caught a glimpse of him coming up the street, and her stomach decided to do a peculiar little dance. It felt like she was on a swing, gazing upside down while her feet soared.

She recognized the suit as the very one she'd seen out the bedroom window of her aunt's house. It was better to meet like this, at her home, with her parents and sisters present to love and support her. *And tease you.* She did not look forward to that. Well, Father wouldn't tease. She'd implored Mother to keep her sisters away from the scene, knowing their presence would fluster her. She didn't want to be flustered, but the situation nearly required it. How does one speak to a man who traveled so far to express such ardent feelings of love in such a serious and bold way?

She saw him pick off the bowler hat and scrub his long, slender fingers through that thick mess of hair on his head. He looked nervous too, his eyes downcast, but his stride was undeniably quick. Hasty even. He was anxious. She could sense it radiating from him.

McKenna twisted the door handle and stepped outside before he reached the porch.

She wore her favorite dress, the purple one with the lace collar and little designs of black and silver across the fabric. She'd never worn it for him before, but this was a special day, the moment equally so. He noticed her standing in the doorway, and he took her in with a slight flush and a look of adoration that made her insides wriggle even more. She realized with mortification that she was trembling and that her voice would follow suit.

"Mr. Hawksley. I mean . . . Professor." She feared her voice was trembling very much indeed. Would he even be able to understand her defective utterances? She swallowed, trying to calm her galloping heart. She started over. "Professor Hawksley—would—would—you come into the greenhouse with me? Where—where we can be—alone?"

Without waiting for a response, she turned abruptly and walked back into the house, only to make a quick turn down the servants' corridor that led to the kitchen and out back to where the greenhouse was situated. Mother had assured her the corridor would be empty when the professor arrived, and she'd been true to her word.

McKenna couldn't hear whether he was following her, but she rather thought she sensed his heavier treads on the floorboards. The greenhouse was made of whitewashed framing planks and old used windows. She stepped through the doorway, and onto the pea-gravel floor of the interior, which she felt crunch beneath her shoes. It was warm inside, the windows having done their service by capturing the sunrays. There were little pots of tomatoes, onion shoots, and an assortment of fresh herbs that gave the greenhouse delicious smells. It was a tidy little place, ten paces by ten paces square. Sometimes she liked to read books on the wicker chairs kept inside.

She turned and saw, gratefully, that her tutor had followed her inside. He gently shut the greenhouse door, looking at her with wonder in his eyes. His cheeks were scruffy. His body still looked gaunt, but perhaps a little fuller. His cheeks were not quite so sunken. She saw his teeth behind his slightly parted lips—parted because of the tender smile he was giving her.

His mouth opened further to speak, but she held up her hand to forestall him. He had shared his heart with her already. It was time for her to do the same in return.

"Professor Hawksley," she said through a throat that was suddenly too dry. She coughed a little to clear it. "I—I really don't *dislike* you, whatever you may have been told. I—I like you. I don't love you—not as you do me—but I do like you. Is it enough for now?" A feeling of lightheadedness passed over her. She better not faint! That would be unendurable!

He stepped closer, not looking offended or hurt in the least. He was still holding his bowler hat in his hands and turned it around in a circle in a fidgety sort of way.

"Your aunt dislikes me. Distrusts me even. You respect her opinions. Her good judgment. But if what you have told me is what *you* feel . . . that is all that I ask to know. I am willing to wait."

She felt her cheeks burning, but she felt pleased. "She isn't fond of you. She knew you would ask me to marry you."

"And I will when you are ready," he said, meeting her gaze with openness. "I promised your parents that I would not pressure you. Not now. Not ever." There was no dissembling in this man.

"That is reassuring, Professor Haw—"

"You can call me Robinson. In fact, you may call me Rob if you like."

She felt a little mischievous and hoped it came across in her tone. "I like it when you call me Miss Foster. But I will permit you to call me Miss McKenna."

"So I can call you McKenna instead of Miss Foster?" he asked with an inviting look.

She felt a little like teasing him back. "Maybe on informal days? Of course. If you wish. Excuse me, Robinson. This is still very new to me."

"I think we will survive the moment somehow."

"Well, in your letter, you said you would like for us to get to know each other better. That would mean seeing each other more than just at Closure for supper."

"I would welcome that, McKenna."

"Good. Now that there is a lull in the war, I hoped we could start our lessons again. For speech and . . . magic."

He started to look a little uncomfortable. "I will not charge your family for a service I'd gladly provide freely."

"That is my second stipulation, then. When I come to visit you, I will bring dinner for you. And you must accept it without arguing. We will share it together, and I will watch you eat until I'm satisfied you are no longer starving."

He opened his mouth to protest but stopped himself. She watched his lips, waiting for him to argue with her. He was a scrupulous man. But on this point, she would not yield. He neglected himself because of his work and his caring for others.

His jaw relaxed, his mouth closed, and he scratched his head. "Why is this a stipulation?"

She lifted her chin slightly. He was so much taller than her, but she felt emboldened. "Because you are one of those men who can't live without a little wholesome tyranny from the women in their lives."

"'*Wholesome* tyranny'?" he said, chuckling.

"I want to buy bags of spiced peanuts now and then and not have you balk at eating your share. I want to care for you and . . . help you with your work . . . and I want you to read books with me and talk about the things we read . . . and share things with each other. And I want you to teach me. As . . . as equals. Well, someday. I don't want you to think I am unable to contribute to your life. That you have to do everything yourself. If we did marry, I would want to buy a Broadwood grand and make you play it every day, even if I can't hear the notes. For me . . . things must go both ways." She stepped closer to him, looking at him sternly, feeling the bowler hat brush against her. "Or not at all."

"A Broadwood grand?" he said, gazing at her with astonished eyes. "My violin is broken, and I despair of ever replacing *it*."

"You should have told me it was broken," she said, touching the rim of the bowler hat. Their fingers brushed together when she lowered her hand, just slightly, and she felt what could only be described as a jolt of magic go up her arm. "How did it happen?"

"It was during the winter," he said. "I was being chased by someone in the tenements. I'd been playing the violin there to try and ward off the attacks. It was the night the new sickness started. I slipped on the ice, and it fell out of my hands and broke."

"Who was chasing you?"

"An Aesir, I thought at first," he said simply. "But my attacker was a mortal. I defended myself with magic. Thankfully it worked."

"I never knew," she said, shaking her head. She wanted to squeeze his hand but felt that might be rushing things too much.

"I'm a private person," he said. "Always have been."

"Well, that must change. Not all at once. But you must share yourself with me. Your hopes. Your dreams. Your fears. I enjoy talking to you. I always have." She looked around at the little seedlings in the greenhouse. "With a little nurturing, some light, I think my feelings for you will continue to deepen."

"Mine are already fully ripe, I assure you," he said with a tender smile. "But I agree to your stipulations. I'd agree to anything, to be honest. You may command me, and I will obey."

"I meant it when I said it should be *wholesome* tyranny."

"A benevolent dictatorship?"

"That sounds about right. I'm joking, of course. Neither of us should be subservient."

"I have another question."

She smiled brightly. "Very well. Although we should probably return to the house before Clara starts peeking through the closed curtains. This is a *glass* greenhouse, after all. We are quite on display at the moment." She swished her hips to make her skirts sway. She was enjoying herself. The timidity and fluster of earlier were gone. It felt strangely right, being here with him. It always had.

"Tell me about what happened on the beach, Miss McKenna. Your accident."

She related the details quickly and concisely, sharing how her mother's letter and Aunt Margaret's words had rattled her. How she'd sought solace on the beach to read the letter, which had perished in the ocean. She didn't describe the strange feelings she'd had then and since. She wasn't even sure how to explain them. Or why the world felt overbearingly warm since she'd been submerged in the ocean. Or why she couldn't remember her dreams anymore.

"It was hearing about your accident," he said, "that prompted me to go to Siaconset. I was so agitated that I might lose you, and that you might not ever learn how I felt. I don't regret going. I don't regret telling you how I feel." He was looking into her eyes, but then he glanced up, his expression changing.

McKenna turned and saw Mother walking toward the greenhouse door, a frightened look on her face.

"Something is wrong," McKenna murmured.

Rob opened the greenhouse door. "Is all well, Mrs. Foster?"

Mother had an anguished look on her face and tears in her eyes. "Come inside, both of you. Come inside."

"What happened?" McKenna pleaded, her worries flaring. Her mother was positively distraught.

Mother put her hand on her mouth, her eyes welling with fresh tears. Rob helped McKenna climb over the threshold of the greenhouse and then took her mother by the elbow to steady her. He looked almost as concerned as McKenna felt.

After she'd steadied herself, Mother said something that made McKenna feel like she'd been struck by a rogue wave again.

"Mr. Swope . . . just sent a message. My sister was found . . . her neck . . . broken. An accident. A horrible . . . horrible accident."

It is possible to introduce errors into the simplest of equations. One digit in the wrong place can have a cascading effect that brings one farther from the truth. Mortals, not the universe, are the source of the greatest deviations. Error is not in the art but in the artificer.

—Isaac Berrow,
Master of the Royal Secret,
the Invisible College

Joseph Crossthwait

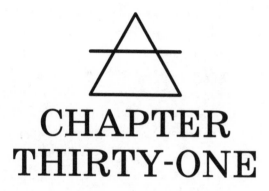

CHAPTER THIRTY-ONE

NEW ORDERS

The locomotivus slid fluidly down the tracks, the scenery out the window marred by dusk. Joseph Crossthwait brooded as he stared out the window, seeing the distant lights of the towns and villages they passed. He still felt uneasy about breaking the woman's neck and leaving her body in a way that would imply an accident. It was part of his duty to prevent injury to members of the populace. But sometimes sacrifices had to be made. Sometimes innocents had to die. Indeed, he was even proud of his ability to administer death efficiently and, usually, painlessly.

He'd sent word immediately to General Colsterworth to apprise him of the action taken on the island of Siaconset. The Semblance impersonating Hawksley had managed to slip away on multiple occasions now. When he'd gone to the man's apartment with Lieutenant Wickins, he'd expected to execute the Semblance then and there, not meet the man's father. But the information provided to him had certainly proven enlightening. The professor had suffered from axioma, which was usually fatal and had indeed killed his brothers. He'd been so sick his parents had left Covesea and come to Auvinen. And, even more interesting, the family possessed an Aesir device they could not account for. Many such artifacts where shrouded in magical glamours that deceived the bearer into believing they had been in the family for generations when, in fact, they were new possessions. It seemed intuitive that Semblances might require devices with which they might communicate their findings back to their people. Such knowledge of the Semblances and their ways was not commonly known. No, it was reserved for those in the upper ranks. Such as himself.

Still, he regretted the woman's death. If she hadn't been so headstrong, he would have let her live. But no, once she'd come to learn, during Joseph's visit, that the military harbored suspicions about the professor, she had decided to immediately depart for Auvinen to warn the family. Joseph had tried to persuade her that it was *his* duty to intervene, not hers, but the aunt's concern for her niece was so virulent that she would not be appeased. There'd been a brief scuffle, and a scream for help muffled by his hand. He'd had no choice but to render her unconscious while he considered what to do. Her obstruction would endanger his mission, possibly warn the professor too soon and cause him to flee. That would make hunting him down even more difficult. It might give the creature that inhabited the body a chance to shift to another newly dead.

And so he'd broken the woman's neck. He'd carried her limp body to the top of the stairs and then shoved it down, all while wearing his cloak of invisibility. He'd watched the housekeeper and the manservant come running. Her body had still been warm, but she was gone.

He squinted against a sudden glare, realizing the locomotivus was slowing upon its arrival at the station. Frowning, he tried to tamp down the unease he felt. In his career, sometimes they got it wrong. Sometimes a person they *believed* to be a Semblance turned out not to be one. The only way to tell was *after* the life had been terminated, when the telltale mist slipped from the deceased's mouth. Until that moment, though, there was the nagging worry about being wrong, about executing an innocent person. He'd heard about Professor Hawksley's intervention at the school of the deaf. It was not in a Semblance's nature to care about the lives of mortals. Perhaps there'd been an ulterior motive, but if so, he couldn't imagine what it might be.

That made killing Hawksley more confusing. More uncertain. But that was the office of the Brotherhood of Shadows—to do the difficult thing. His superior knew the sacrifices that must be made at times for the greater good.

The magic subsided, and the locomotivus connected and locked on the track. Plumes of frost came from the dampeners to chill the metal, causing a billowing cloud of cold smoke to swell on the platform. Joseph rose from his place and noticed a man standing on the platform, gazing at him through the window.

It was Peabody Stoker, a fellow member of the Brotherhood of Shadows. He too was wearing a kappelin. He'd allowed himself to be seen before vanishing in the smoke.

A surge of wariness filled Joseph. He had sent the message to Bishopsgate, and now a member of the order was waiting for him at the platform. Were they going to kill him? Instead of feeling nervous, he sighed and squelched any misgivings. He'd followed his orders as best he could. If the general was upset about what had happened on Siaconset, he would have sought Joseph first to discuss the matter in person. He wouldn't have sent an assassin to kill an assassin. There was a private killing yard in Bishopsgate to handle such secret courts-martial.

He emerged from the traveling machine nonchalantly and started walking toward the exit. He used no magic now. There had been few passengers that night, so there wasn't the need to rush.

"Walk with me to the commissary, Crossthwait," said a voice from behind him. He recognized it as Stoker's.

"I have orders from the general," Joseph answered, not changing course.

"My orders supersede yours. Come now."

Joseph didn't argue, and they walked together to the nearest commissary. Peabody had little hair and a short, trimmed beard. Like most in the brotherhood, both of them were illegitimate children born at orphanages. Lack of maternal bonding had proven to be a great indicator of success for assassins in the empire. Not in all cases, surely, but men like Joseph and Peabody had no family connections. They were instruments to be used. He'd grown numb to that fact long ago. The two men were colleagues, not friends. They knew each other by reputation more than fellowship.

When they reached the commissary, they went to the officers' mess. Joseph was grateful to get a cup of java. They sat at a little table, and after a few sips, he felt his mind become more alert. About a dozen other officers were sprinkled around the mess, but none of them would have felt comfortable intruding on a conversation between two men wearing kappelins, cowls lowered, and carrying visible harrosheth blades.

"The general needs you up north."

"I'm trailing a *known* Semblance," Joseph muttered. "How can this be more important than that?"

"You're to put a halt to that for now. There is going to be an inquest in Siaconset."

Joseph stared at the other man dispassionately. "I did what I had to do."

"The general trusts you were discreet and that the public inquest will reveal nothing. But she was a prominent woman and a wealthy benefactress. Her brother-in-law has high connections and will no doubt avail himself of them."

Joseph knew about the family connections well enough. But still . . . he'd seen a threat and disposed of it. In the grand arithmetic of the empire, one woman's death was insignificant compared with the devastation a single Semblance might wreak.

Stoker leaned forward, lowering his voice. "The general wants you away from the region for a little while. Let the inquest finish uninterrupted. Were you seen by any of the servants?"

"You think I was careless?"

"Were you?"

"I revealed myself only to the aunt because I needed information from her and her alone. She already harbored ill feelings for my quarry. Apparently her niece is being courted by the Semblance."

"Poor lass," Stoker said without any hint of sympathy. "As I said, the general has ordered you to lie low. Let the interviews happen. Let the will be read. I believe Mr. Foster is the executor. It may take several weeks, perhaps a month."

Joseph squeezed his hand into a fist. "That's too *long*."

"Yet there's no rush, Crossthwait. It's an off season. If the Semblance believes it's being hunted, it could find another host body. It's not running from you presently. Biding your time will only help you kill it."

Stoker was right, and Joseph resented him for it. "What is this . . . mission?"

Stoker smiled. "We think we found the ringleader of the sect that's been preaching in Tanhauser about surrendering to the Aesir."

"Who's the man?"

"We don't have a name. They call him the *strannik*. Means *philosophical pilgrim*. Word has it he has some followers in the imperial city preaching outside the palace. The general is sending a few of us north to see if we can find him."

Joseph nodded. It was the general's prerogative to alter assignments. There'd been rumors that this internal faction, these pacifists, were gaining momentum and becoming less . . . well . . . peaceful. Every time there was a war with the Aesir, this idea blossomed again like a weed. Surrender. Be subjugated. It was the only way to survive.

But in that, Joseph did not agree. The Aesir were a mystical and powerful race, but they could be killed. Men like him and Peabody had accomplished it. Saltpetr slowed them down. Bullets of elfshot forged in alchemies could slay them.

It was better to be dead than a slave.

The magic of the Unseen Powers works so well for the Aesir because they are exact in their adherence of its rules. By understanding the true principles governing the order of the universe, they harness incredible power. We may no longer be infants in our understanding of the same universal laws, but we are children, nonetheless.

—Isaac Berrow,
Master of the Royal Secret,
the Invisible College

Robinson Dickemore Hawksley

CHAPTER THIRTY-TWO

Changing Seasons

Robinson hunched over the worktable, using a series of magnification lenses to study the strange device in his hands. The smell of burning pewter lingered in the air, a metallic smell that was pungent but pleasant. Wickins was sitting across from him, tightening the screws on another quicksilver tube. The last one had shattered, and they'd had to evacuate the alchemy to escape the toxic fumes from the gas. McKenna was tidying the other desk, rearranging vials and beakers and organizing the different chymicals and powders and even labeling them. In the two weeks since she'd started helping out, the alchemy had been transformed into a much more organized and efficient space.

"Rob, these papers and drawings were in the dustbin," she called out to him. "I think you should save them."

Turning his neck, he saw McKenna standing on a little black step holding a sheaf of papers, drawings he'd done months ago and then discarded.

He wrinkled his nose. "I don't need them anymore. None of those designs worked." He had a lamp near him on the desk, illuminating his face, which helped her read his lips. She'd suggested that idea too.

"Still, I think it's important to keep them," she said. "Father said that documenting things is necessary in case a patent gets disputed in court."

Robinson shrugged. "He would know. If you want to organize the rubbish bins too, you're welcome to. Speaking of your father, when does he return from the inquest?"

"We're expecting him tomorrow," she answered. "I think it finished yesterday, and he had more things to do as executor. But he said he'd be home before Closure."

The inquest had revealed little additional information. The powers that be considered it an accident, but that conclusion didn't sit well with Robinson. Aunt Margaret hadn't been a doddering older lady with weak ankles. But with the absence of additional evidence, there was only one conclusion that could be reached.

"Blast it," Wickins grunted, rubbing his hand. "I can't get it to turn!"

"They use torsion wrenches in the factories where these are made," Robinson explained to his friend. "You need more leverage is all."

Wickins grimaced and tried it again, and this time the screw moved and began to loosen. Robinson had enjoyed the intimacy of the last two weeks, of working on his invention with the woman he loved and his friend after teaching his classes at the university. McKenna, true to her word, brought or arranged for dinner to be brought every time she came. The three would sit around the small dining table, which was really only big enough for two, but they all fit, and they'd eat and talk and sometimes tell stories. Then McKenna would give him a kiss on the cheek before getting on the last street tram back to Brake Street. In a word—it was pure *bliss*. He believed he sensed some softening and deepening of her feelings, but he feared his hopes could be causing him to misinterpret the signs.

Mrs. Foster, following the interview in the greenhouse, had sent Robinson a brief, heartfelt letter absolving him of any restrictions on courting McKenna. McKenna's frequent visits to his alchemy had only strengthened his feelings for her and her regard for him. She wanted to help, to be of assistance. And now that she and Robinson were courting, it was no longer socially prohibited for them to spend additional time together, so long as Wickins was around—to reduce any appearance of impropriety. Since both he and his friend were in the Invisible College, their reputations were known and trusted.

At McKenna's request, they always spent part of their evenings together discussing magic and experimenting to see if they could manage what had never, to Robinson's knowledge, been managed before. Every day they spent together was a gift.

Wickins unscrewed the end of the bulb and then fixed it to the contraption Robinson had devised. "I think we're ready for the next test, Dickemore," he announced.

McKenna brought the dustbin papers over so she could observe.

Robinson set the device his father had given him down, the round lid open, and picked up the tuning fork he had custom made to invoke the precise complex tone coming from the floating boulder in the park. With the tuning fork, they didn't have to lose time traveling to conduct experiments. Once he had managed to mimic the exact frequency of the sound, the effect worked the same in his alchemy as it did in the park. It was proximity of the device that triggered the reaction and caused the bulb to brighten.

Wickins held the bulb in his hands eagerly. Robinson handed the device to McKenna, and she slipped it into her pocket. Robinson struck the tuning fork, which instigated the dull throbbing tone. The bulb in Wickins's hands immediately began to glow. McKenna gradually stepped backward, and the glow slowly faded.

"Ix apsis spectra," Robinson said, invoking the command for the contraption attached to the bulb. It jettisoned plumes of icy smoke, bathing the bulb with fog. It was a similar invention to what was used

on locomotivuses to cool the moving parts of the engine. They had experimented with hot and hotter temperatures up to just below the point where the bulb shattered or the metal began to liquefy. Now they were trying increasingly cold ones to see if that had any impact. They'd used ice, at first, but that had only allowed the temperature to fall to a specific point. They needed subfreezing temperatures, and cold oxygen yielded the best results.

With the cold fog billowing around the glass, there was no change in the light. McKenna stepped closer, and it grew brighter. The temperature didn't matter, only proximity to the device seemed to make a difference.

Robinson rubbed his bottom lip. He had started to shave more regularly now that McKenna was visiting frequently, but she never seemed to mind when it had been a couple of days since he'd last shaved. His mass of hair was its usual unruly self, and she seemed to like that too and would sometimes run her fingers through it when she was standing behind his chair. Her touch made little shivers go down his back.

McKenna handed the device back to him. "No change with colder temperatures," she said. "Have you tried taking the device apart?"

"I don't know how," he said with a sigh, slouching in his chair. He turned his face to look at her so she could read his lips. He rubbed his thumb along the side of the Aesir relic. "There are no screws holding it together. It was not made by mortals." He stuffed it back into his vest pocket. Then he revoked the spell, and the plumes of cold smoke began to dissipate.

Another failed attempt. But Robinson wasn't discouraged. He was determined to find another way to activate the bulb without his special device. If he could understand how it was interacting with the bulb, he could replicate the effect. With every facet he eliminated, it drew him closer to the truth. He rubbed his mouth. "I wonder what kind of metal it's made of."

Wickins set the bulb down on the table. "I'm famished."

"I brought a basket of cold sausages and cherries," McKenna said.

"Cherries? Are they in season already?" Robinson asked.

"These came from our orchard," she said. "They're a little tart, but they're still good."

They abandoned the experiment and removed themselves to the front room, where McKenna had left her basket. He still had several more hours with her before she would have to leave for the tram. Then he and Wickins would stay up well into the night, working and trying to think up new experiments to test. He wished McKenna could stay, but that would be improper. She went to the basket and brought out the stiff sausage, then handed Robinson a knife to cut the rounds. Wickins found the three mismatched cups they used to drink from and fetched some water. There were crackers and cheese in the basket as well.

They'd all gathered around the tiny table when Robinson heard the sound of footsteps approaching from outside. He lifted his head, and McKenna's flinch told him she'd noticed his reaction. A knock sounded. Firm and rapid.

Robinson pushed away from the table and walked to the door. He opened it with some trepidation and found Mr. Foster standing there, wearing his pince-nez spectacles and a top hat on his head, his suit a charcoal gray with light blue pinstripes. The family carriage was parked not far away with a driver sitting on the bench.

"Mr. Foster!" Robinson said in astonishment.

"Father?" McKenna gasped and rushed to him, giving him a fierce hug. "You're back early!"

"Indeed, and it was an exhausting trip," he said, looking beleaguered but also as though he might be battling other emotions. The look he gave Robinson was rather stern.

McKenna gazed at his face, her happiness wavering when she noticed his expression. "Is something wrong? Have you had any dinner? We were just starting."

"I came to fetch you home. I'll explain it all later. There are concerns, yes. I understand you have been spending much time in the professor's alchemy. There are many toxic fumes, my dear."

"Indeed, but we have the proper ventilation," Robinson said, feeling a prickle of unease.

"Please, Father," McKenna said. "Come join us."

Mr. Foster shook his head. "There is supper at home. Get into the carriage. I'll be there shortly."

McKenna seemed crestfallen. She glanced at Robinson, then at her father, then back again. "Well, you can have all the meal to yourselves, then. I'll be back tomorrow."

She took Robinson's hands in hers and then, in front of her father, went up on her tiptoes and kissed him on the cheek as she usually did. Robinson detected some sparks in her father's eyes when she did so. She went to the table and took up the basket and then smiled at her father and the two young men before leaving.

As soon as her back was to them, Robinson didn't hesitate to speak, knowing that his words would not be overheard. "Something is wrong, sir."

"Astute as always, Professor. I came in person not only to fetch my daughter but also to deliver a message in person regarding our full permission to court McKenna. Due to circumstances, I should like to amend it. I hope you will find my terms agreeable."

Robinson's stomach clenched with dread. These were the words of a barrister, not a doting father.

"I don't understand."

"Of course you wouldn't. You are entirely unfamiliar with certain facts, which, in due time, will be revealed. Professor Hawksley, I admire your ambition, your creativity, your work ethic. When I chose to invest in your future, I did so deliberately and knowingly. But I have also observed some defects of character. Defects that may impact the material happiness of my daughter."

It felt like Robinson had been punched in the stomach. "Defects, sir?"

"Your obsession with my daughter is one of them. You are too passionate, sir. Too hasty. That has caused no small alarm in my wife, and it causes me concern now as McKenna's father. I don't believe your motives are improper. You wish to marry her. You wish to marry her *soon*, despite the conventions of Society. Very well. So long as she is willing, you have our permission. But with conditions."

"Why must there be conditions *now*?" Robinson asked, his throat dry, his anger starting to swirl.

"There is no guarantee you will find success in your endeavors. I merely wish to reduce the risk to myself and my own. I would like you to discontinue teaching at the university and focus on the research we *originally* agreed on. This latest exploration of Aesir magic . . . I do not have confidence that it will be successfully concluded. You have strayed from our original bargain. I feel that your original plan has a stronger hope of success and future financial return. If you wish to marry my daughter, I need to see evidence that you will be able to provide for her and not be a further strain. If you refuse, then I revoke my permission for you to see McKenna and court her further. You have until Closure to make your decision. I hope that is sufficient time to consider what you stand to gain and to lose."

Robinson was dumbfounded. Mr. Foster had never treated him like this before. He had never imposed restrictions on his research. He'd been keen and curious always. Something had changed. Something had altered his, hopefully, future father-in-law's good feelings.

The anger inside Robinson's chest threatened to burst out, but he restrained it.

"Good night, Professor," Mr. Foster said with a nod and gesture with the brim of his hat before turning away and marching back to his carriage. McKenna was gazing through the window, her expression one of worry. She had no idea what her father had just said. She waved to Robinson, trying but failing to smile.

He offered a sullen wave in return, his cheeks flaming with outrage. Give up his classes just as the term was starting? After he'd asked the dean for an advance? Impossible. Give up his research to explore a path that had, in his estimation, even less hope of success than the one he was working on? He hadn't explained every jot and tittle of his side work to Mr. Foster, like his efforts to invent the magical flame that might help McKenna adjust her tone so that she might be taught to sing. And there were other ideas too. Always. He hadn't explained the dead ends he'd found exploring the other path.

The invitation to come to dinner at Closure came with an implied threat. That he would be barred from coming again in the future if he did not obey.

Mr. Foster boarded the carriage. Robinson saw McKenna begin to press him for information, but the man looked implacable as he sat down, gazing anywhere but back at the ramshackle dwelling in a mediocre part of the city.

Emotions warred inside of Robinson.

Something significant had changed. Was it the business the barrister had attended to in Siaconset? Were his own finances in disarray? Was it a combination of both or something else altogether different?

He tried to quell the hot emotions inside him as he heard Wickins approach from behind.

"Sorry, old chap. I'm so sorry."

He turned and looked at his friend's sorrowful expression.

The sting of the humiliation was even worse than the anger, but Robinson didn't look away. He didn't hang his head like a woebegone pup just barked at by a larger dog.

"I won't be treated like this," Robinson said firmly. "Not by anyone." He didn't reject the notion that Mr. Foster had a right to express his opinions on the matter. Even have a say in it. But to tell Robinson what he could research and what he could not?

His mind didn't work on command.

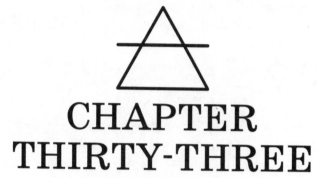

CHAPTER THIRTY-THREE

Seeking Counsel

Robinson's mental anguish and rage drove away thoughts of experiments and teaching methods for his classes and robbed him of his rekindled appetite and desire for sleep. As he tossed and turned on the sheets, he fixed in his mind a purpose. He needed advice. The next morning, he tied his cravat, put on his ill-fitting suit, and walked relentlessly through the streets of Auvinen toward the school of the deaf run by Sarah Fuller Fiske. As he tramped his own path, fixed and determined, he watched the city buzz to life. Crews were still repairing the damage done by the Aesir war, but he could hear the morning choirs singing the protective spells over the inhabitants. Street trams were starting up on schedule, delivering people to their places of work. Until Closure, of course.

It was a day he usually looked forward to, but after Mr. Foster's ultimatum, he dreaded it. Would this particular Closure sever his connection with the Foster family? With McKenna? He was still livid. It was unjust of the man to make such a demand of him. Robinson had tried to puzzle out what could have changed Mr. Foster so, but he couldn't account for the man's abrupt shift in demeanor.

"Watch out!" cried a man, driving a team of horses.

Robinson had been so distracted by his thoughts he hadn't heard the clop of hooves. He stopped and nodded his bowler hat in apology, but the man looked at him and muttered, loud enough to be heard, "stupid git," as he passed.

When he reached Mrs. Fiske's school, he was greeted by the children with such exuberance it made his throat catch. The help he had given them during their crisis had not been forgotten. They petted and jumped on him and made such a ruckus that it summoned Miss Trewitt into the corridor to see what the commotion was about, and it took some considerable effort to detangle one little girl who had wrapped herself around Robinson's leg and clung to him.

"That was quite a welcome, Professor Hawksley," Miss Trewitt said with a bright smile. "If you ever feel lonely, come here at once to be properly adored."

The same little girl looked up beseechingly at Robinson, so he squatted down to be on eye level with her.

"Happy . . . thanks," the little girl said, making the finger signs as she spoke the words.

"Happy thanks," Robinson said back to her, making the signs as well.

The little girl ran back to the classroom, and Robinson straightened again, feeling tall and lanky next to Miss Trewitt.

"I can see why McKenna adores you too."

Robinson cocked his head. "Oh? And she's told you this?"

"Several days ago, in fact. She wrote telling me about your little *interview* in the greenhouse. She asked me for advice, but I don't think she needs it. She knows her own mind."

"I'm afraid that's why I've come. I need some advice myself."

"You came to seek mine?"

"Actually, Mrs. Fiske's. How is she?"

"Her throat was damaged by the disease, but she is making progress day by day. Her doctors expect a full recovery."

"What a relief," Robinson said. Some of the sorcerers, once infected, had lost their ability to commune with magic. That, undoubtedly, had been the aim.

"We're very grateful. You were very brave, Professor. We all think so."

"That is kind of you to say. I just did what I felt was right. No more or less. Can you bring me to Mrs. Fiske?"

"Certainly. Follow me."

Mrs. Fiske was in her office, and she brightened when Robinson entered. Miss Trewitt excused herself to return to the children she was teaching. A faint antiseptic smell still lingered in the air. Mrs. Fiske greeted him by rising from the desk and embracing him.

"What brings you to the school this morning, Robinson? It's so good to see you." Her voice was scratchy and a little hoarse.

He quickly and succinctly explained the purpose of his coming, telling her of Mr. Foster's surprise visit and declaration of the terms by which he would allow continued courtship of his daughter. As he spoke, he noticed the change in her demeanor, the wrinkle of concern in her brow. She leaned back against her desk, looking at him compassionately.

"I'm very surprised by your news," she admitted. "That seems unusual. Out of character even."

"I thought so as well," Robinson said. "I feel I was bearing the brunt of a barrister's demands and not a doting father's care for his daughter."

"If it happened upon his return from the island, then McKenna must have been just as blindsided as you were. Have you spoken to her since?"

"I haven't. We weren't going to meet again until Closure. In two days."

Mrs. Fiske looked thoughtfully at him. "Has anything . . . untoward happened between you and Miss Foster?"

"Untoward" was a polite way of asking if he'd done anything dishonorable with her.

"No! We haven't even held hands. When she leaves, she kisses me on the cheek, but I should think—"

"There's no need to elaborate. I trust you implicitly, Robinson, and I know you would never deliberately injure someone. I'm reluctant to say this, as I abhor gossip in all its forms, but I have heard that the Fosters are under considerable financial strain. They've shut up their home in Bishopsgate. There is a case against a military supplier that has been dragging on in court, a case that has been very pressing and high stakes. And he won't receive his portion until it's resolved. Despite this hardship, he has never missed a promised payment to the school, but I fear he may be experiencing a great deal of professional and personal stress."

Robinson nodded. "Miss Trewitt is close to the family, so she might have been your source of such information."

Mrs. Fiske wisely nodded and did not elaborate.

"And so the prospect of taking on an indigent son-in-law has added to his worries."

"Again, I am only speculating. But it does stand to reason."

Robinson scrubbed his fingers through his untamed hair. "He's already supporting me financially. He knows where I live and would prefer not to see his daughter living in squalor."

"You could come back to my residence," Mrs. Fiske suggested. "I have not found another tenant yet. You two are more than welcome."

"I appreciate the offer. Truly. But moving again would only put me further behind in my work." He did fancy the offer, though. Perhaps, if things calmed down and McKenna was allowed to marry him, they could move back to her basement apartment?

"And how is your work going?"

Robinson sighed. "Tediously slow. I feel I'm on the verge of a great discovery, but I'm baffled by the results."

"Can you explain the dilemma to me? I might not be able to help, but I know a fair number of sorcerers."

"You're aware of the principle powering our quicksilver lamps?"

"I am indeed. When the ambient light decreases, after sundown or from fog, the intelligence embedded within the starter causes a spark, activating the coil within the lamp and causing the vapors within the tube to glow. That luminescence prevails until the ambient light returns, near sunrise, and they shut off again."

"Exactly. What I have found is the same intelligence that is harnessed in the technology of the lamps *also* responds to subacoustic frequencies that barely register with mortal eardrums and in a chord that is not common in our musical arrangements. How familiar are you with musical theory?"

"Some. Try to explain it as simply as you can."

"There are many complex chords given technical names—Dorian, Phrygian, Lydian, Locrian. The chord I discovered is a Mixolydian chord. It causes the lamp to glow based on the proximity of the sound. I believe artifacts of magic, possessed by the Aesir, trigger this response unwittingly. Imagine, if you will, the lamps in the city begin to glow when they detect the presence of the Aesir."

She blinked with surprise. "It would be a means of warning us early of an impending attack."

"It would also reduce the need for as many soldiers on the front," Robinson said. "A chain of lamps could be set up at various intervals outside of the cities, watched by spotters with field binoculars. The glow in the lamps reveals the presence of our enemies. Orders can be given to concentrate forces in those areas of danger instead of putting men in every trench."

"And each year, we could extend the borders of the lamps farther and farther to begin mapping where their strongholds may be."

"I hadn't thought that far ahead, but yes. Early detection will prevent the surprise attacks. I think this idea has enormous possibilities."

"I do as well. There are many military officers who are part of the Storrows. If you would allow me to tell them—"

"No," Robinson said firmly. "I have a device, something handed down in my family, that appears to be the key to unraveling this mystery.

It's one of a kind. As such, it makes it useless since there is only one such device. The lamp only works in the presence of this device. If I can find out how it works or the principle by which it operates, I think I can replicate the effect. This is the project Mr. Foster wants me to abandon in order to marry his daughter." He tossed his hands. "I don't know what to do."

Mrs. Fiske drew closer and touched his arm. "Then you will have to persuade him. I believe in the merits of your invention. Your curiosity and ingenuity have surprised me from the start. It may take time to figure it out. It may take *years*."

Robinson blew out his pent-up breath. "I can't wait years for her. When she's near me, she . . . she calms me. And excites me. And . . . it is a kind of torture when we're apart. I've never felt this way about someone before. When we talk, it helps me think and . . . gives me ideas to pursue. I wish I knew when the puzzle will be solved. But I don't. I can see why he'd be concerned with me marrying his daughter. But she's of age, even if she's not technically out in Society. Isn't it ultimately her decision to make? Not his?"

"I owe a great deal to Mr. Foster. His intervention with the government allowed for the creation of this school. However, that does not mean your contribution wasn't equally important. Your knowledge and your father's method will help these children have more meaningful lives."

"What should I *do*? I don't want to offend him. But I can't let him walk all over me."

"I would advise you to consider this from McKenna's perspective. What would be best for her, ultimately? He is a father. No matter what pressure he is under, he will want what is best for his daughter. That is my advice."

Robinson nodded. "Thank you. I can't tell you how much I appreciate your words. I truly hope you recover fully."

She smiled wistfully. "I have had to step down from my duties in the quorum. Another will take my rank. But that is as it should be.

Positions should be based on merit and capability, not on tradition or connection. I put *your* name in as a possible replacement. They decided on another. Someone with stronger ties to the military."

"You didn't have to do that. Or tell me even."

She nodded. "I know. I just wanted you to know how much I value you. It's only a matter of time, Professor Hawksley. Only a matter of time before the world sees in you what *I* see in you."

Her kindness caused a flutter in his chest, a flutter of warmth. He took her hand and squeezed it.

He returned to his lodgings, and before taking any of the leftover sausage and cheese for his breakfast, he went to his small experiment desk, which still had the aroma of pewter, and began to hastily write a letter.

Dear Mr. Foster:

I dispatch this letter so that you might know my mind before my arrival on Closure. I will still come unless you forbid me. However, I will not relinquish my profession. Nay, I cannot. Unless I find a vocation more profitable to me than teaching (which is unlikely) or manage to train others to take my place at the university. I do confess that I would prefer being employed in other ways, but until such ways become profitable, I cannot abandon that which provides my living.

Should your daughter McKenna come to love me as passionately and devotedly as I care for her, she will surely not object to any work in which I engage myself, on the condition that it is respectable and provides a sufficient living.

I am sorry if you have the impression, through my words, that I do not sincerely respect or value your opinions and feelings. For I do hold you in great esteem.

You are McKenna's father—and I will not urge you to give us—nor would I accept it were it offered—any pecuniary help other than what we agreed upon before you knew of my affections for your daughter.

I am compelled by the circumstances of my feelings to act as I do. I can do no less. If forbearance is a virtue, I implore you to exercise it on my behalf to your fullest extent.

Respectfully yours,
Robinson Dickemore Hawksley

MaKenna Aurora Foster

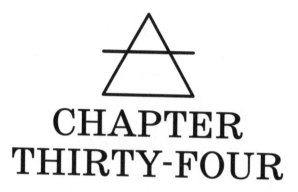

CHAPTER THIRTY-FOUR

Face-to-Face Again

Once more McKenna paced near the front window of the house on Brake Street. It was Closure and her nerves were fraught. The smells of the roast and brussels sprouts were making her nauseous. Father sat in his favorite chair in the parlor, still enigmatic, still waiting to see what would happen. Mother kept peeking in from the corridor, and every time McKenna caught a glimpse of her, she'd scowl in warning. Even Trudie and Clara were too apprehensive at that moment for any mischief.

When she turned around again, there he was, coming up the street. Father had shown McKenna the letter Rob had sent the previous day. She was *so* proud of him for standing up for himself. She had posed the same arguments when she'd found out about her father's ultimatum. As the professor came up the path, McKenna quickly opened the door and met him on the porch. She wore a forest-green muslin dress with tight cuffs. And she had done up her hair in a coiffure that was simple but elegant. She bit her lower lip out of sheer nerves, but she was fixed in purpose. Resolved. And yet her stomach felt as if she were on a swing soaring over a precipice. She loved that word. "Precipice."

"Miss McKenna," Rob said, looking at her with surprise and admiration. He reached for her hand and took it when she gave it to him.

"Might we go to the greenhouse again?" she suggested. The last time, she'd whirled away with hot cheeks and hadn't even waited for an answer, but this time she was determined not to let her manners lapse.

"Am I . . . welcome in the house?" he asked deliberately.

"Of course you are. There are some things I need to say to you, and I would prefer to do so with some privacy."

His countenance wilted and she realized he was expecting to be rejected. He had come to say goodbye. That would not do. Not at all.

"Please, Rob, if we could talk before you worry too much? I think . . . I hope, at least, you will like what I have to say."

Her words clearly startled him, but she squeezed his hand, and she led him quickly through the house, noticing once again her mother peeking around the corner. McKenna nearly stamped her foot with impatience, but she didn't—she wouldn't be petulant. She would be poised. Even if her stomach wouldn't quit somersaulting.

When they arrived at the greenhouse, the plants were even richer and taller. The weather was very mild with just a hint of summer in the late afternoon breezes. Winter seemed very far away.

"First of all," McKenna said, after shutting the greenhouse door and sidling closer to him, "I want to apologize for my father's conduct the other day. I told him he owes you an apology himself, but let me be the first to state that his words were unconscionable."

"'Unconscionable'?" He grinned at her use of the word and closed what little gap there was between them. He looked as if he were about to stroke her hair. A little shiver of anticipation went through her. Instead, he took off his bowler hat and put it down on one of the wooden tables. His hair was a mess, but it was a lovely sort of mess. A mess that needed taming. His face hadn't suffered a razor in days.

She blinked again, trying to master herself. "That's the first thing I needed to say. Let me explain as best I can. Father had just returned from Siaconset and the inquest regarding my aunt's death. It was ruled to be accidental, although one of the servants said she heard a man's voice coming from the sitting room. It wasn't Mr. Swope. There's no accounting for who it might have been, but it was odd enough that an inquest had to investigate the matter. With no conclusive evidence otherwise, it was ruled an accident." She paused, feeling she'd been talking too fast and was a little out of breath.

"I am sorry, Miss McKenna. It's a tragedy, truly."

"Thank you for saying so. Now, the second part. I'm not saying this to excuse his behavior, but Father is under a great deal of stress. I didn't realize how severe the stress was until he returned. After he told me about his conversation with you, I was shocked. He had no right to tell you what kind of career you should have, or to set such expectations on *me*. I was really quite furious. But then Mother explained something I didn't know." She paused again, biting her lower lip. "You see, none of us knew that Aunt Margaret had named *me* as her heir. That was part of the inquest, to see if there were any circumstances that might void her will. Father didn't tell us until he got home. And he was worried, you see, he was worried what might happen to her fortune. It will be in probate for a few months, but then I will have access to all of it."

Rob's mouth hung open at her declaration.

"I think my aunt was worried about you taking advantage of me if you knew about it. So no one knew. She didn't even tell my parents. Mowbray House is to be mine. I told Father that I wanted to use some of the money to help him in his financial situation. He did not feel it was right to influence me to try and solve his problems, but after all he has done for me, for my education, for helping me to *speak*, for finding you . . ." She shook her head. "I can do no less. It would be so ungrateful if I didn't. I hope you understand."

"I'm . . . I'm quite astonished. But happy for you. That gives you freedom, Miss McKenna. Freedom that most young ladies never have."

"I know," she said, grinning. "Now for the last part." She took both of his hands in hers and steadied herself. Her mouth was so dry. "I . . . I love you better than anyone but Mama. Truly, I do. And if you can be satisfied with so much love, then I think . . . I would ask . . . that we be engaged to be married this very day."

"Miss McKenna!" he gasped in incredulity.

She nodded eagerly to him. "You chose me before you knew about my wealth. Once Society learns of my great expectations, I am sure there will be several . . . maybe more than several unscrupulous young men who will desire my hand to get control of it. How can I trust them?"

"Miss McKenna," he murmured, shaking his head.

"You cannot refuse me," she insisted. "You can have whatever profession you wish. I don't care. I think you are a wonderful man, and I believe that you love me sincerely. I . . . happen to love you quite well. I know it hasn't been long, but I don't want to wait. I think I know your character. You've been to Brake Street countless times. I've seen how you are with children, with my sisters, my parents . . . how honorable you are to everyone, even those who don't deserve it. So I really think—"

"Miss McKenna," Rob interrupted. He looked so conflicted as he squeezed her hands. Not conflicted about how he felt, but about what this news might mean. "We *must* delay. Especially in light of such a revelation. There is no need to rush. The inheritance makes no difference to me. But you are still very young. You have . . . you have options now you didn't have before. You haven't seen other men. Please. I couldn't—"

She wasn't going to allow his fastidiousness to interfere with her decision. "Don't you understand? This is my choice, Rob. My parents have left it totally up to me. No one is pressuring me. No one is telling me what is best. Or what I *ought* to do. So I've decided. I. Choose. You."

He pulled one hand away to run it through his hair. "When I came here, I was in the deepest despair."

"I know, darling. I can only imagine. I'm sorry for that."

"I thought I might never see you again. That I would have to say goodbye."

"I want to see you every *day*. I want to help you in your work. I want to be part of it."

He looked overwrought as he took both her hands again. "So . . . you've asked me to marry you? Just to be clear? An engagement?"

"I have. Why shouldn't I? We don't have to hurry anything. Just . . . let's be honest with each other. Always. I care for you. I love you. And I think you will make me very happy."

At her words, he pulled her toward him and hugged her. She'd never been embraced like that before. She could smell the scent of his shirt, of his laundry soap. There was another smell there too . . . something strangely familiar that echoed through her memory. She was stiff, at first, unsure of how to respond, but then she wrapped her arms around him and leaned her head against his chest since he was so much taller than her. And as she pressed her ear closer, she sensed the throb of his heartbeat. The pulse thumping, thumping, thumping. And it made her smile. A delicious, warm feeling chased away her nerves.

He released one of his arms and tipped her chin so she could read his lips.

"They're watching us from the window," Rob said with a soft chuckle.

McKenna turned her head and saw the parlor curtain open. Mother was gripping Father's arm, beaming with happiness. Father had a little smile on his mouth and gave her an affectionate nod. Clara said something to Trudie to make her laugh, but they both looked pleased. In their way, they were welcoming Rob to the family, and that made her heart glad. She buried her face against his chest again and sighed. Then she lifted her eyes to his mouth again.

"You still haven't accepted my proposal."

He took her hands, kissed her knuckles, and then lowered himself down on one knee. Now she was higher than him. That felt strange, having this teacher, this friend, and now lover gazing at her so openly, so passionately. It made her head swim.

"I could never say no to a lady," he said, then kissed her knuckles again. "Everything I have or will have, everything I am . . . is yours, McKenna Aurora Foster." He bent his neck a little, looking behind her.

"What are they doing now?" she demanded, knowing she and her fiancé were a spectacle.

"They are . . . applauding."

"I suppose we should join them?"

Rob rose and reclaimed his hat, which he held to his chest and gave a mock bow to the family on the other side of the windows.

"When may I kiss you?" he asked her.

That was an interesting question, but she didn't want their first kiss to be in the greenhouse, witnessed by the entire family.

"Not yet. But soon."

It happened later that night, on the doorstep of the house on Brake Street, in the shadow of the porch. Bugs were flitting around the glowing lamp. It was a very quick and light kiss, a brief touching of lips. They were both uncertain. Shy. Nervous but eager.

And it gave her the strangest feeling . . .

As he walked away, McKenna felt the moment of bliss was all too familiar. That she had kissed him before. Only she couldn't remember it.

CHAPTER THIRTY-FIVE

Past Memories

McKenna awoke, expecting to find herself amidst the blizzard that was in her dreams. The noise of the wind, so strange in her ears, the sting of the sleet on her skin, and the blood-spattered snow were as real and vivid as anything in her life. She'd had dreams like this before, all jumbled and confusing and incredibly real. Only they never lasted. She always forgot the details, but a disquieting feeling lingered regardless.

Upon waking, she jumped out of bed, rushed to the little writing desk beneath the window, and quickly began scratching words on the paper. *Snow. Blood. Magic. Shrieking. Find him. Find him. FIND HIM.*

And then the images, the memories, were lost again. Snatched from her mind like tart cherries plucked from the sagging tree limbs in the garden. The ink pen trembled in her hand, a large blot of ink dripping and staining the page. She stared at the words she'd written, unable to remember why she'd written them. The dream was gone once more.

McKenna began to feel desperate. There was something *wrong* with her. There had been since her near-drowning.

The sunlight was pouring into the room. The heat was stifling, even though she now slept with the windows open all night. It still couldn't get cold enough. Even sleeping with several of her nightgown buttons undone scarcely helped. Her body *craved* the cold. She didn't know why. Maybe the summer would be intolerably hot this year.

She looked down at the paper, saw the words, and they startled her. She didn't remember writing them, but there was no denying it was in her handwriting. Had she scribbled a note before going to bed last night? Anxiety began to spike inside her chest. Why had she written those words? They didn't make sense. Yet there was a nagging feeling, a frenzied feeling, something that warned her of forgotten things.

McKenna stripped off the nightgown and changed into her outfit for the day. But with each tug of the corset straps, her mind niggled at her, insisting she'd forgotten something important. Something *paramount*. Yes, that was the right word for it. "Paramount."

She was sticking in her earrings when she noticed Mother's face in the mirror's reflection. She was holding a letter in her hand. A letter written in Rob's handwriting.

"This came with the first post," Mother said, smiling. She smoothed her hand through McKenna's long hair. "How are you feeling this morning?"

"Unsettled," McKenna answered, her voice halting.

Mother's smile wilted with worry. "What's wrong?"

"I don't know. I . . . I can't say, but I'm very troubled right now."

Mother knelt by the cushion McKenna was seated on and searched her face. "Darling, I was afraid of this."

"Afraid of what?"

"That you might have rushed into your engagement. It is perfectly natural to have second thoughts."

"You think I do?"

"I don't know. Your behavior of late has been . . . alarming. Darling, it would not be wrong to postpone it. Maybe you need more time?

Maybe we all do? The pressures of Society are intimidating, and you haven't even had your debut yet."

"You think these feelings are because I'm anxious about Society?" McKenna asked.

McKenna noticed Mother surreptitiously positioning the letter behind her back. "Maybe some more time will be helpful. I can take you elsewhere. We can go on a trip . . . to Bishopsgate or . . . somewhere new. Get away from Auvinen for just a few weeks."

As soon as Mother said those words, McKenna felt a spike of panic that made her jump up from her cushioned seat. "No!"

"Darling, what are your feelings telling you? Listen to them."

"This isn't about the engagement at all."

Mother stood and tried to put her hand on McKenna's shoulder, but the feelings churning inside her were so powerful, so charged that McKenna nearly fled from the bedroom. Like that time she'd stood up to her aunt. And now her aunt was dead.

What if it's my fault?

That eerie thought flashed in her mind, adding to her distress. It made no sense, but then again, none of it did. Her mind was a jumble. She wanted to run. She wanted to flee to Rob. She could almost see herself running down the street, hurrying to catch a street tram that would bring her to her fiancé. The urgency of the feeling was so powerful it was overwhelming. She needed to find him. *Find him. Find him.*

She saw Mother try to speak, but McKenna ran for the door. The only thought burning in her mind was the need to get to Rob. They had to get married that very day. She didn't understand why, but nothing else mattered. The force of the conviction brought tears to her eyes. Something was going to happen to him. She was going to *lose* him.

Find him. Find him. Find him.

McKenna sobbed as she hurtled down the stairs. She nearly tripped but caught herself on the banister. Her feelings were so intense she couldn't bear them.

She was nearly to the door when Clara intervened. Her sister interposed herself and gripped the handle behind her, leaning back to block the exit.

"Get out of my way!" McKenna shrieked at her sister.

Clara stood stone-faced. Implacable. She shook her head.

McKenna tried to shove her aside, but her sister was taller than her and stronger. She looked like a woman now, her hair done up smartly, a little hat perched atop it, her violet dress and corset cut in an incredibly fashionable style. Clara was elegant, beautiful, and clever, but she did not yet have any suitors.

"Get . . . away!" McKenna shouted. A spell came to her mind. A spell that would knock her sister and the door away in a burst of fury.

Clara shook her head once more, resolutely.

"Klaximora," McKenna breathed softly, holding out her hand. But nothing happened. Not even the smallest ripple came from her. Not even a sigh of wind.

Mother reached them and seized McKenna. The pent-up burst of emotion fizzled out, and McKenna allowed herself to be led to the parlor, tears dripping down her cheeks. Suddenly she felt ashamed of herself for her outburst. It wasn't like her at all. What by the heavens had possessed her to think she could actually *use* magic against her sister? It was ridiculous.

A few minutes later, McKenna's tears had turned into hiccups. Her cheeks were pink and so was her nose. The wildness inside her had been tamed. She felt herself again, and as her breathing calmed down, the strangeness of the world became normal again. There was the Broadwood grand. There was Father's favorite chair. In her mind's eye, she could picture an evening after dinner with company and Professor Hawksley playing the violin for the family. And her heart burned with pride at watching him swish the bow across the strings so deftly.

Finally even the hiccups subsided. She looked up through swollen eyes and saw the tolerant and loving face of her mother. For some reason, she'd felt like a threat earlier. But that was a wild fancy. No one loved her like Mother did.

"I'm sorry," McKenna apologized. "That was . . . dreadful of me."

"Hush, say no more of it," Mother answered, stroking her forehead. "I still think we should go away for a few days. Your aunt's death. Your engagement. These are all rather sudden."

McKenna shook her head and took Mother's hands. "I don't want to go to Bishopsgate or anywhere else. I belong here, with my family."

"You will always belong here," Mother said. "But please listen to me. I think you should consider—"

"No," McKenna said emphatically. "I'm not afraid of marrying him. No, what's strange is I want it to happen right now. I can't explain it. It was such a powerful feeling. I didn't realize how dear he has become to me." She blinked, amazed at the words coming out of her mouth. "Can I see the letter, please?"

"Are you sure? You seem calmer now."

"I am, truly. I'm not going to run away."

"I was worried you might," Mother said. "I've never seen you that way before."

"I was upset by something. I don't remember what. Maybe it was a dream."

"What did you dream about, darling?" She smoothed McKenna's hair over her ear.

"I don't remember. It's so strange. I haven't been remembering my dreams lately. Not since I almost drowned."

"That was very frightening, to be sure. Each day is a gift. None of us are entitled to any more or less than what the Mind of the Sovereignty has planned for us. Ashes to ashes. Dust to dust."

"Justice claimeth its own," McKenna finished. "Can I see Rob's letter?"

Mother turned her head so McKenna missed her response, but shortly afterward Trudie came in, looking nervously at McKenna. She had Rob's letter in her hand and gave it over.

McKenna gazed at the handwriting and felt a keen desire to read it privately. She knew her mother would want to know what it said, but she felt it should be read alone, by herself. She fidgeted with the letter in her hands. The open curtain revealed a glimpse of the greenhouse outside, so she rose and walked there by herself.

Once inside the greenhouse, she breathed in the fragrances of the tomato bushes and herb gardens that filled the air. The sunlight made it much warmer than the house, and so McKenna opened some of the buttons of her dress, exposing her skin to the fresh air. She fondled the letter in her hands and then carefully opened it. She was smiling before she even started reading it. No blots or crossed-out words this time.

McKenna Aurora Hawksley,

This is the first time I have written those words, words so precious, so sacred to me. To blend our names together is a heady feeling. I shan't grow tired of it.

You must not scold me if I sit up for a little while longer tonight—even if it is very late—to write a few lines to you. My dearest. My beloved.

I could not imagine when I went to Brake Street this afternoon the surprise in store for me in your greenhouse. As I walked there, you seemed to be—shall I say it?—drifting away from me. So far away where I might never see you again. So many things loomed between us. I almost despaired.

Yet I was wrong. Rather than drifting away, you were nearer than ever. If only I could have heard your thoughts whispering hope to calm my fears. I can scarcely credit that you really and truly love me. That you have chosen to be my wife. Honestly, I am afraid to go to sleep lest I find it all a dream. How can I dispel this irrational fear? My remedy—I shall lie awake and think of you.

Life would be so cold and selfish living all for one's own self, one's own happiness. I think a man is only half a man who has no one to cherish. It shall be my endeavor and paramount aim—McKenna—to protect you and to love you. With all my heart. Please do not go away from me. Not anymore. I could not bear it. I must go where you go. We walk hand in hand for now and evermore.

I pray this—that we may be a comfort and support to one another always.

Yours and yours only,
Robinson

McKenna clutched the paper to her bosom, feeling the smooth sheet against her skin. She was blushing fiercely. Her throat felt tight. It was the most lovely thing she had ever read, better than anything in even the best of novels. His feelings were expressed so openly, so proudly, that she could not feel anything but resplendent joy. Her love had brought him such happiness. And he had made her *incandescently* happy. How strange that her feelings had altered so dramatically so quickly. But it was joyous, and she wanted to savor it.

The whirlwind of passion from earlier intruded on her thoughts. But what if something happened to him? What if he died? Agitation swelled within her heart again. She wished he were there, in the greenhouse, wished with all her heart she could press him to her instead of just his words.

No, she would not give in to such worrisome thoughts. McKenna swallowed. She would be strong. She would be determined. They would spend part of every day together.

Nothing would tear them apart.

The happiness of your life depends upon the quality of your thoughts. Therefore, guard them well. Take care that you entertain no notions unsuitable to virtue and reasonable nature. Not every thought that enters your mind is yours.

—Isaac Berrow,
Master of the Royal Secret,
the Invisible College

Robinson Dickemore Hawksley

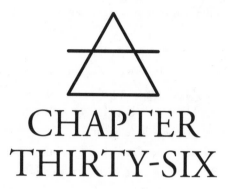

CHAPTER THIRTY-SIX

Aesir Gold

It had been a full day of classes and research in the Storrows, but then McKenna had come with dinner and to help organize things, and the company and companionship were so pleasurable that the hours had shot away. Now it was time for Robinson to escort her to catch the street tram back to Brake Street. They held hands as they walked down the avenue.

"For our honeymoon, I have an idea," McKenna said, her eyes flashing with eagerness.

When she'd arrived at his quarters, one of the first things she'd wanted to talk about was fixing a date for their wedding. Robinson had balked at the suggestion of having it the very next week. Surely waiting until the end of the term would be more pragmatic. It surprised him a little that *he* was the one urging delay.

He turned to face her so she could read his lips. "Oh? I'd rather thought we could visit Covesea. I haven't been there in ages. I'd like to show you where I grew up."

She beamed. "I'd like that very much."

"But what was your idea, McKenna?" He was permitted to dispense with the "Miss" now that they were engaged.

"I want to take you to Tanhauser. You need to see Shopenhauer's opera."

He gazed at her in amazement. "I've always wanted to see it."

"I know. But I would enjoy seeing the look on your face as *you* enjoyed it. You've played the aria for my family many times. I know you love music. And I won't be bored if I'm with you. The costumes are nice. So is the stage decor. Very elegant."

"I've heard they are rather elaborate," Robinson said.

"Especially the costumes. Do you think the Aesir truly dress like that?"

"Like what?" he asked, squeezing her hand.

"I don't know how to describe it. Long flowing robes. Armor made of hide leather. And all the jewelry. Crowns, tiaras, rings, necklaces. So beautiful. But all made of white gold. Never yellow. Why is that?"

"It's part of the legend," Robinson explained. "There's a river in their snowbound lands up north, the only source of white gold. Of course, it's *not* white gold chymically speaking."

She looked confused. "What is it, then?"

"It's an alloy. I think seventy-five percent gold and twenty-five percent nickel and zinc. I don't remember the exact combination, but it gleams like silver with an even greater luster. To the Aesir, it's a sacred metal and the one they embed with magical properties. On the stage, it is probably an imitation. Real white gold is very expensive."

"Then that's what I'm getting as your wedding ring!" she exclaimed.

"No," Robinson said, shaking his head. "I'd be happy with a cobalt band. *You* are more valuable to me than metal."

She blushed at the compliment. "Well, we can consider it anyway. So can I take you to the opera, my love?"

"How can I refuse such thoughtfulness?" he said. "I've always wanted to go. And you speak the language fluently. It would be a dream come true." His words caused a little alteration in her expression. "You made a face. Why?"

"Oh. Dreams. I've had terrible nightmares of late, only I can't remember them when I wake up. It's awful."

"I'm sorry to hear that. Nightmares?"

"Yes, but I can't remember anything about them. I woke up so agitated this morning. But it was all a dream. I even tried to cast a spell on my sister! On Clara! Isn't that strange?"

"That is certainly unlike you. What spell?"

"I don't remember it anymore. But the command came to my mind and I said it. Clara doesn't remember what I said. She thought I was raving mad. And maybe I was. But I feel so much calmer now." She swung their arms in sympathy together. "Now that I'm with you. There's the tram."

Sure enough, Robinson could hear the metallic clop of hooves as it approached down the rail. They reached the street corner well ahead of it, and it stopped to pick up another passenger. They waited at the corner, still holding hands. She looked so beautiful to him. Feelings like bees swarmed inside his chest. If he hadn't borrowed his salary in advance, he would have been tempted to ask the dean for a brief leave of absence in order to marry her. But it was wiser to wait until the end of the term, which was only a few weeks away. Then there would be a gap before the next one started with the onset of summer. He'd never spent a summer in Auvinen, but he'd heard how miserable hot it could be. Covesea was mild. And so was Siaconset, thankfully.

"I hate having to leave you," she confessed, gazing up at him. "Promise me you'll get some sleep tonight."

He sighed. "I won't make empty promises." He brought her hand to his mouth and kissed her knuckles. "Not even for you."

The tram approached. It was rather full, but there was still plenty of room. She leaned up on her tiptoes. He thought she'd kiss his cheek, but she surprised him with a kiss on his mouth. He could still taste the raspberries from their dinner, and it made him thrill.

"Don't stay up too late," she said. "I'll see you tomorrow."

"I wish it were tomorrow already," he said. He watched her climb aboard the tram and stayed until it went out of sight. She took a bench facing him.

He mouthed the words *"I love you."*

She smiled in response, a pleased smile. When she was out of sight, he sighed at the burst of energy in his step and started back to his quarters. He would love to see the play about the most famous legend of the Aesir. He knew the score well, and the thought of it being played by one of the best orchestras in the known world was absolutely thrilling. Tickets to the opera were expensive. He felt a little guilty about it, but it was a gesture of love, and that meant everything.

When he got back, Wickins was finishing up the rest of dinner. The man had a prodigious appetite, yet never added to his weight.

"You've a gem, Dickemore. A gem. I don't know what she sees in you, but thank the Mind she sees something. Her sister is a real catch too."

"Aren't you waiting to become a captain before you marry?" Robinson reminded him.

"It's a sensible plan, and my parents insist I not beggar myself or the family by wedding prematurely. Once I have a commission, I'm free to choose who I will. But I don't think Clara Aurora Foster will wait that long."

He was probably right. Robinson went into the alchemy and sat down at the desk. He pulled out the device his father had given him and examined it again. They'd still made no headway in their experiments with it. He opened the lid and looked at the crystal with the numbers on it. Unchanged, of course.

The little adjustable dials in the middle were concentric circles. Rings. The little markings on the edge were different, suggesting each tracked a different measurement of some kind. The dials were tinged yellow, so he'd assumed them to be copper or brass. Maybe bronze. But, remembering his conversation with McKenna, he had to wonder if they might be gold. They looked burnished, dark, but gold did tarnish over time.

He summoned a light with his magic and then held the piece underneath the lens again. He squinted, studying it closely. The edges of the dials were the same burnished color he'd known. It was important not to expose base metals to certain solvents or it would be destroyed. Yet . . . that had never happened with this Aesir device. Maybe it wasn't tarnish he was seeing but an alloy?

As he stared at the rings, he imagined the one McKenna would buy for him for their wedding day vows.

Wait . . .

What if the metal bands within the device weren't dials at all? Could he just be seeing the edges of them? What if they were rings? It seemed a ludicrous thought, and yet it rang true to him. But if he was right, how could he get one of them out? He had tried all sorts of combinations and nothing had ever worked. He gazed at the device closely, using his thumbs to twist one circle, then another, hearing the little clicks.

He had always had very delicate hearing. Robinson lifted the device closer to his ear and twisted one of the rings. Concentrating, he tried to blot out the sounds of Wickins in the other room. When that failed, he stuffed a towel in the bottom of the door and went back to the desk. He held the device right up to his ear and used his fingers to twist the same ring.

As the dial went around, he heard a subtle but different click. He marked the position of the dial, then spun it around and went to that same spot. He heard the subtle difference again. Excitement began to throb inside his chest. He examined the markings under the magnifying glass, but there was no differentiation between them, so he added a little dab of paint to mark the spot. Then, holding the piece close again, he twisted the second ring. He missed the subtle difference on the first rotation and had to turn it around again, but on the second attempt, he noticed the change and marked it with another color. There were four inner rings with markings and an outer ring without. Well, the outer ring had eight little nibs on it, but it didn't move. Neither did the innermost ring. It was the other four that could be manipulated.

As he worked to figure out the positions that generated the acutely different sound, hours passed barely noticed. Finally, he had four different markings, which he believed were the four combination points required to access the device. The fact that the device did not activate or change suggested he needed to align them in a certain order. Which ring to move first?

Well, there were a limited number of sequences possible. With only four interior rings, he could test those possible outcomes individually. He scratched his trials on a piece of paper on the desk, using the four colors of paint he'd dabbed on the rings as his guide.

It was on the fourth try that he heard a different sound in response to the combination white, blue, red, green. Another faint click happened, a different sound he hadn't heard before.

Robinson's eyes widened. The metal sheath around the embedded crystal moved. It moved!

Breathlessly, with trembling hands, he pried at the innermost ring and nearly came out of his chair when it slid out effortlessly.

It was a *ring*, not a gear. A ring meant to be worn. The other rings appeared to be there only to lock in this one. The band was white gold—or, as he guessed—an alloy of gold, palladium, or some other combination. He turned the little ring over, examining the outer and then inner surface. Smooth, except for the ridged edge of the band on the upper side. On the inner side of the band was an engraving of the symbol of the Invisible College—the compass and square. The piece was slightly larger than one that would go on a finger, so the original owner either had big hands, or it was meant to be worn on a thumb. The inner marking shocked him because this wasn't an Aesir device after all. It had been made by some long-ago sorcerer.

He didn't hesitate.

Robinson slipped the ring on his thumb and instantly felt as if a knife had stabbed his mind. The pain was excruciating.

Wickins! I need your help!

He didn't say the words. He couldn't make his mouth work for the pain. He struggled against the agony, which felt as though it would never subside, and then it did. He blinked, eyes watering.

"My goodness," he breathed heavily, sitting back in his chair. The pain had ended, but someone was . . . whispering. Whispers were all around him.

He blinked again, this time in confusion. He looked around, finding himself alone, the will-o'-the-wisp of magic still dancing in the air where he had summoned it.

The door handle jostled. Robinson turned again, confused, and saw Wickins pushing away the towel that was wedged there.

"Do you have any idea what time it is, Dickemore? I went to bed hours ago."

There was whispering still. Whispering *everywhere*. Words were distinguishable but incomprehensible. The whispers were being spoken in a different language.

"Do you . . . hear that?" Robinson asked.

"Hear what? Why did you call me?"

"I didn't call you."

"You most certainly did. I heard you loud as a bell. 'Wickins, I need your help.' I'm here. What do you want?"

The importance of the moment was beginning to dawn on Robinson. He gripped the edge of his desk. "Go back into the other room."

"Are you feeling well, old chap?"

"Just go. And come if I call you."

Wickins sighed and walked away, shutting the door.

Robinson didn't say a word. He thought it. *Come back.*

The door handle turned. "What?" his friend asked, a little too impatiently.

I didn't say anything. Robinson didn't. Not with his lips. He was using his thoughts.

"You most certainly did!" Wickins objected.

I am not speaking.

Wickins stood there, dumbfounded, gazing at Robinson with a mingling of perplexity and excitement.

You can hear me. Say the name you call me. Dickemore.

"Dickemore," Wickins whispered in awe. "We're going to be *rich*."

CHAPTER THIRTY-SEVEN

Conundrum Explained

A firm knock sounded on the door in the other room. Robinson, exhausted but elated, looked up from the worktable.

"Knock at the door. I think it's your father," he said to McKenna, who was standing next to him, handling one of the quicksilver tubes. She set it down and then rushed out of the room to answer the door.

Wickins was chewing on the end of a pencil, then he scratched a few more notes. He looked up with a grin. "Every single lamp worked. You've done it, old chap. You've done it!"

Robinson felt relieved, giddy, and exhausted. After teaching his final class that day, he had literally run all the way home so they could continue the work. Wickins had picked up the samples they'd needed. The dinner McKenna had brought remained uneaten, due to all the excitement. When he'd demonstrated the results of the tests for her, she'd insisted on sending a post to her father to summon him directly.

Mr. Foster entered the alchemy with his daughter, carrying three bags of steaming spiced peanuts, the smell of which arrived before he did.

"You haven't eaten all day," McKenna said. "And you deserve a little treat after such a breakthrough." She handed a bag to Wickins and one to her fiancé.

For such a taciturn man, his eyes were gleaming with interest and his expression was one of bridled excitement. "My daughter's note was rather too cryptic for a barrister such as myself, but if she is correct, then I suppose some congratulations are in order?"

"See for yourself, Mr. Foster," Wickins said midyawn, while stretching. He was unable to conceal a triumphant grin.

"Why don't you explain things first, Professor," Mr. Foster insisted.

"I'll grab a chair from the kitchen," McKenna offered. She already knew how it worked.

Robinson scratched the back of his neck and then picked up the tuning fork. "As I told you before, Aesir magic seems to conduct at a certain pitch, one beyond the range of human hearing. A deep pitch. The conundrum we faced was that the pitch we were trying to detect would only produce light in the quicksilver lamps when my device was in proximity."

"The device your father gave you."

"Exactly. The device acted as a sort of combination lock, like the kind used in safes. Today, or technically sometime last night, I managed to figure out the combination."

"And how did you accomplish that?" Mr. Foster asked, impressed.

"I've always had a unique gift of distinguishing fine sounds. I had to concentrate, but I was able to discern the difference in the clicking noises made by the dials. I also discovered that there was a pattern to the combination."

"That came after the fact, Dickemore," Wickins said. "He used little drips of paint first."

"Indeed so. The combination, apparently, is three, one, four, one, and . . . ? As a sorcerer yourself, that number should be significant to you."

"It's the ratio of a circle's circumference to its diameter. The last digit should be five."

"Well, it's almost six. I found the last click just before six. This device I've been carrying was invented by a sorcerer, *not* the Aesir."

"Even I knew it," Wickins said proudly. "Tell him what happened next!"

"Once the combination was correct, the crystal at the top of the device could be moved up, and the inner ring came out. It bears the marking of the Invisible College. It's a thumb ring. I put it on and—"

"You did what?" Mr. Foster exclaimed.

"I put it on."

"That was incredibly risky! Handling unknown artifacts is vastly dangerous."

"He's all right, Father," McKenna soothed. "Although it did give him a splitting headache!"

"It still does," Robinson confessed. "You see, it's the composition of the metal that matters. The ring is made of Aesir gold—white gold. A specific ratio of gold, palladium, cobalt, and platinum, to be precise. I have the calculations right here," he said, brushing his hand over a piece of paper before extending it to Mr. Foster to examine. He then scooped up some of the peanuts and ate them. McKenna beamed at him.

Mr. Foster squinted, looking at the calculations. "And it has to be precisely so?"

"Yes," Robinson said. "Apparently the structure of this alloy has certain acoustic properties." He picked up the tuning fork and then rang it against the edge of the desk.

All of the quicksilver bulbs immediately responded, simultaneously, and started to glow. The brightness chased away the darkness from within the alchemy.

"And it still works, Father," McKenna said enthusiastically, "even if the device is kept in another room. It's the *alloy*."

"But how did you figure out the alloy so quickly?" Mr. Foster asked. "It should have taken weeks to determine the precise mixture."

"I presumed so as well, sir," Robinson answered. "I know that white gold is three parts gold, mixed with other metals. All I can say is while I was combining them, the right combination came to my mind through intuition based on each ingredient's unique weight. And it is not so unlike the ratio contained in a circle as well. I must give credit to the Unseen Powers, though. I knew the ratio almost immediately after performing some calculations. I've created several other variants, and they don't work at all."

"And how did you get the lamps to work?" Mr. Foster asked, picking up one of the tubes, capped on each end with metal. But he noticed the different color affixed to the end nearest the glass. "You've added a wire of this new gold?"

"It doesn't require much," Robinson said.

"Which means it will be inexpensive to replicate," Wickins offered. "Any quicksilver tube can be turned into a sensing device. If an Aesir comes near it with magic, the tubes will start to glow automatically, alerting us of their presence."

"This is an incredible discovery," Mr. Foster said. McKenna squeezed her father's arm, nodding vigorously.

"And he doesn't know the best part yet," Wickins said smugly.

"There is more?" Foster asked in disbelief.

Robinson stood up from his chair. "Sir, when I put the ring on my thumb, I began hearing whispers. They were inaudible to anyone but me—or someone else wearing the ring. When Wickins wore it, he knew at once the whispers were in the language of the Aesir. I'm certain they are not voices. They are *thoughts*. When I put on the ring, I was able to communicate to Wickins, even though he was asleep in another room. He could hear my thoughts as if I'd spoken them aloud. And when he tried it on, he began to decode the words. First, let me demonstrate this to you."

Robinson pulled out the device. He dialed in the combination, which allowed him to release the inner ring again. He took it out and then slipped it on his thumb. He gritted his teeth, prepared for the pain, and it struck him with the same force as before. It took him a moment to collect himself, to acclimate to the pressure in his mind. Then he stared at Mr. Foster.

Incombinant Duo, he thought to the other man.

Mr. Foster's eyes widened with shock. He'd spoken a password from the Invisible College. A verbal greeting from one sorcerer to another that would allow each to identify the other as a member.

Robinson slipped off the ring, and immediately the headache lessened. It could take several minutes for the pain to totally go away, which meant wearing the ring permanently was not a realistic option.

"I heard you," Mr. Foster said.

"We haven't tested the full extent of the range," Robinson explained. "But so far it appears to be quite extensive. Not only can I send my thoughts through the aether, but I can receive them as well. We've discovered those whispers are actually communications from the Aesir. This is where the lieutenant was especially helpful. Tell him."

Wickins smiled with pride. "Sir, my specialty in the military is signals intelligences. Sending orders to various troop deployments. Forwarding responses along the chain of command. I have been studying the Aesir language for some time now and recognized it immediately. It is the language of their thoughts. I believe—*we* believe—that we can now intercept their communications."

"It means you can also know where they will attack next," Mr. Foster said. His face became inscrutable, but he was thinking deeply on the implications. "Would they not then be able to intercept your thoughts? Isn't this dangerous?"

"I wondered that at first," Robinson said. "The thoughts we've intercepted appear to be some sort of subconscious commands. Not conversations. The commands continued whether or not we thought something of our own. I think a sorcerer invented this device for the precise purpose of listening in to their communication. The quicksilver tubes can give us early warning of their movements. The ring, and hopefully we can make *more* of them, will enable us to listen in to their command hierarchy. Imagine what we can learn!"

Mr. Foster nodded slowly. He looked from one young man to the other. "This information must be kept in the strictest of confidences. Neither of you can tell anyone about this, especially no one from the military *until* I have submitted a patent for the alloy with the Industry of Magic. I will travel to Bishopsgate at once, this very evening, if you can prepare a copy of your papers and a description of the effects. This . . . has the potential to revolutionize our society."

Wickins took a fistful of peanuts and began to shovel them into his mouth, grinning from ear to ear.

McKenna gave Robinson a hug, gazing at him with happiness.

"You think this is a valuable discovery as well?" Robinson asked Mr. Foster.

The gleam in the man's eyes said more than his next words. "It will shape the future, my boy. In ways we cannot yet see. I was wrong to have doubted you. But this is only the beginning. Someone else may figure out the same alloy. They will try to claim it as their own. It is imperative we keep this confidential until the rights can be secured. Then . . . then we shall see."

So much of what we do is done because we fear the disapproval of others. The inclination to steal is subverted when we contemplate the reaction of a stern judge and formidable barristers knowledgeable of our faults and ready to mete out punishments. We believe in the Mind of the Sovereignty because we cannot, innately, imagine an existence in which there is not an all-powerful witness—in the wind, in the trees, in the ocean—who sees our behavior and will, eventually, hold us accountable for our thoughts, words, and actions. Knowing this unseen witness is omnipresent makes us less likely to transgress the norms of society, less likely to curry unfavorable gossip from our fellow mortals, less inclined to become an outcast from a society we depend on for our daily survival.

—Isaac Berrow,
Master of the Royal Secret,
the Invisible College

Joseph Crossthwait

CHAPTER THIRTY-EIGHT

The *Strannik*

Hunting down the *strannik* had proven exceptionally difficult. But patience wears away stone, and diligence is eventually rewarded. An innkeeper, hungry for coin, had eventually provided the tip they'd needed to find the gathering of men.

They were at the inn now, waiting. Joseph sat at a corner table, picking absently at a loaf of streusel bread. He wore a commoner's outfit, but his array of magical artifacts were hidden throughout his costume. Peabody Stoker, who sat across from him, wore his kappelin, so he was invisible to those gathered within.

Right on time, the conspirators slunk into the inn, known for its tributes to Yverdon cuisine. Many of the patrons spoke the guttural language. The *strannik* matched the description reported by others who had observed him. He was a gaunt fellow who wore a black frock coat with dull bronze buttons. A chain or medallion was around his neck, so it was likely he carried a magical artifact with him. His hair was parted in the middle and slicked with some pomade, but his beard, in contrast, was unkempt and growing wild. But what stood out to Joseph the most was his intense eyes. The passion in them bordered on madness. He led the three others to the corner table, precisely where the innkeeper had said they met regularly and discussed politics over cups of hot tea and bread. The meetings would often last for hours at a time, always with some familiar faces bringing in new members to initiate them. Meeting the *strannik* was part of that initiation.

Joseph picked away at his bread, examining the newcomers passively. The order from General Colsterworth was to capture the *strannik*. If that proved unlikely or impractical, then he was to be eliminated.

That was the only reason Joseph hadn't shot him already.

There were dozens of other patrons in the common room, some banging mugs of beer together and laughing, which made overhearing the covert discussion impossible. Joseph slid the tray of bread away from himself and then pushed back his chair. He rose and walked to the table.

The *strannik* noticed his approach instantly. The paranoid tended to be vigilant. He focused his attention on Joseph for a few seconds before casting about for others in the room. Perhaps he already knew a trap was closing on him. Joseph saw the man's shoulders tense, and then he came to his feet, arms swirling, and invoked his magic.

An invisible force slammed into Joseph and sent him sprawling on the floor. Chaos erupted in the inn. Chairs squealed, men shouted in concern.

Joseph rolled over his shoulder, coming up onto his feet, just as one of the men from the table tried to tackle him. Joseph braced for impact—the fellow was burly—and then hooked a boot around the man's foot, pivoted, and used the other man's considerable weight to leverage him over Joseph's back and then onto the floor. Another man from the table whipped out a pistol and aimed it for Joseph's face, but a harrosheth blade severed the man's hand at the wrist before he could pull the trigger. The victim howled in shock and pain.

The *strannik* was gone.

Joseph cast around, trying to find him, and then saw the flutter of a cloak. Stoker had the *strannik* in a headlock, a harrosheth blade in his own hand at the revolutionary's throat. He did not perform the killing blow, however, for the *strannik*'s hands slowly came up in a gesture of submission.

The man with the severed hand was kneeling on the ground, panting and grunting in pain. The third accomplice was still seated at the table, white-faced with shock, frozen into inaction by the sudden violence.

When the local constabulary entered the inn, the three accomplices were taken into custody. Stoker had a smug look on his face, obviously pleased that he was the one who had apprehended their man alive. General Colsterworth would be pleased.

Within the hour, they had brought their quarry to the military barracks the brotherhood used in the imperial city. They were underground now, in a room lit by a single quicksilver lamp. They'd clapped some nulling cuffs on the *strannik*, to prevent him from casting any further spells, and deposited him on a chair. They'd also removed his gold chain. It was connected to an amulet made of Aesir gold that had been concealed beneath the buttons of his frock coat. The room was heated by an incalescent device. One that was making the room uncomfortably warm.

"What's this?" Stoker asked, handling the piece and then showing it to the wild-eyed man.

"What does it look like, vermin?" the *strannik* said in a thick Yverdonian accent.

"What is your name?" Joseph asked, leaning against the wall. They were prepared to beat the man to get the information the general would want. His confession would be long and involved.

"What does that matter? You're going to kill me anyway. You are leeches. Both of you."

Stoker wrinkled his brow with amusement. "You will be punished according to your crimes, sir. We're not your executioners."

"How comforting. What are the charges against me?"

"Conspiracy. Treason." Stoker shrugged. "You'll most likely be sent to a labor camp. If you cooperate, the sentence might be mitigated."

"A labor camp." The *strannik* scoffed. "I am used to hard labor. I'm not afraid. You poison the people with fear. You make them fear the Aesir when we are their natural subjects. You accuse me of treason when you yourselves are guilty of it. Fealty is owed to the Erlking, not that pampered, arrogant *scheifele* you call emperor."

Joseph hadn't heard that word before, but the tone implied it was an insult.

"Your name?" Joseph asked again.

"What is a name but a construct handed down by parents and traditions? My mother does not define me. My father does not define me. Or the lack of either. I am *strannik.* That is how I identify myself."

"Where do you come from?" Stoker asked with a bemused expression, for surely he'd get another indirect answer. Joseph didn't find it funny. This man was dangerous. Not because of his magic but because of the intensity of his thoughts. He had a sizable following, one that was growing in secret. How long had he been drawing in converts?

"Now you seek to define me by the location of my birth. Next you will try and define me by affiliation with the den of iniquity called the Invisible College. An organization that has subverted the people and made them slaves to the Industry of Magic. You cannot define me, gentlemen. The Awakening is happening, but not in the way you have come to define that word. No, gentlemen. It is not what you think it is."

The door opened and a man with captain buttons peeked his head inside.

"The general sent in new orders, Mr. Crossthwait."

"Does he know about the capture?" Stoker asked. "That we have our man?"

"I don't know, sir. The orders just arrived."

Joseph left the room, but Stoker followed him and caught him in the corridor. "Are you going to Bishopsgate? You'll tell him *I* captured the *strannik*, won't you, Crossthwait?"

Joseph paused and gave the other man a look. "I think he *wanted* to get captured, Stoker. I think he is going to use the publicity of the trial to spread his creed. It might have been better if you'd killed him."

The other man looked insulted. "We had our orders, Crossthwait. And he's not a Semblance. Did you feel how warm that room was? It didn't faze him a bit."

"I noticed. But something about him isn't quite right. What he's preaching is a *lie*, and the more people that hear it, the more it will spread."

"I know that. Just . . . don't take all the credit, Crossthwait."

Joseph looked at the other man disdainfully and then followed the captain to the dispatch office. The new orders had just arrived and were stamped with the general's seal.

Joseph opened them and quickly read the page.

> *Mr. Crossthwait:*
> *You are ordered to return to Auvinen immediately. The Semblance is making a bold move and will gain unprecedented access to the Industry of Magic. Before he causes any more damage, see that the situation is resolved. Report to Gresham College once these orders are fulfilled.*

The orders were written vaguely enough so that the transcribers would not be aware of the nature of them. But Joseph knew exactly what General Colsterworth meant. He understood the implications and importance of the command.

Professor Hawksley would die as soon as Joseph reached Auvinen.

McKenna Aurora Foster

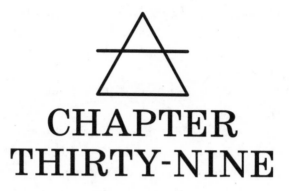

CHAPTER THIRTY-NINE

Fate's Crossroads

McKenna gazed deeply into Robinson's eyes expectantly, but nothing happened. They sat across from each other in the alchemy, full of its curious smells and interesting apparatuses. Lieutenant Wickins was gone to pick up a guest, a military officer who was interested in Robinson's work, so while they were awaiting his return, Robinson had put the ring on again and tried to reach McKenna's mind with his thoughts.

"Why isn't it working?" McKenna said after several more minutes had passed without success. Why was she as deaf to his thoughts as his spoken words?

Robinson slipped the thumb ring off and examined it again. Then he sighed as he put it back into the device and twisted the inner circles to lock it again.

"I wish I knew," he said. "I can't see why the ear damage from your fever would impact this mode of communication. It should bypass it, yet it doesn't."

The disappointment was acute. It probably showed on her face, because he slipped his hand across the table and took hers.

"I'm determined to find a way," he said. "We've tried it at different proximities, so distance isn't the problem."

"Do you have any hypotheses, Professor?" she asked teasingly, squeezing his hand.

"It's difficult to know where to start. What we do know about mortal anatomy is that it seems to be created to filter out information. Our eyes can only see certain bands of color. Our noses have receptors for certain smells, but we're not as complex as canines, for example. Hearing . . . also limited. From what little we know of the Aesir, they are more advanced than us in almost every way. Faster, smarter, more sensitive to stimulation. They can sense the faintest imperfections. There must be something blocking our thoughts from each other, just as we block out certain colors, sounds, and possibly tastes. Each time I put on the ring, it causes a piercing headache."

"I know, I see you wince every time. That troubles me."

"But what if it is that pain that removes the blockage? A sorcerer in the past must have made this device to communicate with the Aesir. I wish we knew whom it had belonged to."

"And your family history doesn't shed any clues on that?"

"None at all. There's no memory of how long it's been in our family, but it may have been generations. It could be from the time when the Invisible College first started."

"What if . . . what if *I* wore the ring?" McKenna suggested.

Robinson looked down a moment but then met her gaze. "I've thought of that. But it . . . hurts. I don't want you to do anything that hurts you."

"I'm willing to try," she said. "It may do nothing at all."

"That's true. Are you sure? It makes me . . . squeamish actually."

"I like that word."

"'Squeamish'?"

"Yes. It sounds like it feels. Language is beautiful."

He sighed. "Well, it can't hurt to try. Actually . . . it *can*, but you know what I meant."

"I'm willing."

He pulled out the device and handed it to her. She had already learned the combination to open it and did so with a grin she couldn't help. The disappointment was turning to anticipation again. But what if it didn't work? What if this was yet another sign that she could not learn magic?

"I'm grateful Father filed the patent," she said, adjusting each ring in order. "He mentioned in his letter about the Great Exhibition happening this summer. It would be a good time to showcase what you've invented."

She looked up at him for his reply, still twisting the rings. "And I agree with him about that, but I can't attend."

Her fingers stopped moving. "Robinson, you should go. You deserve the recognition."

"But I've made a commitment to teach summer classes, the busiest season of the year for the university. The exhibition is during the week of finals *and* it's in Bishopsgate." He held up his hands. "They're not going to change the date for me, so I can't attend because of my previous commitments. Wickins said he can go. And your father can go. I'm not going to be free of my commitment until the summer classes end."

"But what if something goes wrong? No one knows your research better than you do. There will be questions. I think you should go."

He sighed again. "I can't. I made a commitment. I even got my salary in advance."

She saw the stubborn look in his eyes and felt it would be unwise to try to push him further. Father had been upset when his offer to *pay* her fiancé to come to the exhibition had been declined out of hand. McKenna had promised she'd try to persuade him to change his mind.

She turned the final piece and then pushed the crystal with her thumb. She removed the inner ring and gazed at it, taking in the sigil engraved on the inner band. The feeling of familiarity it gave her was odd, but she'd felt it immediately upon seeing the ring for the first time. It was as if she'd seen it before. Of course, Father wore a ring bearing the symbol of the Invisible College, so perhaps that explained why it should be familiar, but this sensation was . . . different. More like kissing Rob for the first time had been.

McKenna summoned her courage and then put the ring on her left-hand thumb.

There was no piercing headache. No pain in her skull. But what she felt, immediately and powerfully, was that she was in great danger. Every instinct screamed at her to flee. If felt similar to the emotion one felt upon seeing a serpent in a garden. Visceral, instant, terrifying.

She plucked the ring from her thumb, her whole body trembling with fear.

Robinson snatched it from her. "Are you all right? What happened? All the lamps in the room started to glow."

"I-I don't know," she stammered. The feeling was still there, so intense and palpable. She wanted to run. But he was right, all the lamps were shining brightly, triggered by the Aesir magical chord.

"Did it hurt?"

"No . . . I'm just *afraid.*"

"Afraid of what?"

"I don't know!"

"Interesting. It triggered a fear response in you. It didn't do that to me or anyone else who's tried it."

McKenna rose from her seat, gripping the edge of the table until her knuckles turned white.

Robinson's head jerked suddenly, and he looked to the door of the alchemy. "They're back."

McKenna's instincts screamed again. "R-Robinson . . . I don't want to see them."

He picked up the device, inserted the ring into it, and stuffed it into his vest pocket. "He came from Bishopsgate. I would feel bad not to at least speak to the man. Your father said it was all right now that the patent has been filed. I think he works for military intelligence."

"I just . . . c-can't. Not like this."

"Stay here in the alchemy, then. Come out when you've collected yourself."

Fear stabbed her again. Stronger. "Don't go out there." She felt a surging sense of dread. What had the ring done to her? She couldn't account for her feelings, but they were very real. The same kind of irrational feelings that had gripped her in Siaconset. And at home. What had triggered it? Was it the ring?

Only, there'd been no ring on those other occasions, just her.

He frowned, not in anger but confusion. "I'll tell them it isn't a good time." He walked to the door leading to the living area, but before he could open it, Wickins walked in with a fellow in a military outfit indicating a higher rank. McKenna was vaguely familiar with the various insignia, but this man also wore a cloak that positively radiated magic. He had other accoutrements of power too, and she sensed the dangerous power they controlled. In the past, she'd never noticed such phenomena. Had wearing the ring altered her senses?

"This is Mr. Crossthwait," Wickins said with a gregarious smile, motioning to the man behind him. "He's so anxious to meet you."

McKenna watched the stranger pull a pistol out of his belt and aim it directly at Robinson.

Everything happened so fast, she could do nothing but stand riveted in place in utter shock. Rob tried to back away. Wickins saw the pistol, gaped in shock, then grabbed the man's arm and shoved the weapon up so the barrel wasn't aiming at Rob. The two men wrestled in the doorway but just for a moment.

McKenna felt the pistol's explosion in her bones and recognized the plume of saltpetr and the flash of fire. Haze instantly filled the room. Wickins slumped against the wall near the door. McKenna saw a bloom of blood appear on his shirt. He pressed his hand to his chest, shocked to see the evidence of violence, and then slumped slowly, dragging down the wall as his legs failed him.

McKenna covered her mouth in horror. The saltpetr stung her eyes, her nose. She had a visceral reaction to it, a wave of nausea that was intense and violent.

Rob looked shocked as well, seeing his friend collapse on the floor, but he moved to block McKenna from their attacker. The man whipped out another pistol from his belt, the first one still smoking, and aimed it at Rob's face.

Rob raised his hands in a universal gesture of submission. He was standing a little in front of her, shielding her body with his own. She wanted to scream, but her mouth wouldn't work.

She watched, in horror, as Robinson stepped toward the dangerous man. They were talking. She couldn't tell what her fiancé was saying, for his back was to her.

Then the intruder stuffed the expended pistol into his belt, grabbed Robinson by the arm, and held the tip of the barrel against his skull in a very threatening way.

Just minutes earlier, they'd been holding hands across the table. They'd been talking about wedding plans before that. About traveling to see an opera and making a new home, before winter, at Mowbray House. Never had she imagined such a turn of events. Wickins bleeding to death. Her fiancé, taken at gunpoint, wrenched away from her.

"Please, no," she stammered, shaking her head and pleading with everything in her heart. "Please don't take him! Please don't hurt him!"

Robinson turned his face to look at her. She saw his mouth form the words *I love you. Always.*

And then the two were gone, her love dragged from the alchemy before her smoke-stinging eyes, a pistol pressed against his untidy hair. She thought she might faint. But she didn't.

She hurried to the injured friend and realized there was nothing she knew that could save him. They needed a doctor, but she had no idea how to find one. His head lolled against his chest, but his eyes remained open and blinking.

The instinct to flee began to fade within her, replaced by the urge to fight. To smash the intruder's head with a fireplace poker. Only there were no fireplace pokers in this place because of the little magical heater that kept it warm. Maybe the ring had awoken something in her after all.

Images flashed in her mind, a snow-strewn battlefield. Bloody snow. So much bloody snow.

She trembled again, this time with determination. Gritting her teeth, McKenna marched out of the alchemy, grabbing a glass tube that was dormant once again. The intruder's magic had summoned the light. That's why they'd started glowing, not because of anything she'd done.

She couldn't hear the way they'd gone. But hopefully she'd be able to find them still and come up behind them with the tube and smash the awful man in the head with it.

Unless she was already too late.

Robinson Dickemore Hawksley

CHAPTER FORTY

The Semblance among Us

Robinson's mind whirled. The man gripped his arm tightly, pistol still pressed to the back of his skull. One squeeze of the trigger and he was done for. With his back facing McKenna, knowing she could not hear his words, he had pled with the soldier. *Don't murder me in front of my fiancée. Do it outside.*

The man had an aura of familiarity, one that hearkened back to a winter's night. It was possible it was the same man. He'd shot at Robinson before. This time it would be at a much closer range.

"Tell me what this is about at least," Robinson asked, trying to stall for more time. He was grateful the man was right-handed and grateful also the device was kept in his left vest pocket. Surreptitiously, he snaked his hand into the pocket. When he'd put the device there, he hadn't redone the combination, so the pieces were loose. Deftly, he tried to tip the thumb ring out of the casing.

"You wouldn't understand it if I did," the man said gruffly. He yanked Robinson into the closest alley, one thick with shadows and rubbish. It was a dead-end alley. No escape.

"I'm part of the Invisible College," Robinson said. He got the thumb ring loose and used his fingers to help slide it on. Instantly, the zing of pain struck his mind, making him shuffle his steps.

"I know that. And it doesn't matter. I outrank you by many degrees."

"What have I done to deserve death?"

"What you've done you've done unwittingly. If that eases your conscience."

Robinson heard the whispers again. Speaking the Aesir tongue. He had started familiarizing himself with the speech, but he had a long way to go before he'd understand the words. Poor Wickins. He'd been duped by this man. And been shot for it.

He extended a thought to Lennox Warchester George, the dean of the college. *This is Robinson. My life is in danger. A man from the military is trying to kill me. I'm in the alley next to my residence. Wickins has been shot. McKenna is all alone. Send help.*

The university was close at hand, and Dean George had been involved in their discussions of the new invention. He also knew Robinson well enough to know that he would not raise a cry for help without purpose.

"I think I deserve to know the reason," Robinson said.

The man pushed him up against the wall. "You'll know soon enough. You're a dead man walking. An abomination. You already died once. Elfshot will finish the job."

"I don't know what you're talking about."

"Of course you don't."

There were Aesir words being repeated over and over in the whispering in his ears. The repetition stood out. *Kill him. Kill him. Kill him.*

He watched with wide-eyed surprise as the soldier's face firmed with determination. And he pulled the trigger.

Nothing happened. No click. No hammer fall.

A look of surprise was evident on both of their faces. The soldier stepped back, lowered the muzzle, and shot point-blank at Robinson's chest. Again the pistol didn't function. Nothing happened. No plume of ignited saltpetr.

"I'm not what you think I am," Robinson said. "I've never died."

"Of course you believe that, but you're a Semblance! You're an animated corpse that retains all your old memories. It is my *duty* to kill you!"

He stuffed the pistol into his belt and pulled a blade from a bracer on his forearm. The ice-cold blade radiated magic. It could pierce anything. He held it underhanded and plunged it down toward Robinson's heart.

The blade paused, quivering, just an inch from the professor's chest. Held back by an invisible force. The soldier's face twisted with frustration. He was putting all his strength behind the killing blow.

Robinson sung a command. The blade flung itself away and embedded into the wall of the building on the opposite side of the alley, just like the maneuver he'd managed with that thief after arriving in Auvinen.

"I am not a Semblance, whatever that is," Robinson said. "I'm mortal. A sorcerer."

"You've been working with the Aesir," the soldier accused. "Telling them our weaknesses. They attacked this city because of you. You drew the stormbreaker to us!"

McKenna entered the alley, gripping one of the glass tubes from the alchemy as a weapon. As she approached them with a look of determination on her face, it glowed even more brightly. The whispers of the Aesir grew louder and louder.

Robinson's worry spiked, and he held up his hand to her, warning her not to come any closer.

"I'm not a Semblance," Robinson said to the soldier. "I know you think my body is being used as a host, but the opposite is true. The Aesir are ordering you to kill me. Their thoughts are subconscious to you, but I can hear them. I have a ring made of white gold that allows it." He tapped the ring on his thumb.

"You're lying!" the soldier spat.

"I'm trying to *stop* them from killing more of us. And they don't want me to do that. Isn't that why you are really here?"

"My orders are to *kill* Semblances. They'll say anything to protect themselves."

"Like you are? Right now?"

The soldier rushed at him, face twisted with rage. Robinson sensed the man was wearing magical accoutrements that enhanced his strength, his speed. If he could not kill Robinson with a weapon, he certainly knew how to do it with his bare hands.

With a thought, Robinson repelled the magic items from the soldier. He wasn't sure how he managed it, but he felt an instinct for what to do buried within him, deep down. The soldier was shoved away from him. He strained against the invisible forces holding him back. He had a murderous look in his eyes, but he could not fulfill that intention. It was hauntingly similar to the previous attack on that cold winter night, when his power had surged, creating a spell beyond what he'd thought himself capable. He'd thought, at the time, that the dog's intelligence had helped him. But where was *this* power coming from? Was it possible, indeed, that he was what the soldier suggested? What an awful thought . . .

Could there not be another explanation?

Robinson stepped closer to his attacker, keeping himself between the soldier and McKenna, who was cautiously approaching them. "How does one become a Semblance?" he asked. "Does it happen quickly?"

"We don't know," the soldier said, snarling. When he stopped trying to attack, he was able to move again. He came around in a circle, trying to get behind Robinson, who pivoted on his feet to keep himself facing the soldier. "It is their highest form of magic. No Semblance willingly reveals the process. They'd die first. Then shift to another host."

"That makes them very dangerous." Robinson could not, out of hand, reject the soldier's accusation. He needed more information. But he wasn't going to voluntarily submit to execution.

"You have no idea."

"And the host retains no memory of dying?" While they spoke, Robinson continued to silently cast spells, weaving them together with his thoughts. Intelligences swarmed into the alley, coming to aid him, summoned by his need for assistance in his crisis. These new ones, including many nocturnal animal intelligences like cats, street dogs, raccoons, and bats, offered a variety of enhancements he could employ. Quickness, hearing, barriers, willpower. Since he'd come to Auvinen, more intelligences seemed to be at his beck and call. Could that be another sign that he had, unwittingly, become a Semblance during the journey from Covesea? Had the illness weakened his health to the point that an alien entity could infiltrate him unaware?

"None of the ones we've caught remember it. But they were always injured. Many to the point of death."

That had not happened in Robinson's case. He was sick, but his axioma had never progressed to a wheezing death rattle, as it had for his brothers.

Also, thinking on it, another explanation occurred to him for his amplified powers. Perhaps the device had helped him in some way. Perhaps it been helping him all along. A wave of intuition told him it was so—and it told him something else as well.

This man in front of him was the very thing he was accusing Robinson of being—the soldier was a Semblance.

"So *you* would not remember if you have ever died?" he asked the man.

The soldier stared at him, realization dawning in his eyes with an expression of surprise.

"If their goal is to hide among us, to gather intelligence they can then communicate to their lord, the Erlking, who would be better than a member of one of the highest circles of power within the military and the Invisible College?"

"I'm *not* a Semblance," the soldier insisted.

"But by your own reasoning, you wouldn't know if you were one. What if you've been killing innocent people all along?"

The soldier looked upset and confused. "There is a way to tell. But it only happens when one is killed."

"Ah, so you have to *kill* someone to be sure, then. What a horrible task you've been given."

"I am *not* a Semblance," the man insisted.

"If you were one, how would anyone know? What is the sign you mentioned?" Robinson heard the shriek of whistles coming from the head of the alley. Whistles from officers of the Marshalcy. It was followed by the thunder of boots running toward them. Then he sensed intelligences coming into the alley ahead of the authorities, like hounds following the scent of a hare. He recognized the one leading the pack as the friendly dog's intelligence. A surge of gratitude filled his chest. This was not ordinary. This was amazing, something he would not have thought possible!

"I've seen it enough times. A breath of frigid air releases from the mouth of the dead. Like the kind from a cold morning, even if it's not cold."

"Their magic thrives in the cold," Robinson said, wanting to stall things further to give the authorities a chance to arrive. "It must be painful for them to live in such warm-blooded bodies."

Robinson began to back away, moving toward the alley mouth and gesturing to McKenna, behind him, to back away too since she couldn't hear the approaching officers. She stood fixed in place with her makeshift weapon in hand. "I've created a shield while we've been talking," he said. "One that will box you in here until help arrives. And now for the final touch." He added one more thought to it, one that would block the harmonic range the Aesir used to communicate, as well as in their magic items.

And just like that, the tube of light extinguished. The whispers in Robinson's mind were silenced.

The soldier looked around wonderingly. He too had sensed a change. "What happened?"

"I think I've blocked the source of their communication," Robinson said. He was convinced it was the device that was helping him channel so much power. It had been the device all along. Its protective powers and capabilities were astonishing. "You can't hear them anymore. Now you are realizing you always could."

The authorities finally arrived, dressed in the uniforms of the night watch, the leader with a glowing will-o'-the-wisp to brighten the way. "Hold there!" he commanded. "Don't move!"

The soldier tried to advance, but the shield spell held him back. He activated magic that should allow him to jump, but the shield was spherical, or near enough. It would prevent the man from leaving.

"Let me out!" the soldier demanded.

Robinson was relieved that help had arrived in time. His silent communication to Dean George had been responded to promptly.

"It seems we have a rare opportunity here," Robinson said as the officers arrived. One of them grabbed McKenna by the arms in a protective gesture. The other two closed ranks with Robinson. "To learn what we can of one another. Perhaps we can communicate directly with the Erlking and end this conflict between our kinds."

The soldier touched the boundaries of the shield with a worried expression. "It can't be," he murmured. But Robinson saw dawning understanding on the man's face, a realization that he was the very enemy he'd been hunting—and his position in the Invisible College was so important to the Aesir that they'd allowed other Semblances to be cut down in order for him to continue to operate as an agent. "It won't work. We've tried that already!"

"Failure doesn't mean something cannot be done. It means we haven't found the right way of doing it yet."

The soldier drew the pistol from his belt again.

"He's mad!" one of the officers shouted, drawing his own weapon.

"Firing that won't break the shield," Robinson said coaxingly. "It will only cause the bullet to ricochet inside there. Officers, stand down. Give me a minute to persuade him."

"You *don't* understand how dangerous they are," the soldier said. "They must be destroyed. *I* must be destroyed!"

"But surely we should learn what we can from them. Maybe this time we'll learn—"

He stopped abruptly as the soldier put the pistol to his own temple and pulled the trigger. The report echoed in the alley, and a plume of saltpetr shrouded him. Robinson was shocked and sickened by what had happened. He couldn't have prevented it. The officers were bewildered at the sudden violence, their mouths widening with the surprise.

McKenna jerked free of the man holding her and rushed to Robinson's side. The other officers gathered around them.

He maintained the shield and came as close to the crumpled body lying in the alley as he could. The tang in the air from the saltpetr was intense, its fumes leeching through the strands of magic. He sensed the dog's intelligence lingering near him, anticipating him, caring about him. If it had been in possession of a body, it would have licked his hand.

Then Robinson knelt near the fallen body, watching the man's face. His eyes were still open. Then his lips parted, and a puff of frosty mist came out with his final exhalation. The mist coiled like an entity, a sentient one, and then slipped effortlessly past the shield spell. Was it looking for another recently dead person? One it could revive into another incarnation so that it might continue its ruse?

"Wickins," Robinson whispered in dread.

CHAPTER FORTY-ONE

A General Apology

A breeze with the hint of lilac came from the open window into the parlor. Robinson and McKenna were nestled together on one of the smaller sofas in the Foster home on Brake Street, their hands entwined, bellies full from another amazing feast provided by Mrs. Foster. Mr. Foster was sitting in his special chair, reading a book and occasionally looking up to observe his family and guests. Trudie was playing a piccolo. She'd become quite proficient at the melody of the Erlking's daughter, and only every twelfth note or such made Robinson inwardly wince. Clara and Wickins were playing a card game at a table that had been brought to the larger couch for such a purpose. Wickins was pale and walked with a decided shuffle, indicating the pain he still suffered, though the injury to his chest was healing, and he had leave from the military to recover from the elfshot. Thankfully, his wound had not been mortal. He'd never lost consciousness, and his behavior and mannerisms were as they'd always been. Clara had taken on the role of his nurse since they'd arrived for their regular dinner on Closure. And the young lieutenant didn't seem to mind the attention one bit. There was a hint of flirting in the card game, observable from the couch where Robinson and his fiancée sat.

He noticed the breeze fluttering McKenna's hair, and he reached with his other hand to slide some strands over her ear. Touching her sent a shivering charge up his arm. She was so beautiful and looked so tranquil after the violent exchange earlier that week.

"Are you getting cold? I can close the window," he offered.

"The breeze is lovely," she answered, leaning her head against his shoulder. "I'm always too hot these days and summer hasn't even begun. Siaconset has a milder climate than Auvinen." She traced a tendon on his hand with her fingertip. "I hope you'll like living in Mowbray House." Then she lifted her head so she could read his lips as he responded. There was an interesting rhythm to their talks, a back and forth, a close attention required to be sure the words were exchanged properly. It was so natural that it was almost unconsciously done at this point.

"I can't imagine not liking it," he said. He was thrilled she would soon become his wife. After the attack, she had insisted they delay the nuptials no longer. They were to be married in the family gardens as soon as Robinson's parents arrived from their cottage farther outside the city. It was a hasty wedding. One that had caused some gossip in Society. He was still in the middle of teaching, so they would postpone their honeymoon for the break in the term. It felt right not to delay any longer. He loved her with all his heart. She meant everything to him. Their brush with death had drawn them even closer together.

She stroked the edge of his hand with her thumb and gave him a loving smile. "I'm just grateful you're here," she said, her throat suddenly thick. "What happened . . . that was terrible. I still don't understand what that man thought you were. He called you a Semblance. I'd never seen that word used that way before."

Robinson nodded, adjusting his shoulder to face her more. "Neither had I. Wickins had, though. He's studied the Aesir language, their lore, more than I have. The word was used in translations from some epic poems written who knows how many years ago. In Tanhauser, the word they use is *doppelgänger*. Do you know that one?"

She thought a moment. "That means *double . . . double walker*? Something like that? I've not heard it before."

"Interesting. A double walker. Someone pretending to be someone else. There is much in the Aesir lore that is fascinating. And terrifying. There is so much more to their magic than we've realized."

"Mostly terrifying. I hope your invention," McKenna said, "will be used to help in the war. Father thinks it will be worth a good deal to the Industry of Magic."

"I would never accuse your father of being wrong," Robinson said. "Except in matters of the heart." He glanced over and saw a glimmer in the glass of Mr. Foster's pince-nez spectacles. The man gave them a wry smile before looking down at the book again.

"Confound it," Wickins said, slapping the last card down. "You beat me again!"

Robinson looked over at the game in progress and saw a triumphant smile on Clara's mouth. She'd won the set, although Robinson suspected that Wickins had possibly *let* her win. His exclamation had been a little too zealous.

McKenna's grip on his hand tightened suddenly. He turned his head to look at her face and saw a growing apprehension in her eyes.

"Are you all right?" he asked with concern.

Then he noticed the quicksilver tubes in the room were all coming alive. After their dangerous encounter, he had been determined to provide more protection at his apartment and at the Fosters' home. The new insights he received from his device had aided in this. He felt the chords of magic begin to swell. The house's defenses had been activated. He was convinced now that the device wasn't an artifact of Aesir magic at all, but one invented by a sorcerer long ago to counter it. It had never fit the mold of other Aesir devices he'd seen, but it had incredible complexity and power, and there was much he could learn from it still.

Mr. Foster set down his book and rose swiftly. Robinson rose as well, and McKenna came up with him and clutched his arm.

Trudie set down her piccolo, looking confused. "What's happening?"

Robinson had installed test lamps in his alchemy and at the house on Brake Street. They were the only people in Auvinen who had the ability to detect Aesir magic.

Wickins tried to stand but winced in pain at the sudden movement. Robinson pulled out the device from his vest pocket, quickly connected the last part of the combination, and emptied the ring into his hand. He then put it on his thumb. The stab of pain struck him instantly, but it also awakened within him a connection with the magic of the house and the devices and intelligences he'd intertwined with its safeguards. He sensed magic coming up the street and also heard in his mind the nearly subconscious growl of his invisible canine friend.

"Professor?" Mr. Foster asked with concern.

Robinson looked at him and nodded. "Someone is coming." Before he could even request it, he sensed other intelligences being summoned by the dog.

"Are we *safe*?"

Robinson considered this thoughtfully before answering. "I think so. I've set wards around the entire property."

Information was coming to him from the wards now. Three men were coming. Military. One had an Aesir cloak, a kappelin. He swallowed with dread, but he did not feel any real fear. Since the attack, he'd learned that the device his father had given him had actually repelled the military man's violence. The blade, the bullet. None of their magic had worked against him. He wasn't sure why, but he'd experimented and discovered that the device had more properties still that he was just beginning to learn about. It had probably saved his life that night in the tenements as well, only he hadn't realized it then.

"Rob," McKenna said worriedly, looking at him with terror in her eyes.

"I think we'll be all right," he said reassuringly. He began weaving a protection spell for the inhabitants of the room in his mind. Intelligences responded to his summons instantly.

The three men crossed the gate to come to the front door.

Clara was seated next to Wickins, gripping his arm in fear. Trudie whimpered behind her mother. A knock sounded at the door, and the butler's footfalls approached it. The tension in the parlor was palpable, but Robinson felt confident he was the master of the situation. The military men didn't know their weapons wouldn't work against him. That made them quite ordinary against a rather accomplished sorcerer who had throngs of intelligences swarming him to offer their aid.

The butler approached the door of the parlor and opened it. "Sir, there are visitors here to see you from the military. A General Colsterworth from Bishopsgate, Colonel Harrup, of course, and another young man in a strange cloak."

Mrs. Foster looked at her husband in concern.

"Send them in, please," Mr. Foster said.

Robinson slid the device back into his pocket but kept the thumb ring on. The general had a mustache that angled sharply beneath his nose, with waxed tips at the ends. Like many in the military, his hair was cropped, quite salted, and he had deep, penetrating eyes. The shoulder lapels of his uniform bore his rank, and a distinctive medallion around his neck was some show of royal favor perhaps. The other man was older, wore colonel bars on his sleeves, and was mostly bald. The third man wore a kappelin and the same attire that had been worn by the man who had tried to kill Robinson. McKenna squeezed his hand hard.

Wickins had managed to struggle to his feet and held a salute. "Sir!"

"Sit down, Lieutenant," the general barked. "Before you fall down. I know you're injured. At ease. I apologize for the intrusion on Closure, Mr. Foster. My name is Colsterworth. You know Harrup, I'm sure."

"We've met on many occasions at civic functions," Colonel Harrup said with a charming smile. "Good to see you again, Mr. Foster."

"This is Mr. Stoker, my adjutant," said the general. Then he looked at Robinson, his eyes keen and interested. "And you must be Professor Hawksley if I'm not mistaken. I understand you take dinner here on Closure every week."

"Good evening, General," Robinson said evenly.

"Perhaps my family should wait in another room?" Mr. Foster suggested.

"Oh no, we won't be staying long, and what I have to say concerns them as well. You see, Mr. Foster, we've made a terrible mistake. A nuisance of the highest order."

Mr. Foster maintained a grim expression and continued to listen.

"What happened in Auvinen should never have happened. I was shocked when I heard of the incident. Shocked, I say. That's why I've come in person, with Colonel Harrup, to apologize for the indiscretion. An inquest is underway, and I assure you that all diligence will be taken to discover the cause and how such a matter can be prevented in the future. It's unacceptable that the daughter of an esteemed barrister such as yourself, and also a highly regarded member of society like you, Professor, came to be in harm's way. For that, I seek your pardon."

Robinson blinked in surprise. It was a fine little speech, very vague, very articulate, but it wasn't exactly dripping with sincerity.

"I thank you for your pains in coming all this way," Mr. Foster said. "I do hope that the results of the inquest will be made available to review by the public?"

"Absolutely *not*," the general countered without hesitation. "Under the Lieber-Halleck Code, General Order Number One Hundred Fifteen: 'All information deemed potentially deleterious to the war effort shall be branded secret, and only those with privileged and authorized access can be so informed.' You are familiar with the Lieber-Halleck laws, Mr. Foster?"

"I am, General."

"Let me not mince words. And this warning goes to the entire family. Information regarding the nature, activity, or existence of Semblances is a secret of strict and vital importance to the security of the empire. The officers who witnessed the demise of my former adjutant have similarly been forbidden to disclose the experience. What was witnessed must remain secret." He stepped forward, his gaze becoming hardened and intense. "You can imagine, sir, the consequences if the public were to suspect there are imposters among us. Imposters who inform our enemies of our weaknesses and vulnerabilities. You can imagine, sir, the distrust this would provoke in Society. The consequences would be incalculable. There is a rank within the Invisible College that is trained and prepared to handle such threats. To discover and eliminate them."

Robinson felt McKenna trembling. He felt rather tremulous himself.

"One infiltrated your own organization," Mr. Foster said. "That doesn't fill me with confidence, General, that you have the matter under control. Is the legislature aware of this internal threat?"

"Those who are part of the Invisible College are aware," the general answered slyly. "On these matters, I report to the Master of the Royal Secret. Not the emperor."

"I see."

"Well, I've made a nuisance of myself here, and I apologize again. Colonel, make sure the Fosters are compensated for any losses they incurred. Be generous, if you would. And Professor, I understand you have an invention coming to the Great Exhibition?"

"The invention will be there," Robinson said. "I will not."

"I hope it does well. These things can make a sorcerer quite renowned. I also understand congratulations are in order. My best to you and Miss Foster." He bowed gallantly, his eyes fixing on McKenna.

Robinson didn't like the way he looked at her.

"Thank you, General. I'm sorry about your officer. I don't think he knew the truth about himself until the very end."

The general frowned. "That is what makes these cases such a nuisance, you see. A Semblance doesn't even know if she is one."

"'She'?" Mr. Foster asked.

"There are all sorts, sir. A great deal *too* many."

MaKenna Aurora Hawksley

EPILOGUE

Till Death Us Depart

Judge Coy Taylor was a formidable man in his early fifties with a well-groomed short beard, which added—with his robes—to his look of distinction. In the center knot of his cravat was a jeweled pin that bore the symbol of the Invisible College. McKenna watched his lips move as he read through the marriage license. She could tell he was mouthing the words, not speaking to her and Robinson, because he was describing the details of the agreement. He looked up suddenly.

"Both parents have signed it on Miss Foster's behalf, although not legally required. You've both decided to alter your names as agreed upon herein. Again, not legally required. You will live at such-and-such residence in Auvinen. Witnessed by both sets of living parents. This all seems to be in order."

McKenna bit her lower lip, squeezing Rob's arm in nervous anticipation. Something was going to go wrong. Something was going to prevent them from being married. So much had already gone wrong. A stalled locomotivus had delayed Mr. and Mrs. Hawksley's arrival by a day. A problem at Father's law office had made her worry he'd ask to postpone. The bridal bouquet order had been misplaced, but thankfully the florist had been able to satisfy Mother with a suitable alternative. McKenna was seething with tension, wanting to leave the parlor and go outside to the garden so the judge, a special friend of her father's, would perform the ceremony.

"*Is* everything in order?" McKenna asked after an undue pause from the judge as he examined the license again.

The judge glanced up from the paper. "Unfortunately I can find no excuse *not* to marry you both this morning. I understand there's a carriage waiting to take you to the station afterward. But we can undergo more pleasantries if you'd like, Miss Foster." He gave her a crooked smile and a wink.

"It was her idea to be married this soon," Robinson said. "And who am I to thwart her?"

"Wisely said until the bills start piling up. Which, by my reckoning, shouldn't be a problem since *she* will be paying them." He gave Robinson a quizzical look. "Mr. Foster related your extraordinary gesture, Professor Hawksley. That you legally signed away all your rights and shares of your invention to your wife as a wedding present. It's unheard of."

Robinson patted McKenna's hand fixed to his arm. "She will do a better job managing it than I ever would."

"If I didn't know Mr. Foster in a personal capacity, I would suspect duress and require an inspector of the Marshalcy to interrogate you both."

McKenna started in surprise.

He held up his hand. "You flinched, Miss Foster; I was only joking. I've simply never heard of such a thing before. There are usually mountains of affidavits and prenuptial contracts determining what to do in the event of the sundering of a marriage. You'd be surprised how many arguments I've witnessed on what should have been days of joy and bliss. I was amazed to hear what you'd done, sir, but from what I've learned about you, Professor, you're an admirable fellow."

"I trust her completely and totally," Rob said. McKenna squeezed his arm. The shares, at present, would not be valuable until the patents Father had filed were granted. But there were investors keen to speculate on their value—and the contracts likely to come to fruition should the military decide to use the devices. Father had already secured a partnership with a major bulb manufacturer to begin using the new white-gold filament that would enable the bulbs to alert of the presence of the Aesir, and many of the up-and-coming sorcerers at the Storrows would be put to work immediately. Full production was to commence within a fortnight.

But there was still enough time before the next set of classes ended to rush up to Tanhauser to see a performance of Shopenhauer's play. If the judge would just get on with it.

"Shall we go to the garden?" Judge Coy Taylor asked. "I understand the greenhouse has special meaning for both of you?"

"It does indeed," Rob said. "May I have a moment with her alone, Your Honor?"

"I'll await you at the greenhouse." Judge Coy Taylor nodded and exited the parlor, leaving them alone at last.

"What's wrong?" McKenna asked, looking worriedly at Rob's face.

He didn't look worried. He looked peaceful actually. In the past weeks, she'd noticed the change in him accomplished by regular meals. His cheeks were fuller, and the vestiges of sickness she'd always seen in him had vanished. The suit his father had brought him after his bout with the inspiratory stridor was actually starting to fit him. Fit him very well. And when he put on the bowler hat, he looked quite dashing when he smiled. In fact, the way he was looking at her made her insides start to jumble around. Was he going to kiss her? Now?

She wanted him to. It didn't matter that their families and friends were waiting just outside the curtained window. They were alone. And soon . . . very soon . . . they would be *very* alone. Her cheeks began to get warm.

He stood in front of her, taking her hands. "I know you've been anxious about today, about everything that could go wrong."

"Please don't jinx it," she begged. "I don't want to *wait* any longer."

"I know," he said, nodding. He grazed his thumb across her fingers. "I just want to . . . savor this moment. You *want* to be my wife. You seem to want this as much as I do. Do you know how amazing and terrifying that feels? That someone named McKenna Aurora Foster . . . wants someone like me?" He looked very vulnerable in that moment, as if he didn't think he deserved her love, and her throat thickened.

"I'm nervous, I'm scared, thrilled, impatient—I have no idea what feelings are coming next. But this I know, Robinson Dickemore Hawksley. I love you. I love you for who you are and what you've done for me, and what we'll figure out together . . . even awkwardly and with mistakes." She paused, breathless. "And you've made me so happy. So very, very happy I want to burst."

She took his face in her hands, rose on her tiptoes, and kissed him on the mouth. Just a little kiss. She anticipated a longer one in the private car she'd secured for them on the locomotivus to Tanhauser.

The kiss was sweet and full of longing.

"Can we please . . . *please* . . . go outside now?" she implored.

He gazed at her with triumph, with delight, with a look of pure and unfettered love and gave her a little bow. Then she fixed the bowler from the tabletop onto his head, linked arms with him, and the two of them went outside to a little bubble of applause. Mother had styled McKenna's hair in her favorite version of Aunt Margaret's style—the Amarynth style it was called. There were Father and Mother, gazing at her, Mother dabbing tears and Father cleaning his pince-nez glasses after brushing something from his eye. Clara and Trudie stood with Miss Trewitt, who was nearly bouncing with happiness for her former charge. Lieutenant Wickins next to Judge Coy Taylor in his dress uniform, looking dapper and handsome. Mrs. Sarah Fuller Fiske stood with Rob's parents on that side as well. She'd given them a generous wedding present already, adding furnishings to Rob's apartment so that McKenna would feel more comfortable living there until all the teaching commitments were done and they could move into Mowbray House. It was unnecessary but so thoughtful. Some of the deaf children had come the day before to help decorate. The widow Robinson had befriended was also in attendance with her children. The oldest boy wanted to be a sorcerer someday, much like McKenna herself, and she'd encouraged him to keep trying.

Even with all the friendly faces around her, McKenna's stomach positively buzzed with nerves. As soon as she and Rob were standing in front of the judge, though, all the anxiety vanished. She felt more than eighteen at that moment. More than the little deaf girl on Brake Street. She was almost his. A strange feeling came over her, as if she could feel the cool morning breeze rustling the hair coiled above her neck. A memory tried to burst through and couldn't.

She was so lost in thought, she'd forgotten to pay attention to Judge Coy Taylor's words. Then he looked at her expectantly, and she realized he was waiting for her affirmation.

"I . . . I do," she stammered, mortified. She was always vigilant in such things when it mattered. The unsurfaced memory continued to nag at the back of her mind, though. Something she needed to remember but couldn't. She gripped Rob's arm, gazing at the judge's mouth as he continued the brief legal ceremony.

Rob answered promptly, and soon it was complete.

"I now call you husband and wife, Robinson Foster Hawksley and McKenna Aurora Hawksley, in the eyes of Auvinen, the empire, and the Mind of the Sovereignty. Till death you depart. Ashes to ashes. Dust to dust. And Justice claimeth its own."

"Till death us depart," Robinson said, and McKenna felt an odd foreboding. A chill went through her heart.

"Ashes to ashes. Dust to dust," she said haltingly, fearfully. "Justice claimeth its own."

"Justice claimeth its own," Rob concluded.

⁂

The locomotivus station was crowded, so they abandoned the driver of Father's carriage, and Rob carried both of their valises, even though she insisted she could have managed the smaller one. It was not as wild as the rush from Bishopsgate after the Aesir attack, thankfully, and she managed to keep stride with her husband through the melee. The bulk of the crowd was going into the largest section where the most seating was located, so once they passed that, there were relatively few passengers, all well-dressed. An agent was waiting to look at their tickets and quickly guided them to their private compartment. He took the valises and helped stow them both in the upper rack.

"Let me know if I can be of any service," he said with a tip of his hat.

"I told you we'd make it with time to spare," Rob said. He'd never ridden in such comfort, but she was grateful to be able to spoil him a little. She was determined to find a new violin for him in Tanhauser.

"Coming from a professor who doesn't carry a pocket watch?" she teased. "I'll be nervous until we're on our way. And even then I'll be nervous because what if we get stuck on the tracks? I don't want you to miss the opera."

"She should arrive in Tanhauser tonight. Even if we get delayed, we'd arrive in the morning. This compartment is big enough to sleep in! We will be fine."

She looked at him with astonished eyes. "Our wedding night on the floor of a train? My dear husband. You have much to learn about romance."

He chuckled. "I didn't mean . . . *that*. The hotel in Tanhauser . . . it's the one you stayed in with your parents?"

She nodded eagerly. "It's beautiful. The fashion is from the Aesir ruins at Ashelterra. They spared no expense copying its style." She walked to the window and gazed outside, hoping they would be underway soon.

Thankfully, there were no delays, and soon the locomotivus was thrumming with power. It levitated off the tracks, and a plume of chilling fog blew past their window. The employee passed by again to see if they needed anything. When he was gone, McKenna locked the door and sat down next to her husband.

"You'd like some privacy, Mrs. Hawksley?" Rob asked, taking off his hat and setting it down on the other side with a wry smile. She had sat *very* close to him.

"I wasn't intending to read a book the whole time," she said, tilting her head. "We must save some things for later, Husband, but . . . I think I should like you to kiss me now. Properly."

"If your hair comes undone, I can't be held responsible," he said. He was gazing at her with such admiration, such need.

They kissed again and again. With the sway and acceleration of the locomotivus, it felt like they were flying. It made her dizzy. And breathless. The soap he'd used—it was intoxicating. And . . . she wanted more but thought it might not be wise to carry on. He was tender with her. Never demanding. Accepting what she gave. He was very patient. And it felt wonderful to kiss him at last.

Sitting next to him on the bench, leaning against his shoulder, her hand on his leg, it felt so natural. Like they'd been together for years.

She noticed his pocket where he kept the device, so she snaked her hand in and pulled it out.

He gave her a doting smile. "I brought some sugared peanuts. I asked Wickins to get them on his way to the house this morning. Would you like some now?"

"Yes, please. I'm glad you did."

He rose and stretched, and while he reached up to the stowed luggage, she opened the lid of the device and gazed at its strange symbols. The inner ring that could be removed and worn on the thumb. The stone in the middle. They still didn't know what that did. The two buttons on the top that didn't work. Or . . . they hadn't yet figured out how they worked.

"I wonder who made this," she said, admiring it. Then she looked into his eyes.

"I think a sorcerer did," Rob answered. She could smell the whiff of peanuts as soon as he opened the valise.

"But my clever husband is figuring it out," she said, gazing at the crystal with the number that never . . .

Changed.

"Rob," she said with surprise.

"Umm?" He juggled both bags of peanuts and was closing the valise, looking down at her quizzically.

"It's all the same number now. Three in a row."

There was a startled look on his face. He sat quickly, setting down the bags of peanuts and looking in her hand.

She was trembling. She didn't know why.

"Nine . . . nine . . . nine," he murmured. "It *did* change."

"What does it mean?" Part of her knew. The part of her she couldn't talk about. The part she wasn't *supposed* to talk about. Her awareness began to shimmer. She blinked, the dizziness this time *not* caused by his mouth searching for hers.

The peculiar feeling came again. The same one she'd felt during the marriage ceremony when Robinson said those words.

Till death us depart.

Fear stabbed her. She shoved the device into his hands and clung to him, fearing he was going to leave her, that someone was going to *kill* him. She couldn't let that happen. Not yet. It was too soon. It was too soon for it to happen again.

A cloud of fog blew past the window. He tried to soothe her. But nothing worked. Her mind was agitated again. She felt she was losing hold of herself. She was drowning again. *Why? Why? Why?* Why was this happening to her? It was happening more and more often. Since she and Trudie had fled to Mowbray House. Since she'd nearly died.

"Hold me," she whispered, burying her face in his shirt. "Hold me tight. Don't let go."

Acknowledgments

I hope you've enjoyed this new foray into my imagination. When I started this career full-time, I did not want to be pigeonholed into writing in just one world. I'm so grateful to have a publisher that encourages me to try new things and for an imagination that gets excited about new possibilities.

My editorial team changed midstream with this novel, but everything still fell into place perfectly. I would like to thank my new editorial editor at 47North, Alexandra Torrealba, for jumping in and contributing quickly. I'm also grateful to my sensitivity reader, Jenna, for providing a helpful and deep perspective on McKenna's deafness. Of course, gratitude is owed to my core team: Angela, Wanda, and Dan, who have unfailingly supported my stories and made them all better with their wisdom and insights.

I'd like to also thank Charlie N. Holmberg, Luanne G. Smith, and Allison Anderson for reading *The Invisible College* in advance and being willing to provide quotes for the book. I'm so grateful for the other authors who have supported me during my writer's journey and for showing up together for events.

And to my readers—thank you from the bottom of my heart for allowing me the privilege of writing books. Without your support over many, many storylines, I wouldn't have been able to invent these stories. There is more coming. Twists you won't see coming. I hope you continue to enjoy Rob and McKenna's adventures together. For those interested, there are two additional bonus chapters for this book, which you can find on my website (www.jeff-wheeler.com/invisible-college).

About the Author

Photo © 2021 Kortnee Carlile

Jeff Wheeler is the *Wall Street Journal* bestselling author of more than forty epic novels. *The Invisible College* begins a brand-new series, set in a new world. Jeff lives in the Rocky Mountains and is a husband, father of five, and devout member of his church. Learn about Jeff's publishing journey in *Your First Million Words*, visit his many worlds at www.jeff-wheeler.com, or participate in one of his online writing classes through Writer's Block (www.writersblock.biz).